The Gathering of Fools
The Crimson Collection vol II

Robert J Power

For Séamie and Jan. It used to be just Jan. But I prefer Séamie. So he gets first mention. The kid has got style... wow... I'll regret this dedication on launch... it's not too late. I can pull it back from the fire.

For Jan and Séamie. You are my light.

Nailed it.

Contents

Previously on The Crimson Hunters

Derian hated the wind. Really hated it. It was a deep-seated hatred emanating from somewhere within his shuddering being. Perhaps as far down as his soul. If he had one. He wasn't sure he had one. In fact, he was most certain he didn't. There was something there alright, but it was no soul. It was monstrous. Taking a moment from hating the wind, he wondered, did monsters have souls? Maybe having a soul and still being a savage prick anyway was the definition of monstrous things. Made him do monstrous things. Think monstrous things.

Perhaps it was the monster within him that hated the wind. Wanted to take it behind a shed somewhere and kick the ever-living shit out of it.

A sudden gust of wind caught him as the airbarge shuddered, and he near lost his grip, and no, he decided he hated the wind regardless of the monster that slumbered deep within his essence. He hated the monster as well. It had been a few days since the beast had woken, took control and made him a right gnarly savage.

Fuk you, beastie, he thought and hoped his thoughts travelled all the way down to where his monster rested, no doubt sated on some fine dining involving a soul and goodness with a little civility on the side.

The monster never stirred, but the pole in his grip did, as it was taken by the breeze. As far as poles went, he was no fan of this one. It was ungainly and awkward, needlessly heavy where the metal hook was attached to the shaft, and catching in the wind as it did, it was likely to get him killed. Sighing, Derian braved another step out along the edge, all the while fighting to keep his balance, thrown off by the wind and the top-heavy pole.

After a moment, Derian decided to hate long poles. Fuken loathed them outright. To the fires with them. Or the oceans. Whatever, really.

Edging himself carefully along, he tried to set his feet, dig in tighter on the impossibly smooth and slippery surface of the airbarge's extended... wings? He didn't know the name of the jutting metal platform he stood upon. Only that there were four of them, one at each corner of the barge, each one holding a set of spinning propellors in place. He decided 'wings' was a decent enough term and he fuken hated them and all.

Fuk you, wings.

As he edged further along, his foot slipped and, with the wind trying its best to fuk him up, he was pulled a half-foot closer to the edge. Instinct saved him. And a hanging chain. Wrapping both arms around the metal chain as it swung lazily in front of him, he let the pole fall.

So much for the pole.

It was no loss.

"Oh, for fuk's sake. Why did you do that, Derian?" a voice from across the precipice called, and he muttered under his breath a fresh curse that was lost in the wind. "What did you say, you little shit?" the voice called, and Derian shrugged and held tight to the chain lest the wind blow him to blue oblivion.

"I said nothing at all...sir," he finally called to Lorgan, his master, his leader, his... friend? Derian wasn't sure about that last part, but that was fine and polished. He trusted Lorgan with his life. There were worse traits to have in a leader.

Saying that, the cur was testing that trust this fine windy morning.

Beyond, Derian could see Lorgan gesturing to Kesta in the cockpit of the airbarge. It looked like he mimed a pole slipping away. She looked pissed, but who could tell with the fuken wind whipping his scarf and cloak around him? Kesta looked like she had words to say, screamed words in fact, but they were lost in the wind. This was probably a good thing as well.

This is how I die.

I really hate this.

"Lorgan," Derian begged, swinging ever so gently with the chain as his feet struggled and failed to grip on the wing. "I'm going to die and you aren't listening," he cried again.

Now, in truth, Derian had always been fond of the right boots for the right task. Largely because most of his life, he'd never had the right boots for the right task. Or boots that even lived up to their primary task of keeping his feet dry and comfortable.

Moreover, coming upon a grand gathering of splendid

new boots in his cabin had near brought his eyes to tears. That some of them even fitted his feet was an even greater miracle.

It was a rare thing to even enjoy the luxury of laces, and the pair he'd donned this morning, with its many needless buckles, had looked quite attractive things indeed. Crimson and black and shined with nothing but love, they positively shimmered in the morning sun. These fine boots were designed for style and allure, and were better suited to sliding down a dignitary's polished hall floor than to keeping a firm grip on a metal surface.

After a moment's pause and a few further struggles, he decided to hate these boots and all. It was something to do while hanging out over certain death with nothing to keep him balanced. Not even a pole.

Lorgan still didn't reply, but Derian would not be dissuaded. "I have a terrible feeling about all this. I really don't think this is a good idea," he called, and felt the wind pull at his cloak. Just a gentle rap this time. A little suggestive tease. A warning of a coming gust, no doubt, like the melon served before a banquet. Derian had never been to a banquet. Nor had he ever had melon. That was a rich fiend's delicacy. It sounded too salty for his tongue anyway.

He gripped that chain harder and heard his boots squeak ever so as they sought and failed to find friction.

"Ah, whisht, young one," Lorgan roared. "I can't hear what that woman is saying with your whingeing."

"I'm not whingeing, I'm fuken slipping. I'm dead, I'm so dead."

"Ah, you're fine. Stop being a little hiss about it."

"I'm not being a hiss. You're being a hiss."

Derian didn't know what a hiss was. He might have asked Lorgan, who looked positively at ease, standing all comfortably on the deck of their airbarge with nothing to worry about but the wind messing up his hair.

I hate this, I hate this, I really, really hate this.

He decided to hate the propellor and the airbarge, and immediately thought better of it. He only hated the propellor for breaking down on them. The rest of the *Fighting Mongoose* he liked just fine. And why wouldn't he? Was it not the pride and joy of the greatest mercenary group ever to march the seven Isles of Dellerin? The Army of the Dead, that is, for until very recently, the airbarge had been theirs. A shudder ran down his back. It was just the wind, he told himself, and not the thought of the Army of the Dead catching up with them for this crime. Terrible name, really, but real fuken good at their job. Real fuken good at tracking down their targets. Real fuken good at doing what was needed. That shudder again.

Derian's own mercenary group had a rather fetching name, if not the legacy of the legendary mercenary group. Derian was part of the Crimson Hunters and they most certainly weren't the greatest mercenaries in any of the Islands. They were a right shit outfit altogether. Even if they were heroes. Even if no one would ever know they were heroes.

But they were good at stealing airbarges. They had a one hundred percent completion rate of such endeavours so far.

A sudden monstrous wave caught in the wind. The spray lifted higher, was carried in the wind, hung for a while, and washed over Derian, soaking him through. He hadn't thought waves could reach this far, but in this breeze, who knew.

Fuk you, wind.

Fuk you, wave.

The propellor suddenly rotated a few times, and Derian froze in terror. Kesta had promised there was no fuel running into this propellor. She'd sworn on all seven gods and demons while she was at it that she had cut the fuel. Even Lorgan was affected by that close call.

"Whoa—did you do that?" he called from the edge of the deck. He looked concerned for a breath and then quickly returned his gaze to the familiar disapproving scowl. There was reassurance in that gaze.

"I did nothing. I'm just hanging out, having a wonderful time, waiting to die," Derian cried, wrapping his arm around the massive chain that was used to hold the equally massive propellor in place when the airbarge was not in flight. "In fact, I've had enough. I'm coming in. We can wait until we make landfall."

The three remaining propellor blades had been working just fine these last few days. A miraculous thing, really, considering the violence this airbarge had suffered at the hands of a grand demon. And this fourth propellor? Well, that had clunked and whirred and fought its spinning fight as long as it could. Earlier, at dawn, it had given up completely, and though Derian was no master of the sky, he could have sworn such a fantastic flying ship could stay afloat with three, or even two propellors.

Most certainly not one propellor, Kesta had assured him.

Definitely not.

Nope.

Regardless of three perfectly operational propellors, Kesta, the grand thief of them all and their only pilot, insisted they needed to do repairs immediately.

Fuk you, Kesta.

He'd argued against it, but she wouldn't have it. Instead, placing the monstrous airbarge a hundred feet or two above the rushing ocean and sending one idiot out along the edge had seemed like the smarter plan.

"Quiet, you!" roared Lorgan. "Just pull away at the debris around the edge and you can come in and have breakfast," he added.

Fuk you too, Lorgan.

"But... I lost the pole."

"That doesn't matter," Lorgan offered without missing a beat. He began stamping on the deck, pointing to the shards of jutting metal that had broken away and become entangled in the deadly blades.

"I can see land on the horizon," Derian cried desperately, even as he edged up over the blades towards the offending blockage. Glancing down, he wondered what had become of his trusty pole that he'd surrendered to the ocean. *A terrible end*, he mused, looking to the grey and white waves far below as they danced in a rushing, eternal sway.

He truly hated waves and all. Big bastarding things, doing nothing more than attempting to mess up everyone who sailed upon them, just for the sheer joy of it.

Yeah, fuk it. I think I'll hate the ocean too.

Derian had always intended to learn to swim properly, but sights like these would take the desire from anyone. The waves continued to rage, no doubt driven wild by the wind, and it was as daunting as staring into the eternal darkness of the source.

The source.

Derian really hated the fuken source. He had tried to explain his adventures into the source to his comrades these last few days, but they were loath to listen, or to try and understand. And really, why should they try to understand things that made little sense? Thinking on the source was akin to the mind hurting as it grasped for rationality in a spinning darkness. It was a place where the rules of known things simply didn't exist. Where time could run forward, backward or everywhere in between if it desired. Upside down too, if it felt like it. Who would argue?

The source was a maze of inexplicable moments and eternities. Where things of miniscule size could be as big as mountains, all in the same breath. Derian didn't even understand what had occurred while he marched through the source, save that, at the time, he had been rather confused by the whole matter; every day since, he forgot a little more of what had occurred. Even now, just thinking of it was akin to drinking so much alcohol one ended up lying on the floor, trying to rise and failing as the world spun something terrible.

He felt some nasty spinning altogether as well as he stared down at the vast ocean.

"Oh, for pity's sake, would you just get it done?" This query was from Natteo, his best friend and disaster of a comrade. Across the deck, he was swinging ever so from the frame of the open galley door, wearing a delighted grin on his charming face. He had taken to the galley these last few days. To deal with heartbreak, he claimed, but also to set his mind to cooking some truly awful meals. Natteo claimed they were "quite the delicacy" in the lands of his hated isle of Castra. Derian thought he was just a shit cook taking every opportunity to slag off Derian for the peasant he was.

"Get clearing the shit from that turbine thing," Natteo added, stepping up beside Lorgan and carefully eyeing the drop into the ocean below. "Whoa—that is some drop. Did you see that drop, Derian? That is some drop." He spat over the edge and it caught in the wind and flew far above and behind him and finally dropped to the sea below. "No one would survive that drop."

Derian agreed, but a drawn straw was a drawn straw and orders were orders, terrifying as they were.

Distantly, they heard Kesta's muffled curses as she struggled with the controls. The wind was wreaking havoc with the beast's hovering flight and she was keen to return to full power. They had not set down again as they travelled across Dellerin these last few days. Instead, Kesta kept to the sky, no doubt fearful that some cur, in the form of an aggrieved mercenary, would find a way to track them down and steal her precious new beast. Those sneaky mercenary curs had done sneakier and more impressive things in their illustrious careers. And perhaps the *Fighting Mongoose* was not the only airbarge at their disposal. She was fast, she was fierce, but she was lesser than some of the behemoths that soared the eternal blue.

Again, Derian looked to the horizon and the thin line of black peeking out above the rushing, endless waves. *Sanity and landing ashore to commence repairs are of little interest to the dark-skinned goddess,* he thought bitterly.

Seren.

It was also Seren's fault that they were still driving forward as swiftly as they could. Her coming had heralded the appearance of a grand demon. Who could be sure there weren't another six of them on the way? Lorgan and Kesta, that was for sure.

Fuken Seren.

She had looked at him without much interest these last few days, and strangely, Derian was untroubled by such a thing. Out on the march, with their lives on the line and little in the way of luxury, it was probably only natural that a ravishing girl without clothing would enamour him, but in this extravagance, Seren's beauty and grace had less of a hold on Derian than before. The more he got to know her, the vaster the differences between them became. He called her a comrade; perhaps he called her a friend. He most certainly called her a girl who might once have occupied his thoughts in the dark, wonderful moments when he was lying in bed with no one else around. But since the emergence of the grand demon, she hadn't been the same. Or, perhaps, she was exactly who she had always been.

Who are you, really?

The last few days, when she hadn't retired to sleep away the daylight hours, she had walked the deck looking out across the sea, deep in thoughts, no doubt, that were not meant for him. She only had time for Lorgan, in truth. And why not? When he wasn't standing at the edge of an airbarge barking out orders, he was quite the pompous, impressive cur. He had masterminded the survival of the town of Treystone, earning himself a little bit of a strut after enduring a lifetime of disappointment. This confidence was a good look to him, and while the rest of the Crimson Hunters looked to him with more confidence now, Seren gazed on him with something else entirely. Derian might have felt jealousy at such a thing, but he liked to think he had grown up these last few days. Besides, Seren herself had claimed there was a girl with nice knees somewhere out there. That was something to think about.

Clutching the chain lest he meet a grisly, water-soaked end, Derian began to stamp down upon the offending shards of metal blocking the blades. With every stamp, the debris began to slide free, yet the blades still stubbornly held.

"Oh, that is some wind, but it's a nice day for it," Natteo said, looking out across the ocean.

"A day for what?"

"Dying."

"Oh, would you fuk off," Derian muttered. "It's freezing out here," he added under his breath.

"It might be freezing, but at least the sun is out. I like sunny days," Natteo added dreamily, and a fresh coldness, not drawn from natural things, came upon Derian. Like a faded memory. Like a whisper of things to come. Like walking in the spitting source. Natteo turned from the clear morning to gaze at his friend's work as Derian placed as much weight as he could upon the blades. "You are doing it wrong," he added helpfully, and Derian hesitated, forestalling his next attempt, and offered his thoughts with a gesture.

"Let go of the chain," Natteo said. "Really lean down on that fuker."

"To the fires with you."

"I already went. I walked it off," Natteo replied. It was a fair comment. He had died. Thrice, in fact. That was one time more than the rest of the Crimson Hunters. Some people were perfectly adequate at dying. It just didn't stick with Natteo. He claimed to have seen something in the darkness beyond, but was wary of talking much on it, lest Derian begin going on about the source and its infuriating physics, which would confuse them both. It was probably a shrewd move on his part.

Suddenly, the shard of metal shunted and fell away.

He couldn't celebrate, though, for without warning there rose a terrible hissing shriek and Derian clung tightly to the chain.

"What the fuk was that?" Derian cried.

Along the edge where the propellors stuck out from the barge he saw a large hole where a panel of metal should have rested. And it was from here he guessed the shriek might have emerged. Peering into the hole, he caught sight of delicate movement and he froze where he huddled.

"I see something," he exclaimed, edging along the housing of the propellor, holding tight to that fuken chain, before reaching into the hole and pulling at a mound of wet, tangled mush.

"Oh, gods, what the fuk is that?" cried Natteo.

Her name had been Keralynn. She had been a bit of a whore. A bit of a bitch as well. She had started as an ambassador for the town, but like an apple turning in a battered barrel, she had revealed a nastier side, eventually leading a rebellion against the Crimson Hunters. A real shitty thing to do, after they had saved their entire town from oblivion. No nasty deed was left unpunished, however, for soon after that, and perhaps because the Crimson Hunters hadn't been in a position to intervene, she had met a grand demon's charge. The impact had thrown her high into the sky, where she'd met the propellors of the *Fighting Mongoose* and been splattered rather messily across the deck. Truly no way to die.

"Oh, spit on me," moaned Derian, staring incredulously at the bloody mess of blonde hair, dripping flesh and diced bone mush in his shaking hand. She'd already begun to rot. To stink. To become stickier. Shaking her away from his fingers was no easy task.

"Oh, dear. Was that some of Keralynn?" Natteo asked.

"I thought you cleaned all of her from the barge?" Lorgan muttered grimly. They had shared a night together. Derian imagined her betrayal had cut Lorgan that little bit deeper.

"I thought we did," Derian said unhappily.

"Don't throw it away," Natteo called. "Perhaps Lorgan wants to keep some of her... you know... as a memento." Natteo braced himself for the crack across the head long before he uttered the words.

Derian didn't keep any of the sludge as a memento. He opened his hand and let it drift in the cursed wind to the sea below, before reaching back in to pull the last of the human gunge from the hole.

As he did, he caught sight of a peculiar thing in the sea below, a large swirling in the water, and he wondered was this the phenomenon that sailors of doomed vessels usually called a whirlpool. He didn't know how he knew its name, nor why it fascinated him, but he couldn't keep his eye from it as it grew wider and deeper.

"What the fuk is that?" came a child's voice, and little Eveklyn stepped in between Natteo and Lorgan to gaze at the whirlpool below.

"That's just a whirlpool, little one," Lorgan insisted gently, turning to the girl they had kidnapped from the fallen town of Treystone.

Kidnapped.

Rescued was a more apt term. The child was an orphan, and Lorgan had taken it upon himself to pull her to freedom and simply not return her. In truth, it was her choice to stay with this unfortunate mercenary group, but really, the Guild would see her as kidnapped. The Guild were sticklers for these sorts of things. They would be in this case, too—that is, until Lorgan and the crew travelled to the Guild, eased a few coins into the right hands and were forgiven their actions. For now, though, Eveklyn was very much part of their merry group and had spent the few days since her "kidnapping" floating through the decks, slipping from cabin to cabin, watching the mercenaries at task. This very morning Derian had overheard Natteo giving her passionate instructions on how best to bake sweetened honey and eggcake, whatever the hell that was. She didn't speak a great deal. Instead, she mostly stayed quiet, listening, soaking up what she could. Sometimes, though, Derian wasn't sure she was even taking it in. He wondered if perhaps she was a little simple. Not that he'd say such a thing to Natteo. And most certainly not to Lorgan, who looked upon her like the child he'd never had.

Kesta, though, he might mention it to. She was no great fan of the child. In fact, whenever Eveklyn stood outside the cockpit observing the pilot in her manoeuvres, her silence unnerved Kesta somewhat. Kesta was rather vocal on that matter. But she didn't stop her. Moreover, she even explained a few techniques that meant little to Derian.

"No, I'm not talking about the whirlpool..." Eveklyn said with a gasp. "I'm talking about that thing beside Derian," she cried, gesturing to the hole.

It was in this perfect moment that Seren roused herself from her slumber and announced herself to the remaining Crimson Hunters with much menace and slamming of doors. Stumbling up the galley ladder and out onto the main deck, she stormed out onto the bridge, screaming as though ablaze. Her dressing gown barely contained her nudity beneath and, just like at their first meeting, she didn't seem to care.

"Help me," she wailed, waving her hands, all a-panic. She staggered along the deck as though drunk, her face pale, her eyes darting in terror. To any casual observer this would have been an alarming vision. As it was, this was the third or fourth time in half as many days she had appeared as such.

"Oh, for fuk's sake," muttered Natteo under his breath.

Her proclamations frequently involved "the coming of dark forces" and "monstrous things emerging."

"It was him... It was him..."

I'm sure it was.

"He knows who I am..."

Sure. Why wouldn't he?

"I stepped upon him..."

Ooh, you probably shouldn't have done that.

Derian sighed and eyed Natteo as Lorgan went to calm her. There were only so many times a girl could shriek about Venandi nighthunters and expect a band of hunters to grab up and go a-seeking, come a-saving.

"He said the demons hunt me," Seren cried at last, then leaned over the barge's edge and threw up.

No more cheese for you before bedtime.

Derian hated the sound of throwing up. He hated the smell and taste of it too. Mostly, though, he hated when the wind caught vomit and carried it his way in the wind.

Oh, please no.

It was a fine heave, flush with the remnants of the previous night's dinner. Plenty of chunks of meat and rice. It floated in front of him and all he could do was flick away the last of Keralyn, hate his life a little and hold his breath. With a dreadful acidic splat, it hit his face, and he smelled the rancid fluid in his nose as awful droplets smeared themselves upon him.

Of course.

"I can feel them. Help me," she cried, and Lorgan reached her with fine, comforting arms.

"It is fine, my dear," Lorgan insisted, cradling her, and Derian imagined she might even get one of Lorgan's pats. Such was Lorgan's blind faith and trust in the mysterious weaver.

"They are so close," she whimpered, and Lorgan held her tight as she shivered. She played dominant warrior something fierce. She also played victim and delicate waif just as skilfully. It was a small matter. Looking away, Derian dug into the hole one more time to pull out the last of Keralynn.

"Wait—hang on, Eveklyn. What thing were you talking about?" Natteo asked suddenly, looking away as Seren fell still in Lorgan's hold. It was a comforting thing, admittedly, his hold. Derian knew that from a long time before.

"The thing beside Derian," Eveklyn repeated, and Derian raised an eye.

And that's when the thing beside Derian attacked, shrieking as it did.

Source of All Evil

Seren stirs in the dark. Her movement is ethereal and slow. She does not like this feeling; she is not certain she is asleep. She is most certainly awake. When she is awake, she is not so cold. Not so tired. She is nowhere and everywhere all at once. She does not like this feeling. It is akin to suffocating. Drowning. To dying, too. It is also similar to getting an arrow shot through her mind at the worst possible moment.

She floats and walks, glides and wades, all in the same breath, without the use of her lungs. She moves well in this dark. Powerful strides, always forward, always deeper. She knows she should slow, should look around and avoid the inevitable, but she is drawn to the cold. Like nothing ever before. She does not know why. She does not like this. She will not stop, however.

"Is there anyone there?" she cries out in the misty darkness, and unsurprisingly, there is no reply. Nor would there be. This may be a dream; this may be her soul form taking a stroll through the source. Perhaps Derian will be here. Stumbling and clawing and killing and reviling. Perhaps Bereziel, with words of trust and truth and love. Perhaps something else. Something that will slay her from this world and the next.

Each night, slumber takes her. Releases her to this darkness. Yet still she rests her head. Does not fight the inevitable. She does not know why she allows herself be taken. She does not know why she desires to step further.

Dreams and the source have no shape nor meaning anymore. They simply mould into each other. She cannot help but feel lesser for this loss. Even if her mind welcomes such things. Within this horrid prison of a place, she is her true self, but also as far from herself as she could possibly be. It makes little sense, just like the source. Just like her dreams.

She feels her ethereal body glide forward and, with it, the dull, inane sensation of footsteps as her senses gather and her dreams become more visceral.

Deep she walks, hoping to find a path, hoping to remember the plan. For there must have been a plan, she believes. Why else would he draw her from the dark? Return her body to the living world where fewer beasties roam? Why else would she desire to return?

With every moment, her mind acclimatises as she gazes upon the twisted vision of many realms. These sights are blinding. Not meant for human eyes. Barely for those of gods, either. Demons, though, can see just fine, for they have lived here longer. She knows this as fact, but cannot remember where such truths were learned. Then lost through the tip of an arrow and a foolish boy. That same boy had such fire, a fire that she longed to unleash. If only she knew how.

"Fuk you, Derian," she whispers with lips barely moving. Barely even there, but she can see her breath slip from these lips.

He does not reply, and she knows now he is not the one she seeks.

Wrapping herself in her arms against the chill that might be in her mind, she strides into the night, seeking her master, Bereziel. Time is both eternal and nothing in this place, and she spends a lifetime and a half gliding into its hazy murk, until upon her path she sees a soul, all a-marching. All glimmering and beautiful, in a godly form. She does not know how she knows this, but she knows not to step upon the path lest she ignite and burn to nothing, such is the beauty. Or worse, edge this marvel from its own chosen path. More clearly now, she sees it walk as a boy younger than she but wise in decades beyond her. She sees purest sorrow in him and she wishes to know him, to bow, such is the indomitable spirit she sees in him; such is the nobility in his very essence.

"This is not for me," she whispers to herself as they pass upon the path. His steps are to greater things. His beauty is blinding, and she steps beyond him, daring not to meet his gaze lest she learn things not meant for her.

And in a breath not taken in the darkness, they pass.

"Good searching, friend," she whispers, and as swiftly as he appeared, he is gone from her mind, and she seeks out an answer to the questions moving in her fractured thoughts.

Ancient time passes from her grasp and still she

marches, wondering were she to wake from this dream might it seem a foolish daze? Might she sit upon the deck with a cup of tea and a sweetened oatcake from the clumsy makings of Natteo and laugh at this foolish dream with lovely Lorgan?

And then she wonders if she will ever wake. Will she find herself imprisoned in here, beaten to submission? To acquiescence. To reverence.

Like before?

And for just a pulse of time, Seren wonders, might she hold her step, slip back to consciousness and enjoy ignorance as her comrades might savour their chosen fates?

And the source must be listening to her imaginings, for in that hesitation she comes upon something darker than a crusted soul, a true darkness, and her heart in her body, in her bed, in her airbarge, begins to quicken.

She sees it as he wishes and still she walks, though this is not who she hunts, yet this is who she is fated to come upon.

"Is it you, Bereziel?" she whispers, though she knows this is a loose thought, a trained outburst, though she does not know why. Does not want to know why. Merely desires to glide closer. Draw upon her darkness that takes both love and joy and hope.

To kill.

To save.

To return.

To make my own.

To love.

She ventures deep into the darkness where no foolish young weaver should tread. She knows this because Bereziel showed her the poison of the Anguished One's true evil. She can almost imagine Bereziel now, clawing for her. Demanding her return. Demanding she draw a fist.

Where are you truly, master?

The dark spreads a mile high and deep and across, and at the same moment, she sees it as no more magnificent than a room a girl could take for her own upon a gliding airbarge. She sees it as a sphere and a cube fuelled by ancient vileness. She knows this is the domain of Anguis's demonic form.

She is terrified.

She is still walking.

"Who is this that drew me to this miserable place?" a terrible voice cries out. "Who speaks this cursed name?" It echoes around her as she steps through. His voice is simply a man's. More than that, it is a man's voice tinged with the voices of others. All speaking as one. All wrapped around the throat of this fiend. Cutting through her. Drawing her forth.

Her heart beats faster, and she knows she has inadvertently drawn the fiercest weaver into the source where she is hopelessly overpowered. Her feet touch upon hardened floor, and around her the vile dark becomes a room of his making.

She hesitates, then finally holds her step as though her limbs are finally her own, and watches this figure appear before her, sitting upon a golden throne of much impressiveness.

Anguis, the Dark One.

What have I done?

Anguis is hidden beneath a heavy cloak embossed with

runes and strange lettering. She can sense the power emanating from the cloak, even as it conceals the pulsing power of the form underneath. His head is hidden beneath a hood, as though he were asleep, and he lies casually across the throne, no doubt seeking comfort in uncomfortable things. One leg is slung across the other; his elbow supports his resting head as though he were bored and disinterested. Perhaps this is exactly what he is. Perhaps this is how he intends her to see him.

He does not look up, for she is little more than a wisp of nothing in this dark. But he speaks again. "What is this?" he whispers.

She will not reply, for there is strength in silence. Why give the cur a thing?

He stretches and allows his hood to fall free and he is young and good looking and so vile to gaze upon. Distantly, she can feel the presence of others. Stirring. Waking. Peering and creeping.

"Ah, yes. Another trick from the source," he spits, and now she sees it upon his throat. A serpent slithering. He doesn't seem to notice. "Is this your making, Silencio?" he growls.

"Are you the Anguished One?" she asks, after another lifetime has passed, and the world appears to quiver as though she were upon a struggling, quaking barge. For just a breath, she wonders might there be some turmoil in the waking world, and as swiftly as the worry struck her, she allows it to leave, lest he dig into her mind and read all manner of delicious secrets.

Anguis sighs deeply, as though it is habit and little more. Smoothly, he steps from his throne and glides towards her, and she is terrified and intrigued. Not even for a breath does she believe him to be luring her with an enchantment. She does not believe him capable of such a thing. She is stronger than that. Isn't she?

"Anguished?" he says after an eternity. There are at least five other voices to his words. This she knows to be true. As though to confirm this, a spider-looking beastie sprints across the floor between them and he stamps carelessly at it. "Yes, dear spectre, I am anguished." He spreads his hands open to her, mockingly. "Love has made me as I am." For just a breath she feels that anguish, but more than that, she feels his strength, and, curses upon her, for just a stolen breath not of this world, she desires this strength. She knows it is a curse of any fine weaver to crave this power.

She knows she is not ready for such things.

Not yet.

But I want it all.

His words echo around the room and he begins to chuckle. An unsettling thing, with so many voices. As though she is upon a stage offering her finest wit for the good of the crowd. "And I am a better fiend for it," he offers. The spider beastie, a thing both human and arachnid, scampers away to lose itself in the dark, and he is closer now. Peering into her eyes. Into her soul.

"I am Seren... of the Crimson Hunters," she says after a time, an age, a patient infinity, and he seems intrigued. There is a familiar glimmer to his eyes, and she is beginning to believe this is a dream after all.

"Tell me... Seren, is this a dream I find myself in?"

She does not understand. "If it is, this is my dream," she warns, and his eyes lose their glimmer.

"You come to this place bearing a dead man's name," he snaps suddenly, and he stands before her and he is no giant. He is simply a human. Taken by demons, for certain. But still human, no doubt. As he moves, his cloak opens ever so and she is drawn to his chest and the dim glow of power emanating from within. She wishes to reach for that power, take it as hers, but she knows she can't. He is enshrouded in much enchantment. Too many enchantments.

This might be no dream.

"I come in search of my master," she replies, and wonders why she willingly gives away such things. She might step away from him, but, instead, desires to reach for him. Tear his thurken heart out.

At these words he diminishes and steps away from her. Not in fear or disgust but rather in thought—and something more. She wants to follow but also flee. Away from him she is more herself. She is Seren of the Crimson. She is fierce.

Eventually, as her wits return to her, he speaks again. "So, you come hunting a dead man? Lost in the source these many years?"

He looks ever so dishevelled now, and around him she feels the presence of her master. Distant and seeking. She desires to call out to him.

So she does.

"Master, where are you?"

At this, he looks around in glee. "Is it really him?" he roars, and around him terrible shadows form up, mimicking his movement. Though with more horns and spikes. "Is this truly real?" he roars, and she feels his excitement, and it is a terrifying thing. "Is this beauty of horror standing before me no dreadful enchantment?" He goes to caress her face and recoils. He spins around and around, and within the darkness she feels them closer now. Scratching and braying. Beasts of ancient times. Licking and shuffling, sniffing and hunting.

Getting my scent.

Again.

"Where are you, fiend?" Anguis howls, and it is terrifying. He spins around the room like a child hunting a hissect. Eager to kill and trap and destroy. And she feels the call of the waking world. No doubt she's been gifted such a thing by Bereziel's will.

She wants to call out to her master and claim her hunt.

She wants to go to war with her master and own it all.

She only needs to join him in battle.

And win.

"I can feel him. So, too, can my... friends," Anguis whispers, and suddenly he pierces her mind and she fights him. An instinctive wall draws up against his sudden claim, and she is terrified but enchanted. She feels his lure, feels the temptation to break. To give in.

She will learn from this.

"They can sense you too... Seren," he says when she fends him off, and he steps away and she is immediately colder.

"Will you set them upon me?" she asks.

"Oh no, dear... Seren. Why would I do that? Why would I need to? They are their own vile kind with their own vile actions. They cannot hunt me." His eyes blaze in threat and fire. His voice is just a man's without the taint of demon. Yet still cold and cruel. "But they will hunt you."

She draws away from him as she fades, and suddenly she is flying. "I can protect you, though," he pledges, and she knows it to be true. Even as she knows he will enslave her for the price. She is terrified. She is cold. She is screaming, and he wails for her as she fades.

She is flying.

No.

Falling.

Seren gazed to the ceiling as she fell, a painful thing. Wrapped in her damp bedding, she struggled to her feet, still sensing the evil things afoot. She had misspoken and revealed the words of Bereziel. Somehow, she knew this to be a calamitous mistake on her part.

As was revealing herself to the demons, for she sensed them still coming. Still hunting. Though why was beyond her. This dream was a thousand times worse than any before, for it *was* real. It had to be. "I am not that valuable," she muttered and felt a terrible pang of dread as the world around her shifted. As though something of great power and horror was revealing itself.

Hunting her.

"What have I done?" she wailed, stumbling from her room into the bright, windy day beyond, for everything was about to take a terrible turn.

And she was right.

THE BEAST FROM BENEATH

It was a cat. A white cat with a big body, very sharp claws and a piercing cry. Natteo was certain that Derian didn't know this when it attacked him. It was a fine leap. It cleared the entire wing, springing across the gap, before landing on Derian's unsuspecting face.

"What the fuk?" he cried, and Natteo could only watch with a held breath. Truthfully, it was a perfect moment to mock his best friend. He could have suggested he'd met his match. Or that he had that type of face that just needed a clawing. Might even have been that the beast was only clawing him because he loved him, and that it hurt the cat more to do it. Really, the possibilities were endless. The problem was the precariousness of the attack and the guarantee that Derian would slip to his watery doom.

"What the fuk? What the fuk? *What the fuk?*" Derian screamed heroically, wavering ever so as he did.

The cat hissed and spat and clawed at its victim, but somehow, Derian remained upright. He leapt away from the propellors, scurried along the thin edge and somehow collapsed back over the edge of the barge onto the bridge. All with the cat still attached, heralding the mocking to begin.

"I think you're winning," Natteo suggested. "I believe in you."

"Get it off me, get it off me, get it off me."

"I think it's tiring. You'll get it in the second round. Keep your left up."

"Someone kill it. Kill it. Fuken kill it," Derian cried, sounding ever the impressive mercenary as he spun around the deck, all to the sound of the wailing feline, and Natteo could now enjoy how hilarious this was, allowing his laughter to ring out.

Even Seren released herself from Lorgan's reassuring grasp to watch the spectacle, and Natteo's eyes narrowed. He wanted to trust her. It would be better for the Crimson if he trusted her, but he simply couldn't. Wouldn't. Something deep within him just couldn't settle. Perhaps he was being unfair to the girl. She'd had it rough. But Natteo's gut went against her. And the fact that she stole from their souls to heal herself was a sin taken too far. The fact that he didn't believe he had a soul didn't matter. It was the principal of the thing. She hadn't even properly apologised. Or given it back afterwards. Oh, no, she had simply grown in strength and barely said a word since. Apart from going on about the source and demons and the Dark One.

Fuk off, Seren.

"What is that thing?" she cried in both delight and wariness, and her hands became thin glowing embers of fire, and Natteo stepped between her and Derian and the impressive cat, lest she scorch the beastie to charred meat.

Natteo fancied himself quite the chef, but roast cat was not a delicacy he ever intended to eat again. Let alone prepare.

Although a nice orange sauce would go well with it.

Another thing that irritated Natteo was Seren's sudden advancement in the Crimson Hunters. Or, more to the point, Lorgan's neglecting to set her to menial tasks. She waltzed around the barge all wistful and spit, while Derian and Natteo were ordered to its upkeep. Cooking food. Mopping the deck. Climbing out on a terrifying wing to clear some obstructions in the propellors under a barrage of flying cats. Both he and Derian had put in far longer a time, earned greater experience than she, yet Lorgan elevated her above them both combined. It wasn't fair. It was decisions like that which edged both Natteo's and Derian's favour towards leaving this shitty outfit. Aye, they were polished as spit at this present time, but like that same gut feeling that didn't trust Seren, he also felt it was nearing time to get gone. That something was on the horizon. Something rightly nasty.

From the source or beyond.

He might have spoken to Derian about it, but the cur would listen intently until Natteo took a breath before launching into his own thoughts on the source. That Natteo suspected both issues could be connected wasn't enough to justifying his enduring the hours Derian would go on about things indescribable. Natteo had visited the source. His visit had been far less vivid and all the more terrifying.

So, all in all, things weren't looking particularly good for the Crimson Hunters, and Natteo wanted out. To the fires with the rest of them. Even if he loved them, even if he'd kill for them, perhaps die for them again as well. Truthfully, Natteo considered only Derian as an irreplaceable comrade. Natteo liked to think Derian thought the exact same thing.

"It's just a harmless cat," Natteo hissed to Seren, who eyed him warily. "Derian is just being a bitch about it." Seren hesitated, but those fingers stayed alight in fire. "You didn't have those in the source?" he asked, and her fingers fidgeted and fell still. "And don't be stealing my soul while you are at it," he added.

If she was hurt at the accusation, she showed little more than a frown before spinning away as Derian's screaming began to match the attacking cat's.

"Get me my spitting sword," Derian demanded, finally pulling the hissing creature from his scratched, bleeding face and launching it across the deck, where it landed gracefully, before facing him with tail straight and impossibly fluffy. It growled as loudly as a hound over a bone.

"That thing is a demon," Derian cried, discovering the blood streaming down his face.

"All cats are," Natteo countered, and loved them for that fact.

"Spit on this. He's dead." The sword Derian called for was Rusty. It most certainly was once a sword. Now it was a dagger. A piece of shit dagger, to be precise. He should have known better than to call for it. They had all manner of swords to choose from deep in the hold. All owned by the mighty Army of the Dead before they were stolen. All bright, sharp and pretty, in every shape and size. Swashbuckling swords. Hefty hammers. Beautiful bows. Masterful maces... and so on, and still, Derian called for a piece of shit dagger, because he was an idiot. Some mercenaries held on to their relics and never knew any better.

New weapon or no, that Rusty dagger could do all manner of harm to any beastie. Even an enraged Anculous demon. Even a cat with little prickly claws.

"Rusty daggers wouldn't be a fair fight," Natteo offered. Derian looked ready to skin the cat with his bare hands, and Natteo wondered if the nasty demon monster-type thing in him wasn't unleashed. He hoped not. He remembered seeing that cat asleep in a nook above Boab's bed when he'd climbed aboard the airbarge that fateful night and thought little more of it. It was no stray; it had mercenary, legendary owners. It was one thing stealing their airbarge. It was an entirely different thing murdering their fluffy comrade.

Eveklyn came alive at the cat's appearance. She chased after the white-furred beast, screaming in delight.

"I always wanted a cat," she cried. All morning she'd studied his cooking without so much as a word, and the first thing he'd heard in two days was this. Typical peasant. Amused by shiny things. That would be the last time he'd take time to train her.

Little harsh.

He thought of the traumas she had endured leading to her "liberation" and felt a little ashamed for his lack of patience. She was still growing into her title as an orphan.

Gliding across to the aggrieved Derian, Seren waved her fingers across his face, easing the pain and vanishing away the fresh scars in a breath. As she did, she stumbled sideways for a moment and both Lorgan and Natteo leapt to catch her lest she collapse. She was light and barely a thing despite her height. Shaking her head and releasing herself from their grip with a weak, embarrassed smile, she ran her fingers unconsciously through her long, dark hair.

"Oh, that feels better," Derian said, feeling his face and discovering only drying blood and perfectly sculptured skin.

"Thank you," she breathed to Natteo, bowing deeply in an infuriatingly charming way before darting off after Eveklyn to catch the white cat. She squealed wildly as she went, and for an annoying breath, the better part of Natteo warmed ever so to Seren and her naïve, curious ways.

For only a breath, though.

The cat would not be charmed so easily. Though it did not screech or growl or attack, it retreated along the deck as Eveklyn cooed and hushed at it, as only children could. Natteo couldn't remember what name Boab had called the beast when they'd first crept into his room, save that Boab was rightly pissed the cat had been in his room "getting up to shit."

"I want to keep him," cried Seren, joining the child's desire for furry things.

Derian, though healed at the expense of no soul whatsoever, was less enthused. "Yeah, well, I'd like to eat him."

With an orange sauce on the side, and maybe a few shallots.

"He might be tastier than some of the swill Natteo has been feeding us."

Eveklyn shot around, her voice concise and angry. "We won't be eating him." Perhaps the cat was a good thing, after all, mused Natteo, taken aback by the child's passion. Perhaps they'd best not eat the near-defenceless creature.

"Here kittie, kittie. Come to Eveklyn," she murmured, dropping to her knees in front of the animal—charming him, no doubt. Seren, unsure of what she was doing, mimicked the child and appeared delighted with herself.

"Meow."

"What'll we call him, so?" Natteo called.

"Lunch!" Derian offered.

"Meow."

"Shut up, Derian," Seren countered, before the child could.

"Fine. Fine. What about Kittie of the Dead," Derain said after a breath. "You know. Because we stole him from…"

"That's really fuken stupid," Natteo muttered.

"Fuk off. It's witty."

"Meow."

"He seems to like it."

"How about Keddy?" Seren offered.

"Meow, meow."

"Keddy it is," Kesta murmured, appearing from the cockpit and eyeing the cat suspiciously. She leaned out over the edge of the barge to inspect Derian's handiwork. She wasn't foolish enough to climb out fully herself. Derian, though, was expendable. Satisfied, she offered a rare smile, knowing her baby would be flying better once more.

Natteo wasn't used to her genuine smile. It was a pleasing thing to be around. Even if it wasn't brought on by his usual wit.

"How in the gods did that thing get aboard?" she asked.

"I think he always lived here," Natteo said, feeling the guilt of stealing yet another thing from his boyfriend.

Natteo had to wonder just how much the Crimson could take from the Army of the Dead before Boab would not forgive him. The cat might be the lynchpin.

Ah, well. Love was nice while it lasted.

"Probably got a right shock when that grand demon took a hold of us," Lorgan muttered, eyeing the hiding hole it had climbed into. Probably knew the ship better than the rest of the mercenaries combined. Probably knew all manner of wonderful hiding places and all.

"How did it survive these last few days?" Kesta wondered, dropping to a knee, and immediately the cat took a liking to her. It jogged on past both Eveklyn and Seren and leapt into Kesta's arms as though they were companions of a decade. "Nice Keddy. Won't you go and hunt all the rats for me, yeah?"

Even the cat is given more responsibilities than Seren.

"Just like our esteemed leader, I reckon… Keddy…" Natteo hesitated, enjoying the moment. "… had a taste for Keralyn." It was worth the slap, but Lorgan really threw what he could into it.

"Didn't hurt!"

It really hurt.

Satisfied that the four propellors were working sufficiently, Kesta, carrying the cat back to the cockpit, soon became surrounded by a giggling Eveklyn and mesmerised Seren, as they welcomed the creature to the Crimson Hunters.

"It is nice to see the little one so animated," Lorgan said, sitting up against the balcony of the barge and watching the trio at the cockpit. Eveklyn had come upon some strips of meat that hadn't been infused with some of Natteo's more exotic spices. The cat, no doubt thrilled with fresher flesh without blonde hair running through it, ate greedily, all to the delight of Seren, who looked less and less likely to burn the beast to a crisp.

"Well, at least it was a decent fight," admitted Derian, finally seeing the humour in the cat attack.

"Just another few moments and you'd have had it," Natteo offered, sitting beside Lorgan and dangling his feet out over the steep drop so he could gaze out across the ocean.

He really thought it a beautiful sunny day.

"Yeah, little Ked had the element of surprise. Caught me cold is all. A cat like that wouldn't have lasted another six or seven rounds."

Lorgan chuckled. A rare thing. "You shouldn't have led with your chin," he noted. "Should have moved those sorry excuses for feet," he added, raising his impressive fists, mimicking a pugilist's stance ever so subtly. For just a breath, beneath that grin, he was away from them. A thousand miles off, no doubt thinking of other things.

"His jab kept me off guard, but next time I'll have the beating of him."

"Course you will, boy, and next time I won't put money on the cat."

"Next time just kick the fuken thing," Natteo offered, laughing. He knew Derian well enough to know that by day's end he would be stealing scraps for Keddy's favour. Derian was a sucker for such things. And Natteo? Well, he was master of the kitchen. That feline beast would be better fed than all of them put together. Natteo would be Keddy's favourite.

Until he returned him to Boab as a pathetic attempt at redeeming himself.

"Nice job, Derian," Lorgan said after a time, patting Derian on the back, and it cut Natteo to the core. Derian was three Lorgan's love pats ahead now. And that was some rightly fuken shit. There was some serious playing up to do if he wanted to get back in the game. Or else do some hard work in his immediate future.

Derian was delighted with the praise and winked at his competitor. He was counting too.

"With a bit of luck, we can get on to Dellerin, maybe pay off our bounty, clear any outstanding warrants... Clear our name of any mutterings... Start earning again," Derian said thoughtfully, patting the edge of the barge that was the source of their increasingly changing fortunes. Clear of a bounty was a unique thought and one they were thoroughly unused to. It was that bounty on their heads that kept them earning lesser contracts on the smaller islands of Dellerin. Get back to Dellerin City, get some nice easy contracts that paid far more, would be polished indeed. Things were looking up for them something wonderful.

Natteo was immediately suspicious of such good fortune.

Looking around and taking a breath, Natteo joined the others in their reveries over the thought of wealth. He gazed out to the land, then down at the growing swell below them, and his stomach took a delicate turn. Probably just the airbarge hitting a little pocket of warmer air. The other morning, Kesta had explained such things to him, but he hadn't really been listening at the time. He'd been working on mixing up an orange sauce.

Looking down, though, he thought the ocean looked ever so threatening: the whirlpool was growing exponentially in size. A mile across at least, with a funnel at the centre that grew deeper and deeper. Real fuken deep. So deep that a ship would be swallowed up in no more than a breath. Around them, the air began to cool. Natteo saw his breath, and a fear took him ever so.

"That's a strange whirlpool," he said warily, and the others looked down to the gaping maw of ocean as it darkened and grew wide, calling all natural things into it. There came a pull in the breeze, and instinctively, Natteo climbed back behind the balcony and immediately wondered about climbing back into the galley, sealing the door, sealing every fuken door, while Kesta brought this beast high and far away from this unnerving thing below.

"What is it?" Derian asked aloud.

As though she, too, gazed down upon it, Seren suddenly spun towards them. "Something is terribly wrong."

MEANWHILE, BACK
IN HELL

Erin took the lead as they marched. A battered duo, captain and private. Her captain. And she, a lesser private. New to this war. New to discipline and all that regimented shit. Most considered little Erin to be cheerful and sweet and useless in war. They didn't know her at all. She was merely *almost* useless. She was fleet of foot, but she'd never been the finest warrior. She was smaller than most, with hardly any muscle to her punch. She'd still happily throw a punch if needed, though. She could swing a sword, and usually in the right direction. She could read like the wind, though, and that was something.

This night, Erin felt lighter than before. As though some absent god guided her step. Rhendal, her captain, still carried his injuries. He was hardened, though, and kept up as best he could. A good man, she believed. Gruff and calm. Wiser than his rank suggested. More than that. He still barked orders, too. Even if they were only whispered.

"Keep your head down, little one," Rhendal warned as they cleared the gates of the house, their sanctuary, and ventured out into the dark streets where all manner of nasty fiends and demons might be creeping. The streets were emptier than she'd ever seen in this city before. Why wouldn't they be, what with all the bloodshed and thundering murder that had occurred? Who wanted to be out in the dark at this late hour? Who was alive enough to want to, either?

The thin, slitted moon glimmered through the heavy clouds, making the path a right nasty trek, but more than that, keeping them better concealed. As far as desperate retreats through a battlefield went, there could have been worse. She told herself this to keep that assuredness. To stop that nasty, biting feeling deep in her belly that things were going to take a terrible turn.

Erin had spent a lifetime traversing in dim light. Any wretch from the streets endured such things. She only needed to see a foot in front of her and let everything look after itself after that. It probably wasn't the finest outlook to life, or indeed to a dimly lit trek, but so far, she still took breath.

"Aye, sir," she whispered, peering into the gloom. Though her steps were careful and lithe, he may as well have been a right thundering boar. She might have said as much. It wasn't like he was going to report her for degrading a captain. Yet still, the words never came. He was badly injured. Perhaps he could be forgiven a little clumsiness. The day's rest, hidden away reading *The Seven: A Dellerin Tale*, had allowed them a chance to treat the injuries, but he needed a proper healer to get him back to his best.

Though she was terrified, there was a daring in Erin this night. It was down to the reading of the book. It still rested in her pack. Heavy and awkward and oddly reassuring. It was a strangely written tale; the author had a talentless flair for prose and over-indulgent description. Still, though, there was something ethereal to its creation. And she couldn't help but wonder about its greater power.

"Any ideas, sir?"

He seemed to appreciate the respectful tone. Perhaps out here, just as she felt safe in a book's presence, he felt better in barking out orders, whispered as they were.

"You are leading us well, Erin," he whispered, and for just a breath, she wondered how he felt to be a captain of one. To have commanded an entire legion and in moments be down to little more than a handful. A moment after that, to be left with only swift-footed Erin, who had been lucky enough to keep her head down by means of stumbling and tripping down behind a battered wagon just as fire came upon them all.

Black, demonic fire.

Shivering at the memory, she silenced the awful screams in her mind. With the cover of darkness as their ally, she crept down through the path, further and further away from Bereziel's long-forgotten lair. Hugging dark shadows, sticking close to whatever covering wall she could call upon, she and Rhendal moved with determined steps. Each one brought them further from the fires of the northern part of the city, away from the fires of the stronghold, away from the Dark One's stronghold.

Just two little shadows, gliding along. Nothing to see here.

For a time they shuffled, sprinted and rested. An agonizingly slow pace, but at least assured. Catching their breath behind a broken wall, they gathered their wits and she looked into the night far behind, to where they'd come from. Again, the screams played their anguish in her mind. Immolated screams as the fire took their breath and innards and the rest of them after. She bit the inside of her cheek. An unpleasant habit she'd learned as a child. The pain was welcome; she focused on it instead of the horror.

"My heart is racing," Rhendal whispered, wiping his brow. "Can't hardly catch my breath, either." Distantly, she caught a sound of a high-pitched wail, but it was lost in the wind. It was no matter. It was a day and a little since the fall of the army. No reason to believe there were still nightmares roaming these streets, seeking out stragglers.

Still, though, looking far back, she was drawn to the fortress. She could only see the great stone walls and the dim illumination of a thousand torches lighting the building within. It had once been a palace. She had seen paintings of it. Now, it was an indomitable fortress. A prison for the vile king. And a cage for his demons. It was also the resting place of the dead. And possibly the revolution. That last thought stung her something fierce. She wondered how many had died after the first wave. If the fire and demons and the Anguished One had charged right back through the city, killing all who marched upon him.

We arrived as a nation.

How many of us still breathe?

She suddenly thought of the book in her pack and allowed her hope to kindle. Without hope there was nothing. Her hands suddenly began to tingle as though dipped in a warm cup of honey tea. Not enough to scald, but warm enough regardless. "We should not delay. The dawn will catch us badly, and we have miles to go," she said.

"Wait—wait a moment. I think I know the way back from here," Rhendal whispered, eyeing the night, and the struggling stars above. Erin could tell he was lying. No doubt playing the part of captain to one private. Out here, in the coldness of the night, it was easy to remember the pain, forget the assuredness of a childish tale. Of the comfort of a hidden sanctuary.

Are you real, Bereziel?

Are you coming to save us all?

Is there still a war?

Am I an idiot?

I probably am.

"How about we aim towards the gates, sir," Erin offered, pointing to the outer walls, to the large gap where the wall had been split open. They were far away, though. So fuken far.

"Aye, sounds like a plan, private," he agreed, and fell in behind her as she scrambled forward through the ruins.

Further in, the path worsened, for away from the fortress the buildings were little more than mounds of rubble. Scrambling up and over one such mound, she caught her step, and helped Rhendal back down into cover.

"This is difficult going, with injuries like mine," he muttered, grimacing as he fought the pain. Three fiends had fallen to his blade as the cost of such injuries. Three fiends that would likely have killed her, were Rhendal not swift with his brutality. She had only hesitated for a moment at the time. Who wouldn't after seeing a gathering of demonic bastards lay waste to a thousand warriors?

She thought again of the fiend. Anguished and eternal and ever evil. Floating upon a cloud of deathly black smoke and black fire that covered the sky and hung there, and it was horrible.

Tripping on a jutting snag, she stumbled ever so and freed herself from the obstacle, only to realise with horror that it was an outstretched hand.

"Poor fool," Rhendal said of the hand, clenched and rigid in its dying grasp. Erin took a moment to gaze at the decoration on the dead hand's fingers. She wondered why ever a woman would paint her fingers with all manner of stars and colours?

"I hope they were your pride, before the world sucked you up," Erin whispered, and, curses on her, she took hold of the freezing hand and squeezed it once. "They were a lovely design," she added.

"We must be scrambling over a thousand and one similar civilians," Rhendal murmured, standing tall and looking around. Erin couldn't tell if it was pride or revulsion in his features and decided on the latter, for really, they weren't the enemy. Not really.

Necessary for greater things.

"A terrible sin on our part, admittedly," she said.

"Aye, but an unavoidable sin," Rhendal said, and she nodded. War was full of many such atrocities. The winners never spoke of such things. The winners never cared about such things, either. Why should they taint their history? Better their people believe them to be superior heroes, doing what they did for the betterment of all. Liberation came at a cruel cost, though, didn't it? Sometimes it wasn't even liberation, but invasion with better word of mouth. And she had fallen for it. In the first hour's march, with a thousand comrades spread out around her, with her sword in hand and a scream in her lungs, she had felt mighty, surging beneath the fractured gates, through the city walls, high and impenetrable by any living fiend, save a grand crustacuus eager for human flesh.

Just like in a storybook.

Or some other similarly terribly written book.

Where murder was reserved for those most deserving.

Erin could not argue with Rhendal on the matter of righteous murder. She had grown up beyond the city, hundreds of miles away. Yet still, these may as well have been her people, and she had no argument with a single one. Their politics were merely different to hers. They were simple people living under tyranny like the rest of the people in the Isles of Dellerin. This close to his lair, they were simply too close to the fire and as a consequence had been unwittingly burnt to charred husks.

These Dellerin City inhabitants weren't alone in their actions or behaviour either. Most people across the seven islands had little interest in challenging this ruthless cur. They paid their exorbitant taxes, they enforced the Dark One's laws, they fell in line and did his bidding where need be. They did what was necessary to keep away from Anguis's gaze. And they most certainly had little interest in offering up troops up for an ill-fated assault on the capitol. Alas, that type of behaviour had attracted the disapproving eye of the demonic king, and she couldn't resent their choices, no matter what.

Apart from Karkur.

She longed to visit that mystical, mysterious place. She'd probably need a sword in the hand and all if she did. Beautiful Karkur. The gem of Dellerin. Rich with forests, runes, waterfalls, valleys, meadows… and weavers. As far from the grey of Dellerin as could be, Karkur took no step back from anybody. Especially a cruel, demonic cur sitting on the throne.

A decade or so later, Karkur still held off the fiend's approach. Some said Karkur had even beaten off his advances at one point. Regardless, the isle stood as an homage to the spirit of humanity when all around it lost their heads. Aye, the beautiful lands were a lesser thing after ten years, but still, Erin couldn't help but feel drawn to the place.

She always had.

If I could just steal myself an airbarge.

Truth was, Karkur's defiance was a major reason for the taking of the city. In a desperate bid to break the shield keeping Karkur protected, Anguis had instructed his airborne armada to lay waste to the great island in the hope of crushing their resistance once and for all. Splitting his armed forces and sending them far across the world was a calculated risk. Or it would have been if word hadn't reached them sooner.

Distantly, there came another piercing cry, lamenting unimaginable things, and Erin froze, mid-step. Rhendal crashed into her. "What are you doing?"

"Can you not hear it? That shrill cry is terrifying." She peered back into the gloom and, unsurprisingly, heard little and saw even less.

Rhendal looked around warily for a time and they waited in silence until the cry suddenly sounded again. "Aye, I fuken heard that one. Probably an injured beast of burden somewhere below a boulder."

Erin glided along the crumbling path, and again she thought of how many lay beneath the rubble. Some perhaps even breathing and screaming, never to be recovered. With a shudder, she pressed on, seeking an escape from this battlefield, careful not to trip up on any grasping hands along the way.

Battlefield.

She almost laughed at the absurdity of it. There had been no battle; there had only been annihilation.

Hearing movement behind them, both weary warriors ducked into a side street to take a breath and keep an eye upon the path, the ruins, even the sky. Leaning against the wall of a ruined building, she caught sight of a smear of blood from Rhendal's wounds on the bricks, dripping down ever so. Again, that piercing cry filled the night. Closer. Far closer. A concerted, piercing cry, like wolves at a hunt. All emanating from the fortress.

"Oh, fuk me—that's no beast of burden," Rhendal muttered, wrapping his tattered bandaging a little tighter. "Oh, no. This can't be happening," he cried, as the colour drained from his face. Might have been the blood loss. "The fuken book has me shaken here," he hissed.

"The book?"

"Your spitting book—the one in your pack."

"What?"

"I've heard them before, Erin. From the safety of an airbarge. Out over Venistra a few years ago. They shouldn't be here. They can't be here. He's not that mad to let them loose."

"You are scaring the shit out of me."

"That's good. Won't help nothing, but at least you'll be ready."

"What is out there?"

"Venandi night hunters," he said, leaning out to gaze down the path. It had taken them a lifetime to come this far, but there were still miles to go.

"Like in the book? With... um... Cherrie?" she said, meaning the unfortunate legendary mercenary who had met the hunters' savageness bravely, after they tracked her down in the night.

"Aye. The cur must have been keeping them in his fuken basement, waiting for the darkness, sending them out to hunt down anyone foolish enough to be on the streets."

"Wait. Like us? You think they hunt us?"

"They hunt fuken everyone, and they will find us by night's end," he cried, then straightened and darted off towards the distant gates. So far. So very far away. He was not careful; he was not silent. Erin could only follow as the savage howls began to increase. As though whatever it was had caught the scent of something rightly delicious.

Rhendal turned to her, urging her on. "Let's go, little one," he demanded.

"Bereziel, help us," she whispered in prayer, and felt all hope diminish as they raced through the night, seeking a safety that could never be found.

The Real Beast from Below

It was no cat. It was bigger. Far, far bigger, and Derian could only gaze in horror at the many-tentacled beast emerging from the depths. The ocean spun. It gushed like a spirit geyser in Brimlore Fields. An awe-inspiring sight, and Derian fell dumb in fear.

Natteo didn't. He stood up beside him. "Hey, remember when we were a rightly shitty group of mercenaries, just fuking around at the far end of nowhere without a care in the world or a win to our name?"

"That was a week ago," Lorgan muttered.

"Aye. The good old days," Natteo said. His voice quivered ever so, despite his grin. "Back when shit like this happened as far away from us as could be." He tapped the airbarge's balcony railing as though regretting the speed they could travel into trouble in this beast. Derian, however, loved the *Fighting Mongoose*. Even if they could swiftly fly into bad luck and bad trouble. Besides, they could also get rightly far away if they decided. Far away from this monster if they decided too. They merely had to decide. Who would know? Who would care?

"Suck it up, Natteo. That's why we are mercenaries," Lorgan declared, all pompous like, and Derian realised that Lorgan had decided they would not be sailing away into the great blue above, but instead, attempting to tackle a many-limbed horror from the great below.

With a fresh piercing cry of nightmare horror, the beast reared its head above the frothy water and oh, it was ancient. And more than that, familiar. Derian's heart sank. The last few days, Lorgan had insisted they study what they could of demons, and grand demons, and every monster in between, in the Successful Mercenary's Compendium. He hated that guide something fierce. Even if it had all manner of helpful tips for avoiding getting killed.

The monster resembled a creature called a puilypus. Albeit, one a thousand times bigger than his book suggested. And according to his ever-so-helpful book, this particular prick puilypus went by the name of Clamamus the Grand Demon.

Fuk this shit.

Not again.

Seren suddenly appeared beside them and gazed down in horror at the massive monster below. "It can't be," she gasped, wrapping her arms around herself as the beast did the exact opposite with all eight massive limbs. "It can't be…"

"Of course it can be," Natteo argued, eyeing the girl with unrivalled disgust. "Since you showed up, if something *can* be, it most certainly *will* be." It was a fair point, and to emphasise this aggrieved point, he spat over the edge at the creature below.

Seren didn't bother to argue. Sometimes that was the safer bet with a Natteo point. Besides, there was a grand demon climbing out of the ocean looking for her. Best to focus on one thing at a time. "He claimed they would hunt me," she added.

Who?

Bereziel?

"Why would they hunt you?" Lorgan grunted, just as the beast released its great tentacles from the salty spray and extended them skywards as though stretching after a lifetime entangled in each other. Perhaps this was exactly what the tentacles had been doing until the Crimson Hunters took this moment to park their airbarge over its territory.

What are the chances?

Derian thought on that moment for a breath, and a coldness came over him. There was no chance at all.

"I don't know why they hunt me," Seren said. "Only that they do," she added weakly, and Derian didn't trust her words. Saying that, for his entire life he had never been able to tell if ladies were lying to him. He found it unlikely that, in this very moment, he had mastered the art of catching a truth. Still, though, she shuffled and looked awfully guilty all of a sudden.

"Well, it's certainly hunting someone," Lorgan muttered.

Though the first grand demon, the giant spider fiend Fiore, was an impressive grand demon, this bastard Clamamus could have loomed over that bitch thrice over.

No fuken airbarge blades would be cutting its head from its shoulders either. Mostly because it had neither.

As the beast's body emerged fully and floated along the surface, causing massive waves to break around it, Derian instinctively took a step back.

"We are dead."

"Shut up, Derian. Get to arms," Lorgan roared, studying the wildly waving tentacles as they rose and dropped, sending thunderous waves in every direction. Lorgan drew his sword. A foolish notion, really, for the limbs of this beast would suffer little injury, even from a hundred drawn blades. Still, it felt better having his weapon in his hand, being ready for war, Derian supposed, than standing here feeling naked.

Fat lot of good Rusty will do, either.

"I don't think our swords are going to do a fuken thing to that monster," Natteo argued. He sprinted off, taking the order regardless, and Derian followed after.

We are all going to die again.

"And it was such a nice morning," Natteo added.

———

Dreams.

Dreams.

The terrible dreams.

Derian had had this exact dream many times in his life. Not a dream of facing a leviathan (though that was a different, terrifying feeling altogether,) but a dream of being left behind. That terrible feeling of having to drop down a ladder three rungs at a time, before sprinting down to the lower decks, all the while being unaware of what was happening above, up on deck.

I'm so late, and we are so, so dead.

Sorry, Rusty.

Time to say goodbye.

Some people wanted to close their eyes as death climbed up around them. Other people faced it head on. Derian was neither of these, but somewhere in between. Most certainly, scrambling through the armoury seeking armour and swords for a desperate battle was not the place to be, yet here he was.

Down here, the engine's rumblings were loudest, but he could still hear the beast's shrill cry as it no doubt set its sights upon them, and for just a moment he considered forgetting the task and getting back above decks, if only to see his doom. If only to wake up from the nightmare. He also thought about climbing into a hole somewhere in the heart of the *Fighting Mongoose* and waiting out the mayhem. He suddenly realised he had wasted these last few days enjoying the lap of luxury when he should have been seeking a hiding place for just such an eventuality. For, really, Natteo was right. When Seren had shown up, chaos had followed.

"We are so fuken dead," Natteo muttered, drawing Derian from his imaginings of climbing into a secret little nook he spotted at the far end of the room. It was all snug and surrounded on all sides by heavy steel. A clever little mercenary could crawl farther in and who knew where he'd end up. He could get so cosy in there.

Spit on this.

Abandoning his dreams of a hiding place, he turned to

the weapons display, seeking any sort of inspiration. It was a rather impressive display: an entire wall upon which weapon after weapon hung from little leather straps. All neat and fetching. All shapes and sizes. Heroes' blades, no doubt, sharp and oiled and ready for killing, to be wielded by greater fiends, and Derian hesitated for just a breath. He might have preferred average weapons, better suited to his level of skill. Might have preferred ones that were less pompous, less extravagant. He craved a simpler blade or two.

Like Rusty.

Taking a moment, he removed Rusty and its scabbard from his belt and placed it among the rest of the weapons. In a way, he liked to think it was the weapon's retirement.

Perhaps Rusty will feel right at home among these fierce, legendary weapons.

These blades had been owned and won and used and earned by right proper heroes, and in that moment, Derian felt like a thief claiming treasures of which he felt utterly unworthy. His eyes danced from one impressive weapon to the next but never lingered. He wanted none of them. He also wanted all of them, the flashier the better.

The barge suddenly shifted, and a blade slipped from its clasp as though shoved from the wall, and landed at his feet. "Aw, look. Just choose that one there, will you?" Natteo grumbled as Derian hesitated over the fallen blade.

"I don't know. It doesn't have any jewels in the hilt. Not much design in the making of it, either," he argued. "If I'm to die, I'd like my sword to look well."

It was a perfect argument, but really, it was the simplest blade upon the wall. Probably a little too simple.

He picked it up and it felt perfectly balanced, and he felt a stir in his soul immediately, like a monster creaking. He waved the blade and considered its finely sharpened edge to be rather charming. He swung it absently and instinctively, even as his other hand reached out for another ordinary blade among the many better pieces. He did not know why he did this, only that in the dimness, the blade shimmered a deep red for a breath, before returning to its cool ordinariness, and Derian wondered if it wasn't laced with some fierce enchantment to trick him into choosing it.

At least it has style.

Natteo stood away from him, his eyes fixed on a dozen whaling poles wrapped in chains. They were long and crude and likely top of the range. "Hmmm. Perhaps we could use these beasts." He ran his fingers along one of the long, jagged barbs, then cursed as he cut himself.

"Have you ever hunted a whale?" Derian asked, fully expecting to hear a tale of Natteo's prowess out along the coast as a whale-hunting child.

"How hard can it be?" Natteo said, and Derian imagined it to be quite the difficult task at the best of times. He also imagined the Army of the Dead having the skills to hunt whales, which were invaluable for their profitable oil.

Perhaps to keep the airbarge flying.

Derian had never seen a whale in his life. He'd heard they were delicate behemoths, uninterested in killing humans. He'd had little interest in whale meat after learning that fact.

Leaving Natteo to gaze at the weapons, he took the two blades for himself, waving them erratically in circles in an attempt to familiarize himself with each perfectly adequate piece.

"So, which one are you choosing?" Natteo asked after a breath. He'd taken a sword for himself, leaving the poles where they rested.

"Both."

"This is not the time to be trying your hand at fancy dual-blade wielding. Who do you think you are? Erroh of the Outcasts?"

"I don't know who that is."

"Just someone from a tale I once heard," Natteo mumbled. "Wasn't a good one, either."

Derian held both blades, and fuk it, but they felt right. "Yes, I think I will dual wield," he declared, and imagined both his swords being very pleased with this.

Natteo didn't appear pleased. "You idiot."

"Hey, look, if one blade isn't going to do a thing against one of those limbs, why not try a second."

Natteo stared at him. "That's stupid enough to be effective. Ah, fuk it. I just remembered—I have a cake in the oven that's going to burn."

"Don't worry. I'm certain we're going to die long before the cake is ruined."

"Ooh, let's hope," Natteo said, strapping his bows to each wrist and slipping his bolts into a pouch on his leg. He whipped back his cloak and popped both his daggers into their scabbards at his waist. Clad in his leather-and-steel armour, he looked rather impressive. "How spit 'n polished do I look right now?" he said, turning this way and that.

"You look like... Erra of the Outsiders?"

"Aye, that'll do, I suppose." Taking both swords, Derian

began to strap on his own armour. Black steel with a fur inlay. Comfortable, effective and real good against the wind. "Sure wish we had some horse armour to call upon," Natteo jested, watching him.

"Hey, it wasn't my fault we left it in the town!"

"We could have stolen the armour. Instead, we stole a kid."

"Exactly. It's on Lorgan."

Satisfied that he looked nearly as polished as Natteo, Derian had just turned to leave when Natteo grabbed him, drew him in close and shoved his forehead against Derian's. "No jest."

"No jest."

"We will not die, brother. Not today," Natteo whispered.

"Of course not, brother. I will be at your side the entire way, always," Derian declared as Natteo broke the embrace.

"Whoa. Did you just try to kiss me, Derian?"

"Oh, for fuk's sake. If I wanted to kiss you, I'd just fuken kiss you."

"You aren't my type. How many times must I tell you."

"I'm into fiends with better knees, anyway."

Stopping to look at his knees in puzzlement and perhaps a little annoyed at the gibe, Natteo began to climb back up through the airbarge, clanking loudly against every rung as he went, and Derian followed after. "You cut me deep about the knees, Derian," he called over his shoulder. "Cut me way deep."

"I'm sorry, but it needed to be said."

"Maybe I'll start shaving them."

"Then we can talk."

They reached the top of the ladder. Natteo was gasping, his face turning serious. "Still, though, we are fuken miles up in the sky. What can a monster like that ever do to us?"

"I agree. We are at an advantage," Derian offered.

They weren't at an advantage at all.

Luckily, they were used to these types of odds.

"What took you two idiots so long?" Lorgan cried as they emerged.

"We stopped for a sandwich," Natteo countered. "Calm down, Lorgan. Is the monster gone? Did we miss our chance?" he asked, looking out over the edge. "No... no... the monster is still there... Nothing to worry about... Thank goodness for that—Ow! I didn't deserve that."

"So, what's happening? What's the plan?" Derian asked as Natteo dropped a bow and two quivers at the feet of Seren, who hung out over the side watching the behemoth gather itself far below. Her hands were glowing fiercely; her eyes squinted in concentration. She looked gorgeous, and Derian once more felt less attracted to her than ever.

Perhaps if she got naked again...

Massaging his hand where he'd struck Natteo, Lorgan looked over the edge. "It hasn't done much, just kind of flopped in the water looking up at us with that one beady eye."

It really was a beady eye. As big as a single-roomed shack in the middle of a doomed town to be exact, and every time it blinked, Derian felt less and less hopeful they'd survive the day. If the eye was bad, its beaked mouth was the spitting worst. It was probably because of all the teeth. Derian might have started counting but would have lost his way soon enough. Each incisor was as tall as a barrel, and from this demonic mouth with its terrible teeth came a squeal of primal awfulness. No creature walking or swimming the world should have made such a sound. It cut through his soul and echoed in the clouds above and came right back down at them for a second go. It grew in volume the longer it howled, and Derian instinctively covered his ears lest madness begin to stir.

I sure could do with a little seeva beast in me... Hey, beast, you awake yet?

He sought the monster inside him and found nothing but silence. He hadn't died in a couple of days. Perhaps the fiend had gone back to its slumber, never to return. He wasn't sure this was a good thing. "At least we are all safe as spit up here," Derian suggested, choosing a little cowardice, eyeing the others, hoping they would agree. "What's it going to do to us up here?"

"Surely if we charged towards Dellerin and informed the Guild, we would be welcomed in with warm embraces," Natteo added. A fine assist on his part. It seemed a silly notion to hover on down there and pick a fight with a creature ten times their size. "I think that's the only plan of action. What do you say, fearless leader?"

Lorgan said nothing. A precarious scowl formed on his face.

Derian jumped right back in. "Who knows how valuable the Guild could find this useful knowledge?"

"Because if we die, and no one lives to tell the tale of the beast... well... that would be rightly useless," Natteo pointed out. It was a polished routine by the two friends.

Lorgan growled under his breath, a hopeful sign that his better senses were returning to him. So Derian delivered the finer finish. "I mean, it's just waiting there. Not hurting anyone. We could just..."—he made a whooshing gesture—"... whoosh away and stay safe." He winked at Natteo, who grinned in agreement.

Perfect.

Lorgan lowered his blade. Kesta looked back to the controls of the airbarge. The omens were good, until Seren ruined everything with nobility.

"What about that ship?" she said, pointing to a large three-sailed vessel floating across the increasingly wavy waters. In that very moment the airbarge shifted ever so, no doubt caught in a nasty wind, and Derian's stomach turned.

Oh, shut up, pretty lady.

The ship in question, no doubt embarking on a fresh new voyage from some nearby sea village along the coast, had been sailing directly towards the surfacing sea demon, but had begun turning back towards shore.

"They're alright. They are making for land," Natteo countered, and cursed under his breath.

"Look at them. They look fine," Derian added. It was one of his weaker lies. The ship was turning far too slowly. Derian could only imagine the dreadful panic on board the vessel as it came upon the sight of the tentacled creature.

"Ah, that isn't great," Kesta moaned as the beast, realising there was better game in its territory instead of a half mile up, turned its horrible body as though catching a scent. Waving a few of its massive tentacles in unison as though it were swimming leisurely, the demon began to gather speed.

"Maybe it's looking to make friends?" Natteo

suggested, then shook his head in defeat. "Can you fire at that thing from here?" he asked Seren, who also shook her head. "Well, can you at least try?"

"Already did." Effortlessly, she released a fierce ball of fire and sent it tearing through the sky, where it died with a sizzle upon the beast's wet, leathery skin. The demon howled in anger but showed little pain. Nor did it slow, and suddenly the distance between ship and death became shorter and shorter. "My fire is not powerful enough... Perhaps if I possessed black fire..." she said thoughtfully.

"Would some of my soul help?" Natteo countered, gripping the balcony. She seemed to think about it.

"Well, we can certainly distract it," Kesta muttered with the confidence of a woman who believed this idea was up there with facing a lecherous demon in open warfare without even a net to call upon.

Lorgan hammered his fist upon the balcony edge. "We can't let the beast sink that ship—and look beyond! That's a town along the coast," he called out, sounding ever so much like the hero every man wanted to be.

"I have this," Kesta cried.

She really didn't.

She sprinted for the cockpit before Derian or Natteo could argue. Only Seren appeared pleased with this turn of events, as Kesta, locking herself in, brought the fourth propellor to life. Immediately, the *Fighting Mongoose* began to drop down towards the beast.

"Airbarge blades only work on monstrous spiders," Natteo cried, gripping the balcony's edge as the airbarge lurched and shunted against pockets of air. "They only work on spiders!"

Kesta wasn't listening. She was too busy bringing the airbarge level with another stomach-churning manoeuvre, before charging after the monster, ducking up and down over the thunderous waves.

"What the fuk is she doing?" Natteo cried.

"I really think you were wrong, Natteo," Derian shouted in the gush of wind and hazy spray as it rose around them, then struck and soaked through them. Spluttering and fighting blindness, he tasted salt on his lips. He didn't want to taste salt on his lips at the end. *What if that was death?* he wondered miserably. An eternity of feelings came upon him, as was common in the exact moment when you died. Terrified, bewildered, angry and tasting of salt was no way to spend eternity.

"About what?"

"I think this is exactly how we die today."

"No, brother. Only you will die today," Natteo countered, but truly, he looked as terrified as Derian. He was also licking his lips.

They drew nearer, but not quick enough. Suddenly the beast was upon the fleeing ship, bent on running itself ashore. Below in the water, Derian could see where the ocean shallowed, and for a breath he hoped the sailors might make it somehow. Might have even believed it with every foot they surged forward, away from the tentacles.

The *Mongoose*, of course, had no risk of running aground. It soared over the water, and then touched down upon the demon with a thundering wallop. Perhaps with its solitary eye, the demon was slow in seeing its attacker. Tragically, and unlike Fiore had done when they'd announced themselves, this beast did not wrap itself around any of the turbines. Instead, ignoring the airbarge, it drove forward at a breakneck pace, waving its tentacles in a grotesque yet oddly calming motion.

So Kesta brought the *Mongoose* down upon her quarry a second time, as though landing upon solitary ground and attempting to bore right through it.

"Alright, what is she doing?" Lorgan cried, doubtful now of Kesta's sanity. To her credit, Kesta looked at ease in her cockpit. Perhaps she believed herself safe behind the reinforced glass.

Derian, for his part, was thinking perhaps he should have hidden in the galley with Eveklyn and the cat. But he couldn't look away. It was as though his eyes were not his own. As though something whispered at his limbs, commanding him to dig in and wait for the treat of the day to be served.

With a terrible screech, the demon spun and Kesta suddenly drew up, avoiding a slap from one of the many appendages. She reversed the airbarge, drawing the monster's wrath perfectly. It waved its tentacles in the air as it slowed, and the movement sent one last mountainous wave of water rushing at the fleeing ship, driving it towards the land that little bit swifter.

Spit n polished.

"Gods, I hate that sound," Derian cried as the *Mongoose* surged upward and a sucker-laden tentacle slapped fiercely against her hull, attempting to grip and crush. And perhaps, were a less skilled pilot manning the barge, it would have. As it was, the airbarge shunted and spun and twirled and hung and avoided the deathly grips. Kesta pulled the machine high into the sky, and had Derian not seen it with his own eyes, he would never have believed it, for the demon jumped high with them and tried wrapping its many tentacles around the *Mongoose*.

"It missed," Seren cried in delight as the beast fell back to the sea, creating a splash akin to an absent god's angry palm to the world.

"That was fortunate," Lorgan muttered, watching the beast spin and wail in frustration.

"We did it," Derian cried.

"Did we?" Kesta called. "I cannot see from this angle."

And for a wondrous moment, Derian believed. Below, the ship ran aground and spectacularly held from breaking into a thousand pieces. Instead, it drove deep into the soft sand, wedging itself firmly and tilting just slightly to the side.

We saved them.

The beast, sensing the shallows, howled one last time and spat in frustration. The vile gobbet soared high into the air and broke into a hundred little blobs of phlegm... that appeared to sprout claws... that appeared to shift in the wind and spread out... and land upon the beached ship.

The beast spat again, and the ship swiftly became covered in these horrid demon offspring that resembled the largest crabs Derian had ever seen. They swarmed and attacked the unprepared sailors, who attempted to fend off the scuttling beasties with fists and measly daggers even less impressive than Rusty. Swiftly, the sailors began to fall to the clicking horde, and it was a horrid sight.

"The book didn't say they did that, Derian!" Natteo screamed in horror. "It didn't fuken say they did that."

The demon turned and looked skywards, and Derian

gripped the deck edge and really wished he had that heavy horse armour from Treystone. He also wished he had an inner monster to call upon that could grant him skill and strength and true devastation.

"Oh no..."

The monster sucked in a deep breath, checked the breeze with a tentacle, and spat up at the flying airbarge. As far as spittle went, it was a good shot.

CHAOS AND LAMENTATIONS

Eveklyn watched the Crimson Hunters from behind the safety of the locked galley door where Lorgan had ushered her right swiftly. She hadn't wanted to go. But orders were orders. And she would answer them, for he was her leader. In her hands was her double-bladed axe. It trembled in her grasp, so she left it to lean at her side and it reassured her. She was safe in here. There was hardly a reason to need a weapon at all, she told herself. Her breath fogged up the glass porthole despite her repeatedly wiping it away. It might have been the cold, or the cold terror. She didn't want to be frightened. Her Crimson companions weren't afraid of anything. Even if they were all screaming at each other as to what to do about the monster below. Eveklyn wasn't worried at all. They had defeated a grand demon just a few days before. They would do it again. She felt it in her bones. Her trembling bones.

"Kill them all," she whispered to the foggy image. She dared not blink too much, lest she miss a thing. She took in their behaviours, their actions, their manoeuvres. She was small. Always had been. But that would change. Best she fill her little mind and body with their teachings and grow to become as good as any of them. Greater than, perhaps. It was a reassuring thing to know how her future was laid out in front of her. From horror and sadness to hope. It's what her parents would have wanted.

Eveklyn blinked a few times, looked away and caught herself before she wept out all over her face, her clothes, over the galley. She saw her parents, as she did most moments of the day, but now she saw them in purest terror. She hoped to forget them. Or at least remember their smiles, their warmth, their voices too. Her stomach churned and she gazed at Lorgan and loved him because that's all she could do. She watched him move and thought him rightly impressive, and again, as always, a dreadful, awful desire to hug him and be comforted in his embrace took her.

"Mercenaries don't behave like that," she whispered, and damn those tears as they streamed down her face. *To the fires with them,* she thought, wiping them away. It was hard enough to study warfare from behind a pane of reinforced glass without a salty layer of tears getting in the way. "Spit on this," she muttered and felt a little better as terror and melancholy gave way to determined faith. At least for now.

For a few breaths she felt better watching them. Until she became distracted by the sudden wafting aroma of delicious things.

The smell of freshly baked cake permeated the room. "He was really excited about that egg and honey cake," she whispered to herself, ignoring the wafting, tantalising odour of honey as her mouth watered. She hadn't had cake in a lifetime. She'd watched him all morning, studied his art in silence, for that's all she could do, as he tended to eggs and flour and all manner of honey and yeasts. She really liked Natteo. He made her feel at home with his incessant talking. She liked to listen. He didn't seem to mind talking, either. Daring to look behind her now, she cursed as she realised the fire was still burning in the stove.

He should have been back by now.

Mimicking his movements, she tended to the stove and discovered the cake was lightly browning, just as he said it should. Careful with the stinging-hot metal platter, Eveklyn took the large baker's mitt in her hand and slid the cake free before easing it up on top of the stove where it would stay warm and finish cooking in its own heat, without the threat of burning.

As he said it would.

He seemed a very good baker and a fantastic chef altogether. She didn't quite understand the differing flavours as they wreaked havoc on her taste buds, but she trusted it was merely her ignorance of finer flavours, her unfamiliarity with delicacies—a thing suffered by most peasants.

As he said.

As great a chef as he was, he was an even better instructor, and she was inclined to listen to instruction.

"Perfect," she whispered, mimicking his tone, easing a veil of thin fabric over the cake lest some nasty hissects get a whiff. That would be quite the tragedy. There were no more eggs left, and she really wanted a slice of the cake. She had earned that slice of cake and all. Her mouth watered and, despite the terror, she contemplated daring a quick grab at the cake, then putting all she could fit straight into her mouth. Who would know?

He will.

Grudgingly, but not before inhaling deeply one more time, Eveklyn left the cake to cool, returning to gaze out across the deck at her heroic comrades, who now stood back to back, weapons raised. She thought it a strange sight. As were the dozens upon dozens of giant crabs crawling and scuttling around. The creatures did not attack at first. They merely circled, clicking their claws open and closed, open and closed, staring with oversized beady eyes like a crowd at a fair. Watching and waiting to be entertained. Watching and waiting for an eruption of movement.

They freaked the fuk out of Eveklyn, and she stepped away from the window, suppressing a whimper as she did.

She thought of that awful spider demon and thought this clicking terribly familiar. She nearly thought more of her mother and father but quickly shut that down.

Her stomach churned, and the only sound was the creatures' collective clicking and the tapping of their shells upon the deck. They moved as one, like an ocean of sickly grey and pink. And the smell of the salty sea was a terrible thing.

I used to like crab.

Delicious with butter and lime and a mound of salt, she thought. All mashed up in a little bowl. These brutes, however, were half the size of her. Perhaps more. There would be quite the feeding in them when the Crimson Hunters killed them all. Natteo would need quite the mounds of butter to serve them up, she mused.

"Kill them all," she whispered to her heroes, and the crabs must have heard, for they charged and she gasped and held her quaking breath. Without warning, fire erupted in her veins and her eyes were near blinded by a painful blaze of light. She ducked away for a breath, covering her face with her hands, but then, peeking out from between her fingers, she found her nerve. She gazed back at her heroes at war.

And then she heard the sound of clicking behind her.

Spinning around, she screamed her most piercing cry, and unsurprisingly it failed to do a thing to help her cause. She could hear the cur but could not see it. Desperately, she scoured the room, seeking out the monster and its click, terrified she would actually find it.

Turns out, it found her.

Far too late, she realised the beast was watching from behind a grate covering a vent in the ceiling. "To the thurken fires with you," she cried, gripping her weapon, as the vent gave way and the scuttling beast dropped heavily through, landing in front of her.

"Help me!"

Her voice sounded empty against the cacophony out on deck. She could hear more scuttling in the vent, as well. No one would help. No one would come for her. She was alone. Again.

Again, again, again.

With far too many limbs, the beast moved sideways, trying to glide up to her and "get all personal, like," as Derian would say of nasty monster curs. She understood his words now, though she had not at the time, as he had been speaking of some nasty things in the source. It was a small matter. What mattered was surviving.

Behind the first little demon from the vent dropped a second and a third after that, and Eveklyn felt an all-too-familiar terror. Leaping upon the nearest chair and then hopping over the chasm of snapping claws in between, she landed awkwardly on the large preparation table. There was a loud crash as her axe slid from her grasp to the table's surface, landing right in front of her but a thousand miles away. She screamed once more and swore she heard the beast hiss in frustration as its swinging claws clanged loudly against the metal legs carrying her weight.

"Leave me alone," she begged, silent tears streaming down her cheeks, and she was ashamed. Tears were for peasants and the dying. The table swung as though kicked by a group of drunken curs, and she could only step slowly backwards towards the galley ladder, hoping to escape the threat.

"Get away from me," she demanded, and still the crustaceans were unmoved. They just kept coming, and that terrible, familiar terror took hold of Eveklyn, taking her fight. She dropped to her knees as the table beneath her shunted and shook, ready to surrender to the abuse. Time stood still but for the thrashing of the table, and Eveklyn could only weep in silence, hoping for safety, for an escape, for a painless end, or for Lorgan to appear at the galley door, eager to protect her.

"Help me," she cried, but her voice was a whisper. A squeak. A nothing. And then the first beast, using its awful spindly legs, sprang upon the table. It landed at the far end with a hiss.

She wondered what Lorgan would do. She already knew the answer. He'd batter that beast to death and keep on swinging. He'd enjoy it too, and that was why he was her hero above all the other heroes. She'd listened to his instructions about technique these last few days, the lessons on swinging her weapon. She'd almost expected him to take her aside, suggest she wait a time before doing so. She'd been rather surprised he'd not even suggested she use a weapon not quite so large or ungainly. But instead, he'd merely accepted her choice and honoured it. It was her birthright, after all. She reached for that heavy axe, still mercifully lying on the table. She remembered exactly what Lorgan had said, and a sudden desire to please her master overcame her. A potent thing, subservience. Easier to do the unthinkable that way.

"Fine," she roared, and the creature hissed again. Gripping her weapon with both hands and launching her body as though casting a heavy load overboard, she swung that awesome axe and struck the beast's shell even as it swung its own dented limb.

The beast didn't die so much as explode from her strike, and she squealed in victory as the second giant crab leapt towards her, striking her fiercely across the thigh as it landed and skidded off the table. She was terrified; she was injured, too, but also, she was furious. Because Lorgan would expect her to be.

She took the torment of her life's miseries and she went a-hunting, for that was exactly what the Crimson Hunters would do. She leapt down upon the fallen beast, axe first, and cleaved the cur in two. It struggled for a few breaths, unaware of its own demise, before falling still with a desolate hiss of hate.

She screamed again in victory, then turned towards the third and final beast and sought its scuttling, shell-covered rear.

"Where are you, cur?" she demanded, and couldn't believe her own boldness. Couldn't believe she did not give up and hide, climb into the rafters and wait to be saved like before. Not once had she regretted her liberation from Treystone, and this heroism on her part simply reassured her that she would become quite the Crimson Hunter.

And then she found the third one.

"Whoa, whoa—stop right there," she warned, and the beast held where it stood. It had climbed up high to the warmer part of the room, where a delicious honey cake was brewing to perfection.

"Oi... I said stop," she added, and the beast eyed her with its creepy beady eyes, before gazing back at the cake.

"No, no, no, no... Look... I'm right here. Let's finish this," she barked, because she imagined Lorgan would say something spit n polished like that.

Problem was, the beast didn't care where she was, or how spit n polished she sounded. There was cake.

"He'll kill me if you ruin it," she warned, stepping towards the crab as it delicately flicked the protective veneer off the top. It might have inhaled.

"Come at me. I'm not afraid," she roared, and it felt a wonderfully deceiving lie. Regardless, the beast ignored her, so, in desperation, she flung that heavy battle axe. It was a wild assault, and blessed by gods, for though it took everything she had, that axe flew righteous and smashed the crab from its perch, dragging him onwards across the room. The blade embedded itself in the wall, splattering the beast apart.

"Oh, thank fuk," she cried, climbing up to check the cake and finding it was not covered in crab meat. Taking a moment to recover the grate above and wedge it tightly shut, Eveklyn took another moment to feel rather proud of herself before pulling the axe from the wall and gazing out at the heroic Crimson Hunters. They were still at war, and she stood a moment and was impressed with their skills.

Until she saw Keddy the cat among the melee upon the deck, away from the safety of the cockpit, the galley or her companions. He was at war with a crab of his own, and she was petrified.

"No!" she screamed, and unlocking the galley door, she charged out into the swarm of evil things and was immediately set upon by a sneaky cur of a crab hiding above the doorway.

———

"We are so fuked," Derian cried as the spittle-spraying monsters surged through the air towards him. Towards them all.

"Spitting is such a terrible habit," Natteo pointed out, drawing his wristbows and preparing for war.

"Gather up, Hunters," Lorgan cried. He looked impossibly pompous and impressive.

Seren, dropping from her place on the balcony, took her bow and arrows and fell in alongside Natteo and Derian. The crabs came in clustered groups and they came in droves, for the grand demon continued spitting.

Kesta suddenly appeared at their side, a crude sword and shield in her hands.

"Em... Who's flying the barge?" someone called.

"She'll stay afloat," Kesta said, falling into formation

with the rest. Derian looked to the capsule and the controls inside; all the while, the propellors spun and the *Fighting Mongoose* continued flying without her steady hand. Derian thought it a curious enchantment indeed. He might have thought of it longer, but Lorgan boomed out an order and they drew in close together in perfect formation. It was one of the very few formations they'd mastered despite the years of practice together: back to back, swords raised, a perfect circle of deadly intent. They needed only to hold their line without worrying about getting stabbed in the back. Or clawed. It was a tactic more commonly used by mercenaries battling greater odds or by groups experienced at being against the ropes, so to speak.

The crabs had no such tactics. They surged across the barge, eager to hunt and kill just as their brethren had hunted the unprepared sailors below. Though the mercenaries were far fewer in number, the sailors upon the beached ship were little more than peasants. Oh, aye, good in a gale, each with nerves of steel, but put a blade in their hands and a group of monster crabs could overrun them.

The clicking of crab feet upon the deck mixed with the frenzied snapping of claws sent waves of fear through Derian. He clutched his blade and ground his teeth as the masses surrounded them and then suddenly fell still. A small group of the crabs scuttled past the first line, eager to seek out prey throughout the airbarge, and a terror for the child took Derian ever so. He knew she hid behind the heavy galley door, but it made little difference. Though tempting, it was never good to leave a comrade behind, and Eveklyn was one of a sort.

"What are they waiting for?" Natteo cried.

"Be ready," Lorgan whispered, and the moment held. An eerie serenity fell upon them, and over it Derian could hear the enemy rummaging in the galley. He tried to focus. To push away thoughts of honour and nobility.

Leave the child where she hides... She'll be fine.

"What evil is this?" Seren asked, coming to stand beside Derian. Her eyes were alive and sparkling, even in the face of threat and fear. She claimed to be built for battles, violence, death. Derian had seen glimpses of it in the town of Treystone. He desired to see her full potential, an even more tempting prospect than gazing upon her naked body again. He really was growing as a boy.

"I have to piss," Natteo whispered. Derian looked to his comrade alongside. He looked wary but ready. "Also, where's the child?"

"Locked away in the galley," Kesta replied.

"Where's the cat?" Seren asked. A fine, distracting question.

"Fuk the cat," Derian growled, and the world exploded in fire. He was on fire, to be exact. Or, more precisely, his blade was. A deathly blast of purest flame ran right down the shaft from tip to guard. He could see the air above it bend and dance, such was the heat, and he thought it a precarious, beautiful thing. "What the fuk? What the fuk?"

Even Lorgan, standing behind him, turned to look. "What is this enchantment, Seren?"

"It wasn't me," she cried, leaping away from the sudden eruption of fire as it reached for her pure, godly dark hair. He'd believed he saw it turning grey before, but that might have been a trick of the light, or the night. Now it was shimmering and perfect, even if she was spinning away, messing it up terribly as she did.

His comrades felt the heat from the burning blade, but it was cool to the touch for Derian, who ran his fingers through the fire as though it were an illusion, or as though the fire chose not to burn his flesh.

"Did you do that on purpose?" Lorgan asked in amazement.

"Of course I did," lied Derian, wondering why his blade had chosen this moment to come alive. It was a marvel. He was in love, and he might have taken a breath longer to appreciate it, but now the crabs, as one, came attacking.

They broke and washed forward like a wave upon a rocky shore, and the Crimson met their charge. Seren fired arrow after arrow upon the shelled beasts and killed with every strike. Some were delivered with such force that they pinned two crabs right through. Between every sixth shot or so, she drew a ball of fire upon her hand and burned back the charging creatures with a fierce fireball.

The smell of burning crab flesh filled the air.

It was delicious.

Derian's blade also delivered fire, fiercely scorching each scuttling fiend without mercy, and it was easy. He was a menace to all things inhuman, and his mouth watered at the prospect of his violence, and for a moment he wondered if his own beast deep down in his soul hadn't come forth and taken his body for a little killing.

This is all me.

Using every skill he'd ever learned regarding hacking, slashing and killing, he met each scurrying beast and cracked its shell, plunged his blade into white slithering flesh and scorched innards to nothing. His blade seemed to have a life of its own. More than that, it obeyed him without delay. It answered his movements effortlessly as though it were weightless, almost pulling him nearer to the action, demanding he stretch that little bit further than he might have, making him step right swiftly before a careless swipe cut him clean. He lost count of his kills in the first few breaths alone, and for the briefest of moments he felt like a true mercenary.

Fuk that.

A true hero.

He wasn't alone, for around him, his comrades went to task just as eagerly. Any bard or storyteller might have gazed upon their actions and believed them to be experts in such things. And for a moment, perhaps they were. They moved as one smooth unit, killing and moving in a slow, stumbling circle, holding the line and winning it back.

"We are winning," declared Seren.

"Course we are," roared Lorgan as any heroic leader would. As though he was used to such turns of victory.

"That's all spit and polished," warned Kesta. "Don't any of you be burning up my barge." It was a fine threat, and Derian kept his blade from touching the polished wood surface of the deck. Who knew how fuked they'd be if a fire were to break out in this beast. A coldness came upon him at such a thought.

"That smell is amazing," Natteo, ever the chef, declared, and he was not wrong. "We will be eating like kings for a time," he added, mid-kill. He was positively beaming. And why not? They were beating back the little bastards. And after?

They only had the grander sea beastie to deal with.

"It just needs a little garlic and butter," Derian said dreamily, and Natteo was horrified at such a notion. They might have further discussed it, but from nowhere the child suddenly appeared.

Sprinting across the deck, battle axe in tow, she was impressive, and Derian's breath caught in his throat as a sneaky cur of a crab, crouching above the galley door, leapt high and landed on her, knocking her to the deck.

"No, no, no," Kesta cried, breaking the line and sprinting through the throng of creatures, swinging her sword, driving them back, oblivious to the glancing blows she received as she did.

Derian did not delay. Despite the threat, he followed after, screaming his most piercing cry, kicking and swing-ing, killing and scorching. Around him, he cleared the deck of sizzling future dinners, and kept running. Even after Kesta reached the child.

Save her.

Kill them all.

We can all survive this.

Derian might have assisted Kesta had the favour of the absent gods been with him, but they weren't. They never were, so he was hardly surprised. A sudden shadow drew over him and the barge, as an outstretched tentacle waved in front of him.

"Where did that come from?" Derian cried, as the appendage disappeared and reappeared a few breaths later.

"To the fires with you," Seren roared, firing a bolt of purest fire down upon the beast.

"That reminds me of a really nasty..." Natteo offered as

the massive appendage disappeared and reappeared once more. This time it struck fiercely against the side of the barge, sending the flying behemoth reeling to the side, and many objects and people with it.

Derian flew furthest.

A foot skywards at first and another couple more after that. He spun and caught sight of his fiery blade extinguishing and clattering along the far deck while he floated in mid-air, as all around him went still and slowed.

"Please, no," he cried, and managed to gaze at the rest of his comrades stumbling and falling, just as the deck beneath him disappeared completely, replaced instead by the rushing colour of blue.

I can't die without a blade in my hands.

"No!" Natteo cried as Derian fell hard against the edge of the barge and kept going. Slipping down along the hull, Derian reached and grabbed and sought any manner of a hold.

"Help me, monster," he demanded, and felt a shift in his soul. Deep down below.

He caught on a snag of metal. A painful thing, really. It caught him in the leg, cut deep and held on his boot. Skin tore and blood spilled freely and he wondered might he ever run without a limp ever again. He took this as a gift of life, though, even if he was in torment. Hanging upside down, screaming in the wind, he scrabbled with aching fingers for any hold and from above there fell a few squealing crabs.

"Help me," he wailed, and above, Natteo's face appeared.

"You aren't dead."

"Fuken help me."

"Thank the gods—I really thought you were dead."

"Fuken help me."

He disappeared and Derian clung to the side as though it made any difference, and still his mangled foot held and it was no sight to gaze upon. Blood seeped down his body onto his face and Derian sought a calmness despite the panic, despite the terror, despite the agony. He sought peace real hard and, despite himself, discovered a little stillness knowing he was this close to death and unable to do a thing about it.

He thought of the source, of the darkness, and the pain ebbed away, to be replaced by acceptance. His head felt dizzy as though he were drunk. His freezing body suddenly felt numb and he was fine with that too. He was rather used to dying. This was easier than the other times they died. At least he would be missed by those who survived, and this reassured him.

"What... are... you looking at...?" he whispered to the wind, to the ocean, to his soul. But really, he spoke to the grinning beast staring up at him from far below. Only then did he realise the creature must have leapt clear of the water to swat them from the sky and he thought the cur most impressive, if not the worst thing he'd ever seen in his young life.

Too young to die.

The grand demon appeared to smile in reply, showing its many teeth and waving its tentacles.

"If we gave you Seren, would you leave us be?" he mocked. He thought on that a moment and decided the beast would. "Well, you can't have her... harbinger of foul things as she is."

The beast roared as though he understood, and Derian fell silent to enjoy this quiet awfulness.

"I'm back... Oh good—you are still with us. Brilliant," declared Natteo, dropping a chain over the edge. It clanked loudly, disrupting Derian's peacefulness, but he welcomed it as it clinked down beside him.

"Alright, real fuken gentle," Derian hissed, wrapping the chain around his wrist, and Natteo pulled with all his might.

"I have you, brother," the smaller fiend cried, pulling the chain, and Derian felt a sudden pressure. With a scream, Derian pulled his leg free, leaving a dreadful smear of blood and flesh behind, and truly he felt lesser for it. Still, knowing Seren could heal him made the pain manageable.

"Don't let me go," Derian begged and began climbing with one free hand and one working foot. An awkward and awful climb, but truly, as he neared the top, he began to believe.

"I think you've been eating too much of my food," Natteo said, gasping, but still pulling him up.

But that bitch of a grand demon wasn't finished with them, for from below, it lurched once more, leapt impossibly and struck more fiercely than it had before.

"Oh no," Natteo cried as the chain slipped, and for a frozen moment, their eyes met.

"You priiiiiiiiick," Derian howled, as he fell fully away from the barge; the chain dangled loose and useless.

He looked to the great mouth far below as it rushed up to meet him. He could only gaze at those teeth and he knew this would be the end of him.

He was right.

It was no small thing to command an airbarge as incredible as this, and Kesta was eternally grateful for the gift to her life. She took it rather personally that one of its engines had spluttered to a stop under her watch, and it was on her to fix the damned thing, which is exactly what she did. She liked technical problems. She understood them. The problem of leaving the child in the galley was not a problem she liked, however. Too many variables. One such variable was the silly little bitch fleeing from safety only to be felled by savage monsters.

That was one serious fuken problem, and, alas, it was on Kesta to fix it rightly quick.

Even through the gathering crustaceans, she could see the child's impressive instincts despite her years. She did not simply lie down where she'd been felled; instead, turning, slithering, fighting and surviving, she knocked away her ambushing assailant before it could pin her, and met it face on, holding her axe to keep it at bay. As she did, she whipped her head back and forth as claws snapped around her, all the while manoeuvring the shell of her attacker to keep from its dreadful serrated edges. It was a sound tactic, and it kept her alive in those first few breaths. That's all it took, too, for Kesta rushed the brutes, tearing into them as though taken by a demon herself. She would not hesitate, for she had seen such dreadful things occur with little ones before.

Not today.

Swinging her blade upon the ranks of shells, she cracked them open where she could, plunged deep into flesh where it presented itself and sliced softer limbs free where they dangled in her vision.

"To the fires with you," she roared, wading in among them, knocking them back until she came upon the child, overcome but still fighting. Screaming and wailing, but living. "Come here," she roared, whipping the shaken girl to her feet, handling her roughly, as she spun around and resumed battering back the beasts.

Though Derian had created a wave of space where he drove through on her flank, it was actually Lorgan who assisted most.

He came upon her as the barge was struck fiercely, and both human and demonic sea life shunted and stumbled enough for Lorgan to drive up beside them and lift the girl into his arms as Kesta went clearing the route ahead.

"To the cockpit, to the cockpit," she roared as the barge veered ever so. Distantly, she could hear Natteo wailing over some matter, but she could only focus on her next few steps. Saving the child. Getting the barge to a higher altitude. Anything after that was manageable.

Lorgan did as she bade, and through the scrambling fiends they waded, driving them back, leaping over invaders, crushing them underfoot.

"Burn in hell, you bastards," Kesta roared, feeling braver with Lorgan by her side. She swung with everything she had, and for a breath she forgot the misery of her life. Instead, she took wonderful joy in the killing and perhaps the living too. Alongside, Lorgan was ever dominant. There was no plan of action; there was only the violence, and he was a torrent of wrath. She loved the violence. She wanted it all. More of it—the sound of blade against demon, severing and slicing and killing and fuelling her decade-old thirst for vengeance that she never knew she still harboured.

"To the fires with you, curs," Lorgan roared, kicking with heavy limbs and knocking away many beasts from his path. Such was their fierceness they soon made a path for themselves among the mayhem. Suddenly, that cockpit didn't seem that far away, and within it waited salvation.

"Where is Derian?" the child cried, as they reached the cockpit, and a coldness took Kesta for a breath, before she grabbed the child from Lorgan and shoved her into the little glass cockpit.

If Lorgan wanted to come along, he never said, nor did he argue as the door shut tightly behind them both. Instead, he charged off into the melee, tearing and crunching a little more.

Immediately, the scrape and crack of claw on tempered glass erupted around them as the crabs sought an easy dish; they seemed mighty perplexed that there was now a protective shield around their prey.

"Spit on you, curs," Kesta snarled, as the crabs battered the cockpit from all sides. A lesser pilot might have panicked, but she knew the sturdiness of this tempered glass. "I doubt even Lorgan could break through with the heaviest axe," she added, mocking the fiends. They must not have heard her, for they continued to try and get in.

"I think Derian fell over the side," Eveklyn said suddenly. She spun around to see Natteo hanging over the edge of the barge, ignoring the violence, wailing, and her heart fell heavily. She wanted to wail with him, wanted to scream as well. Wanted to slap the little bitch fiercely for thinking she was skilled enough to join their fight. "I think it was my fault."

"Shut up, Eveklyn," Kesta said, deciding to merely shove the girl aside so that she might see what she was doing.

"I think he's dead."

"Shut up, little one, and do as I do," Kesta demanded, grabbing at the straps behind the girl, and the girl remained motionless for a moment.

"I didn't want him to die."

Shut up, shut up, shut up.

She could see the cuts on the girl's forehead. A bead of crimson slid down to her chin and she trembled, and for a pulse of her own blood, Kesta softened.

"Listen, if you are going to fight with us, comrades are going to die." She looked over to Natteo and the anguish came anew. She knew that torment all too well. She wondered was it a wonderful silence as Derian fell to his doom, or did he fight it every breath of the way? "Sometimes it will be a blade to the belly." More crabs clawed at the glass and she wanted to kill them all. More than that, she wanted her comrades to escape with their lives. Mostly, though, she wanted Eveklyn never to have left the galley. The child was shaking badly now, likely slipping into shock right in front of her. Kesta slapped the back of Eveklyn's head so that she might concentrate, or at least stop focusing on the fact that her actions had brought about the death of her comrade. "Sometimes it will be falling from a terrible height." The child nodded but did not understand. At least her attention was back on the older, wiser woman. "This is not your fault, little one," she lied. "This is the fault of a great evil, is all," she said, and this perhaps was a greater truth than any lie. "Now, do as I do," Kesta insisted, and the girl wrapped the straps around her before Kesta reattached her own.

"As you wish," she whispered.

Kesta went to task, ignoring the beasts on the other side of the glass. Her hands and feet also went to task automatically, working at setting this beast to flying. She did this slowly so the child could watch. Receiving instruction was probably the only thing that might pull the child from her shock. "It is best you learn all you can, little one." Her hands moved over the choke and the child blinked a few times but watched. She even shook her head.

"All I can."

"Good, because at some point I'll probably be dead as well. Best we have another that can fly this beast."

The child squinted in disbelief but nodded regardless.

Cutting power to the four propellors, Kesta pointed beyond the mayhem and murder to one of the propellors as it began to slow its spin, and immediately the *Fighting Mongoose* began to drop at a delicate pace.

"If this happens..." Kesta noted, "you are in deepest shit."

"I see."

"So ignite this switch here," she said, doing so, and immediately, like a good flying behemoth, the airbarge caught itself, the engines set the propellors turning and the beast eased its fall.

"I see."

"Watch my feet work the levers," Kesta demanded, as her feet, perfectly in sync, eased movement into the

Mongoose as it soared high. Real fuken high. Fast as well, so that the remaining crabs on the deck struggled with the increased elevation as though they were drunk.

"I see," Eveklyn whispered as Kesta brought the beast level.

"Do you feel any better, little one?"

"Not really, Kesta," she whimpered, and Kesta grabbed her shoulder.

"It never does get any better," Kesta said, slipping from the restraints, directing the child to sit in the pilot's chair. As she did, she wedged the controls to hovering and locked them in place. "But that's alright. Because it's good to feel the pain, and the guilt, and the better days." The *Fighting Mongoose* answered the child's gentle movements. A pleasing sign; perhaps the girl had an instinct for it.

"Keep an eye out that the airbarge holds, while I see to the last of the beasts," Kesta said softly.

"What happens if we start to fall again?"

"Just do exactly what I showed you," Kesta said, and after a moment the child nodded.

"As you wish."

———

Seren was suddenly not alone on the deck anymore. Her mind was awash with a lie. A vision of something that had never happened. But would happen. Could happen. She stood facing Anguis the Dark One, and it wasn't real. It was pure fear. And something else. Like a flutterbye, those thoughts flittered away from her mind, leaving her cold and confused.

A crab clawed weakly at her, and Seren lamented her choices that had led her to this very moment for an entire breath, before casting fire upon the crab. "To the fires, crustacean."

She did not know how she knew that word, nor if she pronounced it correctly. Regardless, it was a strange word and it was a perfect word for the monster that burned away in front of her.

The flame passed from the crustacean on through the figure of Anguis standing in front of her, and she told herself again he was not real. Her visions of the future, and of the now, were slipping away from her grasp. Like difficult words. She tried to grasp them, but they were nothing but echoes.

Crustacean.

Anguis grinned, exuding handsome evil, and she was revolted. Revolted that he had an interest in her, that he knew of her. That he would come for her when all seemed lost and the seven gods were a-stirring. He would come for her and would not kill her. Could not kill her, for she was fierce, invincible.

Or would be.

Once Bereziel returned.

And completed her training.

If he returned.

She held that unsettling vision for as long as she could. She held it like a lover caressing naked flesh. She did this, for she suspected she might never have another vision. Every day, the source took from her that gift of foresight.

Everything is tainted and wrong.

She had not envisioned Derian's downfall, though as

she gazed upon him, she knew him doomed. She could weave no enchantment to return to him his life or soul, nor could she even rush across the deck to pull him ashore with Natteo. For she desired to hold onto this vision of Anguis most foul for as long as she could. To study him. To study the moment.

Nothing personal, Derian.

With a terrible ripping of flesh, she returned to the waking world and was pleased to discover herself still killing, even in her own unconscious absence. Her limbs obeyed her desires, even if unaware. She knew this for, as she took breath and lamented the disappearing, vile cur, she still released arrows from her bow with perfect precision, still fired flames upon the crustaceans.

As she returned from the vision, the awful rush of war and hate assailed her. She watched the chain slip free with curiosity, and then came the wailing anew.

It's alright, Natteo. It was probably always meant to happen like this.

Probably.

Drawing three arrows and firing them in quick succession, she glided along the deck and gazed over at the falling Derian. He was beautiful in his death. He drew a sword and all and did not flail his arms, as though such a thing would cause him to slow his descent. He merely gripped his sword, tumbled over and slipped right into that monster's beaked mouth to meet a dreadful end.

She waited for a breath. "And..."

"Derian!" Natteo wailed, and she glided up alongside to see to the rips upon his fingers and how much they bled over the deck.

"... He is..." She took one more breath and felt Derian's soul twist as it was wrenched from his broken body. "... gone."

"I had him! I fuken had him," cried Natteo, and Seren understood such agony, though she had not experienced it for herself. At least not in this life. He hammered his fists upon the deck, ignoring the crabs around them. So she took another three arrows and cleared the way so he might grieve without the necessity to kill.

"He was not afraid," Seren lied. "Merely angry at the world," she added, and it made little difference. She knew she should have felt more anguish for what had occurred, and perhaps, these last few days, with the boy no longer sniffing around her like the craven cur he was, she had felt a little less anger for him. She looked down to the grand demon below and could not shed a tear for him as Natteo did now.

She could only turn upon the crabs and vent upon them her frustration at losing a comrade. She glided among the beasts, no longer constrained by the discipline of Lorgan's orders. Her hands became flame and she fired upon those nasties and scorched them from this world.

And power suddenly surged through her. A delicious, terrible thing, and she felt her soul reach out and take from those around the fuel needed for such devastation, and it terrified her. She couldn't help herself. She drained souls, and it was different to before; it was dirtier, more tainted and bitter, and greater. She attempted to ease this energy from her, but she could not; she could only feel herself grow in fierceness.

"I can't help it," she cried, begging for forgiveness, but

around her, no comrade collapsed. Instead, it was the crabs themselves that weakened, and she watched Lorgan, Kesta and Natteo half-heartedly smash the fiends to a pulp.

How do I know this?

I have always known this.

In that moment, she realised her grand importance to Bereziel, to the rebellion against the Dark One as a whole. For an entire breath, she smiled and realised how she could stand firm against him. Against them all. She drew further strength and the crabs began to tremble and quake, and she'd never felt fiercer in her life as she stole from their cursed essence, and it was incredible. She wondered might she possess enough strength to burn down a forest, move a mountain, take on a grand demon.

She suddenly understood she could master this vile practice and perhaps teach Bereziel the technique.

Lest he become too powerful.

As they killed the last of the monsters, Seren left them to their murder. Instead, climbing out along the edge of the barge, wrapping her burning hand in cold chain, and gazing at the grand demon below, she eyed the beast with relish.

Gathering all she could, she gazed at the monster and cast down upon the beast all her wrath, and it was fierce. The deck creaked and near warped where the fire passed from her fingers in a grand fireball.

"Take this, you cur," she hissed and struck the beast with everything, and this time she caused some injury. A clean strike, but not enough to kill. Just sufficient to maim and enrage, and its howls of pain satisfied the bloodthirsty part of her hidden deeper down where a soul could never roam.

The beast spun and wailed, and she gazed at the strength emanating from deep within it. A different spark of light to that which her dead comrade had loosed. She peered at the light and wondered was it a grand demon's soul, and she very much wanted to take it for herself. She licked her lips and wondered might Derian somehow be alive, and then thought better of it. Derian was dead, but there were wild things afoot, and she had every intention of understanding this vile monster that little bit better.

"It's time to kill that beast," Lorgan roared from beside her. He was a ruin, cut and torn, bleeding and gasping, and she approved of the look to him.

"What will you have me do?" she whispered. She felt suddenly empty, missing the furnace of fire that had coursed through her and wanting to heal Lorgan in that same breath.

"What you just did," he said, and grinned, despite the silent tears spilling from his eyes.

———

All mercenary leaders lost comrades in battle. Lorgan knew this better than most. He had lost a few since the day he had damned the world to hell. A better man would have left the world of mercenaries behind. And he had, for a time, earning a life with his fists. But greater things had brought him back into this world. Foolish notions like redemption, nobility and faith.

And for a time, he had done his part keeping the Crimson marching. Lesser leaders might have considered the name itself to be a curse, but Lorgan thought better than that. Remembering the sins was as important as redeeming the sins. The world needed to remember this name, for better reasons than the truth.

Oh, aye, he had moulded these particular raw, useless warriors, one by one, into a fairly useless unit. But it took only moments for greatness to occur, and for a few moments these last few days, he had truly considered them great, if not a little fortuitous.

It was all coming together.

Lorgan couldn't shake the vision of Derian going over the edge, no matter how hard he killed. What was worse was knowing the poor fool had found a way to hold on longer than most. It was a terrible thing to see Natteo attempt to save the boy and Lorgan too slow to do a thing to help.

This was the price, he was remembering, and it was too much. In those first few moments, with nothing but clicking, vicious little thurken curs to kill, Lorgan fell apart. Fell into himself, and nearly fell in the process.

I cannot do this.

He felt slower, and weaker. His strikes became laboured. The renewed strength he'd had these last few days seemed to diminish, and for a breath he wondered was Seren weaving his soul from his body, and he didn't care. If she killed at the cost of his soul, well, why would a wretch like him deserve a soul anyway?

Still, he killed, and hated with everything he had.

Until his sword was knocked free as he drove it off a stubborn shell.

Give up.

You've brought nothing but ruin to this world.

Without redeeming yourself for the death of the Seven.

"It was not all on me," he growled, but knew it took merely a crack in a dam to flood a valley. His sword clattered loudly behind him and he hated that crab something awful. Hated them all, really. He considered dying at their hands, but Derian deserved far better than that.

That old man had certainly thought as much those few years ago, he mused, almost smiling at the faded memory.

Honour Derian.

He held that thought and it infused him, drove him forward, and suddenly he began to move more quickly. Feeling his way, clenching his fists and driving them upon the shelled horrors. For a breath, he thought again of the doomed warrior going to war in the arena, outnumbered and without a chance. A hero in the making with nothing but fists to rely on. Lorgan began to punch like he hadn't done in many a year. Fine, satisfying punches, really, and with each one he felt more enraged, more fierce, more driven. He suddenly wanted that fire in him, wanted the energy too. He wanted his soul so he could lose it anew killing these fiends.

The crabs were enormous and imposing, but they had no chance against Lorgan in his near prime. He cracked their shells with snapping jabs, violent hooks and impossibly impressive haymakers. His fingers split with the force, adding to his frenzy, and he waded through the monsters and left a swath of clear deck in his wake. Those he didn't daze and shatter, he sent flailing over the edge, and he roared in anguish and triumph and victory.

He caught sight of Seren drawing fire from her body and firing upon the bastard below, and he was heartened by her potency. He wanted to kill them all, even as they faded at his feet and the Crimson Hunters cleared the invaders off the deck. Their deck.

When it settled, Kesta stood out over the dead and cried openly, such was her sorrow, and Lorgan desired to embrace her, wail with her, but this was not the time to mourn. She knew it too.

"It is time to kill the beast," he declared, wiping the streaming tears from his eyes and finding the act futile.

"What will you have me do?" Seren said, beside him. She peered with beautiful eyes into his soul, and he felt a cold shiver run through him. She desired this murder something fierce. Even more than a mourning mercenary leader.

"What you just did," he offered, and this pleased her, for she flashed a most disarming, alluring smile as she spread her hands wide and the crabs around them collapsed completely as though struck by a bolt of lightning.

Seren moaned in deep pleasure and climbed back out along the edge of the deck, her shapely body quivering as though struck with an aftershock of that same bolt, and he couldn't help wonder if she'd killed the beasts by wrenching away their souls. He'd heard tell of such cruel practices, but never once believed a soul could be wrenched from anything more than a living creature, let alone a soulless, demonic crab from the depths of the ocean.

It was Natteo who distracted him. He carried with him a few long whalers' poles and dragged long metal chains behind him, and Lorgan grinned at the thought that the boy would put his wrath to good use.

"Are you well?" Lorgan asked, and Natteo thought on this.

"I'm pretty fuken far from well, but I will have my

vengeance," he warned as though Lorgan might argue against his attempts to slay the beast.

"Aye, little one, that we most certainly will," he lied.

―――――

Natteo refused to believe Derian was dead, even if his trembling tears suggested anything but. He took those tears, though, and ignored them. Tears had never helped him his entire life; why should they help now?

You don't need to cry.

It was fine advice and he agreed. So he wiped those tears and killed the half dozen crabs scuttling around his feet. It made him feel better, killing did. Settled his mind, in truth. Reminded him that there were greater things in his future. Not just his, but Derian's too. He knew this because he wasn't ready to lose his best friend. He'd done that shit before and was no fan. Oh no, Natteo was quite certain his best friend wasn't dead. He was ruined, yes, rightly fuked by that fall, and probably fighting to stay alive in the demonic stomach acid he no doubt found himself swim-ming around in. That was the type of fate Derian would have to face before Natteo stepped in and saved his rear again.

Derian will be alive.

You just need to go find him.

"I fuken know," he growled to himself and the rushing wind.

No matter how shitty a place Natteo found himself in, no matter how low life led him, he'd always believed himself worthy of better times and better moments. Perhaps it was self-importance, perhaps it was self-denial, but since he'd died at the hands of a lecherous demon, he was rather convinced he was destined for greatness. He thought on that bastard demon. It seemed like so long ago.

It was a week or so.

As important as Natteo felt, he felt Derian was just as significant. He too was destined for greatness, for old age, for a family and fatherhood. Natteo would be there when he finally wedded a woman worthy of him, and Natteo knew Derian would walk him down the aisle. Would be his best man. He could be preacher and it still wouldn't be enough of an honour to bestow upon his friend.

DERIAN WILL BE ALIVE WHEN YOU FIND HIM IN THE RUINS OF THE DEMON.

"I fuken know," Natteo lied for a second time, determined to convince himself. It was appearing to work. The tears were drying up. The anguish was numbing to mere horror.

Natteo had a simple plan. He just needed to hunt down the beast, rip open its stomach and pull the grinning Derian to safety. It was a simple enough plan. He knew it would work.

And if Derian was dead? *Which he won't be.* He would recover the grinning corpse and bury it in a suitable grave. Somewhere with a view. Away from any passersby. Ready to break down in the dirt and give back to the fertility of the world.

Natteo left the crabs where they were. They were small fry, so to speak. He had greater imaginings on his mind. He moved in a daze, allowing instinct to carry him. It was a fine thing to be this numb. It hurt less. He descended from the deck, down into the deep hold where the engine whirred and rumbled, and he went to task as Kesta had told him to do. She probably didn't think he'd been listening either.

He didn't bother counting the massive cannisters. One less of the blackwater, or miracle juice, or crude oil, or whatever the peasants called it, wouldn't matter. He took that heavy metal cylinder and carelessly popped the engine cap and poured the black fluid in. Immediately, the engines began to hammer wildly like a heart in flight, and Natteo grinned.

Moving on to the armoury, Natteo recovered as many of the barbed whalers' poles as he could. They were light enough but forged with love and skill. He even managed to wrap a few linked chains around his arms before struggling back up to the deck with murder most beautiful on his mind.

On the deck, the crabs lay dead, and it was a small matter. There was still plenty of murdering to do.

Lorgan stood before him as he dragged his weapons to his comrades. "Are you well?" Lorgan asked, and Natteo thought on this as though thinking of painful things would help his mind. It wouldn't.

"I'm pretty fuken far from well, but I will have my vengeance," he warned, as though Lorgan might argue against his attempts to slay the beast. It didn't matter if he did. Lorgan was a fierce warrior, but Natteo was a miserable fiend unwilling to compromise. He was going to kill this demon, and, curses upon Natteo, if Lorgan argued any differently, he would challenge him there and then for leadership of the Crimson Hunters, and would feel just grand about it.

"Aye, little one, that we most certainly will."

Good answer.

Lorgan did as Natteo did. When he returned with the remaining poles and chains, Natteo was already attaching the clinking chains into holding pegs embedded in the deck on both sides. As he worked, he explained his plan to any who would listen, and truly, it wasn't the worst plan at all.

Though disapproving of his liberties in using up one of the cannisters of black oil to give the *Mongoose* a burst of energy, so to speak, Kesta listened and nodded her willingness to sacrifice the airbarge, all in the name of vengeance. Her tears suggested she believed this was no rescue mission, and Natteo wasn't inclined to argue. Let her be surprised; let her anger sway her hands.

Lorgan, on the other hand, saw right through his misguided faith.

"You believe Derian is alive?"

"Of course I do," Natteo growled.

"So you risk all our lives on a faded belief in a miracle?" he said, and Natteo didn't like that tone at all. Not that it mattered.

Lorgan attached the chains as Natteo did and the poles to each end as before. And Natteo barely contained his rising anger, though his fingers twitched as if he were firing wrist bows.

"So you believe him dead?" Natteo asked.

"Yes, I do."

"So you risk our lives... for nothing at all?" Natteo grabbed Lorgan. He was far smaller and less imposing, but he had some unearthly fire brewing in his belly. He didn't care.

"I risk it because it is the right thing to do," Lorgan snapped, but did not break his hold.

"Then man the fuken side, Lorgan," Natteo ordered, and Lorgan gripped his shoulder with a force much weaker than Natteo's.

"As you wish, Natteo," he offered and patted him gently before turning to battle.

This somehow crushed Natteo. Thinking Derian's final number was three ahead when he died was an awful thing. A few more fine manoeuvres and he'd pass Derian by eternally. It would be a hollow victory. He didn't want that. He really, really didn't.

"Derian is alive. Do not fear."

"Shut up," he ordered to the reassuring voice in his mind. It was Derian who talked to voices, after all, and Natteo had little interest in following in his comrade's madness.

"As you wish, Natteo... for now."

"Perhaps we should make land first, then drop off the child, and maybe the cat as well," Natteo offered, and Eveklyn shook her head from the safety of the cockpit and began to tighten her straps. It was a humane suggestion, for there was a good chance the airbarge would be smashed to ruin where it flew, but in truth, from the moment the child had climbed aboard the airbarge, her fate had become entangled with the Crimson's own. Little point in training a little miss in the better arts of mercenary life if you had to drop her off before every adventure.

"Well, I tried," he muttered to himself, tightening the last chain before turning to Seren and hating her ever so silently. She had probably been a right proper upper-class lady, he imagined, before she found herself in the source with nothing but fragments of memories. Sometimes, in how she spoke, in how she carried herself, she reminded him of the entitled fiends that marched the leisurely streets of Castra. He could recognise one of his own. His own enemy as well. "We will need you to stop those fuken tentacles tearing us apart when the battle begins," he offered, and she nodded. She resonated a burning energy unlike anything he'd felt from her before. He might have asked, but dared not learn how much better she had become at using the souls of his comrades.

Did you rip Derian's soul as he fell? He will need it back.

"It will be done."

"Take from my soul first," he warned, and she shook her head.

"I will not need to."

"Is there something wrong with my soul?"

"You have a beautiful, eternal soul," she said, smiling sadly. "Just like Derian, the idiot."

"So you did take from him?"

She appeared horrified at first. And then relaxed. "I have no need. I am fierce enough without," she offered, and that was good enough for him. For now.

"Well... it is there if you need it," he said, leaving her to stand at the front of the barge with fire in her grip while he looked to Kesta. Kesta nodded her acquiescence and brought the airbarge from its safe height down towards the sea beast at a terrific pace.

Ahead of him, Seren mumbled to herself as she held tight to the edge of the balcony. Natteo did the same but held one hand free to carry the pole. It felt light and reassuring. It was a rare thing to no longer fear for himself. He felt as though a god stirred something deep within him and wondered was this how Derian felt when the monster took hold, or how Seren felt when she leeched a soul.

His stomach lurched as the *Fighting Mongoose* reached a hunting level. His heart quickened but he was chilled and polished. He leaned a leg out over the balcony, watching the rushing water below. At last, he saw the flailing, distracted monster thrashing in the ocean as they came upon it swiftly.

Across the deck Lorgan roared as any leader would. "We have this," he cried.

As if they really did.

The beast's roars were ever present above the rush of wind and spray, and Natteo thought it a rightly sunny day to come. He liked those sunny days something sweet.

"We're coming for you, brother."

Kesta was a master of flight; that was easy to see. The shadows of the great tentacles appeared across the deck, and she did not waver; she merely tipped the barge forward and eased up so the harpoon wielders could go to task.

Five more breaths.

Natteo might have counted them, but instead, he held each breath and savoured the sight of prey. Without terror to take his mind, he studied the beast's thick, unsightly skin and thought it welcoming to a shard of chained steel.

Lorgan didn't count his breaths at all. He released, and Natteo cursed. "You are too far," he roared. It was an order. A threat too, and Lorgan, cursing his own eagerness, left the chain to zip past him as the barbed pole struck, clung for a pulse of spilled blood and fell away.

"Aye," Lorgan managed, grasping his second pole as Natteo leaned into the rushing wind and counted a few further breaths. Past the many tentacles, down upon its head, around its snapping beak filled with jagged teeth, and the world fell still as Natteo let loose.

It was straight, it was true. It stuck that awful flesh and kept going. The chain at his feet shot out after it as though pulled along by a thousand horses, and perhaps that was nothing in comparison to the beast's movements. Regardless, Natteo kept clear of that steaming chain and ran down the deck towards the next waiting pole. They had mere moments to accomplish this impossible task. A lesser Natteo might have panicked, fumbled with the spears. But this Natteo was ice cold.

He watched the flailing beast turn and howl in fresh shock, and then he saw Lorgan finally let loose a second time. This strike was far better; the barb took hold a few feet wide of Natteo's. Kesta, seeing the strikes, immediately went about saving their rears now that they had announced themselves.

Whatever had distracted the beast before was forgotten by this assault from the *Fighting Mongoose*, for it thrashed anew and there was a sudden pull on the barge as Kesta fought the beast and allowed it to win somewhat.

Natteo reached the second pole and, with a calming breath, sent it deep into the flesh as they passed low and wide of the demon. It was a pleasing thing to cast a little pain upon the dreadful monster. Natteo should have been terrified, anguished, broken and careless. But his hand was steady. Perfect for a killer, really.

Across the deck, Lorgan did the same, sending another

barbed pole into the beast. All the while, Seren brought fire to her fingertips and dashed it upon the beast's tentacles in fierce, burning spheres whenever they neared, and it was quite the plan of attack. It was strange, really, it was almost too easy, and really, nothing ever came easy for the Crimson Hunters.

I did lose a brother, though.

"Shut up, shut up, shut up," he growled to himself and lashed the third pole upon the beast and the next after that in quick succession.

As the chained barbs locked in deep within the beast, it fought their hold, but Kesta, with an uncanny array of manoeuvres, somehow matched the beast's struggles and held them in place by driving the airbarge back and forth with perfect precision, all the while avoiding the snapping lines or getting pulled into the water.

And perhaps it was the water that saved them. Were they to attempt this feat on a demon upon land, they would have had little chance of lasting even a few moments before its weight alone dragged them to a shattering fall. As it was, it was like pulling at a heavy log in a raging tempest.

"That's it," roared Lorgan, casting the last barb upon the beast and leaping away from the six lines of taut, steaming chain clinging to the deck. "Back to the harness-es," he roared, and Seren leapt free of the front of the deck, looking both exhausted and exhilarated.

"Come along, Natteo," she said, gliding by, and Natteo, taking a moment to hate the beast with the last of his likely lessening soul, cast the last barbed pole deep into the monster's flesh and stepped away as it thundered and fought.

He looked to Kesta one last time, and both she and Eveklyn were screaming a word at him through the glass.

It looked like "Whoa."

"Are you saying 'Whoa'?" he called.

The glass opened a foot and both screamed, "Go!"

"Ah, fair enough," he said, bowing, before darting off after Seren and Lorgan.

Down through the galley he sprinted, down the ladder into the main room where they'd all collectively gathered to eat, laugh, be fuken merry in leisure. Though there were more comfortable couches, it was the chairs the mercenaries sat in, strapping themselves in right tightly with leather restraints.

Not one of the helpless mercenaries said a word as they did, for their task was done. The chains would either hold or snap under the strain. The beast would be dragged or it would persevere. They would either live or die. Derian would either be dead or alive. It was all in the seven gods' hands now.

And maybe Kesta's.

Behind them, through the back window, they saw the beast struggling in the chains. Through the front window, they could see the distant land drawing nearer. It was here Natteo felt less a god and more a terrified human once more. He felt a sickening grip on his chest where all his terror lay, and he felt tears of sorrow coming upon him. In that moment, he did believe Derian to be truly dead, and he whimpered to himself a prayer of goodbye to Derian, to perhaps life as well.

Suddenly, Kesta rotated the airbarge and all the chains wrapped in its body tightened, and the beast was hoisted a little from the water—not enough that they could carry it yet; just enough to control it.

"Fuk me," roared Lorgan as the world turned around them. Natteo thought it a fine outburst. Fighting her hair in her eyes, Seren appeared perfectly at ease with the manoeuvre. She barely lifted from her seat and giggled as the world returned to its proper level. Around them, anything not bolted or strapped down took flight and then dropped heavily. Natteo heard the deafening clash of the galley's utensils and something resembling the sound of a splattering cake, and he howled as all manner of debris flew in front of his face. Once more the world outside appeared upside down for a sickening moment, and Natteo joined Lorgan's scream until the world suddenly righted itself and the airbarge thrust forward like a mount in a carriage race.

As before, Natteo thought of dragging a massive log across the water, albeit a right nasty log at that point, with branches trying to fight clear. On land, he could never hope to move that log, but across a water's surface, he could drag it along and gather some speed, and that's exactly what the *Fighting Mongoose* did.

"This might work," Lorgan said, as the force of the speed drove his head back against the chair's rest.

"Course it will," Natteo said, craning his neck to see the beast dragged, despite its fury, towards land.

With every breath, the grand demon weakened and the airbarge flew swifter, and Natteo could barely move such was the invisible force pinning him.

"I do not like this," Seren cried.

"Enjoy the ride," Natteo called as the barge shook and the land neared quicker and quicker.

"Here it comes," Lorgan said, gripping the chair seat, and Natteo gripped his own straps lest they fell from him and send him careening into the far wall with an awful mushy sound akin to a destroyed cake.

At the last moment, as the barge came upon the land, Kesta brought the *Mongoose* wide, and for a breath Natteo feared it was a mistake until he saw the smooth, brown sand give way to the rising threat of rocks along the coast, and he yelped in hope.

And with a dreadful crash, the airbarge lifted and climbed higher over the rocks as the beast struck land with a dreadful roar.

The world spun again, and Natteo suddenly fretted that the chains had all snapped, for they shot into the blue sky, spinning fiercely, and he feared the engines were blown.

"What happened?" cried Seren, who no longer found pleasure in this turmoil. She sat holding her hands over her eyes as the land in the window levelled. The barge did not teeter back to land, though; instead, it hung in the air, slowly rotating and dipping so that those in the privileged seats might see what Kesta gazed upon.

The chains had broken free, but only on account of the monster's body ripping apart where it was driven against the sharp rocks.

"I can't believe that worked," Seren cried, slipping free of her restraints. She fell to her knees and gazed in awe at the remains of the creature below, spread out for a couple hundred feet either way like a hissect smashed by an impatient cur.

It wailed and shuddered and died in front of their eyes, and it was a beautiful sight.

"Grand demons nothing, Crimson Hunters two," Lorgan muttered, kneeling beside her.

"Come on," Natteo said, feeling heavy, feeling hopeless, but feeling nevertheless determined. "Let's get down to Derian, see if he still breathes."

Lorgan shuddered to himself while Seren looked up.

She was smiling.

The Twisted Night into Day

Miles. So many miles. Too many miles. Not nearly enough miles, either. Probably not even a single mile travelled, either. It just felt like it, in this gloomy, doomed city. Both Erin and Rhendal scrambled through the mounds of rubble. They moved quickly despite the ache, the exhaustion and the seeping terror that took the strength in Erin's shapely knees. Shapely or no, they were cut and bruised in a thousand places from her exertions. Her hands were equally scraped from stumbling through the ruined landscape. Still, she and Rhendal charged with the fading moon at their backs and, with dawn somewhere ahead, she despaired that they would be taken at any moment.

Hunted.

"We never should have left our sanctuary," Rhendal moaned, skidding over a mound and collapsing to his knees. He climbed to his feet without missing a breath and kept going. A fresh cut above the knee streamed a little crimson as he did, but it would not stop him, for like she, he was carried by fear. A potent sauce that gifted him drive. "We will regret this."

She could see the panic in his features. It was worse than her own. He'd been a rock in the first battle. Holding his shit together all the way. Now he was breaking, and it was no surprise. Erin might have taken hold of the older man, offered positive words, whispered confident things. She might even have screamed in his face to show the depth of her determination, but truly, she was near broken too. Probably had been for a few days. It didn't really matter if they were broken or not; those nasty pursuing beasts were out there, howling, charging, and they didn't care what state they found her and Rhendal in, as long as their blood was warm. Venandi night hunters preferred the kill—that much she knew of them.

"We can make it," she cried, knowing the lie for what it was. The path had darkened; the moon had hidden itself behind a few stubborn clouds, and an eerie, dim glow spread out across the battlefield that had once been a bustling peasant sector.

"We'll never make it," he whimpered, yet, like any drowning man, he still fought for breath, kept running no matter how much exhaustion took him. "Perhaps..." he said, finally slowing, dropping to a knee and bleeding a little more, "... you go on, and I'll wait here a while." His fingers touched his sheathed weapon. Sweat dripped from his forehead. He was a wretch and a doomed man, and leaving him behind was a tempting thing. Especially if he gave her reason to. Permission to, as well. For just a breath she convinced herself it was the better move. Without him leading, she could dart ahead, stay alive that little bit longer.

Maybe even find a small little nook to climb into and hide the rest of the night away. But she could never live with herself.

"If you fall, I will be at your side," she said with as much determination as she could muster. It was a shade brighter than the last of her will would allow. For now, with no Venandi night hunters actually in their sight, she could feign this strength, could attempt to repay his own stubborn determination in pulling her from the black fire.

If I have nothing left, I will have honour.

"Leave me be, girl," he snapped, and collapsed in the dirt. He closed his eyes as though this respite was the greatest pleasure he'd ever known. Perhaps it was.

"Get up, old man," she hissed, but he would not stir. "Defeat is a bad look to you."

"Look at all this horror," he spluttered, pointing to the dark ruin around them. "Look at all we have accomplished. We were wrong to lay this city as we did."

"We have more to do," she said, dropping down to face him.

"I have no more cruelty left in me. I am tired. I look around with eyes wide open."

She didn't like this talk at all. "Then let my death be on your hands," she whispered, and the moon disappeared completely. She couldn't see his grizzled face anymore, and perhaps it was better not seeing the spectre of looming death as it scampered through the ruins towards them, better not to set eyes upon the beasts enraged by nature, trained by a demon. Aye, perhaps it was better not to see them at all.

As though they heard her thoughts, the beasts howled

again, a terrible cacophony of noise that echoed around the city. There were hundreds of those beasts, if not more.

Much more.

Shuddering, she gripped his shoulders. "This is a shitty way to die," she said at length, and he grunted in agreement. Resting just a few moments returned to her a little relief and some of her determination, but dark or no, honour or no, she climbed to her feet.

"Fine. Help me up, little one," he growled, and she hefted him to his feet. "Can't see a thing in front of me," he muttered, and this time she took the lead, shuffling and bracing herself against obstacles. Sitting was recovering, but shuffling forward was a grasping of the spirit, even if every step was fraught with risk.

And within little time at all there appeared distantly, in the gloom, a light. "Do you see that?" he cried, pulling away from her. As he did, the light flickered and disappeared.

"Could be nothing."

"That is divine salvation—I know it is," he cried deliriously. "Like a beacon from the gods," he yelled, stumbling towards the looming building from which it emanated. She wondered coldly if his injuries hadn't become infected, hadn't taken him to delirium. Still, it was a fuken light and she was grateful. She followed after, stumbling on as many obstacles as he.

Their route brought them to the looming shape of a battered building, tall and archaic, older than any others she'd seen, standing proud and surrounded on all sides by building-sized mounds of rubble. The building itself might once have belonged to one of the wealthier Dellerin families. Now, though, it appeared derelict and creaky. Touched by the gods and quite a few of the crushing boulders resting throughout the battlefield, it was a beautiful sight and a miracle among the ruins.

Running up the front and side were massive cracks in the walls. She could imagine the damage a strong gust of wind would do to it, let alone another strike from a flying boulder; nevertheless, she wanted in from the cold.

"Come on," Rhendal cried, running along its outer garden fence. The fence was constructed of long, spiked poles of iron. Tall and sturdy, they looked less a garden fence and more like a prison fence, in truth. Reaching the tall, domineering gates, he discovered they were locked tight and began to climb noisily up and over.

Erin followed after, catching her sleeve and tearing it on one of the spikes as she did. Dropping down on the other side, though, a sense of hope and safety took her. Aye, it was only a fence of steel, against brutish, monstrous, snapping teeth, but better than nothing.

The building's windows were barricaded from within. A curious thing, really, and Rhendal, having used the last of his energy to scale the gate, hobbled from window to window, hammering as he went. "Let us in," he roared, and Erin winced at the sudden volume in the cool night air. Hunters would pick up that noise easily enough.

"Lower your voice, fool," she hissed, watching the night, hearing that howling. She wondered was it in her head. Would it always be in her head?

"Help me, Erin," he cried, ignoring her, and continued stumbling along, thumping loudly, kicking at anything to make as much racket as he could.

Weakly, Erin walked alongside the building, listening

for light-bearing fiends within. "Help us," she whispered softly and imagined her enemy on the other side, already arming themselves before thundering out and hacking them to pieces.

"Let us in, before these brutes tear us asunder," Rhendal continued, until suddenly, there came the screech of wood—perhaps a seeping-oak wardrobe being moved aside—followed by the hissed call of a scared man from behind a window above.

Erin stumbled over to him, raising her arms in a gesture of pleading. "Please, let us in, friend." Her heart began to hammer in excitement and terror; in knowing, as well. The same knowing any prey had when the end of the chase was upon them.

The man looked as shattered as she, and she saw him curse her under his breath. "Friend?" he said in a strong Dellerin accent. It was rougher, more peasantly. If such a word existed. And if it didn't, it deserved to. "You dare come bringing those... those monsters down upon us this morning?"

"How close is it to dawn?" Erin asked as Rhendal pushed past her to gaze at the man in the window above.

"You'll be fine if you keep walking towards the gate," the man said, and sneered. His face was caked in ash and grime. He'd endured war as badly as any wretch could have. His drawn face resembled those of the grinning, ghoulish corpses they'd passed along the way. She couldn't tell his age, but his eyes had seen a hard lifetime—no doubt much of it in these last few days. "You can beat at the gods' damned door all thurken morning, but you won't get in."

"Open the door or I'll set this place alight," Rhendal

warned, and she knew he meant it. Wouldn't take him too long to pick up enough kindling from the surrounding rubble. Let Rhendal do that and *she* would set it alight. Although she was no great soldier or hunter, she was a survivor. More than that, she was the most skilled fire starter in the lands. It was uncanny how swiftly she could bring fire alight. She liked to think she respected flame and it in turn served her. She'd never met a fiend who could set a fire burning with less tinder or more damp wood than she.

Or damp books.

Saying that, she had no interest in setting this building alight. And perhaps a more rational Rhendal didn't either. Fear and heartbreak were a terrible thing to even the fiercest of legends, the mightiest of heroes. The average wounded warrior, too.

"What is this place?" Erin asked, taking hold of Rhendal tightly. The emotional fool must have heard it in her voice, for he fell still. Either that, or he caught the scent of those that hunted them and watched the night.

"This is the last standing bastion in this sector of Dellerin, and you have no right to enter, fiends."

"I think you meant to say *friends*," noted Rhendal. He dropped to the ground as he spoke, and the man spat at him in reply. "Didn't even come close," Rhendal mumbled, and Erin, smiling sadly, vowed to rely on the man's mercy as means of getting in the door, hiding deep, surviving. After dawn, well, they could see about that. Regardless, she'd happily face the gloom of a rainy day and a thousand of Anguis's acolytes over the hidden howling hunters.

And then the beasts appeared. There were at least a dozen, and the rubble-strewn ground began to shake. Each monster was half the size of a proud mount, with bulging muscles and snapping teeth built to dismember. Erin stood quaking as their doom rushed down through the battlefield towards the two terrified warriors. She remembered the description from her book, and it was nothing like these monsters. It was far worse.

"Like savage hounds tainted by a demonic touch," she could only murmur, and Rhendal stood up beside her and gripped her shoulder.

"A fitting description," the man above said, and Erin hated his cruelty, his cowardice, his refusal to grant them mercy. "They might resemble hounds in their stride, but not even a dozen hounds could stand up to a single Venan-di," he added after a time. "I wish you peace."

"I wish you to burn in hell," Rhendal murmured in defeat. And why wouldn't he feel defeated? The dozen quickly became dozens, became a hundred, became a thousand. Or it seemed as much. Certainly, the world filled up with these vile creatures and there was no escape. There was no hiding behind the fence, either. It wouldn't take long for the fiends to tear right through it, then tear right through the two of them.

"They will come for you after us," Erin said after a time, and the cruel citizen began to laugh coldly.

"They will not step into any abode, for the Anguished One has them well on a leash. No, no. Out there, I would meet my doom, but inside, well, it's rightly polished."

The creatures came as a surging flood, scampering through the rubble as though it were a meadow. They roared, they howled, they were impressive, and they were terrifying, and truly, Erin felt a fear like no other. She wanted to wail, to weep, to howl at the unfairness of things. Instead, she spun around and dropped to a knee, looking up at the man in the window. It was easier to gaze at a cur than at certain, snapping doom. The howling reached a piercing crescendo as the beasts discovered their prey. She heard them running up and down the fence, seeking entry, and she dared not face them. "I beg you please," she wailed. "Mercy from such a fate."

"I will watch you die, and you will be a tonic to my soul," the wretch roared venomously. She was surprised to see a sudden grief in his face and wondered was he once a father with a loving wife and family? Had her people taken everything from him? Did he deserve this vengeance? Did she deserve to ease his pain?

Probably.

"Just take the girl in, sir," Rhendal offered sombrely. From his wrist he drew a golden charm. "This might pay her way," he added, casting the charm at the cur, who reached weakly and missed. The charm dropped to the ground below the window, and Rhendal immediately scrabbled in the dirt before recovering it and tossing it again.

"I shall keep this regardless, fiend," the brute offered, clutching it.

"I am a soldier, grizzled with age and knowledge. I know the terrible deeds we are responsible for, but the girl is a simple child. She is a righteous private without any better sense," Rhendal cried, and then the beasts charged the gate. Their feral howls were dreadful up close.

The man seemed to think on this as he pocketed the piece. Erin knew the value in that golden charm. Any fool would. The man might have had nothing to his name, and perhaps a little gold was all it took to sway a little goodness. Her eyes fell upon the door. If it shifted, she'd charge through it and earn them both a respite. She refused to leave Rhendal to face these beasts alone.

"Just the girl—just take the fuken girl," Rhendal said, pulling Erin to her feet and leaning close to her ear. "I don't believe in many things, but you and that book are far more important than a crusty old fiend like me," he whispered desperately.

Erin, panicking now, shook her head against his urgings. Her fingers tingled again, as though a candle burned upon each tip. "No, no," she hissed. She sought a better barter, though her pockets were empty. She had nothing to her name. Never had. "We will both survive this," she pledged as the Venandi began to climb upon each other, preparing to breach the fence. At the door, there came a scraping sound, and Erin began to believe.

"We rush them as it opens," she whispered, even as she and Rhendal embraced, feigning a bittersweet warriors' goodbye. The roar of spitting creatures filled the air and it was a terrible thing. Erin shook from terror and held Rhendal lest the door remain closed, lest the beasts make the successful climb too soon. "Together," she added, and he embraced her tightly.

"Aye, that we will, little one. On my mark," he pledged.

Behind them, the door swung open suddenly, and Erin rushed for it.

Falling into the End

D*on't be scared.*
     That won't help.
     Don't cry out either.
Just die.
Like a hero.
Like a spitting hero.

The rushing wind was colder than Derian could ever have imagined. For just a pulse of blood, he wondered was it the lack of blood in his system that caused such cold, or was it the panic of death as it loomed ever nearer? Perhaps his mercenary guide might have had the answer, but that was lost to him. Like absolutely everything in his life.

Lost, gone, forever. Or at least would be in a few moments, at least.

His body spun upon itself, and the world became a spinning blur of grey, blue, a little yellow and some blue all over again.

He might have fought it. Might have begun flapping his wings in the faint hope that he'd master the art like no human before him. He really wished he could fly. That shit would have been real handy right now. Best he could hope for was a quick landing. He hoped he didn't face the ground, either. He hoped he looked to the sky, saw the blue and that would be it. There were hardly worse ways to go where such terror was involved... or perhaps there were.

Terror.

He held that word in his mind and couldn't shake it. He didn't want to take it, either. Didn't want to allow that awfulness to infect his mind at the end. He'd take madness first. A little madness would be welcomed. He fought that terror and embraced the madness. It was something to do at the end of his insignificant life.

What about the girl with the stones?

What about the other girl with nice knees?

He suddenly felt betrayed and allowed it to fester to anger. Anger was a gift when you had nothing left. He most certainly had nothing left.

His vision spun again as the world of ocean rushed towards him and his belly near exploded all over himself. Terror gave way to shame, and he held that too. Might even focus on embarrassment while he was at it.

No one will know.

My body will not be recovered.

And that's alright.

Tasting bitter bile in his mouth, he held out his arms like a soaring bird of prey, and slowly, Derian righted himself and felt a little better about things. If he wasn't able to hold his vomit during a second assault, then at least he could avoid seeing the end as it appeared from below at an alarming rate.

Fuk.

Fuk, fuk.

Oh, fuk fuk.

He fought that terror again and squinted at the sun as it burned his eyes, and coldly, with a body already leaking itself dry, he decided he was simply watching the sun until the end, and strangely enough, that was a settling thing.

For an entire breath, that is, until he wailed in misery for his fate.

Felt his bowels releasing and held that awfulness, instead of surrendering to terror.

I did my best.

I was loved.

In a way.

I will be remembered.

For a time.

He'd heard people lived an entire night, right before they died. He had visions of his own. Visions of near escapes, of close calls. Of insane manoeuvres that snatched victory from the jaws of defeat. He tried to grasp hold of any and all such things. To seek comfort, to seek distraction. To seek an escape.

But really, nothing helped.

Most of the time he just thought of hats. Hats he owned, hats he'd desired to own. He wished he'd spent longer seeking out hats aboard the *Fighting Mongoose*. Who knew—perhaps, like the enchanted sword of fire, there might have been one enchanted with the ability to fly. That would have been nice.

He looked below to his doom and thought a little more of hats for another pulse and then gave up entirely.

"Where are you, monster?" he roared to the darkened beast living deep within. He felt so very lonely, and a little demonic beast might be the perfect tonic to this terror as it stirred within his essence, crawled from his belly, infecting everything as it did. "Please, come to me," he wailed, and nothing stirred, and he beat at his chest fiercely with a terrified fist, hoping to stir a little more. It was something to do as the world drew closer, impossibly fast. "Come, take me, seeva beast," he demanded, but still the beast refused to surface. He believed himself more powerful under the monster's hold, but surviving this fall was a feat impossible for even a monster as tough as this. And perhaps, because of this, the seeva did not surface to face death openly. It preferred to hide in the dark, facing the end with its eyes closed. "Fuken coward," he roared, and absolutely nothing shifted in his soul.

"Please," he wailed, and fell silent.

For just a foolish moment he wondered if Kesta was aware of his predicament from her place in the cockpit. He also wondered was that magnificent airbarge about to lessen the distance. Was it about to suddenly drop at a terrific rate using its powerful propellors and the ground's impossible pull and get ahead of his pathetic, squirming body?

Yes, yes, keep thinking there is hope.

He wondered was Natteo about to appear in his sightline, grinning and mocking a flapping, drunken hawk before reaching out and pulling him ashore, right as they came upon the demon's nasty snapping beak.

This is all very possible, he told himself, drawing his eyes to the *Mongoose* as it rose far above and continued to climb as he fell forever.

He whispered his last goodbyes to those he loved most and closed his eyes and waited.

And waited.

Until he opened his eyes to face his doom, and oh, he hated this killer something fierce. Below, the crushing waves and a watery grave no longer waited. Instead, the demon waited with mouth agape and tentacles waving.

As he came upon it, the beak snapped open and shut with a crack of thunder and he was through, and he wondered was his fate not to be severed swiftly in two but to keep falling.

"Teeth," he mumbled in rising terror as countless lines of fangs appeared before him, around him, stretching out, filling his vision. They were endless, they were as large as he, covered in drool and seawater, and they stretched deep into the darkness and on into the gullet of the monster.

"I don't want to die," he moaned, and felt that terrible helplessness take him once more. He felt naked and insignificant and alone. He held that loneliness and wondered would it follow him into the darkness. Was there existence after life? Whatever emotion carried in was contained for eternity in the soul.

He really hated that thought.

Fuk off to that thought.

Instead, he wondered would he miss those he loved in the great beyond? Or would he find darkness and stillness? Natteo claimed there was something dark and unnerving beyond. He really wished he hadn't thought that in the last few moments.

Thanks a fuken lot, Natteo.

"I am diminished," he whispered, and the stench of the bitter sea overcame him as the coldness gave way to the dreadful, fetid warmth of his tomb. And further he fell.

After a desperate last few thoughts, he drew his sword as he rushed past the last of the deadly incisors, deep into the monster's gut. As before with the blade of fire, he was drawn to the weapon as though his limbs were not his. He drew the unimpressive blade and gripped it tightly as the teeth gave way completely to pink flesh where the belly likely opened up. His vision blinked from blindness to sight as the beak above snapped open and shut as though chewing, and this was awful.

"Eaten," he gasped in horror as the dark loomed, and he reached out with that sword and slashed into the darkness. There came no flash of brilliant flame. Instead, it merely cut into softness as though slipping through a melting block of butter. As he plunged that blade, it sliced deep and continued to slice as he fell, and suddenly, he felt perfectly fine about everything. His body shook in relief.

I'm ready.

No more terror.

He closed his eyes, held that sword tight and listened to the rush of his fall ending as he hit the darkness hard and it was there he died.

———

It hurt for only a pulse of blood and Derian was grateful for it. Such was the force of his grisly death, though, his thoughts were thrown asunder. They were thrown a few feet from his body, to be precise, and it was a wondrous feeling. The world spun again, but this time it was welcomed. He floated above himself as though held aloft in water, and for a moment more he wondered had he survived, but really, he knew better. This was different to any other time he'd died. This felt perfect and permanent. He felt as a spirit might when staring at their broken body below.

He tried to talk, to yell, to wail, and to sigh, all without success.

Instead, he simply glided across the dimness, staring at his broken body among the ruin of the beast's stomach. It was as any monstrous stomach would be, he supposed, and he hated it. The rumbles of war and gluttony echoed around him. The skeletons of dissolving sea beasts disgusted him as they bobbed in the ocean of acid. His body was not fully submerged; instead, as though beached and dead upon a sandy shore, he watched himself among the innards.

Curiously, his body lay at many unnatural angles, twisted as though a great giant had taken a moment to wring the life from him. His eyes, though closed at the end, appeared open once more, in a deathly gaze, all frozen. There were a few final spurts of blood, which quickly fell still and were lost in the deadly stomach acid, and truly Derian thought this was a terrible and interesting end. The only pleasing thing was his deathly grip on his blade.

I tried to take you with me.

He was still clutching that unimpressive blade, which remained embedded in the side of the stomach where he'd fallen to his end. Such a long gash it had made, fatal to any reasonably sized monster, even a giant. The gash spread far into the darkness of the stomach lining high above, and he wondered bitterly if he might cause the beast to suffer the pain of an ulcer. It was a small victory and he took it.

And then he looked away from his body and felt a compelling dragging sensation.

Pulled to the dark.

Go to it.

He had not believed death would be like this. Moreover, he'd thought it would be hand in hand with the demise of the creature deep within, but he was alone in his spirited form, answering to an invisible current. There were worse things, he imagined, feeling nothing like the spectre he'd been in the source.

Let go and sleep the sleep of the just-got-home.

"I always wanted to fly," he whispered to the nothing and allowed himself to obey the pull. Without looking back, he floated away from his dead body. In a day or two the corpse would be churned to nothing anyway. He would suffer no dignified burial. Such a thing was a comfort.

He moved with an imaginary breeze. He willed himself forward, and his spirit obeyed, and Derian suddenly realised the knot of fear he'd kept in his gut these last few years was gone. Absent, like a god's grace. As were the aches and pains of a march as well. He near felt reborn once more. But more than that, he felt finished and so very at peace. The shock and the horror of his death flittered away and he flittered away with them.

He touched the wall of the beast's stomach and kept going as though it were nothing at all.

I am nothing.

Such thoughts were welcomed. As was this pulling

towards an end. Like a drunkard to a bed, he followed eagerly, knowing the slumber would be eternally welcomed. He already felt himself slipping away into nothing, and he yearned to follow. Who needed thoughts anyway? He sensed a greater purpose in the nothing, and he would serve it. The universe beyond his own imaginings had greater plans in motion, and somehow, he began to understand things greater than himself.

And from the darkness, he suddenly felt a terrible warmth. Something rooted in the source, in this world, calling to him with much urgency. For a breath he tried to remember the girl's name. The beautiful, nude girl from the source. But these thoughts also flittered away. He wondered was she with him now? Calling him from beyond the veil of nothing? Urging him back to this world?

Seren.

"I'm already dead, pretty girl. Let me go," he insisted, and he passed through the wall of a hollow cavern and he wondered what part of the beast it was. He imagined the slimy fluid and skin, and flesh and organ and much fat. He imagined himself slipping through them as though they weren't even there, and then he felt that pulsing cry once more. With more urgency as well. It was not from the darkness; it was from somewhere else entirely.

"Leave me be," he demanded, but his thoughts shifted back to waking. The desire to fade into nothing lessened and he wailed miserably for it.

He answered that call, and through the gloom there appeared a dim light some way ahead. Like himself, the light was not affected by the real world. It passed through the beast like a warning fire over a coast's rocky shore.

"What is this?" he roared, but his voice was weak. He still sensed the pull of nothingness, but that light was all too enticing.

One more adventure before the end?

He soared through further flesh, barely able to take his eyes from the light—a bluish glow that brightened with every foot he floated too. With every cavern of inner monster he passed through as well.

He took his eyes away to gaze at a mountain of crab hatchlings squirming upon themselves, and for a breath he imagined what it was to be human and disgusted. The crabs did not notice him as he passed above them, and he thought this unsurprising, yet somewhat unnerving.

Until, eventually, in a dark room of flesh and horror, he came upon the source of the light, of the call.

Floating towards the blue light, he saw it was a blazing, potent sphere with just enough space for an old man to sit cross-legged. He knew this because that's exactly what he found.

The old man was deathly still. He took no breath, and carelessly Derian reached for the sphere's wall and felt his hand unable to penetrate its vibrant surface.

And suddenly, the sphere shattered to nothing. The man opened his eyes, gasped, stared at Derian and leapt for him, stretching out, grabbing him through the heart and pulling him to the ground.

Derian tried to fight the fiend, but it was like striking an eternal wall of light and spark. Derian fought and wailed and felt the nothing slip away, and then panic began to return, that knot and all. He could only look into the eyes of the fiend who trapped him, and he believed there was nothing but madness behind those eyes. It was a terrifying thing.

"Hello there," the older man said, easing his grip but not releasing his hold. "I've been waiting quite a time for you, dear Derian."

SACRIFICE

The heavy door slammed shut behind Erin as she stepped through. It was only a breath but long enough for her mind to realise something was terribly wrong. She stared around, blinking, and then it struck her. All too late.

Rhendal had made to run with her. She was sure of it.

He was with me.

We had a plan.

Take them all on.

She spun back to face the old oaken door, polished and aged by a hundred years. Thick and heavy, and very much slammed shut, leaving a doomed warrior on the other side.

"No, no, no," she roared at the fiend who was locking the door, triple-bolting it too, before grabbing hold of an older wardrobe and sliding it back across the door and wedging it against a notch in the floor. A sturdy brute could batter all day at such a barricade and struggle to break through. "Let him in," she roared, grasping for the fiend. He was younger and prettier than the ruined man they'd conversed with. He was no more than a few years older, and she hated him. Especially when he shoved her away, while another set of hands pulled her from the door. From her doomed comrade.

"Be quiet, little one, lest we cast you back out into death," a dreadful and familiar voice hissed as he pulled her blade from the scabbard and tossed it to the feet of the doorkeeper. She began to squeal in horror, in frustration, while he climbed a small mound of crates to look back out the small window to where Rhendal remained.

"What are you doing to her?" Rhendal cried from the other side of the door. He was but a few feet away, but through such sturdy barricades, he sounded feeble and distant.

"I pledged a deal for her life," the bitter man hissed. There came a desperate thumping at the door; kicking too, louder than before as her comrade, frenzied and roaring, attempted to get in to her. Or get her out. "I promised nothing more," the cur at the window continued.

"I will not leave him," Erin warned, making for the door again, but the man standing over the locks looked ready for such an assault. He held out a calming hand, offered a gentle nod before shaking his head. He wore the uniform of a city guard. He was not army, though. Technically, though he served the city, he was no enemy. He had cold, grey eyes, a killer's eyes, and Erin feared him in that moment. Almost as much as leaving Rhendal to his fate. She eyed the dagger at his waist for a breath or two.

"Unlock that door," she demanded, and he snorted as though her challenge was impressive. It really wasn't, and she felt a great rage come upon her. Her fingers began to sting as though dipped in a pot of bubbling water, and she felt silent tears drip from her eyes.

Outside, Rhendal wasn't taking this turn of events any better than she was. "I'll fuken kill ye all if you touch her," he warned. And there was that strength she'd known since serving under him. He was no great general but he was a leader of soldiers. Doomed or no, he would spit venom and intimidate all he could. She tried to grab at the wardrobe but hadn't the strength to shift it a hand's length. The guard shoved her away, grabbing hold and tripping her before pinning her to the cold floor. He leaned over her and his eyes met hers.

"That man is already dead," he said quietly, as though revealing some great secret for her ears only. She struggled in his hold, but his strength was overpowering. He grabbed her neck in a deathlike grip and shook his head, a last warning, and feebly, she fought her last and miserably fell still. She was no great fighter. She never had been. Rhendal, on the other hand, could have killed them all, had he bothered to break his word and charge through the door with her. It would have been heroic, foolhardy and wonderful. Both men would have fallen by now, and they would have had a secure sanctuary to wait out the monsters outside. "Be grateful you are inside these walls, instead of out," the man warned, and released his grip ever so.

He leapt to his feet and hammered back at the door and the aggrieved threatening Rhendal on the other side. "She will be sheltered until after dawn and then free to go," the jailor said, and the hammering stopped.

"Do I have your word no harm will come to her?" Rhendal asked quietly.

"I pledge my life on it, sir," the man countered, and Erin shook her head in disgust.

Sitting up and eyeing the cur at the window, she fought mingled panic, horror and relief. "All these deals involving my fate," she snapped. "No one considering my spitting thoughts on the matter." She thought them to be behaving just like generals on both sides. Their words were similar to those of generals and it disgusted her. "I do not agree," she roared after a while.

"Hush, my friend," Rhendal said softly, but she could barely hear him. She didn't want to hear him like this. She wanted him beside her, slaying all these curs, no matter how pretty they were.

"I can't hear you, Rhendal. I can't hear you from in here."

"It's better you survive, instead of a crusty old relic like me," he said, and this time she reached across the furniture barricade and hammered the wooden door, weeping ever so. She did not love this man. Nor did she even know him well. He was but a superior in their army and she owed him her life. Had done on numerous occasions now.

"You… and the book," he added, and it was but a whisper for her and her alone, and a coldness came upon her. This was no sanctuary where mystical things occurred. This was the real world and there was no power in a fabled book. She felt foolish and she felt a fraud. How could he surrender his life for her in the trivial belief that some book held any power?

"I would rather stand with you than listen to you die," she cried, and he said nothing in reply.

"You don't have to listen," the fiend at the window

suggested, dropping down. "You can watch him die if you'd like?" He grinned cruelly and motioned for her to climb the barrels to gaze at Rhendal.

She did not hesitate, scrambling up and over the wooden pieces, scraping herself as she did, getting numerous splinters and twice nearly collapsing the entire structure with her clumsy desperation. At last she reached the top, eager and terrified to look out at the coming dawn.

"Rhendal," she moaned, realising the window was nowhere near wide enough for her to squirm out and drop down to fall with him. He'd probably not have been best pleased with such a thing, but fuk him; better chances of survival with them both. A part of her was also dreadfully relieved she could not join him in their death.

Rhendal sat cross-legged with his back to the snapping Venandi nighthunters as they scrambled upon each other, trying to gain a foothold and find some weakness in the fence. They scurried like ants upon each other, and it was evident it would be just moments before the fiends scrambled over.

Upon hearing her voice he opened his eyes, as though he had been sleeping. Perhaps he was trying to find a moment of peace before the end. Perhaps he was simply finished. Perhaps he just wanted a nice nap while he waited to die.

"I'm really quite scared," he said, smiling and pinching the bridge of his nose. "I have been scared for near two decades now." Slowly, he climbed to his feet as though waking from slumber after a warm season's picnic in a field. "But that fear is all about to end," he said, and she thought him incredible. "So perhaps it's a good moment."

"Not like this. You don't deserve this."

"Look at this city. Look at her ruin. It is our doing. I think I deserve it quite enough." He spoke in the tone of a man who was ready to answer for his sins. Not like a soldier at the end at all.

The beasts began to shriek, watching him, and they climbed high and began to scurry over the top. They were frenzied with fresh, pumping blood so close, and Erin could only scream as he turned serenely from her to face the threat.

"I owe you my life," she wailed.

"You owe the world your survival," he warned, and truly, he believed in her more than she did. It was a damning and dreadful thing. He drew his sword and eyed the first beast as it scrambled over towards him. Each monstrous limb was bulbous with muscle and demonic influence. There was no creature more fearsome in the entirety of the Dellerin Isles. Looking at them from this safe place terrified her. She couldn't imagine the fear Rhendal suffered.

But he showed no emotion. Instead, he offered a delicate nod and held out his blade in front of him. It barely quivered. His stance was not one of terror or retreat; it was imposing and impressive. She'd seen this stance, seen him at war. Despite his age, he moved more swiftly than most others. A man as experienced in their army as he was likely to be adept, she supposed. Especially at the end, when there was nothing left to hold back.

"Come on," he suddenly roared, as though the beasts would do anything but. The first creature, as though earning the right to attack first, took its time pacing towards the warrior. Those who squirmed over after halted now, to watch the kill, to wait their turn.

Erin waited, too, in anguish. She could have looked away, hidden her eyes and covered her ears, but her comrade deserved more than that. Not just for having saved her life before, but because she needed to witness the death of the last remaining soldier in her ill-fated platoon.

They are all waiting for you.
Waiting for me, as well.

The beast roared a threat and Rhendal sprang forward, impossibly swift. His blade was sturdy and thick, oiled and well used, but cared for and razor sharp. He struck out, sending his blade through the beast's throat and pulling ever so, slicing across, before retreating a step as the dying monster continued to bound towards him, unaware of its fate. The beast reared and swung a massive clawed paw as it died, and Rhendal retreated instinctively. The next closest monster immediately charged towards him, snapping and hissing, enraged by the fall of its comrade, and Rhendal met the attack just as smoothly.

Erin studied his footwork almost absently, watched his shoulders move ever so with every strike as he again slew the beast in a few perfect strikes. Conserving his energy, no doubt, to outlast the curs until the sun burned at their eyes, at their skin, at wherever.

Truly, though, no matter how smoothly Rhendal dispatched them, they were simply too many. The beasts roared from behind the fence alongside, but Rhendal barely blinked. He simply retreated along the wall, meeting the next Venandi and the one after that. Each time, with the barest flick of his wrist, he felled the attacker and met the next.

But the monsters kept coming, in a never-ending rush as inevitable as a tide. One could only hold firm against the breaking waves before the water swallowed all; this Erin knew all too well. She wanted to scream, to yell at him, praise him, curse the beasts as well. Mostly, she wanted a bow and arrow to rain what distraction she could upon the creatures.

Instead, she watched in grim silence as the garden between fence and house became flooded with brutish, demonic monsters hissing and howling, lunging and hunting.

Waiting.

He must have been so fierce in his heyday, she thought, watching him battle inevitable death. Always moving, always swinging, always killing. With the sun beginning to rise, she nearly believed for a moment that he would hold firm. Endure impossible odds like in tales of unlikely heroes and impossible miracles, set down in dreadful prose. Oh, aye, in open ground, he would have been dead in a few breaths, but confined as he was between building and barricade fence, there was a slight advantage and he took every foot of it.

The bodies of the brutes became a rampart of sorts, slowing the Venandi as they climbed over their dead, all eager to take their own vengeance. She counted a dozen before the beasts slowed their attacking and formed into a sort of dignified queue. Now, they howled a little more, snarled and spat, and came at him in groups of three.

Rhendal, however, changed no tactic; he simply continued retreating, slicing and cutting as he did.

"Is he still fighting?" a voice from below asked warily.

"Has he killed many?" another voice asked, and she dared not look away to answer lest her gazing was the enchantment keeping him alive. Oh, if she had the power, she would have chosen fire as her enchantment and sent it down upon them all.

She imagined her fists as balls of purest magenta flame, burning and sizzling as she cast fire upon the monsters, charring them to a crisp. As she did, she felt burning upon her fingers. Felt it as though it was real. For just a breath she looked to her fingers, near expecting them to be alight. Unsurprisingly, her hands were as unimpressive and grubby as usual, and that warmth she imagined dissipated to nothing, leaving no scarring whatsoever.

"He must be doing well," the wretched bargain-maker hissed, and she didn't reply. "Hope they don't catch our scent while he's taking time dying."

"Well, they haven't entered any house so far," the keeper of the door uttered, and her breath caught in her throat. "I doubt they will start it this morning with the sun rising," he added, and still she wouldn't look away. In that moment, she didn't care if they came after the house.

But they didn't come for the house at all.

They were too content with their impending victory.

It happened in a breath, and by the time Erin wailed a warning of a skulking Venandi slipping behind him, it already had its jaws plunged deep into Rhendal's neck.

He did not see his death, and perhaps it was a blessing, as was the blow that felled him. She thought of a wildcat, wary of losing a caught bird to flight. The bite was swift and perfect. His shoulders slumped, his sword dropped, but he did not fall. Instead, the beast held him where he died and the rest of the monsters swarmed the defenceless corpse, snapping, barking, howling and chewing.

Only then could Erin wail one last time as she looked away from the awfulness. But not before seeing the beasts rip and tear what they could. They fought amongst themselves over the ruin, and it was a dreadful sight. She wept for his bravery and her loneliness before slipping away from the window to the floor below, where, falling hard, she rested upon her knees and wailed for her loss. The memory, she knew, would be burned into every nightmare forever, too.

She was alone now, and outnumbered, and no misguided belief in a fuken book was going to pull her from this nightmare.

Arturo and Edel

"Who are you?" Derian cried, struggling in the old man's claw-like grasp. He was unusually strong for a man his age. His face was drawn, each wrinkle suggesting a life of much cheer, or frowning, or just heavy ale drinking. His hair was long, unkempt and as white as snow. Derian had always wanted to see snow. Perhaps he would. Perhaps it wouldn't be as cold as people said it was.

As old and feeble as the man was, his eyes burned vividly. Derian couldn't be certain, but he thought they shimmered. Perhaps all eyes as mad as those shimmered, for they were a madman's beady eyes. He grinned with perfect teeth, suggesting the cur had never smoked tobacco weed a day in his life. Had never spent a day chewing eucal leaves either. Perhaps, even, he wasn't too heavy an ale drinker at all.

Such things shouldn't have mattered to the captured wraith form of Derian, but here he was, thinking it all the same. A shrewder thinker might have been using his thoughts to discover how this cur had trapped him as he did. Or if he was even human.

"You are Derian, are you not?" the old man asked in a croaky voice. His grin faded ever so. "Oh, thurken hell... Don't tell me I climbed out of my shell for a simple doomed sailor...? Oh dear, oh sweet goodness, honey of... oh dear..." he added, and released Derian ever so, and immediately Derian was overcome by the desire to fade into nothingness.

"Perhaps you should be on your way... hmm... yes... That seems best," the old man went on.

"I am Derian," Derian wittily replied after a breath. Though wary, he wondered if truth was the better tactic at this point.

The old man certainly thought so. "Are you absolutely sure...? Oh, wonderful. I knew making that mistake thrice was too much—far too much, in fact—but these things happen, you know, in such a big world," he mumbled, and a sphere of purest white suddenly spun from his fingers, and he groaned in neither pleasure nor pain, but some-where in between. His demented eyes suddenly narrowed, staring through Derian as though scrutinizing an unlikable insect. "You can't imagine how awkward those conversa-tions are when you aren't Derian at all... You could try, I suppose..." He looked distant for a breath. "You could wait around a while... Um... you might even see a non-Derian all shocked and surprised to be alive... when really they *are* dead... and oh, the pleading, the soulful weeping of loved ones... when they realise they are in fact dead after all... Dreadful, really." He suddenly grinned. "Some even pretend they are Derian as they flitter away... Bye, bye." He waved his fingers in the air and the glimmer of light appeared to flitter away. "Yes, you look like Derian... so I'm rather sure... um... *We* are rather sure you are indeed you."

"What the fuk is happening?"

"Language, boy. Such fuken delightful language," the demented man said, and grabbed at the side of his head for a breath. "She must like it too... Keep your demented, delicious language to yourself, dear Derian... or else she'll climb out and make us all regret it."

"Please, what is all this?" Derian cried. "Is this death? Are you from the dark? Are you to bring me into death?" Derian thought about this last part and imagined a coldness taking him. "Are you death?" he asked slowly, afraid of the answer.

The old demented man thought this was marvellous. He began to chortle uncontrollably, and Derian felt the urge to disappear and float away, answering the call.

"What a thing that would be...? Oh, to be death. Silent, it would be... After I killed her, of course." Without warning, he raised his hand and Derian was pulled fiercely to the old man. And all thought of disappearing, well, disappeared. "Not yet, foolish boy. You want to sleep with death, don't you? We all do... Or we just crave silence..."

"I am so confused."

"So is the universe and all spinning things, unless you tell it what you want... make it spin for you."

Derian couldn't keep his eyes from the old man, and terror took him. He knew he was dead. He was really pissed about that. But what if there was no rest in the darkness beyond? What if it was an oblivion with this lunatic as his comrade? And the only thing to gaze upon was the innards of this demon?

Just my spitting luck.

He suddenly thought of the world beyond, and, for the first time, remembered the battle still raging. Only then did he hear the rumblings from beneath this beast's innards. A further terror took him at the idea of a half-consumed *Fighting Mongoose* appearing in the beast's belly. Of his friends struggling and falling. Of their shimmering souls already flittering away into nothingness, leaving him behind.

Alone.

"Fuk this shit. I've had enough of this," Derian snapped, and the old man grinned again.

"Ah, yes. So you do have fight. She knew you would. That's why she's going to ensure you remain dead."

Dead.

"I said I'd had enough of this."

The sphere of light spun brighter and the old man scrambled away from his shattered place of rest. He beckoned for Derian to follow, through a fleshy route deep towards the dark into the demon's lesser parts.

"I am Arturo," the old man said. "Know this face, this behaviour, trust this... scrambling fiend," he mumbled, climbing through a dark cavern of foul skin and innards. Within, there hung a great organ that Derian couldn't quite recognise from his studies. It might have been a spleen. Or a liver. Whichever, really. It was awful to gaze upon.

"It is interesting to meet you, Arturo," Derian said warily.

"It is... about time I met you, Derian," Arturo said, stepping below into a darker cavern where the only illumination was the dim glow from his sphere of light. "*Time.*"

He giggled. "As if I've had anything but time to pay my way." A strange grey cloak clung to his thin body. It was oversized and not at all complimentary to the old man.

"Are you a weaver?"

Arturo began to laugh as though this was the greatest jest ever whispered. "Weaver? Pah... I hunt weavers. Illusionists and enchanters... She and I... that at least we agree on... or we used to..."

"I don't understand."

"I don't mind if you don't."

"Why are you so strange?"

"She would not like you saying that at all... Because then she would be agreeing with you... She doesn't want to agree with you. She doesn't want to know you. She doesn't want to like you, either."

"Do you know Bereziel?"

Arturo shot around. He reached in and took Derian by the soul and held him as though he were stone. He placed his finger to his lips and looked truly terrified.

"They listen for words and figures... In all times as well... If you whisper it now... perhaps it was heard, perhaps it is to be heard..."

"What the fuk are you talking about?"

"I don't know, but the source does... or at least it will... or already has... or always knew..."

"This makes no sense."

"Exactly."

"You make no sense."

"Karkur, dear Derian... Karkur."

Derian didn't know what any of this meant, either.

Arturo suddenly released Derian and resumed his stumbling pilgrimage through the demon's insides. "Don't say names that make little bells ring... Little bells bring about the beginning of all things... or the ends... whichever..."

"None of this makes sense," Derian exclaimed. He was so confused. He was so terrified. He was so lost.

"In other words, just shut the fuk up about naming names when we are in this realm..."

Derian suspected the foolish man spoke in a code unfamiliar to his own feeble thinking, or else he had spent so long in this demonic prison that he'd lost the ability to speak. Regardless, he followed the fiend as though compelled. The darkness of sleep did not pull at him any further, and he hoped this was a good thing.

In the next cavern, they came upon the crabs, and the old man drew a sphere of blue around himself as he walked. The crabs paid little attention. Their clicking, without the frenzy of war driving them, appeared docile. Even harmless. Saying that, from his spectral place, what did he have to fear from them anyway? Apart from an oblivion with this strange character, that is.

"Can I go home?"

"Do you have one? I'm sure you could float there, if you could withstand the pull of that dreadful darkness," Arturo offered.

"Up there, among the clouds, is my home—with my family."

At this Arturo, stopped and smiled. "Perhaps you are Derian after all... Perhaps you will."

A glimmer of hope took Derian and he held it close. He was used to dying, used to returning. Perhaps he was foolish to think he was done with this world, but he knew better.

There weren't enough perhapses in the world to bring him back. This, Derian was certain of.

Sort of.

Perhaps.

Sliding through another cavern, waist-deep in a sickly red, Arturo drew a blade and cut into a membrane so thin and sickly that, were Derian able, he might have retched. Green bile spilled into the river of blood and Arturo waded through, barely keeping his feet under him.

"Didn't like the smell. Didn't desire to wait so very, very long like a... like a man in a whale..." Arturo offered as Derian slid through the wall as though it was nothing—or, to be precise, because *he* was nothing. This thought unnerved him again. Thinking on it too long was likely to take his nerve, break him. So he concentrated on the madman, the potential of family and home.

"I see," Derian offered as they came upon the stomach where he'd died.

"Oh, look—there you are. Well, part of you... the savage part... all growling... hissing and spitting... probably pissing too..."

Derian floated above the figure in numb silence. He looked upon a form of himself in all his grisly glory, giving fight to the demon from within. "What have I become?"

Arturo might have answered. Instead, he took a pause. It was the finer move on his part, for Derian's dead body was no longer simply Derian; he was grotesque. A painting of a savage cur's divine idea of what a human could be in its most terrible incarnation. His fingers were longer, sharpened into bone-thick, dagger-like appendages. His body had grown more muscular in every place where it counted, and his loose-fitting garments were now tight, transforming his usual self into a perfect, animalistic specimen. His teeth were bucked now and sturdier than before, as though a surgeon had implanted vicious incisors upon his lesser impressive set. And those teeth were going to task as they sought to tear apart the demon from within. Ripping and tearing, the monster known as Derian was a blur of frenzied wrath, slashing into flesh, inflicting ruin upon the monster.

Only then did Derian feel the turmoil of the demonic beast: the ground Arturo stood upon became unsteady and only the sphere of blue kept him upright.

"You are beautiful, Derian," the man mumbled. "Just beautiful... Um... not you, Derian... the *other* Derian... The of-this-realm-Derian... Look at that savagery and how he... *you*... feel it, and it is wonderful..." Arturo was in a daze, watching the horror.

"What is this nightmare?" cried non-monstrous Derian, as the monstrous Derian spun suddenly, aware of the new presence in the room.

With a howl, the blood-covered creature turned and leapt across in one mighty bound. It skidded in the flood of blood and bile, howling at Arturo, and then suddenly it stopped and sniffed the air and whined tragically.

"There, there, beautiful Derian... Is it a maddening thing? It must be a maddening thing... It's alright. You are doing fine work... Good hound..." Arturo turned to floating Derian. "I think he likes being called a good hound."

"I cannot watch this. Why are you doing this?"

"Look at his hand. It's a fine sword... Good for..." Arturo made a slashing motion. It mimicked the actions of the beast, who sliced and tore when it wasn't ripping and biting into flesh.

"What does that have to do with anything, you fuker?"

"Delicious language. Just like her."

Derian began to weep and wail. His moans echoed the cries of the monster, who spun around and dropped onto all fours. It wailed, sniffing the air in puzzlement.

"He can't see you, but he knows you are there… so perhaps he can see you… or smell you… Perhaps souls emit an aroma… I never thought about that… That makes perfect sense… but also none."

"What are we doing here?"

"Ah—at last you ask a question… The answer is unimportant… I would just… be interested."

"I've asked you plenty…"

"I wasn't listening… I blame her… She talks so much…" He tapped his forehead with long, spindly fingers.

Derian floated in front of Arturo and begged. "Can I return?"

The monster suddenly gave up searching and returned to attacking the larger monster from deep within. Derian thought it a fine distraction from thinking about himself.

"You know, they will sacrifice everything when they find this beautiful, savage Derian… I wouldn't think they should… but they do…"

"My friends?"

"And the world will suffer because of it… and the world *has* suffered… suffered under a fist to the lands, wielded by a darkness greater than the seven gods… The seven grand demons too… And everything comes in circles and begins and ends… And sometimes stops… or begins… What was I saying?"

"I hate this. I hate you. Fuk you… Absolutely fuk you… Give me back my body," Derian wailed, and his floating body quivered.

Arturo simply smiled. "If you returned, it might be the end of the Anguished One."

"That's a good thing, right?"

"If you do not return, the Anguished One will remain atop the tower."

"That's a bad thing, right?"

"But what if the Anguished One serves a greater purpose?"

"What do you mean?"

"What if an anguished fiend capable of such power is the only thing fierce enough to stop a greater darkness?" For once, he appeared to choose his words carefully. It might have been a trick of the light. "The universe doesn't know how to spin this one… So, how would I?"

"So you won't return me?"

Arturo grabbed his head, screamed and began to laugh. "Oh, Edel… I feel you scratching at the door… Don't you want to end this? Find a nice quiet darkness… just you and me…"

"Who is Edel?"

He stopped and looked at Derian as though he'd just stolen his honey cake.

"She is part of me."

"Am I speaking to her?"

He looked as though Derian had defecated on said honey cake and returned it.

"It is no matter at all. What matters, in fact, is you... Or not... Well, you do... in a way... Part of a machine that spins and turns..." He began to grin again, and around them the room of flesh began to shudder something terrible. Whatever was occurring beyond was certainly causing all manner of unease to this beast. "Look at yourself, Derian. Look how brave and heroic you are."

"Who is Edel? Who are you?"

"We are your killers, and your life givers... all in one... One of us wants this world to burn... One of us wants the universe to turn."

"I see," Derian whispered and began to float from this cur. He didn't see at all. He'd had enough. He wanted to see the sky again. See what had occurred outside of this beast. To the fires with Edel, and with Arturo too. He didn't understand any of this. He didn't want to. He wanted to be free from this place and wait for the reassuring darkness and be done with it.

"If you leave now, she is victorious, and everything you know will burn," Arturo suddenly called, his voice sharp and direct. *A fine thing to behave like you're mad when you're perfectly coherent,* Derian thought. A trickier thing to behave like you're sane when the mind is little more than a demented ruin.

Monster Derian began to howl as non-monster Derian slipped away from Arturo and his mania.

"Dearest Derian, I wager a day's payment you don't know that you are a hero..." Arturo suddenly squinted and slapped at his forehead. "Hush, Edel... You had your opportunity," he muttered, and for a breath he appeared satisfied with himself. Suddenly, he clawed at his old face and scratched himself deeply with his nasty, long fingernails. "Are you done fighting me, woman?"

"Who are you talking to?"

"I didn't say anything bad about you. I simply stole the truth before you could sour it... No, I'm not going to tell him that... Please... just... fuken stop... will you?"

Derian watched the madman argue with himself. It wasn't the strangest thing he'd seen that day.

"..."

"..."

"I think..." Arturo said quietly, "she is satisfied to leave me to my words... I shall be quick and you should listen... Who knows how important they are... Well, I do... and they really aren't." He began to laugh again. "You are a hero, Derian. You always have been... It's in your blood."

"I'm a coward."

"How many fights have you run from?"

"Plenty."

"When evil really stirred... were you not compelled to fight?" Arturo hissed. It was a convincing argument, and truthfully, though Derian was always terrified and always threatening to leave, he never actually did.

Suddenly the entire world spun and Arturo with it. He didn't appear too concerned either. He simply spun as the wet, sloshing room around him rolled. Monster Derian, however, was dashed and thrashed against the wall, torn and broken as though ripped apart by an Anculous demon. He gripped his sword, though, and in his dying breath plunged it into the flesh around him as the sky appeared, torn away like bedsheets after a messy night.

The battle is done.

My comrades have won again.

The stomach of the demon was dashed against a great wall of rock that appeared from below, sending bile and blood and bone coursing out against the stone and beyond it onto the sand, deep into the rushing waves of water, and Derian looked upon his body once more gripped deep into flesh in its dying grip. It looked eerily like his first death. Gone were the bulging muscles and demonic appearance. Better his body be buried like that, he imagined. Still, though, such a thing was unsettling indeed.

"You are special, Derian," Arturo said as the world fell still and the light of a soothing, warm sun touched the beached monster. He slipped from his shield and once more drew Derian to him. "If I told you that saving the world at the cost of your life was a worthy cause... I fully believe you would answer that soothing call to the darkness... Am I wrong?"

"You ask me a question? You give me a choice?" Derian said wearily. He wanted to live. Perhaps this demented cur was indeed a guardian of the darkness, willing to grant him life, willing to grant him a chance again. It hurt his head to listen to him speak, though, to understand his thoughts, to recognise him as friend or enemy, or somewhere in between.

Still, though.

That pit of fear was gone and it was a welcomed thing. It was a small solace after leaving this world, for he knew he did not belong here anymore. He turned to bow. To say goodbye and state his choice. He only hoped it was no ruse. "I want to live, but I would choose death."

There came that laughing again, and a terrible rushing feeling came upon him.

And with it the fear returned. Deep down, where nasty things like monsters and hatred of wind still reigned. He was soaked through. His body was quaking as though he had been refilled after a dreadful emptiness. Arturo stood over him. His face blazed a fine shade of madness.

"Choice? You think you ever had a choice, dear Derian...? Oh no... You have far too many interesting things to do... and we do wish to see where it leads us... And we will have our vengeance on the Anguished One... regardless of the cost."

SHIPWRECKED

Natteo's stomach finally settled, but his vision took a few moments longer to catch up. That didn't stop him from releasing his straps and falling to his knees in front of his reeling comrades. He gripped the ground as it spun beneath him, as though he'd spent a hard night entertaining in the pleasure rooms of Castra.

"What are you doing, idiot?" Lorgan murmured. His gaze was upon the smaller mercenary, but his eyes were dancing as though he were playing at a roulette table. "Let the world settle and be a little patient," he added, but Natteo didn't want to follow the good advice, and he most certainly didn't want to wait any longer than needed. He wanted to dart off into the bright, warm morning, seeking his best friend, and piss-all mattered after that. Problem was finding his feet first, and this he did terribly. Standing upright and daring a step forward, he walked straight into a wall and fell on his rear.

"I told you, didn't I?" Lorgan said, grinning.

Climbing again to his feet, Natteo caught sight of a crimson-covered Seren releasing her straps. Like him, she collapsed on the floor and moaned painfully. Her forehead, where an arrow could perfectly penetrate, was once again ripped open.

"Ooh, that looks nasty," Natteo offered to the injured girl.

She seemed to agree. Her eyes danced as Natteo's did, but there was a blankness to her. Beside her lay what had been one of the last surviving plates from Natteo's assault in the town. Now it was like its brethren. Shattered and useless. "I was hit."

"Yes, you were. Perhaps you should stay here a while and heal," Natteo offered, gripping the doorway for stability. Exhilarated by survival but petrified at the thought of the discoveries to come, he took a breath to shake the dizziness, to find his feet.

"Aye, and you could help us with this incessant nausea while you are at it," mumbled Lorgan.

"Seren is... I am too weak," she offered, lazily holding her blood-covered fingers in front of her face. "I am spent with weaving for now," she added, and Natteo wasn't surprised. Usually, after releasing her most powerful weaving, she was utterly exhausted and appeared to have aged. He did not understand weaving, but it made sense that there was a limit to how much ethereal energy could pass through a human vessel before they needed a nap. He might have offered a rag, or helped her through the decks as she returned to herself, but he didn't care about her minor injuries this very moment; nor did he need her healing abilities. He had greater and more terrible places to be. So he left his comrades behind and did not feel bad about it.

Stumbling and knocking against every obstacle he could, he reached the galley and the many shattered dishes. It was here he spared a moment to lament the cake, which had been splattered against every wall. "Quite the death," he muttered. He stuck a finger into the nearest remains and tasted it. "Needed less honey," he added, trying to remember why he had taken the cake out from the stove at all. Eveklyn would be crushed, he imagined. She'd appeared terribly interested in the process and the bowl after. At least now she could take all she wanted while cleaning the sludge from the walls.

Climbing out onto the deck and with the fresh salty air striking him, he finally recovered his footing and marched along the boards, looking out across the ocean helplessly and hopefully. Hearing a heavy, metallic pop, he turned to see Eveklyn and Kesta removing themselves from the cock-pit. Kesta looked positively glowing, and why not? For the second time that week, her ability at flying had brought about the demise of yet another grand demon. In any other mercenary group, she'd be considered a legend. Their entire group would be. Alas, who would believe they had captured lightning twice?

Certainly not the Guild.

No matter how many teeth we provide as proof.

"Is everyone alright?" Kesta called.

No, everything is fuked and I'm terrified to seek the truth and unable to delay a moment longer.

He shrugged. "I think Seren ruffled her hair, and Lorgan is lamenting a broken nail. Don't know about the cat… but it's probably fine," Natteo declared. He didn't want to add that Derian was still missing, still likely dead. "You flew well," he said. It was an understatement. She'd flown like a goddess born with wings. "Um… nice job," he added weakly.

"She flew well," Kesta offered, tapping the glass with pride. She was a little shaky on her feet, but nothing as bad as Natteo had been. Eveklyn, on the other hand, managed three steps before collapsing among the corpses of the crabs and then threw up all over herself. Natteo wasn't surprised at all.

"I've to go see about a brother," Natteo said, leaving them to recover. Grabbing the rail and slipping over the edge, he gazed at the ruin of the sea creature and it was quite the sight. Where the airbarge had landed, the signs of a mighty fleshy explosion were spread out on all sides.

Here lies the grandest demon of all.
Smushed by the Crimson and their airbarge.
Next.

Already, dozens of eager gulls were beginning to pick the innards, and their frenzied squawking cut through him, reminding him of demonic, squealing things. He shuddered, realising how close they had come to death once more, and put that thought from his mind right swiftly.

There is no talk of death today.
Only heroism.
And crab for dinner.

Sliding down and dropping to the sandy, squelchy beach below, he ran towards the largest fleshy form that had met its end against the jagged rocks. He only managed a dozen water-laden steps before the stench overcame him. In a more foolish time in his wild youth, he'd taken up a job for a summer season down by the Castra harbour. He'd lasted nearly a full shift before the evening catch-trawlers made land and he went to task loading the fresh fish. It wasn't as much their dead eyes or spilled guts; it was the old stench of the sea. A dreadful, infectious odour that climbed into his lungs, his pores, his better underwear, and never released itself.

Deep down, though, he knew it wasn't the terrible smell that took him now. It was the dreadful knowledge of Derian's fate.

Sprinting through the breaking waves, kicking up innards in the white rush with every step, he already knew he would be burning these fresh pants. Shaving his head as well. The Crimson had copious water reserves, and he would be scrubbing in a bath for quite a time with some of Boab's finer oils.

He held the thought of Boab tightly. And caught movement in the water alongside.

For just a breath, he believed.

He almost smiled, and prepared a fist so he might thrash Derian's face for terrifying him. And then his heart rose and fell, like an airbarge upon a spider's head.

They came from the waves, splashing and struggling, huffing and wailing. Some had wide eyes and were covered in scrapes and bruises. Some carried their hands, missing a digit or two; but none of them seemed to mind such infirmities. Perhaps it was shock; perhaps it was knowing their skins had been saved by an unlikely source.

Shipwrecked sailors.

Natteo couldn't help himself. He rushed out into the

freezing water even as it caught him in the chest. It was a fine distraction, really, from the terrible knowledge that his friend was dead. Bitten, chewed up and dissolved in the fetid stomach acid that layered the ocean's surface.

"They just stopped dragging me to the depths," one frantic sailor cried, reaching Natteo and continuing to wade through the sea of ruin and bile.

"They all stopped moving when the beast was driven ashore," another said. He was weeping and laughing all at the same time, and he embraced Natteo, who, for a precious moment, took the praise and felt a little better about himself, despite the horror of the day. "They just stopped moving."

We did a good thing by not running away.

He waded out, pulling as many as half a dozen ashore before the tainted sea became somewhat still. Some exhausted sailors collapsed in the sand, crying for their woes and their luck. Some grasped him and embraced him as a brother. Others rushed from his grasp, offering tears and prayers to absent gods.

Only as their feet touched solid ground would they appear less shaken. These sailors wailed and roared in triumph as they reached land, and he forced a smile at a task well done.

Distantly, he saw Lorgan, still unsure of his feet, make landfall. Seren climbed down with him. Her injuries looked less serious than before, and he left them to it.

Instead, he waded through the awful water to where the beast's most bulbous centre had once been; it was little more than a wreck. "You did your part," he whispered to Derian, wondering if his comrade were a spirit, floating around him. He doubted it somehow. "You were brave, brother," he added and ground his teeth irritably. He didn't like that train of thought at all. That was the thinking that made you discover the mangled corpse of a loved one.

And then he saw a sailor stranger than the rest. He sat upon a large rock, staring intently at the water, where something mushy floated. He looked impossibly old for a life at sea; his clothing was archaic and regal, and well, weaveresque, but he knew this only from the pictures he'd seen of them. He'd heard tell of enchantments wrapped up in a weaver's cloak and he thought the notion preposterous. Clothing that made you weave better? That was some peasant talk right there.

"Ahoy there," Natteo called, in the words of sailor speak, and the old man looked up with a start. And then he leapt to his feet, his eyes blazing in delight.

"This is godly and wonderful," he cried, rushing across the rocks, kicking up splashes with his loosely fitted cloak along the way. "It seems I've come to the right place," he roared in delight. "A god... Wow... Oh... Godly..."

"It's alright, friend. You are safe now," Natteo assured the old man, who took hold of him and looked past him, yet straight into his soul. A peculiar thing. At his touch, Natteo felt a strange shudder of energy course through him, like he'd just worn his most flamboyant outfit and rolled on a carpet before touching something metal. A peculiar and unpleasant feeling, in truth. Nevertheless, the old man was strong, and somewhat mesmerizing.

"Ah—a friend? Oh... yes... Of course we are... I am friends with a monster..." He pointed back to the pool of mush, and Natteo saw now that it resembled a figure from this angle. "Why shouldn't I be friends with someone like you?"

"Someone like me? What do you mean by that?" Natteo snapped, shoving the old man away. The man gave a bemused smile.

"No… that's not right at all… Some… *thing* like you…" He pointed to the side of Natteo and, again, looked directly into his soul. It was dreadfully unsettling altogether. "Ah… Forgive me… It has been such a time since I spoke with some… one like you." He thought on these words for a breath and then nodded, as though they had been correctly chosen.

"Uuuugh… Fuk me…" came a familiar voice from the distance.

"Hello?" Natteo called, leaving the old man to his ramblings. He knew that voice. His pace quickened, his heart doubly so. He splashed through the water, afraid, excited, disbelieving, hopeful, all at the same moment.

"Uuuugh… Hello?"

"Is that you, Derian?" Natteo cried, reaching the pool of flesh that was cleverly concealing the body of Derian, who semi-floated in the shore's current. "Fuk me, it is," he cried, dropping down to his friend, who, in that moment, found his consciousness.

"What state am I in?" Derian suddenly cried, rising to his knees, grabbing at his face, stopping to stare at his hands. He reached into his mouth, appearing to pull at his teeth. "I'm me, aren't I?" he demanded, clearly feeling the effect of a little digesting. He looked around as though drunk. Perhaps he too was feeling the nausea that Natteo had endured. He'd been inside the belly of the beast. That was probably a worse place than being strapped to a chair in a hovering airbarge. When everything settled, they might swap tales of throwing up. Might even allow the fool to irritate him a while talking about the source.

"You are fine, you are... fine... How are you so fine?" Natteo asked. "Wait—did you up and die on me and come back all healthy-like?" he said, and Derian froze.

"I was dead."

"That doesn't seem to afflict us with as much seriousness as most people," Natteo said, leaping on his friend and embracing him. "What the fuk is up with your leg?" he said. The leg in question, which had been near severed, was now fully healed. His trousers were less so, but it was a small matter. Natteo was a fine touch with a sewing needle if need be.

"I think I was dead. That lunatic brought me back, Nat... At least I think he did." Derian was looking around frantically as his senses returned. The old man stood over them, watching with an inane grin as though this was the finest sight in his day. Perhaps it was. Natteo was wonderful to gaze upon.

"See, Derian, I knew you would be happy to be alive," the old man declared.

As the friends embraced, Natteo resisted the urge to batter Derian for the terror he'd caused him. For dying as well. There was plenty of time for that later.

"Hello," the old man said, interrupting them. "My name is Arturo... and... grand things are about to occur... I think," he proclaimed, and Natteo shook the hand he offered. As their fingers released, there came again that shocking pulse of energy, though tenfold the first time. "It can't be," Arturo roared, turning to see Lorgan strolling across the beach with a dizzy Seren in tow.

"Are you alright, old man?" Natteo asked, as the old man grabbed his head and screamed.

"No, Edel... I am in control," he bellowed.

"Um... what?"

"Do not sway my hand," the old man roared again, spinning towards Lorgan. From his fingers came a strange light like a fork of lightning, spitting and crackling off every finger, and he twitched and shuddered as sparks formed around him. "I am *me* to control," he roared, but he was already away from Natteo, charging across the water, waving his hands as those shards of lightning hissed louder, crackling as though building to some dreadful thunderstorm. "I am in control."

"What the fuk is going on?" Natteo cried.

"I don't know, but I don't think Edel is a good person," Derian exclaimed.

"Who the fuk is Edel?"

It was a good question.

TOTALLY WRECKED

Derian shook his head and the world began to become clearer. Everything had been a dream for a time. Dying, floating, waking, talking. Everything seemed different. As though he had been living in a dream, or a nightmare. He tried to gather his thoughts as he spoke aloud of important things, but none of it made sense, and then it suddenly did, and like dipping into a freezing lake when half asleep, he was suddenly awake, and sharp, and apparently running. Running on instinct, to be more precise.

Something is terribly wrong.

Something terrible is about to happen.

He charged after the old man, who was impossibly fast for his older bones. Each stride he took with cloak flowing out behind him through the waves was assured and driven, as though some invisible force instilled his movement with vigour and youth.

Arturo was screaming.

Every second howl was a curse.

Derian's mind was still awash with thoughts of life, death, monsters and floating. Adding to this, the lightning emanating from the fingers of his new saviour puzzled him somewhat. He'd never see a fiend conjure lightning, never even read about it in his Mercenary guide either. Yet here it was, flowing and consuming his saviour, and in his own young bones, he knew it was not a good thing.

"To the fires, Edel," Arturo roared, stumbling despite his enthusiasm. He suddenly appeared laden with some invisible struggling, drunken child. His arms became a blur of white and crackling, and the hiss in the air could be heard above the din of raised voices, the wash of the sea, the squelch of wading and the beating of his heart.

"What the fuk is happening?" cried Natteo. He ran alongside, appearing thoroughly confused. And why wouldn't he be? Only moments before, they were all spit n polished down by the beach, making new friends, and suddenly they were rushing after a madman consumed in lightning shards.

"Fuken something is happening," Derian cried. "Though I don't exactly know what!" And then something did happen.

Arturo screamed Edel's name one last time, and then his arms shot out in front of him. From them, two fierce forks of lightning shot out across the beach and struck Seren dumb mid-step.

She managed a weak squeak as her body contorted and shuddered like a hare struck with an arrow. Her smile was frozen on her face and her eyes rolled as he struck her a second time, and a terrible scorching smell filled the air. The force of the blow sent her flying backwards, at least a dozen feet into the sky, where, spinning thrice, she crashed among the rocks and sand a distance back.

What is this lunatic doing?

"No," roared Lorgan, who, no more than a dozen feet from her attacker, drew his sword and charged. An imposing thing on any battlefield, he towered over the cur and swung upon him, and somehow, Derian knew it would be blamed on him.

Arturo did not move. He simply delivered the same fork of lightning directly at the charging Lorgan.

We are all going to die, all over again.

Again.

This time, however, perhaps because Arturo desired to conserve his energy, the electrifying strike was delivered from one solitary finger. Nevertheless, the same shard of lightning shot out and felled Lorgan as though he were the tallest tree in an open plain. His body convulsed and for a breath he was engulfed in the same sort of energy Seren had endured. He did not fly off into the heavens and come to a sickly end twenty feet away though. Instead, he merely stumbled, crumpled and toppled back into the water, shaking and cursing loudly as he did.

Strangely, Arturo then gripped the larger man and heaved him upright in the water before dragging him ashore. He was still screaming Edel's name as he did this; however, the frenzied cry was lessened somewhat. It was only then that Derian surmised the madman who claimed to be a friend was indeed a madman taken by two separate personalities. He'd heard of such things happening and knew that most of those afflicted with the curse ended up in the sickhouse in Dellerin City or out working the fields of

Brimlore, spending most of their days babbling about inane things. They were mostly harmless. This fiend, however, possessed skills he'd never heard of and was anything but harmless.

Leaving Lorgan to his recovery, Arturo skipped along the ocean's current. As he did, he cursed loudly and only then did Derian see the crazy man's folly. He was hunting the wrong person. "Daria, where have you gotten to?" he roared. "I will burn you from this plain." He fired again upon the dazed ruin of Seren as she crawled among the rocks. She moaned as a few bolts connected with her and deflected off into the earth around her, possibly saving her life.

"Who's he talking about? What the fuk is he doing?" Natteo screamed, rushing ahead of Derian, drawing his sword, plodding out of the waves, reaching dry land, charging towards a kill, and Derian followed after.

Suddenly Derian caught sight of some very confused sailors as he ran past. They had been washed ashore and sat silently in a group, watching these terrible things unfold across from them. They must have thought this was perfectly acceptable behaviour among mercenaries, for they made no attempt to intercede, even at the expense of a seemingly innocent girl being scorched to death by unnatural lightning.

Pissing peasants.

"Hey, old man—over here," Natteo roared, rounding up on the old demented bastard, drawing his attention from the scorched ruin of Seren.

"Arturo, you fuken lunatic, you are attacking the wrong person," Derian cried as Arturo spun on Natteo and, with a delicate flick of his finger, sent Natteo high into the sky. He dropped back into the ocean thirty feet behind Derian.

"Sorry about that, my friend," called Arturo, or Edel, to the stricken Natteo, and seemed entirely unperturbed as Derian gripped his own blade and sought vengeance on the man who had given him an entirely new life.

"Please, friend," Derian cried, slowing his run, playing nice, hoping to lull him to distraction before gutting him swiftly from behind. People took issue with knifing a cur in the back. Derian didn't. Dead was dead and a deed was a deed.

"She is not your friend," Arturo warned.

"Is it Edel you speak of?" Derian asked.

"She fights me for control," Arturo warned, and suddenly a dreadful surge of light struck Derian and sent him reeling. He did not fall, nor was he scorched as Lorgan and Seren had been. Instead, he floated further away from the melee in a rather leisurely manner, just as Natteo had done.

This is much better than lightning.

As he floated away from the battle, he caught sight of Kesta rushing down the side of the *Fighting Mongoose*, and he wondered if she believed she had any chance where the rest had failed. She might have been better advised, he mused, to heave the *Mongoose* into the air and drop it all demon style on the fiend and worry about his reasoning after.

He dropped down beside Natteo, and the two men helped each other to their feet, even if they were gloriously outmatched. It should have reassured them that in most victories they were outmatched, but it didn't.

"Any ideas, Nat?"

"Don't get lifted up and dropped in the ocean."

"Sounds like a plan."

Natteo hesitated, his eyes studying the fiend, as Kesta reached him. "Who in the fires is this cur?" he hissed, loading his wrist bolts.

Derian gripped his own unspectacular blade, and felt a strange hunger come upon him. "He's a deranged weaver, I think."

"He's a right fuken prick, that's for certain," Natteo pointed out, just as Kesta pulled a crossbow from her shoulder already cocked and loaded. Without breaking stride, and looking impossibly impressive as she did, she raised the weapon and fired from a dozen feet away, sending the bolt careening a foot wide of the demented weaver.

"That was hardly worth the wait at all," Derian muttered.

"She's a great pilot, but a shit aim," Natteo added. He was already running again and Derian followed, holding his sword out in front of him as a makeshift shield against the lightning.

Before Kesta could fire a second time, Arturo waved both his fingers wildly and what appeared to be a sheet of ice rose from the ground and encircled her, snapping shut and imprisoning her snugly.

"Lightning, wind and ice?" Natteo cried in disbelief. *What are these mysterious displays of power?* Derian wondered.

"And giving life too," Derian pointed out between gasps.

"What was that?"

"Never mind."

As Kesta howled and beat at the sheet of imprisoning ice, another comrade was determined to avenge her.

"Oh no, not the kid. Please, not the kid," Natteo howled, as Eveklyn appeared along the beach and rushed the weaver, screaming all her wrath.

For just a breath, the world stood still as Derian marvelled at the child's foolish bravery. She did not hesitate; she did not stop by the sheet of ice to cleave into it with her deadly, oversized war axe. Instead, she charged the old weaver and managed to swing once at him.

"Who are you, demon child?" Arturo roared, stepping wide of the axe and shoving the child from him. His fingers were electric once more and for a breath Derian feared she would be scorched as Seren and Lorgan had been. Even a blow as weak as the one that had struck Lorgan might be fatal in one so small.

"I'll kill you if you hurt her," Derian roared, daring Arturo to face him instead. Each step through the waist-high water was an eternity, though. He tried his best, but he was too far away.

I could do this if I was part monster.

Are you there, monster?

Is the child's life a worthy reason to stir?

Arturo stared in disbelief as the child roared again, giving her most inept war cry. It was little more than a squeak. Taking this as a challenge, he retorted with a roar of his own. A finely bellowed, bruising roar. It echoed unnaturally across the entirety of the beach and must have been intimidating up close, for the child hesitated. She might even have taken a step back, but Derian couldn't tell from this distance.

"I can roar too," Arturo, or Edel, declared, staring at the child, who looked ready to flee in terror.

Instead, that step back was merely a rebalancing of her foot, and she kicked forward and embedded the massive blade into his shoulder. If Lorgan had delivered the strike, Derian fancied the cur's entire arm would have been severed clean off. Alas, it only went an inch or so into his shoulder. Hardly a killing, disarming blow at all. Arturo wailed and grasped the spot where the axe head had cleaved his collarbone in half. Eveklyn roared again, for she was fantastic, and Derian screamed in terror for her.

"You little witch," Arturo cried in horror. The axe remained embedded in him and he began to scream louder than before. Spinning away, and pulling the piece free and shrieking as a spurt of crimson followed after, he spun back to the unarmed child and held his hands out as they blazed white.

"You spitting cur," Natteo cried, and fired. But his power was weak at such a distance, and the bolt met its death a few feet from Arturo, lost in the rising tide.

The child took to the sky and flew back towards the airbarge. Almost delicately, she was held in an invisible grasp and placed gently on the main deck, where she screamed a final war cry.

"Just... fuken... leave me be...will you?" Arturo warned Derian and Natteo as they waded pathetically ashore. "It'll all be over and... then it will all begin..." With Lorgan still hunched in the wet sand, and Kesta unable to breach her wall of ice, he marched upon Seren and there was no one to stop him.

To her beaten credit, Seren did not go into the darkness in silence. She fought with what weakened will she had. A dreary-looking sphere of fire appeared on her quivering hands and she cast it upon her hunter.

"Still fight in you," he snarled, spinning away and pulling his cloak up to cover his face as the flame engulfed him. It burned for a pulse of time before dissipating, leaving little more than smoke. Coughing, he took a deep breath and the lightning formed on his fingers again. This time, his entire body shook as though he were a heavy rain cloud, laden with thunder, ready to wreak havoc.

"Do not do this," Derian wailed, reaching the shore a step ahead of Natteo, but it was already too late. He could hear Seren's agonizing wail as he punished her with all his venom. She fought the lightning. Her body became encased in a shield of blue for a breath, before the cur shattered her defence and tore into her.

"I've waited a lifetime to do this," he roared deliriously, and she shuddered and shook under his assault. Again, the smell of burning flesh filled the air and Derian sprinted towards her killer.

"To the thurken fires with you," Seren howled, and began to die as he burned her apart. Derian reached him and kept going. Though the fiend was covered in jagged bolts of lightning, he still charged. Leaping, and feeling his entire body torn apart, he knocked the old man away from Seren. For a breath, he wrapped his arms around the cloak and the brute underneath.

"Get off me, comrade," Arturo cried, but Derian held

firm, even when the lightning was turned on him. "You don't understand. She is evil most vile," he argued, and fought Derian's hold something fierce. A breath later, Natteo was upon him as well, striking and clawing. There might have been some biting as well.

"Fuken get off me," Arturo cried.

"Get fuked."

"Get him, Natteo. Fuken get him."

"I fuken *am* getting him, Derian! Can you not fuken see?"

The three struggled and, between them both, Natteo and Derian pinned Arturo to the ground. Derian, on the bottom of the pile-up, took the weight and also endured the strikes of the ocean as the gentle tide drew in, splashing over him. Through the stinging, salty haze, he caught sight of Seren among the rocks. She was barely alive. Her entire body smouldered as though she were a swine upon a spit. She crawled towards the shore, no doubt hoping to ease the pain from her charred skin. Her dress was ruined, cut open in parts and smoking and melted. Much of it had burned onto her skin—or indeed, her skin had melted against the dress. Her long black hair was lost to the scorch as well, and her bald skin was a bubbling ruin of horror.

And suddenly they were afloat again. Beside him floated Natteo, a long shard of lightning surrounding him, similar to the agonizing chain of his own.

"I'm so sorry, my friends. It'll all be worth it," Arturo offered. "Just a few more moments... I pledge this," he said in delight, as both Natteo and Derian were released and allowed to fall back into the water a dozen feet from Seren. It should have been an innocuous fall, but Derian managed to land on his drawn sword. It went deep into his leg and numbly he stumbled from the water, watching it tremble and bounce with every single step out in front of him.

Take the pain.

I can't fuken take this.

Well, take it out, then.

He knew better than to pull it out immediately, lest he had severed an artery. So, carefully gripping the sword lest it come loose, he hobbled once again towards the shore, moaning under his breath at what a shitty day it was.

Arturo saw none of this.

Though he still spoke to Derian and Natteo, his eyes were upon the fallen Seren, his hands busy tending to her. "Just give me a moment... comrades... friends... or allow me to take a moment... You can have it back after..."

Seren struggled into the waves. From his waist Arturo drew a blade and, gripping her head, brought it to her throat. "I've dreamed of this," he hissed, and something strange happened.

It was a fist, but it may as well have been a hammer. His body flew as though taken by an invisible, electrified hand. Dropping the knife, he fell away from Seren, who stumbled into the grasp of her saviour, Lorgan.

"I think he's dead," Natteo decided. The old man lay outstretched, battered and bettered by one of the finest punches Derian had ever seen. If Arturo did live, he most certainly would be missing teeth. Maybe all of them.

If Seren lived, well, she might well be able to heal such things.

"There, there, little one. You will be alright," lied Lorgan, for she was long past rational thought. A tragic thing, for were she capable, she might have begun some healing of herself. As it was, her blind eyes rolled, her scorched tongue rasped, and Derian, careful not to strike her with his bloody blade, knelt beside her, wondering would he see the light in her eyes diminish. He didn't want to, and none of this was fair. But he would look anyway.

And then her hand shot out and took his in hers. A sudden exhaustion overcame him, and he knew she drew from him, and he didn't mind. She gasped and gripped tight and released, yet the pain still ached. Then he realised she held tight to the grip of his sword. A strange thing, too, for she clung to it as though it gave her life. Stranger, her skin began to recover. He might have taken her hand again, but instead, allowed her to weave from his soul and clutch the sword sticking out of his leg.

"Get the chains," Lorgan hissed to Natteo, who stood dumbly, watching the great healing of a scorched, doomed healer.

The Quiet

Erin huddled into a corner in the dim room. She wanted to stand, to draw a weapon, to lash out. But that moment had come and gone, hadn't it? And she was alone. And very fuken lost. The floor was cold and she placed her fingers on the marble surface. This had been a stately home at some point, no doubt. Now its finer architecture was not simply impressive to the uneducated eye, but for its ability to outlast the rest of the buildings in this entire area. Marble floor and sturdy strong walls. It was no surprise this unsettling place had taken boulders and continued to stand. Like people, some buildings were built to take more abuse without collapsing on themselves.

Breathing slowly and deeply, she felt impossibly small and unimpressive. She could still hear the echoes of his massacre in the garden outside. The tearing and the howls of ecstasy reached a piercing crescendo, and oh, she wanted to scream aloud, to wail away those sounds and not commit them to memory forever.

But she would always remember Rhendal's final moments. And the day or so before. It was all she could do.

She eyed her sword, which was hanging above the door, teasing her to reach for it; to have a go at these bastards who had denied Rhendal his life. She couldn't fathom the kind of hatred that would allow a man meet such a fate, even if they considered him an enemy. It was foul, classless, typical of peasants in a war zone. Only looking after themselves.

Alone.

She wanted to damn Rhendal for leaving her alone in this place. She also wanted to wail aloud, words of purest gratitude. Instead, she hid in the corner, shaking ever so, fearing the worst. Looking out across the horrors beyond, she saw the sky come alive in a watercolour sunrise. The rays penetrated the gloom as they shimmered through, illuminating the room and making the dust floating in front of her sparkle. She breathed in that dust and felt no difference in her breath.

This was no regal place at all, she realised. It was a wretched, dark place where the doomed people came to wait for their fate to reveal itself. Where the selfish few bartered a life for a trinket. Where savage curs listened as a brave man was torn apart.

The piercing cries had fallen to nothing, and this silence was almost too much to bear. She held back her last tear, wiping a few streaks of dark from her cheeks. War was no place to wear face paint, but a habit was a hard thing to break. Especially the habit of batting her eyes at pretty things. She might have smiled at the good-looking man watching the door, but truly, she hated him. Somehow his good looks made it even worse.

Across from her, the bearer of bargains wore a snide grin. "How long have you fought with the army?" he asked, before climbing back up to the window and gazing out with a satisfied smile. Visions of the tearing skin struck Erin's mind again, and once more she fought back tears. She hadn't enough face paint to spare as it was.

She gazed at the cur with unrivalled hate. It was a fine enough answer.

"I am Florian," the good-looking young man offered. "And that is Otto," he added, pointing to the man at the window. "And this is—" He indicated a group of women working in a kitchen nearby, before falling silent at Otto's hissed insistence.

"She doesn't need to know our names. Only her victims," Otto suddenly cried in an explosive voice. She'd heard similar voices in the training trenches, back when the recruits were driven to near madness with tasks and labour. Back when they tested the weakest and sought out the strong ones for the greater heroic days. She might have heard similar outbursts in the field of battle as comrades lost their will to fight, but all of her comrades were killed long before they began to suffer from battle fatigue. *A blessing,* she thought grimly.

Otto wasn't finished, and her silence only added to his frenzy. "Let me tell you of my wife. My beautiful wife... Her name was Lumi. Remember her name," he snapped in that same unsettling tone, and Erin didn't want to know the victims or their names. She might have said something but knew better. He continued to talk. To spit. To lament and hate. Each word louder than the last. "She was crushed by one of the boulders, so she is one of the luckier ones, for she has a grave."

Erin could only stare at the women preparing breakfast in the other room. She did not want to meet Otto's eyes. Did not want him to continue on his ramble as it grew precariously.

Let him fall still.

She looked to the far room curiously. The stove was barely lit, no doubt burning away the leg of some unwanted furniture. The aroma emanating from three cooking pots was closer to the wet stench of steam than savoury deliciousness. The three women looked broken and disinterested as they toiled over the pots.

"Hush, Otto," Florian said suddenly. He walked to Erin and eased her backpack from her back. He did it smoothly, as though taking from a soldier was of little concern to him. "Is there food in here?" he asked.

"There is nothing," Erin replied, thinking of Otto's sorrow of knowing love and seeing it crushed beneath a thundering boulder. She remembered the mammoth beasts of wood and iron wheeled out from the cover of the forests on the first day of the encampment. So terrifying and awesome these war machines had appeared as they thundered along, each one dragged by a dozen mounts, each accompanied by flats of boulders drawn by at least twice as many beasts.

Fine machines and necessary for war, she had been told, and watching the boulders take flight that first terrible night, with a hundred airbarges raining fire down upon them all and a thousand cannons booming in reply, had been a sight for the ages. And then the charge. And the killing.

And then the emergence of the anguished, demonic king.

Florian began to root through her belongings and she protested weakly. At the mention of food, her stomach clawed like a beast at her innards. She felt a grumble and, grabbing her belly swiftly, silenced it. "No food at all," she murmured as he tore at the pockets, muttering and cursing as he did.

"Not even fruit," he hissed, and dropped it, revealing her copy of *The Seven: A Dellerin Tale* in his hands.

"If I had a thing, I would share," she offered.

"Oh aye, you would," Otto countered. "Just as you would expect us to share what we have," he hissed, looking at the treasure in his hand that had once belonged to Rhendal. He didn't look like he'd share that wealth with her at all. Something beyond suddenly caught his eye and he grinned. "The beasts have tasted the burn of the morning sun."

"Are they leaving?" she whispered.

Florian still held the book in his hands, mesmerised. "They leave as soon as they can no longer take the heat... or light... whichever, really."

"Like the fuken demons they are," Otto snarled, spitting out the window.

"They are no demons. They are simple beasts, born for the night," Florian argued, taking Erin's book to a dusty old couch leaning against the wardrobe blocking the door. "Bastarding things, really," he added. Taking a seat, he opened the book and began to read.

Rhendal died for that fuken thing.

"I will not share that book," Erin said, with as much steel in her voice as she could muster.

"Books are meant to be read," he countered.

"I will want it back."

"I can't eat it, so I think it'll be fine," Florian mumbled. He turned a page, his eyes dancing swiftly across the words.

Swifter reader than me.

She wanted to snap the book from his grasp, to hide it back in her pack with the rest of her useless items. Instead, she remained still. She was fearful he might discover the possible enchantment concealed within the words—or perhaps he might cast it into the fire to help with the cooking.

Part of her, though, allowed thoughts of the book to subside, and with that a terrible burden was lifted. She hadn't realised just how much of a burden that book was on her soul.

Rhendal's soul too.

"Lumi didn't believe in your war, girl," Otto suddenly cried, dropping from his place at the window. His eyes were wild and he stood over her with fists clenched. She'd seen murder in eyes before; this was no different. She offered her chin, despite her terror. She was not sure if she was a prisoner or no, but a grim strength took her. "Nor did my son... Leon," he added, and quivered for just a breath. And then he struck her fiercely.

"Get away from me," she howled as he charged her again, his fists flying from every direction. She blocked what she could, but he was taller, quicker, wilder. In defence, she struck his chin, but there was no give, and she took another blow to the head for her trouble, knocking her sideways.

"Leave the girl," Florian shouted, looking up from his book. He did not rise, and she thought little of him.

"My boy was killed by one of the death squads in the first charge," Otto snarled. He slowed for a breath, leaned in close, and she could see the tears in those broken crazy eyes. "Were you one of those fiends who struck him down?"

Death squads?

"I'm sorry for your boy," she howled, and he struck her again, with an open palm this time, as though the fear of knocking her senseless and lessening her pain suddenly occurred to him.

This reassured her, even as he shoved her to the floor. She'd been hit a thousand times in her life, and a slap was no matter. "I should gut you where you lie," he roared, and she stared at him. Her tears matched his own. For just a breath he turned pale, as though suddenly aware of his actions. Still quivering, he dropped his hand to hers. He looked almost contrite, and she took his hand as he pulled her to her feet and she kicked as fiercely as she could.

She was no match for him physically; that was a common occurrence where men were concerned. Perhaps because of this, the absent gods had created in every brutish man a reliable counter to even the footing and put them back in their place.

He howled as she struck him between the legs. It was a satisfying strike. He collapsed in a heap, and immediately her training came back to her, guiding her actions. Though her instinct was to run, she knew the flaw in such a tactic. Even if she was out in the world with no one around, sprinting would be the end of her. It would be only a matter of a time before he recovered and came after her, fuelled by his anger and his greater running speed. Soon after that, he would catch her, and no second strike would save her. She could see his throat was right there to be crushed. All she had to do was stamp down and finish the job. A man who had lost it all was likely to take relief in the dark, she told herself, and stood over him.

Look at his agony.

She followed her lesser instincts—those that embraced love, hope and better things not suited for her—and instead of killing him, she backed away from the moaning man. All the way to her sword, which hung from a hook beside the door. Again, she considered heaving the wardrobe aside, unlocking the damned door and sprinting into the dawn, hopefully avoiding the beasts as they returned to their domain.

"I would not leave this place too soon," Florian said quietly. "Lord Anguis's zealots will be out soon enough, combing the ground. Best you stay in here until afternoon at least," he added, and turned a page. "And survive the bombardment."

"And of Otto?"

"A lesser man might have gutted you the moment you stepped in the door." At this, he looked up from his engrossing read to gaze upon the pathetic ruin of Otto, who lay moaning and weeping for all he had lost. "Perhaps you had a little bit of that mild beating coming."

"I killed no child; I cast no boulder into the sky."

"You stay with that argument, girl, if it makes you feel any better."

It didn't.

Otto recovered himself and, carefully eyeing her and the weapon attached to her waist, slumped his shoulders and gave up the fight.

"Terrible things happen in war," Erin argued, but Florian wasn't listening anymore. He simply turned the next page, and she watched him until he turned the page after that.

"Can I leave?" she asked the room, and only Otto replied as he crept gingerly back up to the watch window.

"You can leave anytime you like. We aren't killers or kidnappers. But I wouldn't advise it," he said. After a moment, he began to laugh and ducked in behind the window frame. "Perfect timing as well. In fact, feel free to step into the dawn's light, girl," he said, dropping down from the window again. With a slight hobble, he marched past her to the kitchen and went to the stove, where he greedily spooned helpings of foul-looking gruel into two bowls. Grabbing a couple of spoons, he passed one bowl to Florian and took the other for himself.

"Are they out there?" Florian asked.

"Aye, a dozen, snaking through the rubble while they can. Not headed our way, but best not warn them." He looked at Erin coldly. "You aren't welcome to it, but if you want a bowl for yourself, feel free."

She was no less starving than before, but now Erin was more interested in whoever skulked around. Her comrades, perhaps? Had they taken this quarter of the massive city? Was this nightmare over?

Could she take her book back?

She started to climb the boxes and Florian hissed at her. "Those out there aren't your friends, girl."

"My name is Erin," she snapped, and Florian shrugged.

"Couldn't give a shit what your name is. Just stay silent a while and let Anguis's zealots be on their way," he said, and a terrible fury took her as she remembered the zealot's deeds. They were so many and her comrades had been so few by the time they had reached the palace.

And then Anguis had come upon the battlefield, and were it not for the fiend disappearing amidst the flame and horror, well, she most certainly would have perished. As it was, she was alive despite the terrible odds, and despite their sneaky hunting.

Weakly, she walked into the kitchen and took the bowl offered by one of the women. If Otto appeared mad, this woman appeared without emotion. She was twice the age of Erin but looked at least tenfold that in her eyes alone. Erin could tell a lot about people by their eyes. Most people could. Problem was, they never thought about it long enough to recognise what stirred behind a person's gaze.

Gladly, she accepted the gruel, which was little more than warm salted water with a few slices of nettle, carrot and perhaps a few strips of precious salted meat.

She took a seat by the doorway and tasted what she could of the meal. There wasn't a lot to taste at all. Still, the warmth was welcome in her belly.

"Pity those bastards took their dead with them," Otto said wistfully, before spooning a mouthful.

"You would eat such a creature?" she asked in disgust.

"Had they left any of your comrade, we might have

boiled a little of his leg," he countered, sniffing. "Hunger will do that to you, girl," he added.

"They are unholy beasts," she said.

"Aye, but meat is meat. Come to me a day from now and you might be singing a different tune."

"Meat is meat," agreed Florian without looking up. As she had once been, he was entranced with the book and she wondered might it be a blessing. "This is a rather interesting read," he said after a time, then muttered something about Heygar, inept weavers and the lighting of candles.

"I won't be here in a day," Erin argued.

"No, I suppose you won't," Otto said, and the building suddenly shook with a dreadful roar and Erin screamed in terror.

Taking Off into Thunder

"Oh, that's right, baby. Right there—you have it."

"Yeah… you like it like this?"

"Oh baby, that's exactly how I like it. Just… um…"

"Just what?"

"Could you twist it a little more? Would that be alright?"

"Of course, my love. However you want it, I'll do it."

"…"

"Is that working for you?"

"Oh, that's it—perfect. You have it. Oh, you have it."

With a clank of metal, the valve slid back into place and Kesta sighed in relief and delight and a little satisfaction. She was on her back, stretched out with her arms above her head, all tucked in below the machines, and she was very much alone. How else could a girl tend to her duties in such circumstances?

"Oh, you are perfect, darling," she whispered seductively to the stubborn valve as it went about its duty, doing what it did best.

"No, no," Kesta replied in a slightly deeper sultry voice. "You are the best."

"Of course I am. I'm your fuken bitch, aren't I?" Kesta replied, and smiled as she slid back from underneath the great mechanism and listened not to the imaginary voice she gave her truest love, the *Fighting Mongoose*, but to the heart and soul of her wondrous beast as she purred from Kesta's handiwork.

"But… but, where are you going?" Kesta asked herself in that same sultry tone. It probably wasn't the finest faux voice she could have given her airbarge, but mimicking all manner of accents was Natteo's gift, not hers. "Will you be coming back soon?"

Sniggering to herself and fighting the giddiness that came with a long task finally done, Kesta shrugged and blew a kiss to the machine. "It was fun. I'll be seeing you."

And then, like a thief in the night, she slipped away from the engine room and glided through the underbelly of the beast.

Around her, she could hear the happy cries of children at play and she ground her teeth in mild irritation; it wasn't just the *Fighting Mongoose* that had spent the last few days recovering. She, too, was weary and battered, and the giddy shouts grated on her nerves.

There's trouble in them.

Admittedly, Lorgan had argued that the Crimson Hunters would have made better time by continuing to fly towards Dellerin City and the Guild, where they could seek proper repairs in the relative safety of the Guild's massive airgarage. Aye, it was a strong argument, but the *Fighting Mongoose* had bested not one but two ancient demons in less than a week. She was a fine flying beast, but that shit took its toll on the most stubborn of engines, and Kesta didn't fancy another patch-up job while in flight over the sea. And there had most certainly been quite a collection of dents and cracks to patch. Thankfully, Kesta knew her bird inside out and was familiar with every mechanism required for the *Mongoose* to fly.

Fly.

While there was a wonderful calmness in tending to repairs, the hour was late. It was time to feel the perfection of flight once more.

Taking a moment to wipe a black smear from her forehead, she made her way up through the reassuring corridors, enjoying the sensation of carpet under her bare feet after the cold steel of the last few hours. Knocking at Lorgan's door, she allowed herself a satisfied grin at a job well done.

When he answered, as per usual he looked wild and unsettled, as though the very act of remaining still was a grand test of his nerves. His room was a mess. Books on the arcane lay strewn across his bed, his floor, and everywhere in between. To be precise, every book on the arcane that Seren wasn't studying in her own quarters lay strewn around his quarters. Both mercenaries had been quite studious these last few days. It was something to do to keep the mind active when things were out of one's hands, she supposed.

"Is it done?" he asked, snapping his book shut. "Are we finally good to get off this beach?"

"Aye, my friend. We can lift off whenever you desire."

At this, he clapped his hands in delight and gave her a rare smile, followed by a relieved chuckle. "See, I was right about staying here, Kesta. There was piss-all to worry about," he exclaimed, grabbing his boots and leather cloak.

It was a rare thing to see him jest, so she allowed it. "Thank the gods for your better judgement and decision making."

"I'll make sure everyone is aboard," he said in excitement, and she couldn't help but smile at his enthusiasm. The man was terrified of staying still, a trait he'd probably had all along, even before she'd known him. She could now understand this: he suffered from a dreadful affliction called responsibility.

She had once been as he was, but that was in another life. For just a spark of agony, the sadness took her and she was back there, among the smouldering ruin of her town on the last morning, wanting to die but unable to complete the deed herself.

Stow those thoughts a little longer.

"Aye, send word up and I'll bring us high," she said without blinking, without dwelling on the cutting horror of losing an entire family in a manner of days, without the shame of having been too inept and unprepared to do a spitting thing about it.

Holding the smile lest her darkness seep out and take his mood, Kesta turned on her heels and slipped out of the room.

"Where are they, by the way?" he called after her.

"They're down in the deep playing at warfare," she said, and Lorgan muttered a curse under his breath. He wasn't happy with how things were unfolding in the lower decks either. But it made sense, even if it could end in tears.

As she had done a hundred times already these last few days, she took the long route back up through the *Fighting Mongoose* towards her cockpit. Allowing her hands to touch the walls as she passed, she hummed a few notes to herself. A soothing tune, really, and one she only sang when she felt somewhat happy. And truthfully, in this great machine, she was happiest. An even greater truth was that she didn't care if she spent the rest of her life aboard its metal body. The land was for the dreamers and thieves and peasants and cowards. Up in the sky was for the ruthless and daring. Those ready to die as well.

Off the *Mongoose*, she was Kesta, inept mercenary. On board, well, there was probably no greater pilot in the skies. Hadn't been for a generation, and she liked to think for at least a generation to come. And if she did come upon a pilot who bettered her in the days ahead, well, she would find a way to blast them out of the sky.

Ruthless and daring.

"Are you thinking of getting me cannons and harpoons?" a sultry voice whispered, and she smiled in reply.

I killed two grand demons without a weapon to my name.

Imagine what I can do with a cannon or two.

"Let's see how things go in the Guild, yeah?" she pledged to herself. On top of stealing the grand airbarge from under the noses of the finest mercenary group in the world, they had also "inherited" quite the treasures, which were now stored on board. A girl could buy a lot of cannons with just a handful of the jewels she could call upon. "Then we can have an easier time of it against the next sleeping demon who comes chasing," she whispered, and a coldness came upon her. That same coldness she'd suppressed the last few days while she'd worked exhaustively on repairing the barge.

There is something greater coming.

"Spit on that," she cried, climbing out through the galley and feeling the cool ocean breeze on her face and the damp deck on her feet. She could feel the wind in her hair and she felt alive. Breathing in the ocean air one last time, Kesta walked the deck, glancing over the edge every now and then. Deep below, through the portholes and reverberating through the longvoices, she listened to her comrades readying themselves.

Admittedly, she might have taken a brief respite after the final few fixes, but Lorgan's patience wouldn't be tested. Besides, she could catch a few hours' sleep once they touched the great blue. One hardly needed to worry about running into another airbarge in a sky so big. And if they did, and the hull ruptured, sending them all into a fiery wreck below, well, that was simply the actions of gods at work and a fine way to go.

She ran her fingers absently along the deck rail, loving this beast as she usually did. Her eyes fell upon the long, rotting ruin still lying upon the beach, and she grinned. She could prove herself the greatest pilot if need be.

Little bit of luck as well.

"Aye, the most skilful usually find the greater luck," she muttered, glancing out across the beach to where the ship had departed a few days before. She had enjoyed the sailors' grateful company for a time. They drank the world down and perhaps, after all their endeavours, a few nights' reprieve was welcomed among the Crimson.

As was the trophy Lorgan had strapped to the front of the barge. "As proof," he'd claimed as he wrapped three long incisors for the rest of the world to see. They had no memento of their victory over Fiore, but with this monster, there could be little doubting the greatness the Crimson Hunters claimed as their own. Besides, it had been something for Lorgan to do when not pacing back and forth in his cabin, trying to make understanding of impossible things.

Terrible things are coming.

Shrugging, she ignored that gnawing feeling in her gut and continued her cursory inspection of the barge. These last few days had reminded her that it was better to simply wake every morning with a little desire in her heart, a little drive in her rear and a little warmth in her soul. It wasn't a lot, but enough to allow her to seek joy in her day.

And if she did die this very day, no doubt crushed by a third demon intent on their destruction, well, that was alright too. She wouldn't fight inevitability, nor would she fear it, nor would she run towards it, nor would she run from it. She would simply strap herself in and see what happened. It probably wasn't the heathiest outlook on life, but it was better than what had warmed her hollow husk of a soul before.

Nearing the front of the main deck, and gazing at the polished teeth and gritting her teeth in reply, she turned back towards her pilot's cabin and the waiting child.

"Come along, move your rear, little one," she hissed,

and the child, sitting on Kesta's chair, began to climb out of her throne to slip into her own place. In her movements, Kesta saw herself as a child, thrust into a life of responsibility. She had trusted herself then. Why couldn't she trust her own gut now? "Actually, fuk it," she said, sniffing. "Stay where you are. I'll watch this one."

Eveklyn hesitated, turned a shade of pale and began strapping herself into the pilot's chair. Grinning, Kesta reached for the longvoice and whistled loudly into the funnel piece. For a time, she heard nothing but mutterings and movement in the lower decks, so she whistled again.

"Galley here," Lorgan called after a time. He waved over from the window and she nodded.

"Where's the cat?" she asked.

"It's not here."

"Go find the cat."

"It's not my job... This is no place for a cat."

She said nothing more, and suddenly a piercing whistle came through the cabin and made Kesta squint, and Eveklyn covered her ears ever so.

"Um... lower... deck here?" Seren said, after a time, and there was a clumsy crash as the girl, who was completely unfamiliar with the mode of communication across wires, muttered a curse before returning. "What do you need?"

"Kesta needs the cat," Lorgan from the other open line said unhappily.

"I don't need the cat," Kesta interrupted. "I just want to know where the stupid thing is."

"Why?" Seren asked.

"So we don't leave it behind."

"Is the cat outside?" Seren asked.

"No, I want to make sure the cat is not outside. I want to make sure the cat is safely aboard," Kesta said, watching Eveklyn flick a few knobs and engage the levers to ignite the engine. She tapped the girl to hold the ignition, but offered a thumbs-up to signify that she'd completed the first part correctly.

Eveklyn offered a careful nod, placed her fingers on the controls and fell unblinkingly still as though in a trance. Kesta knew that anxiety all too well. The girl hadn't yet brought the beast up unaided. Many young pilots killed themselves and everyone aboard in the first few moments of their debut flight. Kesta had been certain to instil this knowledge in the young orphan girl. To terrify her, to instruct her, to help harden her as well. To help her fuken grow.

"I don't have the cat," Seren said, and dropped the funnel of the longvoice as she returned it to its place.

"Guess that's that," Lorgan said, knowing it was anything but that. After a breath he whistled loudly, and, distantly, Natteo came on the longvoice.

"Natteo's pleasure house, deep in the depths of... Ah, fuk it... Nat here, in the depths. You want the cat?" he asked. He too was in the furthest part of the airbarge where he really shouldn't have been, but no one said a thing about it.

"Find the cat, Natteo," Lorgan ordered and hung up the longvoice. Immediately the loud whistle returned.

And came a second time and again after that, and Kesta smiled, knowing what was coming next. Sometimes Natteo couldn't help himself, and Lorgan, well, Lorgan just played along as the disgruntled leader.

"Fuken… galley here," Lorgan shouted.

"Natteo here. Just confirming you want the cat?"

She stepped out onto the deck as the voices argued back and forth, only to come upon the hobbled form of Derian at the edge of the barge, looking down at where he had fallen over. He still looked pale, paler than Seren, and why wouldn't he? She had leeched his soul, and he was lesser for it. There had been accusations thrown when both had been returned to the airbarge in their comrades' arms, but even the matter of Seren healing his wounds once she was capable had meant little to Derian or, loudest of them all, Natteo. Seren had wept and claimed she had cast no enchantment, instead pledging that it was Derian's sword that had instilled her with life. An unlikely story, but in this world, who fuken knew what the truth was? Regardless, he was looking shaken this morning, but better than the day before, and the day before that. Perhaps that was something.

He smiled as she approached, and she patted his back weakly. "Lorgan just said we are leaving. Thought I'd take a look at the ground one last time," he said.

"Ah, don't worry. We'll be back in Dellerin in no time at all," she assured him, and swiped a fly from his shoulder. Above them the sudden rumble of thunder reverberated. She stared at those clouds and raised an eyebrow. They weren't really dark enough for such thunderous weather, but she wasn't right about everything always, she supposed.

Eveklyn leaned out the front cockpit door. "They found the cat. Was in Derian's room… I think it was throwing up… Well… that's what Seren just said… I don't know."

"Of course the cur was," Derian said and gripped the rail.

"Remember what I told you, Eveklyn? Before you embark, ensure everyone checks in, and then take her up," Kesta ordered.

"Will you watch over me?" Eveklyn asked, before whistling as loud as she could down the mouthpiece.

"I'll be here with Derian. Not too high now, but enough to see if we can breach that cloud cover," Kesta warned, and the child nodded as she received word of their comrades.

"Is the child ready for this?" Derian asked.

"Not at all, but that's how she will learn. There are no trees to clip, and there is always a soft landing if she plunges into the sea. I call it a satisfying risk. Also, she is my pupil."

"And you are a good master?"

"I am a terrible mercenary, but I earn my worth in the sky."

"You didn't answer the question."

"I am the greatest pilot of all time."

"Still didn't answer the question."

"I'm getting better at instructing."

Derian looked as though he had more to say, but the *Mongoose* suddenly came to life. The child stretched her arms, took a breath and, gripping the controls, brought the beast high into the sky at an impossibly swift pace. It was a remarkably smooth lift-off.

"Oh, my stomach," moaned Derian, gripping the rail as the land beneath them disappeared and the air immediately began to thin. Kesta knew that sickly feeling all too well and she welcomed it. Always had, since she began flying.

She'd been pretty much the same age as Eveklyn was now, funnily enough.

"Watch the counter or we'll all die, Eveklyn," Kesta warned as the world around them disappeared into a grey mist and the rumble of thunder sounded again, nearer now.

Eveklyn offered a thumb of agreement and only then did Kesta feel the beast already begin levelling and easing forward at a perfect take-off trajectory. The child was a natural.

More than just a kitchen aid.

"I'm going to give her a few more breaths to break through," Eveklyn called out, and Kesta nodded in approval. If they could breach the sky, they could get some decent miles travelled. If they had to fly below the storm, a smarter move would be to delay the journey altogether.

As though the gods listened, they broke through the clouds and stunning blue filled the sky, and immediately Eveklyn tilted the airbarge forward and began charging west as advised.

"What the fuk is that?" screamed Derian as a thousand large shadows suddenly appeared across the deck and the roar of thunder rose to a deafening crescendo.

"Get out of my seat, child... Move, move," screamed Kesta, sprinting towards the pilot's chair, knowing they were but a breath from disaster.

And that's when they hit something really big.

The Kids Are All Right

"Get out of there, you little bastard," Lorgan hissed at the cat, which lay on its back playing with the remnants of what might have been a rat. Keddy's paws ripped, flipped and flung its treasure, and it looked positively delighted with itself. The cat didn't react to Lorgan standing in the doorway. The black mush of fur and bone and blood strewn across Derian's bed held its full attention, and Lorgan couldn't help but feel a little insulted at the beast's disinterest in his orders. In fact, with an insulting purr, the beast flopped on its side and began pawing the dead rodent with renewed intensity in an attempt to stir it into fighting or running for its life. "Sick little fuk, aren't you?"

"Meow."

It wasn't much of an argument. The cat made a good point.

"Come on," he said, feigning a charge, and the cat took the hint, leaping a few feet straight up and then sprinting past Lorgan and disappearing through a vent in the side of the wall. With a callused hand, Lorgan wiped at the ruin among the sheets and flung the remains out the door, where it would meet an end by the returning cat, or under the boot of a mercenary passing by. It probably wasn't the most hygienic act, and Kesta would likely be pissed at him for dirtying up her airbarge, but it was better that than leaving a nasty surprise for Derian to come upon. Doing that little bit extra, he dabbed at the sheeting with a wet cloth from Derian's washbowl before laying the sheets out in all their damp glory.

The things I do.

It was a hero's number of things Lorgan did for his comrades, many of which went completely unnoticed, and this was just another. Truthfully, since Seren had leeched from Derian, he hadn't been himself. Usually easy-going, if not a little irritating, he had been quick to anger these last few days. More than that, he'd studied in relative quiet, which was a rare thing, and Lorgan couldn't be certain the boy wasn't feeling a little defeated by the world. Every day, though, he seemed to lose a little of the pallor, which perhaps meant his soul was replenishing after his demise in the belly of a grand demon. Or else he was just getting a tan. Regardless, he still wasn't himself, and discovering the innards of a mouse on his bed would be enough to rightly undo a day or two's improvement.

He went to report the discovery of the cat at the nearest longvoice when the stench of burning copper reached his nostrils and he sighed irritably.

The things I worry about.

Setting off, he stomped down through the decks and then climbed the ladder into the furthermost hold, where he was greeted by the delighted clamour of excited voices. He usually stayed away from the activities down here, as he tended to fear the worst.

Suddenly there came a terrible explosion, and Lorgan cursed loudly as a second roar reverberated through the dark hallway. The noise came from behind the heavy metal door, which was swinging gently with a delicate creaking sound. He didn't knock, though he might have warned them, lest he take a careless strike sticking his head through. It was a large beast of a hold, and suitable for holding a few mounts rather comfortably. Now, however, it held something else entirely.

Kids at play.

It was a fine nickname he and Kesta had conjured. But it was anything but play among these reckless fiends, although they attacked with the carefree recklessness of children. And despite his better intentions and sense, Lorgan allowed it, for how else could children learn? How else could they improve?

"Oh, hello, Lorgan. What brings you down to the fun?" Natteo cried from inside the ill-smelling room. He hung from a pipe on the ceiling that looked important, and most certainly not suited for anyone to hang from. It creaked as he released himself, and, dropping to the floor with a clank, he grinned as though it was a divine dance he'd just completed. Really, who knew what went through that boy's mind at any given time?

"Get word to the upper deck that we are ready to embark," Lorgan said, looking around and frowning as the stench grew in his nose. It was bitter and disgusting. Mostly, though, it was unnatural. "Look, we allow this foolishness from you." Their faces immediately darkened. He sounded like an old man, their expressions suggested. "But for the love of the gods, will you keep the doors closed in case you stink out the entire ship?"

"Sorry, Lorgan," Natteo said happily. "Sure, who needs to breathe? We warriors can hold our breath for each session. No problem at all," Natteo mocked, and Lorgan near laughed.

"You are a jailor in this place, and little more, boy," he countered.

"On the contrary, I keep them both from killing each other," Natteo said without missing a beat. He tapped one of his wristbows, lying idly on a barrel beside him. It wasn't even loaded. "It's a tough task I have."

"Isn't that true of most jailors' tasks in a prison?"

"Aye, perhaps so. But I doubt they look as spit n polished as me when I tend to my duty."

"Just stop talking, Natteo."

Seren, who up to this point had been kneeling, stood up and breathed deeply in the awful stench. She looked nearly as ruined as the first time Arturo had attacked her with that first bolt of killing electricity. Her dress was ripped in places, her hair singed and her skin lightly charred. Along her thighs there streaked a line of ice as it gently melted. "I'm no prisoner," she argued and gestured to her opponent on the other side of the room to hold off another assault.

Opponent?

Prisoner?

Comrade?

"I wouldn't dream of chaining you up," Lorgan offered.

He didn't like seeing her in this sorry state. It went against every part of him that she did it to herself purposely as well. The ice was a different look to her as well.

"Course you would. Sure, she's gorgeous," Natteo offered helpfully, and Lorgan clipped the boy around the back of his head. There were certain days when there was an annoying glint in the little cur's eyes. The boy had so many things going for him until he opened his fuken mouth. Lorgan had said as much many a time, and it usually ended up with the fledgling mercenary doing everything to annoy and irritate. If Lorgan could have found a way to bottle such chaos, Natteo could be quite the ally. As it was, the excitement of taking to the sky was enough to set Natteo off in a right irritating way.

"What did I just tell you, idiot?" Lorgan warned.

"To shut up."

"Will you do it?"

"Of course I will, fearless leader."

Across from Seren, Arturo stirred from his smoking ruin. He looked as battered as Seren. It was a good look to him, for unlike the rest, Lorgan did not quite trust this fiend just yet. Arturo's hair gently smouldered, releasing a little plume of smoke, and he gasped as the exertion took him. His old cloak, on the other hand, looked untouched by fire, lightning, or ice for that matter.

"I have my breath again. Whenever you are ready, we can continue," Arturo mumbled in a broken voice. Each word was a rasp and spoken with care as though every breath was something to be savoured. The pace of these training sessions was taking its toll on both weavers, but in the prisoner's case it looked to be killing him. His bindings rattled as he struggled to straighten up. One binding, to be more precise. Seren argued that she could improve more swiftly when facing a weaver without hindrance, but Lorgan would allow only so much lunacy aboard. One of Arturo's arms remained locked in chains, while the other was free to cast whatever enchantment he desired, or whatever defensive enchantment he weaved as Seren went attacking.

I don't trust your words, weaver.

Arturo claimed innocence where the attack on Seren was concerned, and Lorgan thought it convenient that the old man claimed he'd merely mistaken Seren for another fiend. After Derian, it was Natteo who had taken to him next. Seren had soon followed after those two idiots. It was the warrior in her, and despite himself, Lorgan approved of such daring even if it would all end in tears. Perhaps it was also a morbid curiosity about why exactly he wanted her dead that drew her to the old man. Lorgan held little faith in any apology or dutiful blood pledges Arturo gave that he would not attempt to kill Seren again or attempt to enchant any other comrades. They had actually tried to outvote Lorgan when he insisted on keeping the cur in chains, as if they had a voice on such matters involving precarious things. He had taken the decision himself, despite their protestations, and felt perfectly fine about that. It was a small consolation that Arturo agreed heartily to such bindings. Nor did he argue against teaching what he could to the younger woman.

Lorgan looked at the wristbow again and remembered Natteo's guarantee that he would keep it aimed at the old man as they went to war with each other. And they did go to war. For hours every day they fought to the symphony of cries and howls, applause and curses. There was little point arguing with Seren on the matter, and so far, there had been no repeat of the initial assault. It should have made Lorgan feel better, but it really didn't.

A better leader might have forbidden such practices altogether, but the Crimson did everything differently, didn't they? A few days in, he knew Seren was becoming fiercer.

That's a good thing, right?

"So, come on, Lorgan. Will you watch us kill each other? It's a rather interesting spectacle, and I know you will enjoy watching," Seren said, winking, before taking her place on the far side of the room. She stared down the weakening weaver before beckoning him to strike.

Lorgan liked it when she winked. Lorgan knew he was far too old for one so young. Still, though, it was nice to be winked at. Lorgan bit the inside of his cheek but said little more.

"I love this part," Natteo said. "I bet they use the floating weave."

"Shut up, Natteo," Lorgan muttered, leaning against the wall, partly to ease the weight in his feet, but also to make himself a slightly smaller target.

"I can't help it, boss. I'm in a chatty mood today," Natteo declared. "Oh, wait—looks like lightning."

With a deep breath, Arturo brought his entire body alive, and a bolt of lightning appeared in the palm of his remaining hand. He appeared to age in front of Lorgan as the illumination highlighted the creases in his leathery skin. Seren, on the other hand, appeared to glow from within, and she stood ready in a fighter's pose with her arms held out in front of her.

"Scorch her rear," shouted Natteo, leaping upon the hanging pipe once more, grinning dangerously as he swung like a drunken munket over a bonfire. He enjoyed this a little too much. As did Derian, who frequently watched, though in silence, for he and Seren were not on speaking terms just yet. Lorgan thought it an interesting thing.

Immediately the hairs stood up at the back of his neck as Arturo released a bolt across the room that consumed Seren completely. For an entire pulse of time, she looked scorched, before the lightning was ripped from the air and formed into a sphere of light around her quaking hands.

"She has you, Arturo. Reckon you need Edel to rear her lovely head," Natteo cried, and Lorgan peered curiously at Seren. He also wasn't sure how he felt about a weaver who claimed there was a darker personality hidden deep within his mind.

"Hush, Natteo, idiot," Seren gasped, and though her arms began to burn from the electric force and her hair stood on end, Lorgan could already see the improvement in her technique, even if he had no idea exactly what she was doing, or how she was doing it.

"I do have you, comrade," Seren roared defiantly. Arturo began to scream in agony as the electricity passed between them. A better weaver might have broken the connection as she attempted to turn the tide of power, but Arturo understood his duty. More than that, he understood his penance, for the girl began to scald him something awful.

"That's actually really impressive," Natteo said, dropping from the pipe and stepping in beside Lorgan. "Terrify-ing, really," he added, and it was. A few days before, she had burned at the hands of this fiend, but now the tables had been turned, it seemed. Lorgan had fretted ever so when Arturo claimed his own abilities were little match for those of Anguis's older acolytes, let alone the dark master himself.

Seren must have taken her failure personally, for the agony she had endured to get to this moment was some-thing indeed. Even if Lorgan didn't approve, it didn't mean he was right.

Though Arturo slumped in his chains, he held that lightning and delivered what he could. He moaned aloud, and Lorgan was once more impressed that he allowed her to practice and learn at his own expense.

And then she weakened. It began as a crack. She gave a slight yelp as her hands quivered and a shard of light-ning slipped wide, striking the wall behind her and leaving a scorch mark in the surface. This was going to piss off Kesta something awful were she ever to venture this deep into the *Fighting Mongoose*'s belly. Thankfully, she rarely had these last few days. Playing the part of mother, she'd allowed them free rein on this level, letting them do as they wished. She had no desire to know what exactly they were up to, or the damages they did to her baby.

"Wait, now. Look at this, folks," Natteo cried. "It's not over yet."

But it was over. For her, at least. Sensing her weakness, as he likely had a hundred times before these last few days, Arturo stood upright and roared as he sent a renewed drive of lightning down upon her, engulfing her in a dreadful spitting flash of brilliant white. Screaming, she collapsed under the counter.

Roaring again, Arturo punished her for a few breaths before releasing the agonizing electricity and slumping in his chains once more. "And your undefeated winner is... Edel... or Arturo... or whoever," Natteo declared, clapping his hands passionately over the broken Seren, who smoked at his feet and squirmed in pain a little bit.

Shut up, Natteo.

With a quivering heave and an anguished shriek, Seren tried to rise, but the agony was something awful, and Lorgan stepped forward to help her. Arturo dropped to a knee and released a light from his fingers, and immediately, the wounds on her skin began to recover. As she healed, Arturo weakened further still. He dropped back against the far wall, moaning ever so. "Healing is the toughest," he rasped, and his eyes were dim as though his life were about to be snuffed out.

"I'm alright. I can take it," Seren called, climbing to her knees and regaining her strength. As she did, she brought up a blue shield of light around her to block his weaving. "I said I'm fine, Arturo," she repeated, and for a few breaths more they battled wits and weaving as she forsook his healing, no doubt so that he might conserve his soul's precious energy.

"As you wish," Arturo said, releasing the weaving but remaining where he sat, broken and exhausted. This too was part of his punishment, though it was self-imposed. Seren insisted she needed only a little healing to catch her breath, to take care of herself, but Arturo appeared hellbent on fuken himself up, in an act of contrition. Lorgan had wondered in the first days if he wasn't simply playing on their better judgement, hoping to steal himself a little good-will, a little freedom as well. Now, though, he wasn't sure the broken old man wasn't determined to undo the sins of his actions. Just a glimmer of trust stirred deep within, and Lorgan suppressed it immediately.

Not yet.

Not until I know for certain.

"That was well fought," Seren said, and Arturo nodded as he caught his breath. For all of Lorgan's mistrust of these barbaric behaviours, there was something to them, alright. He hated being wrong. He hated having to admit as much, as well.

"It was an impressive battle," Lorgan said quietly, and she met his eyes and grinned in delight. "Come on," he said, turning to leave. "Give word I kicked the cat out of Derian's bedroom and we are good to fly." At this, Natteo whistled and the piercing hiss went through Lorgan's head like a knife. He thought these little enchanted things quite wonderful; he only wished they had bells or something less intrusive, but it was no matter.

Climbing up through the deck, he felt his belly lurch as the ship left the ground. He was growing more comfortable with this flying beast altogether. Eager to catch sight of the sky disappearing, he reached the main deck and stepped out just as the screaming started.

"Oh, fuk me," he cried, falling out the galley door as the barge struck the largest airbarge he'd ever seen in his life.

This is how I die.

Meanwhile, Back at Dellerin City Gate

Sabina felt old today. Older than she'd ever felt before. That was the thing with getting old. It just fuken happened at some point, usually in the morning, and then that was it. You were simply old and crabby. She felt at least twice her three dozen years. This morning at least. Only a couple of weeks ago she was wild and fiery, and a proud soldier. Just a soldier, without any responsibility, going where she was told, doing what she was told, killing whomever she was told to kill. She took orders just fine and felt just fine about it.

Scratching her head lest the oncoming hangover catch up too soon, she glanced at herself in her bedside mirror as she rolled out of the sheets and thought she looked as old as she felt. She was still pretty, still lean in all the right places, but in war, there came a tiredness and many a bad hair day too. Her bushy brown hair was even wilder than usual, and the thin line of shade she'd applied to her eyes the evening before had faded and probably run all over her bedding.

Wanted to look my best as the bombs dropped.

"Oh, fuk me," she moaned, then stretched and grimaced at the smell emanating from her. Grabbing a damp cloth and applying some much-needed scented oils, she scrubbed under her arms and a few other key spots before washing her face in a small water basin and immediately felt a handful of years younger. Outside she could hear the rush of thousands, and the call of duty crept into her mind once more. "We didn't die after all," she declared to the tent, and there came no reply. As far as tents went, it was positively luxurious. Far better than the tight confines she had spent many a year squirming in. It had enough space for an entire wood-and-straw bed. They had even erected a wooden standing shelf upon which she could rest her books of war and strategy. They didn't know her at all. She stored her good boots on the shelf, so at least it wasn't going to complete waste. She looked around the rest of the space and decided the sitting stool beside the outside flap was the only other decoration she needed.

"I think I did," came a voice from somewhere outside.

Sabina stepped tentatively from her new tent and the blazing sun met her unimpressive eyes and burned them. Her perfectly unremarkable head, already thumping and splitting from the excesses of the night before, felt larger than usual. It was probably just age catching back up with her. Or else there had in fact been a bombardment that had crashed through the sky and struck her in the head. She'd have probably felt less pain were that the case, she mused, wiping her eyes, regretting the booze and wondering was there any more for the evening ahead.

She tripped over a pair of feet and recognised the owner immediately.

"Are you actually still alive, Nikolai?" It was a fair question and he grumbled in reply. "Hello?" He was splayed out in the charred grass, using a clump of turfgrass as a pillow. Strewn across him were a few handfuls ripped from the ground and dumped upon his chest in an attempt to stave off the cold. She couldn't remember if it had been cold last night, only that it had been on fire. "Nikolai, you morfuk, do you hear me?"

He could hear her just fine. He murmured something incomprehensible and turned on his side, losing his blanket of grass in the process. Resting his arm over his eyes to stop the sun's assault, he did his best to not hear her anymore. He was a pathetic sight, and it was no place to sleep during a battle, but he looked impossibly comfortable. Everyone with a fierce hangover usually did, and in the same breath, they also appeared impossibly uncomfortable. At his head lay the last bottle of sine, long emptied, and she cursed him under his breath. He'd claimed the well had run dry, pledged as much while creeping out of the tent a few hours before. She struck him lightly between the legs with just enough force that he sat upright, howling.

"Couldn't just leave me to die here, could you," he roared and, gripping his manhood in one hand, attempted to strike her with the other. It was a lazy, hungover strike and she dodged it, and in the process, her own stomach churned and she nearly threw up at his feet.

"Get up, you lazy bastard," she ordered, fighting the spinning. She focussed out across the battlefield. It shouldn't have been a battlefield at all. It should have been a sanctuary to the invading army. In the light of the morning, the devastation was more evident. Fewer fires burning now than there had been in the night admittedly, but they left their own ruination behind.

"Fuk me," she repeated, cursing the ruin inflicted by those fiends in the sky. Though the battle had long since passed, some exhausted and soot-covered soldiers were still at task putting out the flames. Sabina could see the wretched corpses that looked better suited to be skewered upon a monster's spit than to be buried with wailing, prayers and sorrow. So many bodies, and their stink was dreadful in itself. "Get up, or I'll put you to work with the rest of those poor souls fighting the fires."

"Aw, spit on me," he groaned.

That was a job she'd never desired to involved herself in. Her hand fell to the fresh patch on the left shoulder of her shirt and she grinned ruefully. At least her rank would keep her from such tasks ever again. More than that, she could order fiends to tend to such things. Or just simply threaten them to make them do her bidding. Specifically, to be her closest companions in the grim warfare today. "We have things to do," she murmured.

"Aye, aye, captain," Nikolai whispered, and the simple act of talking seemed to take a tremendous amount of effort.

"I can't hear you," she countered.

"Aye, aye, captain," he replied with more vigour. "Well, nothing crushed us... again," he said, accepting her helping hand and climbing to his feet.

"Just the drink," she countered.

"Aye. It's one thing to wait in horror as bombs fall around us, but it's another thing having a glass of sine to stare at every now and then." It was a fair point.

If Sabina was a betting woman, and she was, she would have considered it an awful amount of luck if they'd died last night. The fact of their being settled on the outer reaches of the massive camp allowed the threat of assassins to be a worry, but in the event of a sky bombing, well, the centre was where most bombs would drop, and the previous two night's had been no different. And from their vantage point, they had watched, for what else could they do? They had no desire to get in the way of those defending, those fighting fires, those attempting to heal.

It was no life being a soldier, yet it was a life Sabina enjoyed. Even during war; especially in war. Most wars she fought had been mere skirmishes across the Dellerin Isles. She'd fought under a Venistra flag for most of her career before seeing the light, as they would say. She'd fought in secret as they'd wiped out what enemy numbers they could, attempting to rouse the locals, enlist the youth, somehow find value in the misguided belief they were ever going to march under a proper banner. They called themselves rebels, but she considered herself something far more. Most loyal soldiers did too. And she was loyal. Not to any real flag, for the banners changed frequently, but to war itself. And it had brought her to the gates of Dellerin, and it wasn't looking like it would stop anytime soon.

As long as we knocked enough of their fireflies out of the sky last night.

"Fukers blasted the hell out of us," Nikolai said thoughtfully. He wasn't entirely incorrect. Two days before this, they had set camp in front of the city gates. Theirs was the largest army ever assembled, gathered from across all the Isles of Dellerin. Marching, flying and floating. They were a strange gathering of an army. They had no uniform; they barely had a banner. And even then, that was something that they'd been barely able to agree upon. The Unified Free Islands were no impressive thing in the eyes of the few politicians, but collectively, they were a force. Anguis would see that now, if he appeared again. Oh aye, the Dark One must have watched with much terror as these great numbers gathered.

For a day or so.

"Well, we rightly blasted the hell out of them in reply," she snorted, wiping her nose. She needed some fried bread. A clever new captain would have taken care of feeding his troops the night before, but few had thought of cooking as the fireballs rained down upon them. She thought again of gods or demons toasting people upon a spit, and her stomach churned once more.

"Didn't see nothing like it. Not even in Karkur," Nikolai murmured. From his satchel he drew his cannister of water and drank deeply, and she immediately snatched it from him when he offered it.

"You fuk, I was looking for this," she hissed, drinking deeply for herself.

"Share and share alike," he declared, kicking at the empty bottle of sine they'd shared.

"Come on, let's go to work," she barked, and set off. He raised an eyebrow. She wasn't used to giving him orders, and he wasn't used to receiving them. They'd been friends their entire life, and there was no better friend or comrade she called upon. Though they were similar in age and neither one was too ugly to gaze upon, they had not found themselves in bed together just yet. Such friendships were built on less.

"Perhaps I can run ahead of you, shitting out roses to clear your way."

She grinned as he fell in beside her. She considered herself the better soldier, but he might have disagreed, and might not have been entirely wrong. He might well have earned a few promotions for himself, but he argued the pay wasn't any better for the added responsibility. In fact, there wasn't much payment at all. Still, a girl liked salutes when she walked. And the perks, like a bigger tent and a shiny wooden shelf. Not to mention a striking woven patch on her shoulder. A girl liked these things too.

Spread out before them was their massive camp. Spread out across the entire breadth of the Dellerin gates and halfway along the wall both ways, it was an impressive thing. A larger force had likely never been assembled. A couple of days before, these had been neat rows of tents and weapon ranges, livestock encampments and all manner of cavalry and infantry gatherings, waiting their turn to storm the city and beat back their defences. Come this morning, after two brutal nights, these things still remained, albeit diminished in number and somewhat less orderly. But among them also were their spoils of war: the land was littered with the charred ruins of many Dellerin airbarges that hadn't survived those continual barrages.

Didn't fuken expect that, did you Anguis, you fuk.

She grinned, thinking how perturbed the Dark One might have been seeing this army give such impressive fight to his mighty airborne brigade. It was enough to draw him out for a time as well. She hadn't seen the rumoured black fire with her own eyes either night, nor had she seen the marching of demons that a few battalions had supposedly faced. But she had most certainly heard their squealing roars in the battleground above. And for a time, his demonic voice had been muttering all sorts of things that meant little to her. She'd been stationed in Karkur. She knew it to be a simple weaving enchantment of the voice. Barely any soul juice consumed at all.

"How did we survive this?" Nikolai wondered, and she knew. Numbers and ammunitions and Anguis's misguided belief that weavings alone could decimate an army. The cur should have expected a few Karkur weavers to march towards war with the rebels. And if he didn't? Well, that was just naivety, the misguided belief that his laws still held merit against those who opposed him.

Aye, the attackers had taken a blasting, but it was his precious Dellerin that had come off the worse for wear. And though Sabina suppressed the guilt for the innocent lost, they were his people; their deaths were a necessary sin.

"Worst night ever," Nikolai proclaimed, matching her step.

"I wouldn't know. At least we were ready for them this time," Sabina offered, and her companion nodded. That first night had been dreadful. They didn't need to talk about the sudden assault. She had lost friends in that cowardly attack. Burned alive in the middle of the night as they slept was no way for a soldier to die. Better to see it coming. Better to have a chance, any chance at all. So she drank and faced it.

Both weary soldiers passed among younger soldiers who looked shaken and pale as they donned their armour for the day's incursions into the great city. They need not have looked as shaken as they did. Their assaults would meet little resistance. Their task now was more about patrolling the areas they already controlled. Countless battalions had ventured deep in the first night, she knew, but nothing so brazen had been attempted since, such were the losses. Some remained dug in, holding territory, wiping out stragglers and citizens, but there was little she could do about that. Atrocities occurred in the taking of things, unpleasant as it was.

As for Sabina, her orders were to simply break Dellerin hearts before a second massive invasion occurred. It seemed as good a plan as any other, she supposed. They had numbers, they had supplies, and Dellerin didn't even have running water anymore.

Hunger and thirst caused more surrenders than any number of inexperienced soldiers flexing their muscles, gritting their teeth, praying for no escalation in violence.

"The young ones look rightly wrecked," Nikolai pointed out.

"Every day will be easier."

"For those that don't skip away in the middle of the night, you mean to say."

She frowned. "I wouldn't blame them if they did," she whispered.

"Not a very captain type thing to say, but I agree."

Those not hastily tending to duties or preparing themselves for a careful match were quick to move out of their way. Sabina avoided the healing tents. That was the first thing any soldier learned to do when out on a march. No good sounds ever came from those shitholes. After hunger and thirst, it was the agony of war that took a soldier's heart most fiercely.

The battles had been incredible, waged mostly across the sky while most could only look on. It was no surprise most green soldiers were still shaken come the light of day. They had probably spent those awful dark hours looking up at the horrors above, praying to absent gods that the sky didn't fall upon them. They certainly hadn't spent the entire night drinking alcohol in the privacy of a tent with their best friend, ignoring the terrible crushing roars around them as chance favoured the unfortunate one last time.

"What was that song you were singing?" she asked, and Nikolai chuckled ever so. He was no singer, he never would be, but bless his drunken lungs, he went for it when the right amount of drink was taken.

"Oh, fuk me. I forgot about the singing."

"Something about a battle between gods," she offered. As far as his terrible songs usually went, this one was slightly less awful than most. It was still awful, though. "And some wooden man."

"Aw, I don't know where these things come from," Nikolai said. He began to hum a few notes and shook his head. That wasn't the tune at all.

"And it had tricksters and shit, all killing each other," she added, and he shrugged his shoulders. Alcohol delivered gifts and took them away just as swiftly.

"I was so hammered you could've built a wall with me."

"Well, it was a shite song anyway," she jested.

"My songs are spit n polished."

Above them, a shadow appeared and a sudden eruption of movement stirred as though a flock of birds had suddenly taken flight. She looked up and caught sight of a large airbarge circling overhead. She might have turned to flee, lest it be the enemy, but Sabina trusted in her own fate. She'd happier die where she stood than attempt to outrun an inevitability. She'd never live down the shame of running straight into the splash damage of a bomb. Oh no; better to stand and be cool and see if the gods doomed her. Perhaps it wasn't the cleverest tactic, but as with the countless battles before, it served her well. For some reason, Sabina always believed she would know the moment of her death was upon her, long before the strike. This, however, felt far from death, even as the airbarge dropped suddenly as though it were on a bombing run.

"Is that ours?" Nikolai asked casually. He shared her stoicism. Perhaps they'd even spoken of it from time to time. He'd lived through enough to recognise that some-times standing still was enough. He stood still and looked up as, around them, the army panicked.

As many had in the first incursion into the city.

The Dellerin airbarges all flew under his darkest banner, and there was a near regalness to their flying monsters. They were the shiniest pieces, the best armoured and had the smoothest manoeuvres. They were greater in number and they were rigidly disciplined, and when they took flight like a swarm of hissects covering the sky, they were a daunting, impressive thing.

For as long as their armour held and their munitions were fully stocked, of course. She had to believe they'd used up most of these the last two nights.

The United Islands, on the other hand, relied on what they could get their hands on, particularly with their own air brigade. Fierce and hardened and captained by wild lunatics, though fewer in number, they still held court with the larger numbers. They shouldn't have had a chance in the greater schemes, but they did their part.

Many of the Dellerin Air Brigade found sanctuary near the palace. Others stayed miles away where they could tend to repairs. Others simply scattered to the clouds above. Keeping an eye out, staying in formation. Safety in numbers. Not all could stay flying once the damage inflicted became too much, of course, and this airbarge had the look of a Dellerin bird that lost the will to stay afloat.

"It's too hard to tell if it's friendly, though it most certainly looks as if it's on a charge," she said, shrugging. Looking from the airbarge across the city, she could see the dim sheen of a dome sparkling ever so against the burning morning sun. "I see no flag, but it could always be some wayward mercenaries, just taking a look, wondering what the fuk is going on if they've been out mercenarying all over the place," she said, looking not to the city itself but to the city within the city. The Mercenary Guild, to be exact, and he sighed in reply. The Guild was the one moving part in this war that had yet to play its card. Though weavers were outlawed all across Dellerin, come the violence, that bright blue shield had appeared right swiftly, covering the Guild all the way across like the great barriers surrounding Karkur these last few years. The enchantments required to keep such a shield alight were an impressive thing. Sabina wondered what Anguis might have thought of such a blatant display of defiance.

Anguis might well have had issue enough to bring his

argument to their unwelcoming doors were he not contending with an army at the gates.

"Well, if it is the Guild, let us hope no fool fires up at them," Nikolai offered. A fair point. The Guild were a force that rivalled any army. They were far more than just the stronghold that sat deep in the city with a few thousand hardened and incredibly skilled warriors to call upon, for these fiends were entrenched in every island throughout the rest of Dellerin. Only a fool would incur their wrath. They were neutral, at least for now. She'd heard whispers that they'd chosen sides. Engaged in warfare the night before. She'd heard they had fought for both sides and considered it simply desperate trench talk.

"Our lads down here wouldn't have been foolish enough to attack a Mercenary barge," Sabina offered as the airbarge turned in the sun and she saw no flag. She would consider it a justified defence, and they were within their rights to blow it out of the sky if it didn't rightly fuk off soon. Still, though, no soldier wanted to incur the wrath of the Guild by their own hand, regardless of the rumours.

Around them, soldiers went to task arming a sky cannon. A foolish thing, for there were better-suited weapons to take the beast out. "Easy, lads," she called, marching towards the young warriors. They were just as raw as any other green soldiers. It was likely the two nights' firing into darkness that had taken its toll, not to mention that they were hoping to avoid killing themselves or their comrades with falling debris. "There's only one of those birds in the sky. The chances of striking it are slim," she said, pointing to dozens of similar air cannons pointed directly into the sky. None of their gunners were loading the weapons with flak bombs, either. And why would they? Against a thousand flying birds covering the sky, these cannons were invaluable. But there was barely a need for aiming, such was their awkwardness. "See, they have it," she added, and the soldiers nodded while many ballistae crews armed and set themselves ready.

"Ah, spit on this. It's a Dellerin bird," Nikolai called as the airbarge dropped in a charging run, spinning and dodging as the first bomb was released. "To the fires with them."

"Fools," Sabina mumbled as the first bomb landed in a sphere of flame, burning a few tents and their unlucky occupants. "They won't last long," she added as the first volley from a hundred long ballistae bolts shot straight up with perfect accuracy.

The airbarge completely disintegrated as the bolts seared through the heavy hull, the four propellors and every deck within. A breath after that, the tanks of blackwater caught and the entire machine exploded.

The flame grew and then fell away, and deadly shards of debris spread and fell all across the camp. She did not run for cover as debris fell around her. Nor did Nikolai. The young soldiers did. They hid their heads, they feared the worst, and some of them took shards of singeing metal to their arms and legs.

Sabina and Nikolai remained unharmed.

"Come on, let's get to work," Sabina ordered, and Nikolai followed without word, offering a respectful nod to every ballistae crew they passed for a task well done, even if it was a task expected of them. She thought it a tragedy that some nameless comrades had survived the night, only to be burned alive as they slept. Their last thoughts would have been relief that they'd survived one more day. That was the luck of it, but sometimes luck was a right thurken bitch altogether.

They moved through the infantry parts of the camp as the soldiers roused themselves; though battered, they were still plenty. Still well fed, still hopeful. She hadn't expected the invasion to go smoothly in any way, and it most certainly hadn't. Seeing the cloud of airbarges had taken her nerve ever so. Not enough to show on her face, but enough to drive her to numbness. She would have much preferred to be part of the first advance battalion into the city, but the gods of luck had blessed her. She avoided being part of their spectacular losses. There would come a time when her command advanced, and she would lead a garrison. Until then, she would return to her duty of bombing the ever-living shit out of Dellerin until there wasn't a single fuken building standing.

As she approached the first great trebuchet, she could see the exhaustion on the faces of those tending to it. Many might not have slept since the previous day, and that was fair. Sleep was a thing reserved for those with the nerve to take it.

Especially with a little alcohol.

They looked well worked, well versed, and they might have been firing the great boulders since first light. She had a keen eye for these massive machines, a second sense for angles and distance. She'd ruined more than enough defences in her day and now as captain, her word and orders had led to wonderful successes.

She stopped by one of the many ammunition carts and

absently counted the boulders remaining. It took a few dozen mounts quite a time to pull each massive cart, laden with man-sized boulders, out onto the field of battle where nine behemoth trebuchets stood. It took only a dozen skilled soldiers to load each shot, however. And those dozen soldiers were now at task along the boulder run preparing the next strike.

"Slow down, lads. No point in breaking a nail out there," Nikolai shouted. "The city isn't going nowhere," he shouted to the boulder runners at task upon the imposing mechanism. "At least not today."

Sabina was a fan of the invention, and had been since their creation no more than a year ago by some ingenious brute who believed one solitary shot from a trebuchet just wasn't devastating enough.

Crush it all.

Any usual trebuchet took an age to load. And such loading was precarious and arduous and treacherous during the hours of battle. A boulder run was a long construction connecting trebuchet to ammo cart by way of thick beams of heavy, smooth steel. By using gravity and skill, runners could roll the heavy brutes into place in no time at all.

Aye, locating so much ammunition was a right nightmare, as was the loading of the carts. This was done far away from the battlefield and under the cover of night, long before the first cracks of war rang out. It was a difficult task, but such things were necessary, even at the expense of a few injuries here and there. To her knowledge, they'd lost only a solitary soldier to a crushing error on the first night. Most certainly a tragedy, but again, necessary.

"They must have been firing a while," noted Nikolai,

and she nodded in approval. Unlike in most regiments, the runners worked at their own pace, in their own time. There was a limit to the number of boulders each of the ten trebuchets could fire in a day before needing to resupply. They were doing their job perfectly. She'd always admired captains who appreciated the little things like efficiency, especially when it was carried out at a soldier's own pace. She would treat her soldiers as she would like to be treated.

Unless they began to fuk around, and then she would set Nikolai on them swiftly.

"Fuk me—it's still standing," Nikolai noted of the solitary building in the third sector.

She cursed herself as she watched the great archaic structure standing brazenly among the ruin of the rest of the sector. She took it as a bit of an insult. Truthfully, such devastation was disheartening to even the stubbornest of defenders, and that building meant little to the war effort. It was probably empty as well, but she still took it personally. Nikolai too. So too did the runners throughout the battlements.

"You've done well, lads," she said of her boys. They were tending to the trebuchet and, with a final heave and a few cheers of relief, a mighty boulder rolled into the great steel basket with a dreadful crash. She knew if she survived the next decade, she would be inflicted with deafness, such was the noise of loading such beasts. She didn't care; she loved that roar, loved the whoosh as the beast sent its missiles forth as well. A little deafness was worth it if it brought victory.

"How have you not taken out that fuker over there,

though?" Nikolai called, pointing to the offending building and saying exactly what a captain could not.

"We hit it thrice. The bitch won't stir," a soldier replied and spat in the dirt in disgust. As he did, a few soldiers on each side began winding the great war machine in preparation of another strike.

"Well, don't waste all your shots trying to make it move," she muttered, playing the part of wise captain, even if it irritated her as much as it did them. "Carry on," she said, offering a bow as the soldier went back to setting the degree of flight, setting the angle. She could see immediately he aimed not at the solitary building, but deeper into another sector. No doubt to show her that the next shot, at least, would be aimed into more populated buildings.

After she left, they would no doubt waste all manner of ammunition attempting to knock the building down, and she didn't have any issue with that whatsoever.

For the rest of the morning and into the late afternoon, both comrades waded through the army, overseeing the rest of the trebuchets raining nightmares down upon the city. Some moral fiends claimed such barbaric behaviour was nearing war atrocities, but Sabina thought differently. Let them shout their aggrievement about dishonour all they wanted. This was a safer tactic than charging in with weapons raised and no idea of what to expect. Oh, no—batter the bastards back, deeper into the city where the boulders couldn't reach, and go about pinning them in where hunger would do just as much damage.

Eventually, with her head easing its ache and with the sun far across the sky and even more of the city in ruin, the trebuchets began to empty of ammunition. It was a tragedy to gaze upon war machines as devastating as these without teeth to bite. Immediately, the soldiers disengaged the great weapons from the boulder runners and began rolling the far lighter carts back into the cover of the forests where they would no doubt begin resupplying. She'd always believed there was a certain archaic dignity to it. Some leaders desired to drive into helpless infantry upon crushing mounts; others desired to have the feel of mud underfoot and cold steel in their hands. Some desired the terrifying sky above, to meet other flying threats. Sabina, however, believed in throwing rocks until everything was smashed to smithereens; it suited her down to the ground. And she would argue with anyone as to its merit.

She came upon the first trebuchet, which had done quite the job all day, laying waste to another sector on the northernmost part of the city. The soldiers tending to it had returned to firing at the solitary building once more. With folded arms she stood in silence and subtle approval as they measured angles and let loose. She counted one more strike, and immediately they began reloading, and she willed them to strike true.

The gods of chance must have listened, for the strike was true. It bounced once in front of the building and struck it fiercely enough that the front of the structure near exploded. She held her breath as the building wavered, teetering as though blown in a storm. For just a breath more, she imagined the enemy camped within and thought herself unlikely to be that lucky.

With a roar that was distant enough to be a whisper, the building collapsed upon itself in a grand puff of smoke. The soldiers cheered ever so and patted each other's backs, and she smiled.

"Well, now that that's done, what next?" Nikolai asked.

She didn't need to think. She already knew. "Come tomorrow morning we'll have them bring the beasts a hundred feet closer and we'll go again."

"A fine plan, Sabi—I mean Captain."

"Come on, brother. Let's celebrate with a fine feast."

"Might you procure a fresh bottle from the quarter-master to enjoy as war occurs above our heads?"

"As long as it's for the war effort."

"See, I told you you'd make a good captain."

Shadows in the Clouds

They weren't merely shadows in the clouds at all. And Derian stood numb and dumb as a countless number of the dark beasts appeared around him from all sides. They hummed and rushed through the wind, and his ears reverberated with their noise.

This can't be good at all.

They were an airborne legion, a grand mass of airbarges, and they filled the sky like a flock of birds frenzied by a threat. The Crimson were no threat, and neither was the *Fighting Mongoose*. In fact, as they crashed into the massive airbarge above them, they caused little damage at all.

"Move," screamed Kesta, shoving Eveklyn from her seat before grabbing the controls as they fought the inevitable. Kesta ran like the wind and flew even better, but she couldn't help the collision.

Oh, fuk me.

Once more the airbarge shunted fiercely, as though taken by a great tentacle, and Derian was thrown asunder and the squeal of metal against hardened metal pierced his ears and he feared death. Again. As usual.

"Fuk me—not again," he screamed as the force drove him into the sky and he was weightless for a pulse of time. The world froze for a breath, and he couldn't help but wonder if Arturo would be pissed that he'd gone to all this trouble, sitting around waiting for him, only to lose him immediately. In the exact same way.

Better than a cart of mercenaries to the head.

"No!" screamed Lorgan behind him. As Derian spun, he saw Lorgan spin with him. Blessed with heavier armour and probably better reflexes, Lorgan merely flew a few feet into the air, somersaulted forward and then crashed back to the deck, while Derian, ever the unlucky, took flight as though lifted by Arturo himself. Or Seren, going by the improvements she was making to her weaver skills.

For the love of the seven absent gods, will someone catch me this time?

"Sorry," cried Derian, feeling somewhat responsible for getting himself killed yet again. For a breath he saw nothing but the grey of clouds below him.

And then he saw the deck again as the airbarge, spinning from the crash against the larger barge, came into his view. More than that, the guardrail. With reflexes reserved for only special moments like this, or for a thundering horde of invading Canis demons, his hand shot out, he grabbed mightily hard, and was pulled back in, before crashing painfully onto the deck. This was an improvement over a dreadfully long fall through the clouds.

With a terrible screech, the *Fighting Mongoose* spun away from the larger airbarge, taking splinters of wood and shards of steel, and Derian, lying prone, could only marvel that such a monstrous machine was even capable of flight. Stained in the darkest black of the Dark One's banner, one of its four propellors was the size of the *Mongoose* itself. Unsurprisingly, Derian could see little damage to the hull of the dreadnaught airbarge, barring a few dents and scratches, as they drew up alongside. The *Mongoose*, on the other hand, looked positively battered.

Swiftly, a dozen or more airbarges immediately broke from their formation and surrounded the *Mongoose* like a boar in a mesh net. It was a peculiar thing, for they behaved as though surrounding an airbarge was instinct. Such a thought brought shivers to Derian's neck. They behaved as sky pirates might, and that was never good at all.

"What the fuk is going on?" Natteo cried, appearing from below. "Oh, dear," he added, seeing the massive airbarge hovering beside them, and then the surrounding humming brutes. "Looks like the sky is a bit busy today."

Derian shouldn't have felt as unnerved as he did. Truth was, no brigade was going to start any shit with them, for, were it to come out that a Dellerin army had attacked a mercenary airbarge without provocation, that was cause for war. No one wanted war with the Mercenary Guild. Not even Anguis, the Dark One.

"We should be fine. They are probably taking a look," Lorgan said, standing up and waving all nonchalantly.

After he had done sufficient waving to the gods knew how many sets of eyes, he turned to his knee, which he noticed only now had an odd appearance where he'd fallen on it. "Get back down there and free the lunatic," Lorgan growled, easing his knee straight with a painful pop. For a breath he cursed loudly. Then he grunted again. Then he stamped on the deck. Then he cursed one last time. It was an effective way of dealing with a dislocated knee, Derian mused.

Natteo didn't seem to care about Lorgan's misfortune. "Wait—are we getting boarded?" he asked, as though such a thing was a curiosity and little more. "They can't do that. We are the Guild."

"I reckon they have a right, but we won't make it easy," Lorgan growled, and cursed again a few times for good measure.

"They really shouldn't be doing that," Natteo decided. "And I'm not even looking my best," he added.

"Did you hear my order?" Lorgan shouted as the airbarges drew in around them, making escape an impossibility.

"Um... you want me to free the hostage, right?"

"And be spitting swift about it."

"Does it really matter if we have him chained or not?" Derian asked, above the rush of nearing turbines. They were daunting and all encompassing. They put the *Mongoose*'s turbines to shame. Kesta wouldn't have liked him thinking that, but facts were facts and they were impressive.

"A man in chains claiming innocence might well have reason to think us slave traders," Lorgan muttered. He tested his leg and remained standing under the obvious pain. "That's reason enough to give any army permission to detain us, all legal like."

"Fuk them. They have no right to board us or go searching through our things," Natteo retorted. "There are... certain items... I would rather nobody take a look at," he added, and Derian shuddered at the thought of the salacious items Natteo had no doubt procured for himself.

"Just fuken do it, you spitting cur," Lorgan roared. He had that tone that even Natteo usually backed down from.

Finally, Natteo appeared to grasp the seriousness of the matter. Not a lot, but a bit. "Alright. I'm on it, I'm on it... Spit on me, you didn't need to shout," he shouted, disappearing back down the ladder where his mutterings faded away under the rush of engines and wind and growing menace. That feeling of being spit and polished and being protected by the Guild was ebbing away ever so, because things never worked out for the Crimson Hunters for very long, and things had been working out a little too smoothly recently.

With heart still hammering, Derian roused himself and stood away from the edge of the barge as the great behemoth drew in closer. It was a good thing he did, for a harpoon from another bird struck the barge right where he stood, piercing the side of the vessel. A moment after that, a second and third chained harpoon struck along each side. "What the flying fuk?—Incoming!" Derian cried, and Kesta fought the first chain as it went taut and snapped. "They can't be doing this! They can't be starting a fuken war over nothing," Derian cried, watching the other chains go tight as the *Mongoose* fought the hold.

"I think you should tell them," snapped Lorgan. "I think they'll listen to you." He looked fierce and fuming, but he did not react. He had no hand in their actions, nor Kesta's. Derian, though, was desperate to figure out a way of escaping this. He thought and he thought, real spitting hard, and came up with nothing more than watching on.

Kesta tried her best. She dropped a few feet, angered like a fish on an angler's line, and held any boarding party for a precious few breaths more, until another dozen harpoons from all sides struck deep, embedding themselves, and Kesta howled in frustration as the barge fought their hold and began to lose.

This is all wrong.

They can't be doing this.

The Guild is going to be pissed.

Heads will roll.

Hopefully not ours this very day.

The engines roared, the scream of splintering wood and tearing metal pierced the air, and yet another dozen or so chained harpoons struck and pinned them securely from all sides.

Kesta fought the hold. She screamed all manner of threats and indignant profanities as she did. It was rather impressive, really, and Derian learned a term or two in those first few outbursts. She reared like a mount aggrieved at mistreatment as chains snapped and shot across the deck and sky, sending airbarges rearing in every direction, sometimes near colliding with their comrades around them. Alas, though Kesta was fierce and skilled, the hunters were simply too many. Given their tight formation and now their controlled assault, it was becoming more and more obvious that taking a solitary airbarge like the *Mongoose* out of the sky without damaging it was child's play for them. A fresh coldness came upon Derian; drops of sweat pooled under his arms.

Who would live to tell the Guild?

It felt like an age that the *Mongoose* raged against the inevitable, and Derian was mightily impressed with the power she showed under such duress, but the deadly barbed projectiles became too many and Kesta struggled to fight their hold. Soon the attackers began to get the better of their quarry.

"I think they have us," Lorgan warned, leaning against the edge. He sounded more enraged than fearful. He drew no blade, but his fists were clenched white. "Are we done?" he called desperately, and Kesta nodded and cut the engines, and all four propellors fell still. Derian expected a sudden drop, but the bird remained airborne, trapped in the enemy's net, as stable as though she sat upon land.

For a breath Derian imagined what the grand demon must have felt as it was hooked and taken by so many. He looked out to the sky of blue above the clouds, caught his breath and was rather pleased to see no mountain looming nearby that they could be dashed upon.

Natteo appeared once more, dressed for war. He carried a few swords, and offered them to Derian. "Seemed like the thing to do," he said coldly, counting the lengths of taut chain sticking into the barge on all sides. He dropped the swords on the deck at their feet, and despite Derian's terror, he reached for his own blade, and though it hurt, Lorgan stepped on it.

"Don't anybody raise a fuken sword," he snapped.

"They think they can come on our ship and we won't put up a fight?" Derian countered.

"Yeah!" Natteo agreed.

"You think we have a chance if we start killing these

curs," Lorgan said quietly. The anger was slipping away to thoughtfulness. Historically, those thoughts of his would turn to plans that would never work, although recently, he'd had a little more success. Derian was willing to follow the cur regardless. "I'm certain Kesta would approve of your aptitude, and your attitude in greeting our captors."

Kesta, still sitting in the cockpit, looked fit to join Natteo, such was her anger at the manner of their taking. Beside her, Eveklyn looked shaken. Derian wondered would Kesta blame herself for allowing the child to lift off. In her defence, there was a lot of sky in the world. And it was real fuken bad luck they'd flown straight up into the middle of this flying armada.

"We've been in worse positions. Let's stay calm and try diplomacy," Lorgan hissed.

Across from them, where the massive dreadnaught airbarge hovered, a large door opened and a few heavily armoured curs leaned out with crossbows cocked. "Well, I'll feel a lot better about it if we kill a few before they capture us," Natteo said, reaching for his wristbows. As he did, he slid up behind Lorgan, no doubt attempting to use the larger man as a shield. Natteo would argue against such a notion, of course, and he would be rather convincing and completely lying on the matter. The fuk knew exactly what he was doing, and he knew exactly how immobile Lorgan was with his knee injury.

"You think there aren't a hundred crossbows aimed at us from every barge?" Lorgan muttered, and Natteo shrugged, and Derian left the sword where it lay. "We might have flown into their path, but these curs were too fuken swift to entrap us," he added, and it was no lie. While they had reeled from striking against a thundering menace, the armada had gone to task pinning them down without needing to relay orders to any other airbarge.

The Dellerin army doesn't do this shit under normal circumstances.

What is afoot?

How can we escape it?

Looking out across the flotilla of birds, Derian saw that many of the barges were sleek and sterile and similar in looks. They were the finest airbarges a king's money could buy. But among them, still flying in formation, were lesser machines, likely under mercenary ownership. That coldness came upon Derian once more and dropped into his belly. Up here, there were no unspoken agreements in place. Up here, no cur gave a shit about how precarious it would be to start some shit with mercenaries. Nobody would find out what had happened up here.

Up here.

The crossbow wielders suddenly separated and a long, thin, metallic platform appeared from within the behemoth's innards. Countless hands placed it out along the gap between two airbarges and, with no surprise whatsoever, Derian saw it was a perfect fit from one vessel to the other.

"They've done this before," he warned, and Natteo nodded.

"They've probably only taken peasant barges. All in the name of the king, without the Guild's protection. They've never faced a group like ours," Lorgan hissed, but his eyes were cold and calculating. He was clearly beginning to doubt their intentions.

"We'll send the cat after them," Natteo offered.

"Let's not be the fools starting a war, just yet. They should see our intentions and leave us be," Lorgan whispered as the dreadnaught's exit hatch filled with at least a dozen heavily armoured invaders ready to cross the great expanse. Their faceplates were thick and all covering. Derian couldn't see the eyes behind them, or the expressions either. Killer faceplates, in truth. That sinking feeling began to take him in earnest as the armoured figures began to move towards the skybridge.

From somewhere among them, a new figure emerged, and he was as tall as any of them. He differed in that his faceplate was absent and a silken cloak waved stylishly out behind him.

"We, of the Royal Dellerin Air Brigade, hereby seize this airbarge in the name of King Anguis," he bellowed, and Derian really hated his tone. It was always worse when the fiends were good looking and their voices were grating. He was older than Derian by a decade at least. He wore a pompous insignia across his chest that might have been a general's rank. Derian might have asked, but the call of that blade was whispering in his ear.

Kill them all.

"As a member of the Guild, you have no rights to such a thing," Lorgan countered, carefully stepping to meet them where the ladder invaded their territory. Despite his knee, he stood proud and tall in challenge. He wore no armour and held no weapon, but he was an intimidating sight. He spun to Natteo. "Don't draw a weapon. Use only fists if they attack," he whispered, low enough that the fiends across the bridge would have lost his words in the rushing wind. "A fistfight is allowed, but murder is the end of us all."

The fiends began to march across, three brutes apart, with their leader marching alone in their centre.

Natteo eyed the edge of the platform with fire in his eyes.

"Don't you dare, Natteo," Derian warned.

"I mean, who would know?" he countered, shrugging. "We could say they just fell."

"Shut your mouth, boy," Lorgan hissed, stepping forward to meet the invaders with diplomacy and tranquillity. "We can still get out of this," he added.

"We really can't," Natteo muttered and kicked half-heartedly at the edge of the bridge. Like any half-hearted kick, it did no damage at all.

The invaders must have taken umbrage with his show of petulance, for they began to rush across, their boots hammering loud against the thin metal platform, and in his panic, Derian couldn't help but think of a pole far below, in the depths of the sea.

"We mean you no harm. We are here to negotiate," the brute along the bridge yelled, and the dozen armoured invaders pulled heavy clubs from their belts in perfect unity. Derian was no fan of such clubs. Too agile, too devastating, too fuken unexpected. The club bearers charged towards their side of the deck, and Derian wondered just how painful negotiations with the Royal Dellerin Air Brigade were about to become.

Rather painful, was the answer.

Oh, Please Natteo, Shut the Fuk Up

Natteo left his wristbows unloaded. Despite himself, he knew Lorgan was right. It would be a satisfying thing to let loose and send one of those bastards to the ocean below, or the fires of hell thereafter, or else to simple nothingness, but living was a better tactic. He hated the Dellerin army, fuken hated them. He hated killing, really, but the Dellerin army were a special nasty. They weren't people at all.

Fuk the Dellerin army.

"There's no need for violence," the tall trespassing fiend offered to the three mercenaries, who stood in line blocking their breach of the barge. "We can be civilised."

"In the name of the Mercenary Guild, I forbid you entrance onto this barge," Lorgan roared, and still they marched forward across the precarious skybridge. "We will not draw blades, but we will display our grievance."

"Clubs aren't fatal. This is perfectly legal," argued the Dellerin spokesperson. He shared the despicable tone of a thousand and one politicians Natteo knew from his youth.

He wanted to break that skybridge something terrible, warmongering be damned.

"As long as the beating is all dignified," Natteo pointed out, gritting his teeth. He had such lovely teeth, and a better smile. He didn't want to lose them to a careless swinging club. "Maybe not in the face."

"Aw, spit on me. This is going to hurt," Derian muttered as the brutes raised their clubs in unison.

"Where the fuk is everyone else?" Natteo hissed, meaning the rest of the comrades. They could put up a fight just as pathetically with a few more on their side. Three against a dozen was hardly fair. "At least get the cat to back us up."

"To the fires with diplomacy, so," warned Lorgan, giving them permission. "Fight fiercely, and fall bravely, but do not kill under any circumstances. They don't want to start a war. We really don't want to start a war." A fine point. There was already a bounty on them as it was. Natteo cringed at the fine they'd have to pay to clear their name if they started an entire war.

"Aye, sir," both young mercenaries roared, as the shadows of menace came upon them.

"You were warned," Lorgan roared as the fiends entered their territory.

"I think this will all end in tears," Natteo cried.

"Mostly tears," agreed Derian, raising his fists and wincing as though he called upon the hidden beastie within him. A risky necessity, Natteo mused. He'd seen that monster fight right savagely. Bruises and blood were one thing, but loss of life was the beginning of very bad things. And Natteo couldn't help the feeling that everything was about to go terribly wrong and the Crimson were about to lose it all.

He wasn't entirely wrong.

Three sets of fists against a dozen swinging clubs was terrible odds, but mercenaries never counted such things. They merely went to war and hoped for the best, and more often than not, came out the other side.

The Crimson Hunters, less so.

Lorgan led the defence, striking the nearest invader directly in the face. With a metal clank, Lorgan's fist struck out and sent the brute's head snapping backwards. Despite the armour, he was knocked out cold. Lorgan grabbed the toppling brute and shoved him to one side, lest he accidently tip out over the edge to his doom.

"Show us your grin, you prick," Natteo cried, kicking a brute between the legs, then following through with a second blow to the cur's unprotected nether regions, leaving him gasping upon the deck.

Good thing it wasn't a woman.

Facing the next intruder in line, and certain his initial attacks wouldn't be as successful, Natteo leapt upon the man, screaming in his face as he wrapped his arms tightly around the fiend's neck, before dragging them both to the ground, squeezing as he did. It wasn't the best tactic, but Natteo was half the size of the armoured opponent, who struggled in his grip, and he didn't have the pugilistic skills of Lorgan, or the possible demonic savagery of Derian. He only hoped he could hold on long enough to put him to sleep. His other hope was that Derian could get in the way, taking a blow or two, and give him the time to leave the man limp.

"Go night-night, friend," he hissed as the larger fiend struggled earnestly. "Shush, shush. Stop struggling, and I'll let you nap," he whispered. The fiend didn't listen. He fought hard and struggled to his knees and Natteo wrapped himself tighter. He closed his eyes and awaited a strike to his back, or neck, or head, or wherever, really. It was all he could do. He was committed to this act.

Moments passed and another attacker fell in silence, his armour dented where Lorgan had smashed him. Feet surrounded Natteo as Derian fought ineptly against three larger brutes. It was something to do while this bastard withstood his brutal grip.

Just a moment longer.

"Please, enough of this," the lead attacker cried, and Natteo finally felt his victim fall still. He timed it perfectly, for a boot struck the diminutive mercenary on the side of the head, breaking his hold in the same moment.

"Ugh—that was a cheap shot, you spitting cur," Natteo gasped, grabbing his face, feeling the world darken and waiting for the savage pain to land. He caught sight of Kesta among the melee. She was just as ineffectual as Natteo, yet she struck and kicked at all before her and took hearty blows for her trouble. She was enraged and cursed the bastards something impressive, until a club caught her at the back of the head, knocking her to her knees, where a second strike knocked her out cold.

It was over in a few breaths, but the Crimson kept fighting. They hadn't realised it yet.

Derian managed to drag two curs with him across the deck, suffering winding blows to the belly as he did. He fought well without ever releasing his inner monster, but the clubs kept striking him until, with a sickening crack, his face exploded, teeth went flying and he fell clumsily to the deck, taking one of the battered fiends with him.

"In the name of King and war, I demand an end to this," roared their speaker. His cloak caught impressively in the wind as he stepped carefully aboard. He made no attempt to raise his fists or reach for the sword at his waist. Instead, like a disappointed parent, he waited for the children to cease their aggression.

"But we are winning," Natteo cried as another blow from behind him struck him senseless. His neck exploded in agony, and he was certain he heard a worrying snap as his body fell limp and he collapsed. For a breath, the world was still, and then they pulled him upright and he thought them complete and utter bastards. "You missed me," he mumbled drunkenly as they held him in place.

"You shouldn't have been up here," screamed Eveklyn, who appeared at the edge. She carried her axe and Natteo could only smile as she swung ineffectually against the nearest armoured cur, then fell to the ground as her axe bounced off the thick metal sheeting. "There should have been nothing but sky," she wailed, trying to rise.

"You need a better-suited weapon, darling," Natteo called across to her, and received a blow across the face from a gloved fist. "For fuk's sake, that wasn't even a funny enough jest to merit a strike," Natteo howled, dropping his head, counting his breaths and the dots in his eyes and forming what hate he could in his mind. When he could raise his head again, he gazed at the fighting child and was proud of her determination. Until a strike from a club knocked her silent and still.

You fuks! I'll kill you all, war be damned.

It wasn't just Natteo who was aggrieved, for Lorgan, somehow still fighting, lost his mind, and whatever restraint he might have had. He thundered through the club-wielding brutes, swinging recklessly with devastating combinations. His hands were a blur in the midst of a spray of blood, mostly his own, and Natteo saw the broken bones protruding through the skin. It didn't seem to matter. His rage gifted him wrath and it took all of the remaining curs an astonishing number of club blows to restrain him. Even then, they could only hold him on his knees where, semi-conscious, he fought, struggled, spat and cursed. Were Natteo capable of rising, he might have followed the cur all the way into the night.

The child stirred, and she might have wept, and this too enraged Natteo further. A deep anger from deeper within. An anger he hadn't called upon in a lifetime. Though adrenalin surged through him, he simply wasn't built with the necessary muscle mass to accomplish godly things like Lorgan did, or like Derian did when in his monstrous form.

Give them nothing but bile.

What he had was his wit, and his hate.

It had carried him through trying times. It would carry him now.

"Are we done," the speaker asked, standing over Lorgan, who snarled with unrivalled hate. "Will we discuss the manner of bartering?"

"I'd like you to piss off and play with yourself... you absolute dickhead," Natteo offered, and the speaker turned on him, waving cloak and all.

"And who are you, little pretty boy?"

"I'm a rather important passenger on this bird," Natteo lied, grinning. As he did, he felt a little give in one of his front teeth. "Very, very important. They call me Natteo, but you can call me... Natteo."

"Oh, just a passenger? So I can just throw you over the side, without starting a war?"

"I wouldn't do that. I'm the king's cousin. Loves me, he does," Natteo whispered, and there came a fierce strike to his temple. "More like a brother, really," he lied when the darkness cleared.

"Hold that tongue, boy, lest you make matters far worse," the fiend hissed, and shook his head as a brute stood over Natteo ready to strike a second time.

Natteo had every intention of making matters far worse than they were.

"Ah... no... I don't think I will... Fuk that—I'm only getting started," Natteo decided, and with his tongue he felt that tooth give a little more. Wherever the fuk she was, when she did appear, Seren could go about repairing his tooth first. Well, after the child, of course. That went without saying.

"You are not mercenaries at all?" the cur said to Lorgan, who spat on the deck. "This barge is well known. This barge is registered to the..." The Dellerin spokesman hesitated and tried to recall the most famous mercenary group in the world "... to the... Army of the Dead." He looked around as though some great reveal had occurred. "Now, I know few mercenary groups in Dellerin, but even I know that outfit, and you gentlemen are most certainly not the Army of the Dead."

"We are far better," Derian declared, struggling to his

knees, where immediately he was gripped by two fiends. A stream of blood covered the side of his head and he was pale from the beating he had taken. "Those fuks have nothing on us," he added weakly.

Both friends exchanged silent gazes that said more than enough.

"Think we are rightly spitting thurked."

"I'd say we are rightly thurken fuked."

"I'm rightly fuken scared, Derian."

"Fuken me too, brother. I don't think we'll live through this."

"You were supposed to make me feel better, not confirm the inevitability."

"Sorry, brother. I thought it was your turn."

"Nope. Can I add we are dead?"

"Not at all. We are going to be laughing about this in an hour."

"I feel better already."

Natteo dropped his gaze and tongued that loose tooth a little more. It moved enough that he could catch it in his smile, and he smiled really hard, and with a dreadful wrenching and near silent clunk it came loose. "Fantastic," he cried, and spat the tooth at the leader of the invaders; it fell upon his boots, leaving a little blood on the soft suede finish, so that was something at least. "It's a peace offering," Natteo declared with a delicate lisp, all the while smiling his most devastatingly disarming smile. Less effectively than usual, what with the bleeding gap and the streaming blood erupting from his mouth.

"Fuken peasant," the leader said with a sneer.

"Come say that to my face, you ugly, smelly bastard," roared Natteo, emphasising his lisp as heavily as he could.

"Enough, boy," the cur snapped, and spun on Lorgan. "My name is Clementine, and I speak for King Anguis."

Natteo wanted to mock him. The words formed on his lispy lips. Such an easy, cutting jest that wasn't worthy of his better wit. Still, he needed to keep aggravating the cur. He didn't know why, only that giving him a moment's respite seemed a terrible idea.

Say something wittier about his name.

"Sounds like a stupid fruit," Derian mocked, and hearing that exact mock from another set of lips reassured Natteo that holding his tongue was the smarter tactic. For Derian's "wit," he was struck with an open palm across the face. A lesser jest deserved a meeker punishment. Natteo approved and determined to get all his teeth knocked out.

Boab might not approve at all.

Then again, Boab might very much approve.

Regardless.

"Aw, come on. That mock hardly merited a strike," Natteo argued, and was struck for it. A weak enough strike. A warning too, no doubt. Shuffling on his knees and discovering wonderfully that his neck wasn't terribly broken and he still could walk, Natteo struggled a little more. "Wow, that is one hist of a strike." He fought them harder now. "My boyfriend is a bit of a bitch. Arms like onions. But he beats me harder than that."

They gripped harder. A few of them told him to shut up and he began to laugh.

"But he's got a shed-load of really impressive friends, and when he finds out you fuks assaulted me, you are dead…" Natteo fell silent, and his eyes went serious. "Every one of you ugly fuks is going to die."

At this a brute struck him in the belly. That fuken hurt, and curses upon himself, he yelped as his breath escaped.

"Leave it, Natteo," Lorgan ordered, and with all his strength, shoved his keepers away. He stood up and remained still. "No more violence, just amicable negotiations," he offered, and Clementine raised his hands and all hands released their grips.

"The Guild are going to find you all," roared Natteo, remaining on his knees. "You are all dead, so dead. Oh, you are fuked."

"Can you shut him up?" Clementine asked of Lorgan.

"Why shut him up? He speaks the truth," Lorgan warned. At this he pulled a tooth of his own from his mouth, inspected it in the light and flicked it at the Dellerin leader, who recoiled in horror, and Natteo thought Lorgan rightly polished in that moment. More than that, Lorgan had just given him permission to keep nattering away.

Lorgan can see how much it is unsettling them.

"You can kill us all you fuken want, but there is no hiding one of the most recognisable airbarges in Dellerin," Natteo mocked. "Oh, you fuked up. You are going to start a fuken war."

"There's no need to talk further of war. We are within our rights to commandeer this barge," Clementine countered and appeared as any weak card player might when gambling a pot. The trick was finding out first if he bluffed or panicked. After that it was a case of draining him dry.

"Speak your terms, and be on your way," Lorgan hissed, finding strength in every word. It was one thing to assassinate a group of mercenaries in a remote town where word would hardly spread. It was something else entirely to do it with a few thousand sets of eyes watching this unfold. Oh aye, armies spoke of such things and word would spread of a little murder of mercenaries upon a famous airbarge. Not to mention the spies within the army itself.

"I have orders from the King, himsel—"

"I highly doubt that," Lorgan interrupted.

Clementine continued after a breath. "... Orders from higher command that all airbarges without banner be taken into service for the good of the nation."

"I hear your argument and counter," Natteo declared. "How about you get to fuk, you smelly, ugly fuk duck muck herders."

He was rather proud of that one, and for his troubles he received a devastating blow to the face that knocked him to the deck painfully. He could only laugh. "Yer all dead. Every one of you. The Guild will know of this. They'll fuken know and fuk you all up."

"Stop fuken saying that," one of the assailants roared. He stood over Natteo and stamped down upon his chest, breaking at least a rib on the way, and despite the agony, the tears, the gasping, Natteo could only laugh. He would not be bested. Would show the level of strength a mercenary had, even one as inept as he, even at the end of his life.

"Stop fuken saying that," the cur screamed again and continued stamping down upon Natteo violently until his own comrades pulled him away.

"Go on, you bastards. Throw me over the edge. You may as well. You've gone way too far as it is. You can't kill me—I'll fly right fuken back at you all," he bellowed, coughing up blood. It might have been from his tooth, possibly his lungs. He'd never been more scared in his life, but he'd never felt more alive. More in control. Angrier. Aye, he would likely die, and probably for good, but he would tear their souls apart along the way. He didn't know why he thought as much, but it felt right.

Struggling onto all fours, he crawled towards his assailant, laughing, coughing, gasping. Determined and intimidating.

"Enough of this," Clementine roared. "Throw them over the side. We'll burn the barge where it flies," he snarled.

"That won't work. I'll fly right back. Wave my fuken wings and come for you!" Natteo screamed in defiance; in desperation, too. "You are all dead. I fuken know this, Clementine, but do it you ugly fuk. Fuken do it and wait for the gallows," Natteo pleaded, and they dragged him to his feet. Dragged him to the edge of the barge.

And threw him off.

Fuk.

After the Murder

Lorgan watched his comrade go over the edge and he lost all rationality. Perhaps it was the concussion finishing him off. Tearing away from the grip of his keepers and leaping for the nearest sword, he took hold and felt immediately better about himself. It was better to rage and kill than to accept Natteo's demise. He was old, and he felt older. He was used to losing warriors under his command, although it was never easy. In fact, every death by his hand took away from whatever pitiful bits remained of his soul, and now there was little left.

Natteo's loss was tenfold the horror, for the boy's spirit was a breath of fresh air to Lorgan's tiring lungs. He was more than a comrade. He was closer to what Lorgan imagined a son might have been. Derian too, admittedly, but he'd never tell either one of them. Natteo, however, was a different beast to Derian and the smouldering potential that he possessed. Natteo was a fire, and he caught every single one of the Crimson's branches and burned brighter with them. Why? Because he was a born leader, even if

Natteo didn't see it himself. But that was alright. Lorgan had long believed the boy would grow into the role. Become more than a quick-witted, charming cur. He was but a step from greatness, and as they beat him down, Lorgan was prouder of him than ever before.

Natteo led with his defiance; he cut their souls apart with his grinning words. In killing Natteo, the fiends committed a true act of war. The Dellerin Kingdom allowed the Mercenary Guild to act out in defiance against the King by the simple act of indifference. And the Mercenary Guild, though outnumbered greatly, would never back down. But killing one of their own was no act of indifference any longer.

You struck first and I will live to tell of your atrocity.

The blade was Derian's. There was little chance it would erupt in fire and ferocity, for it carried no such hidden enchantment. It had an impressive history, however, and had embedded itself deep in the belly of a grand demon. Not to mention Derian's unprotected leg.

"You all will die," he roared.

Enraged, and filled with shock and grief, Lorgan broke away and charged the nearest guard. He heard screams of warning and wariness and he grinned as he raised his blade. Let the pricks be wary. He wanted to kill, to tear, to feed and to destroy, and he wanted to wail for his last lost comrade, lost over the edge.

In his mind, Derian's pledges of Arturo's deeds rushed through his mind and a cold horror came upon him. To Arturo, Derian was more important. Natteo was no godly hound. Were Derian to go back over the side, it would be Arturo who would insist they find him. Even if he were dashed to pieces, the strange weaver would insist that the boy was not lost. But nobody believed Natteo something special.

It really wasn't fair at all.

Gathering his strength for one faithful charge, and full of determination to kill them all, Lorgan went to war. The blade was unimpressive, like his leadership, but in his grip, he felt stronger, fiercer... fresher? He knocked the fiends away as they attempted to grasp him and towards Clementine he charged, roaring as he went.

Out the corner of his eye, he caught sight of movement and the flash of a silken red dress.

Seren.

And to the other side he caught sight of another flicker of movement, but it made no sense. A screaming figure waving and floundering like a fish upon an angler's hook, or an airbarge caught by speared chains, and it floated ahead of him before falling roughly before his feet.

"What the fuk?" cried Natteo, gasping, panting, bleeding all over the boots of those who had murdered him only moments before.

It can't be, Lorgan thought, hesitating for just a breath at the sight of his young comraded floundering on the sturdy deck. He looked wild and frantic and no doubt shaken to be alive. Lorgan knew the reason had to be an enchanter's gift and was grateful for their prisoner's freedom. He imagined the old cur, hidden among the decks, seeing Natteo's flailing body pass by through a porthole and thinking the better act was saving the cur after all. Lorgan had been loath to believe Arturo's protestations of innocence. That Seren wasn't at all the person he'd believed her to be, and therefore posed little further threat to any of the mercenaries aboard. He thought again of the many comrades he'd lost or sacrificed or downright damned through weak leadership and he couldn't help imagine he was using up a lifetime of a mercenary's better luck over these last few days.

Nobody can kill a Crimson Hunter anymore.

"What is this?" demanded Clementine upon seeing the young mercenary fall back on the deck. "Who are you?" he cried. "What are you?"

Lorgan didn't wait for Natteo's cutting reply. With thundering shoulder barges, he hammered through the four soldiers separating him from their leader, earning just a moment's breath, before finally raising his sword and swinging upon the army general.

It was an easy kill, worthy of starting a war and thus placing a price too steep upon his mercenary group. The brute was distracted by the sudden reappearance of a young man he'd committed to death. Not even his thick armour would withstand the blow Lorgan sought; he struck towards the neck where leather and fabric held too thin a plate of metal veneer.

"It was the wind that carried me aboard," Natteo cried in his ear, laughing manically, his words protecting the hidden weavers aboard, although with an unlikely reason. Only then did Lorgan see another mercenary swinging for Clementine.

He felt the fire from Derian's sword scorch his hair as it passed beside him, blinding and cutting.

"To the fires with you," Derian wittily roared, and both

his and Lorgan's sword exploded in a sheen of blue and bright yellow sparks as they struck in perfect unison.

Flying.

Spinning.

Falling.

A dreadful shudder of lightning shook Lorgan to the core as it lifted him high and sent him careening back across the deck where, moaning in agony, he sat upright and held the quivering blade out in front of him.

Around him all soldiers and mercenaries lay as dazed as he. Everything was silent and high-pitched all at the same time, as though a grand sky cannon had erupted right beside him. The world was unfocussed for a breath, and for a breath more nothing in the world mattered but the stillness all around them.

That and the two lone figures who walked side by side upon the deck.

One of them was female and she was gorgeous. As though a veneer of his mind had been torn away, he knew immediately that something was different in Seren's very being. She strode confidently, and were he to believe in such hallowed things as a soul, he might swear in that moment he saw her encased in a shimmer of magenta haze that gleamed like the soul of a god. In a flash, though, it was gone, but her red silk dress caught in the wind and she was mesmerizing. Her hair rushed wildly about her head, and suddenly, he did not fear for his comrades or regret causing a war. She looked likely to tear each of these beasts from the sky with a flick of her wrists, with a wink of her godly eyes.

"Who are you?" Clementine called from his place among his stunned comrades upon the deck.

"We are just... travellers," Arturo declared, standing by her side. As magnificent as she was, he was a whisper of a man. There was no sheen; there was only a glimmer of a rotted, hollow shell. "And who might you be?" he asked in a croaky voice.

In Lorgan's youth, he had seen a rather impressive gathering of weavers as broken and withered as this man was now. That was the cost of wielding from one's own essence, he remembered learning. The greatest weavers could barely stand. Aged decades before their time, with young minds and failing bodies. It was a cost few were eager to accept. Lorgan thought otherwise. He hated getting old every thurken day.

"You are spitting weavers, aren't you?" Clementine sneered. "Take them," he roared.

"Less of that language... um... please," Arturo said, and raised his arm, pulling at his collar.

There came a dreadful whoosh from all around them, a piercing hiss that any mercenary would recognised as death most probable.

Bolts and arrows.

As there had been countless eyes gazing upon the events from the surrounding barges, there were also most certainly dozens of archers primed and ready, and the explosion of weaving prompted the curs to let loose. Perhaps it was instinct, perhaps they heard Clementine's orders, for Lorgan closed his eyes, covered up, waiting for the hiss and clunk of arrows and bolts as they struck everyone upon the deck.

This is the end.
Goodbye, pretty world.

I tried my best.
The end.
The absolute spitting end.
Any breath now.
Any breath now.

Moments passed and there were no screams; there was only the rush of wind and the steps of the two weavers upon the deck, and Lorgan dared to face the cloud of projectiles that hung in the air.

"How can this be?" demanded Clementine, but Lorgan most certainly knew.

It was Arturo who caught them in an invisible grasp. He held his quivering hand in the air and the projectiles answered his command, or perhaps embedded themselves in an invisible forcefield.

"Nobody desires there to be war this day... although there is probably war... though not out here... not yet, at least," Arturo called out, and with his other hand he caught a second volley of projectiles. "Now, now, friends... There's no need for that," he said, and his voice was carried on the wind. It boomed out across the entire flying armada and it was a terrifying thing. With steel and less dreaminess to his words, he spoke again. "There will be no more assaults upon us, lest we... burn you all from the sky."

Nobody fired another bolt, and Lorgan wasn't surprised. His body still quivered from the tones reverberating through him. Arturo appeared weak and diminished, but that voice was a godly thing. Who knew if he could indeed burn each airbarge from the sky with just a flick of his fingers.

Sighing, Arturo walked over to Clementine.

"You will not live through this," Clementine warned, gathering his wits, completely unperturbed by this show of force, and he was determined to start a war, or at least kill them all. Lorgan had to respect his blind dedication. The man simply did not realise he was no longer the fiercest force in the clouds.

Or else he knows the exact amount of power Arturo is capable of producing.

Perhaps he suspects Arturo is at his limit?

"I might not live to the end of another moment… but, until then… I will live them well," Arturo insisted. Looking around like a painter surveying a landscape, he suddenly gave another deep sigh, then allowed his hand to drop, and a few arrows were released from his hold. They tore across the deck and embedded themselves in a group of the attackers. Clementine took one through his shoulder and he howled in angry agony. "Are we… calmer?" Arturo asked, eyeing the unlucky group as they squirmed and struggled with protruding bolts and arrows. He did not kill a single one, and Lorgan was grateful for his mercy. He didn't know how this was going to play out, but it most certainly seemed beneficial nobody was killed.

Just a little stabbing is all.

"I am compelled by law to take you, swine," Clementine growled, but he was losing the will. He held the bolt as Seren stood over him. Until now, she had remained silent, instead studying her battle comrade as he held fast an entire air brigade.

"That injury could become serious," she said quietly.

"What? Who are you?" Clementine spluttered. After a breath, he didn't care. "Fuk off, girly," he added. Around him, his guards remained stoic and careful. They didn't speak for him. They had seen enough and were willing to answer to Arturo.

"I am… Seren," Seren wittily countered, and raised her hand, and with it, all Clementine's soldiers were lifted skyward as though it was no effort at all. All but Clementine, that is, who stood to face her wrath without blinking. Without being impressed either. Seren simply nudged all of the soldiers out over the edge, then released them all to fall a few feet before holding each again in her invisible grip.

A potent bargain without any words, but Clementine remained unmoved. Lorgan was no longer impressed; instead he thought the fool brazen and zealous.

"You think I care about a single one of these fiends?" Clementine roared, and his voice carried. It echoed across the armada as Arturo's voice had. "I would let them all fall before I bow to you," he roared, and it echoed, and he seemed perturbed there had been an enchantment placed upon them without his knowledge.

"Oh, I think we have made our point, dearest… Seren," Arturo decided and stepped to Clementine, revealing his rolled-up sleeve as before. "I think we have paid them back enough for the anguish they have caused our friends."

From his arm there shone a golden tattoo similar to the demon mark that had marred Seren's perfect porcelain skin, though with less decoration. This one, however, simply glowed.

"My lord," Clementine howled, dropping to a knee immediately. Seren recovered each of the soldiers from the fall and returned them back to the deck. She did not offer any healing. Perhaps Clementine had ruined their chances of that. Regardless, the recovered soldiers all dropped to an obedient knee as Clementine had, recognising the mark of the Anguished One and understanding his authority immediately. "Forgive my actions," Clementine begged, and perhaps Arturo had every intention of offering mercy. "I and my soldiers are at your service. What will you have us do?"

The soldiers Clementine had been willing to sacrifice seemed not to be as contrite as their leader, judging by their scowls as they knelt in front of Arturo, all casting dangerous glances towards Clementine.

"I think you fukers need to begin by taking those spitting harpoons from my baby," Kesta roared, and Natteo cackled in delight at this sudden change of events. Once more, Lorgan wondered what godly luck was walking hand in hand with them these last few days.

And when it would run out.

Soon enough, was the answer.

The Breaking of Rock

The thunder reverberated loudly around the room. It sounded like death. A dreadful symphony of crushing music, dreadful and awful all in the same moment, and one to be stuck in your head all day and in your mind all your life.

Erin lay crumpled in the corner. It felt like the only safe place to be, dusty and cobwebbed as it was. With her hands over her ears, she whimpered a prayer to absent gods and fought the urge to relieve herself.

"You can hide away all you like, but it matters little," Florian said from his seat. She could see he neared the end of the book. He was a swifter reader than she. Perhaps he was a skimmer. Erin was no skimmer. When she read a book she studied every spitting line, every thurken word at that. She lost herself in every tale. Florian had the look of a man who missed plenty as he flipped from page to page. That flipping increased in speed as he eagerly neared the explosive finale. She knew he neared the end, for she watched him closely. There was nothing better to do these last few hours than stare at his good-looking features and wait.

"Aye, if this building falls, there will be no safe corner to hide in, girly," Otto said. He remained on top of the boxes, where he'd been for the past few hours. Probably all he could do to distract himself from the thundering noise. Watching the shadows of giant boulders as they careened across the sky crushing the magnificent city of Dellerin was a sight he shared with Erin every time it occurred. It didn't help her nerves. "Oh, here comes another," he suddenly cried, and the piercing whistle of a thrown boulder filled the air. There was a booming crash and the room shook, but there came no awful crack of rock on stone. "Ah, your comrades really made a mess of that one," he added as the world fell silent, leaving her with a slight ringing in her ears.

By the light in the sky, she knew it was well into the afternoon and the boulders would be stopping their barrage. How her nerves had lasted to this hour was a miracle in itself, but with every strike that shook the house, they were becoming rightly shredded.

"They should be finishing up by now," she whispered, listening to the distant rumbling crash of more successful strikes.

"Aye, that may be true," Florian said, and turning a page, looked at her for the first time in hours. "You will have the good grace to wait until I finish this rather impressive tale," he said, before returning to the book. It was a question, but also a warning. Some people became dreadfully aggravated while reading this book. It wasn't the first time she'd seen this. She hoped it wouldn't be the last.

"You still have plenty of hours to reach the front gate

before the hounds come a-hunting," Otto muttered, his eyes on the sky again. He seemed to relish the abuse the building was taking. Every time a solitary boulder struck the old building, he whooped and jeered, sneering that her distant army comrades "couldn't break through" because of "Finest Venistrian stone." She knew Venistrian blades were tempered to perfection, but she'd never heard much about their stone. She wasn't inclined to argue the matter at this late hour. He probably knew better. In the time they had shared since he'd struck out at her, he had displayed a little restraint, a greater calmness, and just a taste of politeness as well. He was still taken by a madness she hoped she'd never endure herself, but his rantings were more civil as they faced the barrage, his intelligence quite obvious.

"I will take my chances when the time comes," Erin murmured and rubbed at her aching legs. Though the room was still dimly lit, one of the dozen or so strikes had caused a great crack along the wall to separate wide enough that the sun shone through. Such a crack in the wall worried her greatly, but none of the others seem worried. "And what of any of you?" she asked the room and met silence. "Would you flee with me to the gates?"

"And what life would that be?" Otto asked. "I would take a look at the first soldier and likely lose my temper; my head after that."

"Your family would want you to live," she countered, and he stiffened. It was probably not her place to speak of such things. Even if he'd shown a little sanity on his part. He clutched the edge of the window and she near expected him to leap down and thrash at her again.

"Perhaps they did. Perhaps I want to live as well," he said softly.

"It is only a matter of time before they take this building down. We can leave when the barrage eases," she offered. They were not her friends, nor even her comrades, but this tomb of a tower was no place to die.

"Perhaps I do want to die after all," Otto replied. "Perhaps I wish to meet my family," he said after a time. It was a fair reply. "Besides, I know this beauty of a building can take it just fine."

"What of you all?" Erin asked of the women in the far room, who, as they had all day, ignored her completely.

"Don't bother talking to them. They are enduring their own torment in silence," Florian said. He looked from the book to the women in the room and he appeared sad. "Whatever agonies they've endured these last few days have taken whatever will for life they had.

"All of them?" she asked.

"They spoke a little the first day," Otto murmured. "Among themselves."

"Less and less since then; I expect it's all that keeps them moving, keeps them breathing," Florian added.

"All these horrors placed upon the citizens, and for what?" Otto asked, not unkindly, merely wistfully.

"The King is an evil man, and we are justified in this war," she countered immediately, but her words were hollow in this room. Their world had been torn asunder for the crime of living in the grandest city on the continent. Everything they knew and loved was lost because generals, without their knowledge, had decided there were more pressing things afoot.

Erin could see the world from their tragic point of view, or at least witness a glimmer. She could have argued more, offered righteous hyperbole, but simply fell silent. If they came with her when she broke for the gates, they would be taken in, cared for. Treated humanely. It was better than waiting out the siege, surviving on what they could. Waiting to die.

With a deep exhale, Florian snapped the book shut and leaned back in his chair. "Well, that was a read," he said, holding the old tome in his hands before stretching and offering it back to her. "There is something to it," he said thoughtfully.

"Perhaps I should read it," Otto said, and peered out into the afternoon. "They look to have spent most of their ammunition. There aren't as many taking flight."

Reluctantly, lest he gather her into his arms for some reason, Erin took back the book as though it were an unwanted gift. The burden of its importance fell upon her once more, and she couldn't help wonder if it was all in her mind. Upon touching the book, she felt a surge of fire in her fingers again, though this time it emanated from the leather cover.

It burns like fire.

Dropping it in shock, she instinctively reached for it a second time and took the burning heat for what it was.

A warning.

"I have to get out of here," she suddenly cried, stuffing the tome into her pack and reaching for the door.

"Be still, little one," Florian hissed. He stood up beside the wardrobe and leaned on it. "You should wait a little longer. The boulders are just about finished."

"They are finished, let her go," Otto called.

"I have to go. I have to get out of here."

"Open the door, Florian," Otto conceded, dropping down to the floor again, and she felt the panic rise. There was death coming. She knew it in her bones. Her aching, aching bones. "Let the girly out into the day."

"She could still be crushed," Florian argued.

"Ah, whisht. If you liked her so much, you should have tried charming her the last few hours instead of reading a fuken book."

"I think we are all in terrible danger," she cried manically, sprinting away from the arguing, doomed men. She turned to face the silent women. "We can all escape. I can promise you safety in the army," she cried, grabbing at the blouse of the closest one, hoping to pull her from her silent distraction. She received nothing but a blank stare, before the women returned to their bubbling vats of watery gruel. Behind her, at the door, Florian pulled at the wardrobe. It screeched something terrible as he eased it away from the door.

"We most certainly will be in terrible danger the next few days," Florian offered. "Be it from King Anguis's demonic fire, or the barrage of your army storming through the palace." He shrugged as the door opened, delivering safety, uncertainty and daylight, all in the creak of an old oak door. He gestured impatiently for her to leave lest a giant boulder sneak in while he wasn't watching. "But I would rather take my chances digging in here until there is an accord."

To the fires with you all.

Get out of my way, get out of my way, get out of my way.

Will you come too?

She couldn't stay a moment longer. She couldn't convince them otherwise, so, grabbing her pack, Erin darted through the doorway out into the freedom of the precarious day. They slammed the door behind her, and the scraping of the wardrobe across the door stirred her to move. She was alone with a simple plan. Anything was better than being cooped up like a clucking hen, waiting for slaughter.

"Take care of yourself, girly," Otto called out, and she did not look back. Her eyes were upon the marred ground where Rhendal had impressively slain so many. Had fallen too. There were no bodies left behind, nor was there a sign of the valiant warrior, and she felt his loss anew.

Sprinting past the human bloodstains, she leapt through the break in the fence where the fiends had torn through and she kept running. The sunlight burned her eyes, as did the dust from the rubble. All around her the land had been levelled. A strange thing to come upon in a once bustling city. Behind her, the tower stuck out even more than before, and she wondered if her army comrades, safe outside the wall with rocks so sturdy, saw the standing tower as an offence to their menace. They had dashed it a dozen times this day alone, and still it stood. She knew soldiers who would take offence at such defiance.

Skidding over the rubble, she charged towards the flattest area she could find. Easier thought than done, for the land was still unstable and precarious where she stepped. Keeping an eye to the sky as she moved, she felt her heart begin to settle, her nerve begin to return, her hopes to stir potently.

Distantly, above the ruined streets and blocked walkways, she could see the gates beckoning to her. By now, the attacking army would hold them securely, no matter what the air brigade threw at them. A costly thing to those who died, but that was war. The inhabitants within suffered, but so did those with righteous beliefs. The King needed to topple. The world could recover after that.

As long as the newer king has a soul.

Suddenly, a shadow came upon her, looming and awful. She looked to the sky, to where the sun should have blinded her eyes, and froze in horror to see a great boulder above her head, near silent but for a high-pitched squeal as it spun and cut through the air. The boulder neared and fell towards her, dashing the ground in front of her and erupting in a debris-laden explosion.

Drop.

The rock filled her vision. It was ten times the size of her. It could have smashed her to nothing and nobody would ever have known she was below it. No one would ever have known she had once been alive before an awful, awful end. She might have reached out and touched it as it bounced once and then shot upwards again to crush all in its wake. Bless her luck and reflexes, for she followed her instinct and dropped as it neared her.

This is the end.

The world went dark as it careened over her, missing her head by a foot or less before bouncing behind her, rolling for a time, knocking against similarly thrown boulders and then coming to a stop in the ruined landscape.

She lay in the dust as it settled around her, tears streaming down her cheeks, and knew that this was the moment she had feared while inside the room. Somehow, she had known a boulder was near destined to take her. Sitting up and coughing away the dust from her gasping lungs, she climbed to her shaky feet.

Distantly, she heard a mocking cheer from Otto and she dared a smile. She must have looked like the most pathetic of idiots, running straight out into a boulder's path. She spun to bow mockingly in reply and, in a way, to say goodbye to the companions whose greed had allowed her to live. She should have hated them, but she understood them, just as Rhendal had. He had accepted their need to punish immediately. He had been willing to balance the sins of his army.

"You should have stayed in here, girly," Otto called from the window.

She dared a laugh. And why not? He was probably right.

And suddenly another shadow appeared around her. Another boulder, shooting across the sky at a terrific rate.

"Woohoo!" cried Otto as the deadly projectile struck the building head on. Fine defiance altogether. She marvelled for a pulse of time before she realised the boulder had continued on its way—right through the window he had stood in.

With a terrible roar, the large structure imploded upon itself, and she could not look away.

OUT OF THIS OUTFIT

"Damn you, Arturo," Lorgan roared, and the entire table rocked as he struck it fiercely. Those sitting around it jumped. Derian, who was closest, probably most of all. He was rocking in his chair at the time, listening to its squeak, and nearly took a spill. It was something to do while Lorgan caught his breath and thought a little more about throwing Arturo over the edge. Derian knew this because the thundering mercenary had begun the meeting with that very statement. No one had argued; they knew to stay clear of a whirlwind as it moved across their path. Also, they weren't rightly sure if it wasn't the correct move. Though he'd never met the man and likely had no argument with him, they were fairly certain Anguis the Dark One was not a stand-up fellow. That one of his acolytes had stolen aboard under false pretences was bad enough. That the fiend had earned their trust was near unforgivable. He claimed he did not serve Anguis. Moreover, he claimed to desire a place among the Crimson

Hunters. But that's what a nasty little spy would say, wouldn't he?

He could have killed us all ten times over these last few days.

He could have left me to die.

Evil fiends can come good, can't they?

The world these days certainly didn't think so.

Lorgan fumed and for a breath, Derian wondered if the mercenary was even capable of following through with his threat. Arturo was weak as fuk, but who knew the level of sorcery he was still capable of.

"You should have told us," he roared, and those fists drove down hard once more. Kesta opened her mouth to protest the behemoth abusing a perfectly innocent table but then fell silent. Perhaps she thought the breaking of a table was worth the wrath the old weaver was facing. Perhaps she preferred Lorgan take his fierce temper out on the table rather than an old weaver. They were all alive, thanks to the old cur.

"Aye, I should have said so many things... wonderful things..." Arturo replied happily from his chair opposite. He offered a smile, but Derian could see his eyes were weak. He was less the simple old man from a few days before. Now he was a withered creature looking to the end. His jawline was more pronounced, as though his wrinkled skin was pulled tighter across his grinning skull, like the skin of a corpse. He was hunched over, as though he'd gone a month without sleep. Perhaps that was what death was—an inability to escape such dreadful tiredness. Derian had died too quickly to understand the finer details of stepping into the dark. "About many wonderful things... but I say them now… And I say them true… I believe," Arturo added, shrugging weakly.

"Spitting fiends concealing greater things," Natteo said bitterly. He sat beside Derian in the galley. Unlike the rest of the comrades, he had a mug of steaming tea in front of him. Fate-deciding meeting or not, he would ensure he had a beverage to call upon. Derian licked his lips. He wouldn't have minded a mug himself. Little shit should have offered as he brewed the tea, adding two spoons full of honey while he was at it. They said the king of hell liked his tea with a little honey too. Natteo was as far from a hell king as one could be.

"We should be done with you," Lorgan warned, but did not strike the table a third time. Derian knew that dangerous tone all too well. Not even Natteo's antics could hook that tone. He'd heard it rarely enough these past few years, but knew it was murderous. Few survived that tone. Arturo looked ready to take his chances, though. Perhaps he trusted his enchantments. Perhaps with Seren as his unlikely ally, he was in little peril.

"This is such a… lovely airbarge… Would you have brought me aboard… with such knowledge…? I think not… and it is very important… very important… so very superbly important… that I fly with you," Arturo countered. He looked around at the Crimson Hunters and smiled. "I am among friends, and you are all friends to me… I was never a friend to the Dark Anguished One… but yes, I served him… but no more… He wouldn't even remember me… such are the years." He made a gesture with his fingers, fluttering them like the wings of a butterfly. "Lost in the wind… and weaker for it… but here…" He rapped his knuckles on the table. "Here... I am home again."

"How are we to know it wasn't you who had these fiends entrap us in the sky?"

Arturo frowned, thought for a long enough time before answering and seemed perfectly happy with his reply. "That wasn't me."

Lorgan spun away, fit to kill, fit to do something stupid. "For the love and hate of the seven gods, would someone shut this thurken fool up."

Natteo winced and made a throat-slitting gesture. It wasn't looking good, and the old fool wasn't helping himself. They were still flying in formation with the armada, but there was land below on which they could drop him off. Perhaps they'd even go so far as to land first.

Regretfully, Derian hadn't placed a wager on the outcome of the meeting. Natteo would claim death. Derian would have claimed banishment at worst. He also suspected that once Lorgan thought on the matter a little and shouted a little more, he might even welcome the cur into the Crimson Hunters. They were already breaking the law with having a weaver. May as well double down.

"Shut me up...? Hmmm, yes... A good idea... But I have so many things to say... not many of use... but some." With outstretched arms, he pleaded with Lorgan, but the effort appeared to take a lot out of him. His fingers quivered unnaturally with the type of shake belonging to a drunkard begging on the streets when you have only an apple to offer. Certainly, Seren's lessons with him were paying off, but at what cost? It was she who had caught Natteo, prevented him from falling to his doom. She was a far cry now from the girl who dared to command a little fire a week before. And nothing at all a week before that. Overall, her progress was rather promising.

"Tell me why we shouldn't send you off with the armada," Lorgan muttered.

"We should have said something," Seren suddenly said. "I know Lorgan would not have killed you for simply being marked with Anguis's sign," she offered.

We?

Seren appeared positively radiant, sitting beside Arturo, staring down Lorgan with an uneasy, intrigued gaze, as though aroused at seeing this pure anger for the first time. Derian knew such things tempted some such girls. Saying that, just as many probably found reassurance in gentle, kinder tones. Everyone was different. Trying to predict with any accuracy the emotions of any person was a futile game at best. Seren did not blink, and Derian could swear there was a deeper redness to her cheeks as she watched the older man—and he was old enough to be her father... or a step-uncle—storm around the room, filling it with his temper.

A week before, Derian would have been jealous of such a gaze, but since the slaying of the second demon and Seren's taking of his soul with her healing, he was very much colder to her than ever before. More than that, Natteo's suggestion that she had cast a charm lure upon them all was growing more plausible every day. Now that he was aware, it would wear off soon.

They always wear off, right?

"It's alright, Lorgan," Seren said. "He told me when we first sparred," she said, and Lorgan struck the table and stormed fiercely up to the girl.

"How dare you keep such a thing from me?" he roared in her face, and for an entire breath she stood firm in his gaze before faltering beneath him. It was an impressive thing and a reminder of who ruled these mercenaries. He might not have the enchantments to call upon, but there was a different force to him. "You storm through this barge as though you own it. You care only for your own thoughts," Lorgan shouted, before marching around the table and driving his fist against the wall behind her.

"You've done it now, Seren," Natteo said aloud. He looked positively thrilled. Lorgan was dominating both weavers with nothing more than his voice alone.

And a few punches of inanimate objects as well.

"Know your place, chosen one," Lorgan roared again, and she wilted completely. She quivered as she held his gaze, and her eyes watered up as though not understanding that her actions (or lack thereof) had brought about this wrath. Derian had tasted these screaming challenges a number of times these past years. As good as the Lorgan love pat was, the "Lorgan screamed wrath" was a thousand times worse and far more effective—as fierce as Seren was, and capable of terrifying feats, Lorgan's scream was enough to tear her apart. Derian almost spoke up for her. And thought better of it.

This needs to happen.

She needs to learn.

This is a good thing.

Kesta didn't think it was a good thing at all. "She is new to this world, Lorgan." She met his eyes, her motherly instinct to protect overcoming her own weariness and anger. "Give her a little freedom to make mistakes," she said, and winked gently at the weaver.

Lorgan's face turned a cherry red and for a moment, Derian remembered a recurring scene from his childhood: his parents sitting over dinner arguing over some scrape Derian had found himself in. He remembered the wrath of his bitter father and the calm kindness of his mother, who would ease her husband's wrath by redirecting his rage at more important things, like the latest trades being worth absolute shit, or the ever-rising cost of tin in the surrounding villages.

"I did not know... I wasn't thinking... I thought... um..." Seren countered, and his hand suddenly dropped to her shoulder. Powerful hands. Perfectly capable of thrashing her against the wall until she was knocked senseless. But also, tender enough to hold a mounting panic attack, or to ease the fears of a girl unsure of what a panic attack was. Derian knew well what such an attack was. He wished it on nobody but his enemies.

"You must learn our ways better, girl," Lorgan suddenly said, and once more Derian wondered if she hadn't cast an unspoken lure under her breath to win his favour. He wished he knew more of weaving in that moment, wished it something fierce. He might have asked Arturo, might have asked Seren too, but he was not part of their world. He was his own monster, without the gift of enchantments. It was enough for him. It was far too much.

"I am learning. I just thought about bettering myself," she said, with a breaking voice like a child's, and again Derian was reminded how new to the world she was.

"What will become of me?" Arturo asked.

Derian always wanted to look on the better sides of people, even if he hated them as a whole. He was complex and deep that way. It was a shame the women didn't see him as such.

"Back in chains," Lorgan murmured.

"I pledge my fealty to you," Arturo offered. It wasn't the first time he'd offered such words. This time, though, there was a dreadful pleading to his tone, as though he knew he would never emerge from that room again.

"You pledge out of desperation and selfishness," Lorgan countered.

"Are there any better ways to pledge?"

It was a fine and truthful answer. "Do I appear as though I can offer much of a threat aboard this barge?"

"You roasted Seren something fierce," Natteo offered helpfully.

"That is true godly one," Arturo whispered. "I no longer possess such fierceness... Seren would no longer burn as she did..."

"I can better him," she said in agreement, and eyed Lorgan curiously.

"You could barely survive his attacks before," Derian countered, and she winced.

"I was holding back... didn't want to kill him."

"We could vote," Natteo said delightedly, getting up from the galley table. His eyes were on the main deck and the returning fiends as they scampered back across the airbridge.

"I will choose," Lorgan warned.

"Oh, come on, boss. You know he's harmless to us. He just wants to join our merry group, and I, for one, would like him on our side when Seren turns on all of us... No offence, Seren."

Seren looked confused for a breath, then hurt, then confused again, and then she grinned for the jest it was. "Yes, Natteo. He can protect you all from scary Seren... aagh... Spit on this... I mean... scary me. He can protect you all from scary me." She muttered a curse under her breath, lamenting that her words had become fuddled again. For some reason, she could recall most of her language, but every now and then, her words ended up in the wrong order, or with the wrong meaning. It was rather endearing seeing her curse herself for an issue so small.

"See. That's it," Natteo declared, standing up suddenly. He decided to rush the matter, seeing the sudden departure of the carpenters and armourers back across into the massive dreadnaught. There were no goodbyes, no last orders or instructions, for these fiends had spent a full day resealing the outer shell of the airbarge and reinforcing it with weapons worthy of a dreadnaught, and were eager to get away. They did so, because Arturo ordered it.

"I second that," Kesta agreed.

"Me too," Derian offered, standing, eager to be done with this nasty business. He was happy to see the old weaver free. A man so old and close to death shouldn't spend his remaining days chained without dignity. Also, Derian hated cleaning his chamber pots. The cur had the strangest diet. "He is one of us."

"One of us," Seren offered, hopefully.

Lorgan, too, saw the labourers depart. He also looked to have argued his points and tired himself out. More than that, he didn't appear to desire to be the thug a moment longer.

Upsetting Seren had taken his wind. Derian didn't think he would have behaved similarly if he and Natteo had played their sorrow as Seren did. It must have been her charm.

"I call an end of meeting. Come on, Derian. Let's go play with the new toys," Natteo said excitedly.

"Ah, spit on all of this thurken shit," called Lorgan. He went to strike the table again and fell still. "Fine. For now, you may walk free," he mumbled, watching the upper deck as Natteo and Derian did. Probably a finer tactic keeping the acolyte free, what with them still flying with the massive army.

"Does anyone know where Keddy is?" Seren asked. "There is apparently an enchantment of good fortune, and I wish to try placing it upon him." Everyone stopped at the table, including Arturo, who looked wary that she spoke of such strange things openly.

"Don't blow up the cat, yeah?" Natteo called.

"Of course not," Arturo offered with a deep bow. "It's a simple charm of a lure. Little danger at all," he added.

"A charm that will give the cat good fortune? I wouldn't mind something like that," Derian said.

"It isn't something I've actually done before... but yes... very little danger... to a cat... a good cat... a lucky cat," Arturo offered.

"So what? He'll get good at cards," Lorgan said warily. He didn't like the cat, but he didn't want it exploded all over the ship's lower decks.

"I don't think Keddy plays cards," Seren said sincerely. Then she thought about it. "Does he?"

"Well, have you asked him?" Natteo said.

"Cats can't speak..." Seren murmured and looked terribly confused as her dizzying and dazzling mind thought on this for a certainty. "Wait... do they?"

"So what exactly does good fortune mean?" Natteo asked. "I had a rabbit's foot... It was very tasty."

Arturo thought on this. "Less chance of getting skinned... alive," he said.

"But not dead?" Natteo replied. "Can you do it on me?" Natteo asked.

"It wouldn't work on... you," Arturo said, looking at Natteo unblinkingly.

"Just cats?" Natteo asked warily.

"And other such things," Arturo said, shrugging.

"What about dogs?" Derian said, and Arturo spun around and laughed.

"Wouldn't work on you... friend."

With a shake of the head, and losing the last of his rage, Lorgan addressed the gathering. "Just be careful with the cat, Seren." He looked at her long enough to ensure her fear had diminished. "Everyone else, just go and fuk off so," he said, and Kesta, who had also seen the dreadnaught's airbridge release and pull away, marched past Natteo and Derian and made swiftly for the cockpit. The beast had remained hovering along as they commenced the meeting, but now with disengagement occurring, the *Fighting Mongoose* needed to remain in formation with someone behind the controls.

Free at last and richer for it.

"Come on, Derian. They have four of the fuken things," Natteo cried, leaping out through the galley door and scampering out along the deck to the first longshot secured into the deck. "Fuk me—look at these things."

Natteo had every right to be excited. Suddenly, the *Fighting Mongoose* was a fighting force in the sky, all for the price of a few orders delivered by an aging, weak weaver. There was now something that looked like a large crossbow, a small ballista with a swivelling support holding it a few feet off the ground. Natteo held the massive grip and stared down the aiming sight and looked positively delighted with himself. "I'm in love again." At his feet, equally attached and secured, were massive barbed poles, at least forty of them. There was no wealthy peasant in Dellerin who could have afforded such a weapon, let alone four of the death machines at each side and on the rear of the airbarge.

"It is rather polished. Smooth as well," agreed Derian, watching Natteo spin the giant machine in a full angle with no effort whatsoever. Fitted with weights and counter-weights, and a thousand little steel balls wedged in beside each other, it was more manoeuvrable than anything Derian had ever seen, despite the heavy steel it was constructed from, despite its terrible weight, despite it being almost twice the size of Natteo.

"But can I load it," Natteo wondered, pulling one of the long harpoon bolts from its holding. Easing the long pole into place, he began turning the mechanism, and all too swiftly, the weapon's long, thick draw set and locked. "Apparently, I can," he declared, spinning the weapon skywards, pointing it to where the dreadnaught flew along-side, and a wariness came upon Derian.

"Don't be an idiot," Derian cried, gripping Natteo's shoulder. It was less impressive than Lorgan's hold.

"Arturo will quell their aggrievement. He'll calm all the shit down," Natteo said coldly. His body was rigid. He only needed to fire at the curs with their own weapon.

"We don't need a war, brother," Derian argued. "Remember?"

"They didn't seem to mind," he hissed, and eased his finger over the trigger for a breath before releasing the draw without firing the bolt. He groaned at his own show of mercy and Derian breathed heavily.

"Besides, Clementine already paid the price."

"Oh yes, the... accident." Who knew a general of the skies would simply fall overboard from his dreadnaught in the middle of the night without any explanation?

For a breath neither said a thing as they enjoyed the sight of a thousand airbarges stretched out across the sky, flying in perfect unison towards the grandest city in all of Dellerin, wittily named Dellerin City.

Natteo stretched and looked around the deck to ensure they were alone. "So, brother, can we trust him?" he asked, leaving the great machine's front to slide into a ready position.

"Arturo?"

"Aye."

"I have a terrible feeling we are flying into a right nightmare, and I think Arturo is aware of this."

"You think he intends to bring doom upon us," Natteo asked.

"On the contrary, I think it just as likely that he might keep us alive."

"You are never right about these things," Natteo said as, side by side, they ambled to the front of the barge.

Distantly, through the breaking in the moon-illuminated clouds, Derian could see the dim lights miles beyond.

"That is true, brother," he said, watching as the dreadnaught's horn emitted a loud blast and immediately began to descend through the cloud towards the lights. Kesta, though not part of the army, steered the *Mongoose* in its wake.

"I hate it when he calls me godly, you know. It unsettles me; it really does."

"Why is that?"

"I don't know."

"Poor old Natteo, afraid he's got an elder man's affections to contend with. Are you afraid he'll cast a lure on you? Make a man out of you some dreadful night while you sleep?"

"I'm a light sleeper, and besides, I'd just break him in half, and besides... Boab."

"Boab will never forgive you."

Natteo recoiled for a breath and composed himself. "Course he will. I've a lovely manhood."

"Yes, you do."

"You don't believe me?"

"I believe you; I've seen it many a drunken night when you declare such a thing to whoever is foolish enough to be listening."

"That's what I thought," he said, patting his groin. "There, there, little Derian. Big stupid Derian meant nothing there," he whispered loudly.

"I hate when you call it that."

"That was his name long before I met you."

"I'm going inside," Derian mumbled.

"That's normally what little Derian says as well," Natteo said and his face became serious and he grabbed him. "Ever get the feeling we are just players in some demented god's game?"

"No, I don't." But Derian did. He really, really did.

"That we are being manoeuvred across the world... not being allowed to die..."

That's exactly what Derian felt, and Natteo spoke it true.

"Maybe it's no good thing to speak of such things," Derian offered, looking around conspiratorially as though someone listened.

Nobody listened but the demented, absent gods.

Their airbarge fell in with the air brigade, and as the barges neared, the humming grew louder. Derian would have preferred they find their own way to Dellerin, but Kesta argued the value in flying within the wash of the dreadnaught; it conserved fuel against the wind, or something along those lines. It made sense how she said it, and besides, she was captain of this bird, and who was Derian or indeed Lorgan to argue the potency of aerodynamics or whatever she called them.

"You and me, we need to get the fuk out of this spitting outfit, right quickly," Natteo said, gripping Derian's shoulder, and fuk it if it wasn't a leader's grip.

"But we have a barge, we have riches, we have two fuken grand demon kills to our names," Derian argued. Truthfully, though Natteo had suggested such a things a hundred times in the season—usually when they were running in the rain, or about to do something stupid—this time it was rather tempting.

"I feel things are going to end real fuken bloody soon."

"That's usually not a problem for us," Derian countered, but he felt it too. Dellerin was calling. It would all end and begin in Dellerin, and as they gazed at the oncoming lights of fire, Derian felt just as Natteo did.

"I think the fiend who commands our step will reveal himself, and I think it will be the Crimson Hunters' end," he hissed, and it felt like the truth.

"I think so too. What do we do?"

"Let's get to the Guild, no matter what. Nothing can get us there, right?"

"Right."

About the Author

His name was Bereziel and he was not of this world. He is not of this time either. He will find no place in the world to come.

The world spun as the old weaver pulled himself away from Anguis's grip. His old heart hammered wildly, but he did not fear a stuttering stop and a quick drop. It was not his time. Not in this world, either. Perhaps, had he never stepped into the source all those years ago, such a fate would have befallen him, but he did step in when the world was at its darkest and Karkur was finally breached. And in the source, he aged a millennium and lived a shadowed life twice as long, and now, it was time to end it all. To leave. To die. To find the fight in himself once again. While he still could.

Bereziel wandered through the darkness of the source like the spectre he was. With every step he became more corporeal, as though he were waking from a deep slumber. And the source was like living in a dream. Perfect sense and understanding, despite the rules of time and nature falling upon themselves.

An eternal, unending dream.

Until you choose to wake.

And the understanding and the acceptance slipped away. Seren always thought so too, and truly, in the moments when he felt her absence, he missed her terribly, as a grandfather should. Even if he was not. He was so much more. And so was she.

She was fierce.

She is fierce.

She will be fierce when the right moment occurs, and it is close.

His mind spun with visions of things to come, things long since transpired, and things occurring in this very moment. He was but a man in his soul, but more than that, he was a watching wraith split across the lines of time. The lines of a dream. He could barely influence all that he saw before him, but he could whisper. Just a few whispered words is all. Words that travelled through time. Barely anything, really. Barely enough to change the world. But enough.

Oh yes, Bereziel had watched infinity from end to beginning and every way around. He had seen the birth of the gods and their creation of the lands; he had witnessed the breaking of the gods; he had endured the breaking of the land too, and such things had taken his mind near to madness. He had seen the taking of the world to coming darkness beyond the Anguished One, but that was an event not determined just yet.

"I have created my own dark world, though," he whispered, and his voice echoed across time. He followed his own voice towards dawn, where the world would welcome him in fire and war and the great turning of things to come.

The Lure.

With a tongue that had not found itself yet, he cursed that tainted word for all its damage. He cursed the broken weaver who carelessly doomed an entire world to darkness for the price of duty, friendship and, aye, a little gold too.

So I fled.

I am fleeing.

I will flee into the source to escape and to prepare.

And I return now.

"I am returning from this woven dream," he whispered.

The path felt sturdy underfoot, and he knew the hour was upon him, and he quickened his pace. He looked away from the City of Light and all its perfect beauty, back to his own world, his own universe. He, among very few in the history of the world, could do this. It was a trait reserved for him. Better than most, but at one time he had wanted more.

"Like Anguis, I wanted it all."

Unlike the Dark One, though, he had stolen from no demon. Just from his own wretched soul.

"I stayed ahead of you, hidden," he whispered, and he knew his voice whispered to the Anguished One throughout time. Warned him of his returning. Invited him to a fight. He needed to do this.

He could not meet Anguis in this dreamlike place. All weavers or gods who stepped through the source had their own affinity to it. They had their own inherent skills too. Bereziel understood the spinning of the source better than any fiend before. He knew this as fact, for he saw the past and no weaver had bettered him before. He saw the future to the end of it all, and no cur would master the knowledge as he did. Anguis, however, like a bastard cheating cur, stole more, and could see far and wield fire farther.

So, no. They would not fight in this place.

Upon the plains of Dellerin, their war would wage. Could only wage. And it would be beautiful.

Bereziel took an imaginary breath and felt the ever-dawning reach of Dellerin calling. The book was read, the lure was spinning and grand things were afoot.

And I whispered.

I whisper.

And they hear.

Bereziel remembered the sight of a broken mercenary with a soul destined for great things. That stubborn man had not welcomed his intrusion at all. For many years, Bereziel had battled with that fiend's better senses, to get his words to him across time.

I whispered to Lorgan.

I am currently whispering to Lorgan.

I will whisper to Lorgan and he will hear and he will forgive himself.

Some day from now.

And oh, that moment, as Lorgan slept and his mind relaxed enough that Bereziel could pollute him with calls of duty and ease him towards action. Away from the indignity of brutish fame among the pugilistic gentry, towards something godly, towards marching with comrades, towards pulling glorious fools from the pleasure courts of Castra, and beyond.

You were a hero.
You are a hero.
You will be a hero, Lorgan.

It wasn't difficult to grab that divine child from the grubby hands of those less pleasant. Lorgan never knew what possessed him to do it as he did, but he did it regardless, and Bereziel watched with care, and worry and silent glee.

And those who followed Lorgan were content, even when the world was against them. Because Bereziel whispered reassurances where he could.

And Lorgan endured all the misery in the world, until he grew into the hardened hero that he will be today.

A man needing redemption.

Bereziel gasped and felt the calling of dawn upon him. It wasn't dawn at all, but it most certainly felt like a fresh new day. And that day was on fire.

Bereziel continued to walk from the darkness. From time itself. And the road ahead was welcoming, and terrifying too.

He thought of those further whispers. Whispers that carried the hero across the world until he came to a little village whose people worshipped the old hounds. The beasts of the gods. The most deadly and fierce and loyal.

A lost race.
A godly thing.
Seeva blood.

And it didn't take long or much convincing to tame those poor helpless fools, to convince them to take the child in. To care for the manbeast, or more accurately, the boybeast. And the boy had grown in a home split by love and disdain. For a time, he might well have become some-thing more impressive. And it took longest to break through to the child. He was still growing. Still becoming something. Becoming her guardian.

Will become her guardian.

Will become her everything.

If he opens himself to her.

From a distance, Bereziel grew to love these Crimson Maniacs. He fretted for their complete failures. Rejoiced at their lesser failures. Watched as a doting grandfather might, whose edge was softened by time.

And yet, for all his sight, Bereziel hadn't seen much of the flying witch, for her soul was so broken and lost. She was a wraith, and slipped easily past his eyes. Her appear-ance, though, was a welcomed gift. And now he saw her clearly, for there brewed a glimmer of a spark with her thiev-ery, with her calling, and Bereziel was much impressed with her fierceness and her actions to come.

They were all lost.

She was most lost.

She found herself first.

The path became easier, and Bereziel fell into a steady march, and immediately the greater knowledge of all things happening in the very same moment began to fade as he woke from the dream. He should have feared the coming unknowing but instead welcomed his future ignorance, as no doubt his fledgling must have.

Seren.

He thought of his companion these many years. The twisted, fearful, angry girl who had become so much more, once she lost the darker parts of her tendencies. Once she surrendered to the greater workings of the source. Once she dropped to a knee at his feet. Once she won his favour, and once he earned hers.

She became Serenity.

He loved the great woman she had become. He respected her. He hoped for her. He resented that he would not reach her in time, but that was the spinning of things, wasn't it?

———

His name is Bereziel and he is a legend of old. He is the former Weaver of the Seven, and truly, greater than any who fight with them. Even if he is but a human and no mere god.

Bereziel's steps slow as he feels the dawn of the day just a few steps further. He feels the world burning and bright, and he imagines the taste of ale, of a woman, of a honey cake laced with cream, and he begins to remember what it is to be a human. To touch, feel, taste and desire. To endure pain as well. He imagines his body quivering and he remembers Karkur and the battles and the godly, unborn soul of two gods. Such things can spin a lure into all manner of chaos, and that is exactly what is happening throughout time. Throughout all times. All worlds. And it is his fault. It always will be.

I cast a lure and it grows with each death, multiplying upon itself. This lure will only break when HE dies. But what if HE creates life with SHE within the lure and a new GODLY spirit becomes more and all of the rules shatter upon themselves?

Bereziel holds that thought, much as he holds the last days of the Seven in his mind, and now he does quiver and he feels the taste of battles throughout time. He feels Fiore of Karkur rip and tear at him and escape into a future to meet her doom.

And it is beautiful.

And it was his doing.

It will be the defining moment of the world.

And the lure that was cast will break.

Because if it doesn't, then there was never any hope anyway.

He thinks more of the child of Karkur, and Arturo, the young man, split in two and torn asunder, all for the cost of seeing the truth of goodness and honour.

He sees the Anguished One in Karkur, and he fears the wrath. Such a wrath. A wrath so great that Bereziel can do little more but take those stones, grind them to ink and enchant upon a book and await the reading by the one who spun the lure and the world and absolutely fuken everything after that.

I see you, girl, and you are beautiful.

I am coming for you.

And for The Seven after.

Bereziel will step towards dawn, even though it feels like night. He will be excited as the memories fade. He will breathe with lungs that won't have tasted breath in many a year. He will feel the touch of his feet upon solid ground and it will be unsteady. He will suddenly feel scared, enthralled, liberated and hopeful. But mostly he will feel scared. He will feel demons and anguish and he will feel the darkness close in around him and everyone else as he conceals himself, as he recovers. He will be man again upon the burning dawn, and all around him will be ablaze. He will taste fire and flame and death, and this will not be what he is expecting. Not what he remembers will occur.

The world is spinning a new horror and there is death and war and the end of all things.

He will try and will fail.

He will fail.

And the Anguished One will know a great victory this dawn.

This night.

Welcome to Dellerin. Wipe your Feet

Derian gasped as the emerging lights of Dellerin lit up the land. Walking to the front of the airbarge, he leaned out on the guardrail and marvelled at the sight set out before him. It was beautiful and lonely all at the same time. He thought himself quite the poet thinking this way. He might have said it to Natteo but feared his comrade would have mocked him. He would have been right.

"Stunning," he said.

"Aye, always is," Natteo agreed as their barge, following the trajectory of the armada, cleared the last cloud and glided seamlessly down towards the awesome city in one great web of humming things. "I really wish we'd arrived here on a sunny day," Natteo said thoughtfully, his mind elsewhere, no doubt. "I've never seen the city from the sky this way. I would have liked to see it in all its glory."

"Perhaps, when we leave, it will be daytime. It might even be sunny. We'll ask Kesta to fly this bitch around the city a few times before we go."

Natteo hummed to himself a moment. An eerie tune. "I just have a terrible feeling we won't be leaving here... I don't know why," he said after a moment, and Derian shivered.

"Then let's enjoy this moment of silence while we can," Derian offered.

Derian had not seen the city in nearly two years or so. It could have been more. Any march melded into one contin-uous slog when one was away from one's home. Derian considered the Guild his true home these last few years. The city was merely its shell. He strained his eyes to see beyond the glow, but the Guild was nowhere to be seen just yet. As they neared, though, her lights would be brighter than all others. Derian liked to think of those great lights as a beacon, welcoming its battered brothers back home to rest, recuperate, pay their bills as well. He also thought them whistling in the face of the king. Reminding the Anguished One that not everyone was intimidated by his ungodly strengths and terrors. It was a fine ruse, regardless.

"Pretty," Seren said, appearing from the darkness. Her eyes were alive and alight with the youthful excitement of a child who'd never seen such a thing. And why wouldn't she be excited? This bright glow against the eternity of the night was quite the sight. Her fingers flowed in the air as though dancing with hissects. She saw what it took a breath more for Derian to see. His mind was on other things.

"So, did you and Arturo blow up the cat?" Natteo asked warily. Unlike Derian, he seemed to like Keddy. Unlike Derian, the cat appeared to tolerate him in response. They had a better relationship than most cats and their owners, Derian thought. Derian also thought he wouldn't mind if the cat was blown up. It was the hound in him.

"The cat, Keddy, is fine. Hardly any singed fur left at all," she replied, and beamed a wonderful smile suggesting she'd managed a wonderful jest for the ages. It was a fine jest. It was a perfectly acceptable jest.

It was simply a jest.

It was one of her better ones.

That was something, and she beamed as Derian and Natteo politely smiled at her wit before looking back to the nearing city.

"Wait, is that right?" Natteo asked.

Dellerin's glow spread out further on all sides than last he recalled. Half a mile wider than usual, to be a little more precise, and as they drew nearer, he realised the lights they gazed upon were a hundred thousand individual lights, spread out and illuminating the night like a swarm of fire hissects on a warm season's night. He might have said that to Natteo but held his tongue. Natteo would have agreed.

"No, that doesn't look right at all," Natteo said, leaning forward against the balcony rail. "Perhaps that cur was wrong about the numbers," he added, remembering Clementine's talk of a small army amassing and marching slowly upon Dellerin City. Even though his armada had been summoned all the way from the siege of Karkur, Clementine hadn't appeared particularly worried about such things.

He'd seemed rightly confident in the hours before he "fell" from the deck of his dreadnaught. Wasn't that the way with most zealots? They couldn't see the factual truth beyond what they believed as certainty.

Wonder what he would have thought of this?

Like the Dellerin air brigade, this rebel army had no mercenary dealings. In fact, the Guild would happily stay clear of this conflict. Even if war was bad for business.

"They look like... flutterbyes... on fire," Seren said and Derian could only nod.

"They look like too many fires, is what they look like," Natteo said, tensing as they dropped further towards the lights. The fires. The campfires. The army campfires.

So many.

Too many.

We should not be here.

"Surely, that can't be the pathetic rebel army we heard so little about," Derian cried, looking out across the waves of flames surrounding the city on all sides. "They are probably double the number of citizens within."

"That's no invading army at all. That's a pissing *nation* invading," Natteo cried.

"They are our allies," Seren cried in delight.

Are they really, though?

"Your allies, perhaps, Seren, but we are mercenaries and we have no side," Derian suggested. It wasn't the first time such words had been spoken, and she simply nodded as she usually did, choosing ignorance. "And allies or no, we are flying in the middle of their fuken enemy," Derian added, watching the airbarges tighten in together as though in a warring formation. "Anyone else think we shouldn't be flying with their enemy?"

"Oh, I don't know, Derian," Natteo countered. "I think they'll be able to differentiate between us and the thousand others out here. We'll just wave at them." Natteo began to wave into the darkness, but Derian could see he was worried too.

Let's get the piss out of here.

Distantly, they could see the great gates of Dellerin, and they were awash in flames. Squinting, Derian could see a mass of soldiers manoeuvring along the front of the Dellerin walls, charging through the burning gates and then crumpling to each side like logs on a fireplace. Further in throughout the city, he saw plumes of smoke rising up against the night where fires were already burning, and his stomach clenched. They had not come upon a besieging army; they were watching a full invasion.

From the front line, under a far from neutral banner.

"They're taking the entire city," Natteo cried in horror. This wasn't the first time rebellion had stirred. Some, historically, had even reached the gates. This, though, was a monstrous campaign. Decades in the making, no doubt.

Derian felt a churning in his belly. A gnawing to release the monster within. He did not want to be part of this war, but he felt it inevitable. Much like he felt flying with these barges, bearing down upon the invasion, was a dreadful error on their part.

Let's just blame Kesta, if the Guild ask why we flew into battle with the city air brigade.

"This war is inevitable... It always was... It always will be," Seren countered. She was positively beaming that Dellerin was taking a beating. Perhaps in one of her visions she saw this. Was prepared for this.

Well, you could have warned us.

Natteo thought so too. "Did you and Arturo know about this? Did you send us directly into a war zone?"

Natteo cried. He spun around and gestured to Kesta. "Get out of this formation," he roared, but she was already attempting to raise the barge above the vast single grouping of barges, covering the sky like a sickly webbed net. She had already seen the problem before the rest, for from above there came a dreadful roar as the dreadnaught lifted high above the line of airbarges, trapping them in, and held its course. A dozen airbarges now protected its underbelly, and the *Mongoose* was one of them.

They did that on purpose.

Bastards.

"What the fuk are they doing?" Natteo wondered, and the deck shook something terrible as the larger beast's propellors stole the air from their bird. Everyone upon the deck near lost their footing as Kesta fought the down-draught and the whirling propellors around them. Derian's teeth chattered and his limbs felt shuddered to a milky ruin, yet still, he remained upright, hoping the dreadnaught would pass over and gift them an easier retreat.

"What is happening?" Lorgan roared as his head appeared outside the galley. His face was rose red and he looked fit to kill once more. It was a good look to him.

"Ah, it's fine. We are just crashing," Natteo helpfully offered.

"We're what?" he cried.

"It's alright. We'll be fine. We mostly survive death. Mostly," Natteo said, as Lorgan stumbled across to the balcony and saw the army as they did. And then he saw the dreadnaught above them, and like Kesta's, his curses were most enlightening and creative.

"... Fuk," he concluded. His voice was barely audible

above the rushing thunder of the larger airbarge, which had edged just a little too close for comfort. As had the barges on either side, and the many flying directly behind them.

"They've penned us in, and I can't see anything below us," Kesta cried, her head shooting from side to side as she looked backwards and above. Her hands danced over the controls and despite the terrible reverberations, she managed to hold the *Mongoose* in perfect formation. "Are there barges below? Can any of you fuks lean out and see?"

"I can't see shit in this dark," Natteo said, leaning perilously over the side, as though he'd no fear of simply slipping over and dropping to nothing below. Derian, for his part, had seen the *Mongoose* from below. He wasn't going to be looking over anytime soon.

"Fuk it, just drop and let them go by," Lorgan ordered. "It'll be fine—trust me." It was a fine order, and she nodded warily. She eased the barge a few feet further below, away from the dreadnaught, and the vibrations immediately lessened, then diminished again when she dipped half of the barge ever so to get a view of those below.

"Everybody hold on," she warned as the world dipped, and Derian fought that awful queasy feeling of unnatural motion.

From the barges on either side of them, there came a cluster of movement as soldiers dressed in jet-black uniforms appeared along the decks, preparing for battle. Some attached themselves to the longshots, while others moved to the rear carrying torches. In the time it took Kesta to dip sharply and see mostly nothing beneath, the sky became alive with countless torches.

"That doesn't look good, does it?" Lorgan said.

"Real pretty fire flutterbyes," Seren offered, gazing in delight at the fire around them, and it was stunning. It matched the style of the fires far below. Those without torches took to rolling large bulbous spheres of grey fluid to the rear of each barge, and Derian's heart dropped.

"Is it just me, or does that grey shit look rightly combustible... around torches?" Natteo said.

"I've a terrible feeling about all of this," Derian cried, and the barges began to slow, and then the bellow of that signalling horn filled the air, near deafening Derian, who grabbed his ears in agony.

"Don't drop down," roared Lorgan suddenly as the soldiers lit those fuken spheres, and Derian realised their awfulness as the airbarges ahead of them passed across the first lines of lights in the camped army below.

"They're dropping those pissing things," Natteo cried, and Kesta could only shrug in frustration as she pulled the *Fighting Mongoose* back into formation. He'd never thought he'd see an airbarge stuck in the middle of the sky. Typical that it was his barge that it happened to.

Suddenly, there came a terrible, piercing hiss of a thousand falling things and Derian looked to the fiends in the barge across from them as they lit and released the glass spheres and rolled them over the rear edge of the barge. All of them were at it, and it was a potent first assault on the defenceless city beneath.

Clementine didn't fuken mention a bombing run when he spoke of the unimpressive numbers.

Derian was horrified at such a dishonourable act. War should have been fought between worthy opponents. This murder seemed shallow and truly cruel.

"You have to find a way out of this," Natteo cried, but Kesta wasn't listening. They were trapped from above by a dreadnaught covering itself, and unable to drop below lest a bomb fall upon them. It was desperation that drove Kesta's will. She sped up and brought the *Mongoose* up behind the two nearest barges in front.

"Be easier to fit through a peephole," Natteo cried, watching in horror as Kesta squeezed the beast into the miniscule space, all the while careful not to fly into a bomb as it dropped just a few feet from the ship's front propellors. Suddenly, light flickered in the silent world below, and Derian could only watch with trepidation as the accompanying boom of the first explosion filled the night.

They will end the war this very night.

"None of you should look upon this horror," Lorgan called, gripping the edge for strength. He seemed to shake at the murder occurring beneath the armada.

"I cannot allow this to happen," roared Seren, forming fire upon each hand, and Natteo grabbed her, screaming in her face.

"You'll get us all killed if you fire on them. Moreover, you *will* start a war," he cried, and she struggled in his grip, cursing him in nonsensical words.

"Look around, boy. There is already war."

Arturo must have sensed her threat, for he appeared on deck now, eager to stem the wrath of the young woman. He did not seem surprised at what was happening, and perhaps as an acolyte, or former one, this was exactly what he had expected.

He might have warned us.

He might have wanted us to be in the middle of it.

"We cannot fight an entire armada alone," Arturo shouted. "What have you learned, Seren?" he hissed as an instructor might, and she fell silent, but there was a rage upon her as she stormed away from the deck.

"I must look at this horror," Derian said, stepping to the edge and looking down at the awfulness. The world below began to explode in places, as the volatile solution from the deadly spheres ignited, each shot spreading flames in a fierce fireball that consumed everything in a hundred-foot radius. That wasn't the measure of its destruction either, for even from this high up, Derian saw bodies blown high into the sky, such was the force.

Some were alight and squirming; some were torn in half or worse; others screamed as their last few moments were filled with agonizing knowledge that death would meet them where and when they landed.

That is the worst type of death, he thought, remembering his agonizing wait before dropping into the belly of a grand demon.

The land below erupted in frenzy and panic as terrified soldiers sprinted through the many pathways of the camp, tripping upon themselves and any obstacle as they went. They scurried like ants enduring a violent assault from an angled glass goblet in the sun. He remembered doing such things as a child and still felt shame to this day.

The screaming rebel soldiers tried to run from the hell above. Some escaped, but many simply ran straight into landing bombs and were consumed by a raging, sticky fire all around them.

Of all the horrors he saw in those first few moments, it was the sight of a young girl waving a banner that struck him most. She looked to be no older than Eveklyn, but as the adults stumbled around her, she took the largest rebel banner and began waving it fiercely. It was all she could do, and Derian could only stare at her display of courage, determination and perhaps leadership beyond her years. She waved that damned banner as everything around her burned, and it was an impressive thing.

"That is incredible," Natteo said in awe.

"That is heroic," Lorgan agreed.

"That is beautiful," Derian declared.

Other soldiers saw the banner and it seemed to quell their terror; their panic too. They reached for shields; they began barking orders, and she played her part. Derian wanted to hover around the defiant child and see if she survived the night, or at least survived the first wave. He wanted to watch on as she spurred her comrades to defending themselves, but the bombing run would bring their airbarge over her. In a few moments, she would be gone from his sight and he would probably never know.

"Go with the gods, little one," Derian cried as Natteo, flinching with every word and every bomb, leaned against his best friend for support and followed Derian's gaze.

"There aren't any gods with them," he whimpered in a strange voice, and flinched again as a fresh set of bombs was released from the barge across from them.

"It's a really nice banner, isn't it?" he said, and truly, he wasn't jesting. It was a nice banner. Sometimes banners were barely anything more than a smudge of red upon black fabric. Sometimes, though, they were beautiful, and this banner was startingly rousing, with a rich green outline and an accompanying gold of such richness that—

...

...

The flash came first.

...

...

And then the boom.

...

And then the fire.

It raced across the land in front of them, immolating everything in its path, including the gathering of defiant fighters, including the child, including her banner.

She was there. And then she wasn't.

"Aw, god, please, no," Derian cried, seeing the vast nothingness where the cluster of bombs had dropped.

"It's not fair. It's not fair, Derian. They need to die. All of those curs need to die," Natteo roared, stepping away from the edge and marching towards the nearest longshot. He looked a man possessed, and perhaps he was. His limbs were rigid. His eyes were wild. "I don't care. That's just fuken it. To the fires with everyone. Piss on this. Piss on it all."

Derian might have stopped his friend from starting some shit that nobody wanted, but his heart was too heavy. He, too, felt the loss of the innocent. He didn't bother trying to calm his friend. Not even when he began strapping himself into the restraints before loading the weapon.

Lorgan took the savagery badly as well. "These thurken murderers," he spat, slamming his fists upon the rail. The hour was late, particularly for soldiers who slept through loud noises. Derian wondered if some were never aware that the thunder infecting their dreams was the bombs landing among them.

Suddenly, Kesta clipped one of the airbarges ahead. The scream of metal on metal was fierce, and for a moment it drowned out the awful hiss of bombs.

A moment after that, and the awful hiss of bombs was drowned out by something else entirely.

"What is that?" roared Lorgan as a thundering boom erupted around them. The world flashed a blinding yellow, like a rabid sun had spitefully engulfed an airbarge just ahead of them in its terrible embrace. With a second deadly, thundering boom, the barge disappeared in an exploding sphere of fire.

This is so much worse.

Kesta had neither the time nor the space to manoeuvre them from the debris path, so she charged right through it. Derian ducked his head as a hail of exploding smoke and fire mixed with burning metal struck the deck, the propellors and the Crimson themselves.

"The entire airbarge blew up," Natteo cried from his place at the weapon. "What the fuk can blow up an entire airbarge?" He too shielded himself from the deadly hail storm, screaming as shards grazed and scraped him as they passed through it. "It got me. It pissing got me," he screamed, but Derian's own scrapes were worse, as were Lorgan's. Lorgan had taken a shard to the knee. Bending over, he swiftly pulled the steaming, jagged shard from his flesh and tossed it casually over the side. He may as well have left it at his feet, however, for the *Mongoose*'s once pristine deck was now covered in red-hot metal and steaming lumps of unknown debris. For a dreadful moment, Derian wondered if it didn't smell like charred steak.

"I'm alright, Seren," Lorgan hissed as she went to healing him. She didn't listen to him. A good thing too, as it looked a right nasty wound, even if he played at being the tough man.

Great explosions of black powdery smoke appeared around them, and the barge shuddered as it took a hit in the lower decks. Derian looked out to see similar clouds of smoke striking other barges and exploding on contact.

"What is this bastard smoke?" he cried.

"Fire powder," muttered Lorgan, grasping the balcony edge.

Derian's mind raced. He knew the name but little of its combustion history or effectiveness. He knew it was used in various cannons, but most importantly, he knew it was damned expensive and each explosion was costing the rebels a right fortune. A mercenary paid close attention to such details. Down the road, a mercenary group might make a little fortune for themselves charging a rebel army through the roof for services rendered, knowing they had the funds to pay. Should it come to that, of course.

The explosions filled the sky and Derian wondered just how many cannons sat far below, for they blackened the night completely. A dreadful stench akin to burning oil filled his nostrils.

Any moment now they'll blow us out of the sky, and I'm not sure Arturo will be able to put us back together again.

Arturo took that moment to draw a sphere of blue around him as fresh shards of burning metal struck. Derian dipped his head lest he lose an eye, until the accompanying smoke took his breath.

"This is the fuken worst," gasped Natteo.

"Surely having the shits in Castra was worse," Derian argued, heaving for breath and spitting some foulness from his mouth.

"Or catching that... 'gift' from that weasel of a cur outside Fayenor," Lorgan offered.

"The shits were worse, and Phillippe was worth it," he countered, wiping the smoke from his eyes and the blood from his forehead. He looked a ruin, but at least he had calmed down enough not to fire into the air brigade.

Suddenly, another explosion took a chunk out of the side of the hull and the barge shunted skywards, clipped the dreadnaught and tipped to one side before Kesta levelled up and all were knocked from their feet. "Spit on this. Will you all get down below," roared Kesta from her reinforced cabin. As she did there came a thunderous crash from the lead airbarge as a flak cannon struck the underside of the great machine directly, yet miraculously, it stayed aloft, even as flames erupted from beneath and within. "You'll get cut to ribbons out there," she roared, and it was a fine order. Problem was, there now appeared a dozen figures from the depths of the damaged airbarge in front. They swarmed through the lower hatches, from the galley and from the pilot's cabin itself and rushed up on deck.

"I really don't think it's safer below deck," cried Lorgan, and that too was a fair point, for each of the fleeing soldiers was fully engulfed in fire.

"Oh, that's terrible," cried Natteo. "I hate them, but that *is* the fuken worst."

Their screams were burned away in their throats, but not before Derian heard them briefly. They waved and shuffled and outright danced as the fire took them, and it was a terrible sight to behold.

"You know, I think I'd rather take my chances up here," Lorgan added as the burning soldiers fell to the flames. Some leapt over the edge, no doubt preferring a swifter death, and Derian couldn't imagine the terror they all must have felt as the corridors and rooms were engulfed with a wave of fire they were helpless to fight. That was no way to die, he decided; better to stick to the cold air and dreadful sights upon the deck. And when a cannon shot took them out, well, that would be that.

The fire spread and inevitably struck the blackwater reserves, and the airbarge exploded in a terrible flash of light. The *Mongoose*'s deck shook as though she'd been taken in a godly grip, and Derian's teeth chattered loudly and his stomach lurched again as he struggled to the far end of the ship, where Natteo still waited. If he were to die, at least his brother would be at his side, distracting him every final step of the way.

"There might be a little space to manoeuvre," Kesta cried. "I'm going to try to get through this," she roared, and Derian had never heard sweeter words.

"Find something to hold on to," Lorgan cried, strapping himself into one of the longshot holsters. As he did, Seren, lost in the fire and all manner of horror, glided up beside him. She watched him as he strapped in and when he was secured, she took his arm in hers and wrapped herself around him, digging her head into his shoulder. She took his words literally, no doubt, and again Derian was unmoved by her growing infatuation with the older man.

Or else she just craves a father.
That's definitely it.

She whispered a few words that Derian couldn't make out, but Lorgan nodded as though comforting her, shielding her from scarier things. After a time, he wrapped her fully in his arms as she shook in terror, and Derian smiled and had no idea why. Perhaps she could see now the value in his leadership. He was an old seeping oak. Reassuring and comforting and fine to find shelter in, even when facing a demon horde, a demonic demon queen, a sea monster, too. A flying wall of exploding fire was probably little to him. Lorgan only had to whisper that it would all be over soon and it would be alright. No wonder she snuggled her head into him.

Around them, the barges began to break formation, as the horror of the explosions no doubt affected the countless pilots watching their friends perish. As they did break, alas, they were set upon by ballistae from below.

Within a breath, a dozen further airbarges were torn to pieces, and Derian wailed in frustrated horror. Kesta, for her part, merely cursed a few times and held the barge back in formation, all the while searching for an escape. Derian watched with awe and respect; he couldn't imagine the terror she must have felt in that moment. He considered himself to have decent nerves, but he would have frozen up by now, buried his head in his hands and wailed that he wanted out of this shitty outfit, off this cursed airbarge.

"Aw, fuk this, Derian," Natteo moaned, seeing the barges ripped to pieces by the defences from far below.

"They were ready for this. They batter us all when we are clustered together and just wait until we break to pick us off… I hate this shit. I fuken hate it," he hissed, and Derian had no words to argue or disagree. This was no way for any mercenary to go out. It wasn't fair. It really wasn't. "This is the end, Derian. I feel it in my bones," he said coldly, and reloaded his longshot, which was far less impressive than the countless rebel beasts below. He looked both pale and red-faced all in the same breath. A skill, no doubt.

Silence fell between them, and he spoke again. "Well, aren't you going to argue?" he asked.

"I thought it was your turn," Derian said.

"The last time doesn't count, so you have to go again," he said.

"That's not fair," Derian countered, but he could see that the light in his friend's eyes was diminishing. That would be a catastrophe. For them all. "Utter nonsense, brother. We'll live through this. We've been through far worse," Derian offered, looking out over the edge to the horror below. "Well… perhaps not worse, but I've a real good feeling about this one," he added, trying not to count aloud the many cannons aimed skywards, firing up at them again and again.

"You have reassured me," Natteo said weakly, but he smiled. That was something, at least. "It would be a little bit of an anti-climax to go out like this after we just killed two grand demons."

"Exactly. We need a little fanfare."

"I want some pissing fanfare," Natteo shouted at the fiends below. And again at the airborne fiends as well.

And then he brought his longshot skywards to the great

behemoth of an airbarge above them using the lesser barges as cover.

As he did, Derian counted three times that the behemoth was struck by the cannons. The strikes left little more than a mark upon its armoured hull, and Derian cursed the general aboard who allowed lesser barges to burn and explode rather than covering them with its impenetrable armour.

Cowardly peasant bastards.

"Don't fire," Derian warned, but he didn't disagree with Natteo's motives.

"Who would ever know?" Natteo hissed. He released, and the bolt shot out into the night where nobody would indeed ever know, and it embedded itself in the hull of the dreadnaught, which unsurprisingly, made no change to its flight whatsoever.

"You feel any better, idiot?"

"Aye, I really do, asshole," Natteo said, immediately reloading, as a terrible crash sounded from somewhere ahead. Directly in front of them, a large airbarge shunted and began to waver. But not before they saw the flapping, ruined body of a soldier, lanced upon a longbolt, as it skimmed past them. In the wake of the body came a splattering wave of crimson. As though flung by an invisible paintbrush, the blood carried across the *Mongoose* deck and struck both mercenaries across their faces. Neither said a thing for a breath. They merely stood saturated in blood, no doubt wondering if the body had been alive as it passed them. Probably not.

"No, Natteo, I think *that* was the fuken worst," Derian declared.

"Why is it always us that gets it so spitting shitty?" Natteo asked, hacking and spitting a few globules from his mouth. Derian could only shake his hair a moment and feel the wet slop of dead soldiers' blood against his skin.

Another near explosion.

Another near flash of light.

Another scream cut short from somewhere.

But they remained quiet, defeated, accepting all in the same moment. It was a welcomed numbness.

"Reckon that pilot had it far worse than us," Derian said, spotting the projectile-proof glass in the barge beyond. The unbreakable glass was shattered and bloody where the massive longshot bolt had passed right through, dragging the pilot away as it did. The barge hung for a breath, and Derian couldn't help but hear fresh screaming as it suddenly dropped, smashing and taking out another barge along its way.

Natteo looked into the smoky darkness around them. "How did that bolt travel from way below, and then straighten up, and then go shooting past us?"

Derian thought on this. A fine thing to think about as the world ended all around them. "Um, a good shot?"

"The wind?"

"Enchanted?"

"Friendly fire?"

Both looked to the darkness from where the longshot had come. "You know, in this light, who knows what could be hiding the skies above, just waiting to fuk us up," Derian said after a time and felt no better about himself.

"And still, they continue to drop bombs."

"While everything around them burns."

"Orders must be followed."

Two airbarges behind the *Mongoose* suddenly collided with each other as though they had suddenly lost their pilots. The birds spun apart like leaves in the wind, and Derian spotted a handful of soldiers being thrown asunder around the deck. Some were flung over the edge into the night, and he thought that was no end either.

Where are you, monster?

I'm so fuken scared.

Not like this.

The land sucked both airbarges towards it, faster and faster, spinning them wildly, and Derian could only blink and look away as they careened into each other and exploded to nothing in a burning mound upon the battle-field below.

"I seriously don't want to be on this spitting bird a moment longer," Derian hissed, wrapping his bloody hair in ponytail. If he was knocked clear, he wanted to see his end as it came upon him. Somehow taking control in such a way made him feel better.

With the destruction of the two airbarges there appeared a minute break in the line of vessels behind them. Derian could only stare dumbly at the gap in the net, but Kesta saw it immediately and dropped the *Mongoose* back and slipped into the space they'd left.

"What's going on?" a sleepy voice called from somewhere behind Derian. It was Eveklyn, peeking up from one of the ladders and looking the worse for wear. Wiping her eyes, she climbed upon the deck and for a split breath, the world went still. Then, suddenly, their line of airbarges cleared a break in the bombardment and they glided off over the lights of Dellerin. "I was asleep and I think we hit..." She thought on this for a moment. "Turbulence... bad wind... Was it a bad wind we hit?" she asked suddenly, eager to learn, to understand. "Why are you covered in blood?" she asked as the last of the sleep left her and the realisation of terrible things took her.

"Get over here. Fuken get in," Kesta suddenly cried as the airbarge dropped back another dozen feet from the leading line. "Get in," Kesta roared again, but an invisible force took hold of Derian and the child as the barge cleared the tail end of the dreadnaught before shooting high up into the sky above. As it did, the thunder of bombardment and fire and thunder and death fell away to the scream of rushing wind, and Derian, upon the floor of the galley, could barely rear his head, such was the invisible force sucking him to the floor.

"This happens because we are going fast," Eveklyn pointed out, crawling away from Derian along the deck, towards the pilot's cabin. "You will have to find your own place to secure yourself, Derian... What about the other longshot?" she suggested as the barge suddenly levelled out, the air became a little more difficult to breathe and the light of the moon upon glistening cloud lit up the sky.

We are safe.

"Yes, yes, I'll get my own restraints. You get yourself safe, little one," he gasped.

Limping out to the deck Derian struggled to breathe but was grateful for the silence surrounding them, muffling the distant thunder of war below.

"This is good; this is very good," Lorgan declared. "We can wait out the horror up here." He was upon his knees with Seren once more locked in his embrace. He made fine restraints altogether, and as he released her, she kissed him once upon the cheek, then across the lips before stepping away and adjusting her dress and hair, and Derian could only grin at the redness in Lorgan's cheeks, lit up by the glimmer of moonlight.

And then Derian could only shriek in fright as a long-shot harpoon from nowhere struck Lorgan through the chest, pinning him to the edge of the deck.

"What the fuk?" Natteo screamed as six large shadows appeared around the airbarge.

"Oh, this is not a good thing at all... very bad," Arturo declared, and he was right.

NEARING THE END OF THE MARCH

Erin scrambled towards the rubble as the smoke overtook her. Her eyes stung with the dust, her lungs burned as she gasped for air, but she could not stop herself. Mercy and misery compelled her.

Duty, too. She heard no screams; she heard no desperate pleading for help. She only heard the eerie sound of the dead.

"Despite everything, you wouldn't want me to leave them, would you?" she whispered to the wind. To her dead comrade, too. A decent man, and a man who understood war, understood the vengeance required to be exacted upon him, just to save her life. He had seen this as justice immediately, and he had not condemned the curs for it. Rhendal had needed to die at their hands, not because he had deserved it, but because they deserved revenge. To hear his final howls, to commit a little murder on their part, all the while delivering mercy to little Erin. She would not hate these poor fiends who had put her comrade to death.

It had taken longer for her to see it, but she saw it now,

and this rubble before her was not what they deserved at all, either.

"Is there anyone there?" she yelled, climbing carefully in among the debris lest there be a ruined basement she hadn't known about, lest her next step be her last. "I came back for you," she moaned, though she knew there would be no reply. No desperate scratching where fingernails attempted to break through the mounds of brick, mortar, slate and tile. Those things were hardened, heavy, and capable of crushing a man.

Crushing two women, too.

She should have turned away and left them to their grave, but that terrible burning was upon her. Like a fiery vice, it no longer settled in her fingers. Instead, it roamed through her body, compressing itself into her very being. That fire demanded she release herself, but it also compelled her to move. To tend to grisly duties on the chance that she somehow saved a soul.

They are all dead and I should not delay.

Coming upon a break in the bricks, she began pulling at rubble, eager to find a miracle in the middle of nowhere. She called out for them as she did, each by their name, though she knew this act as hollow. Yet still, she pulled and laboured, and when she reached the sandy ruin of crumbled wall and roof, she dug deep with her bare hands, calling out for the dead. She knew the truth, but chose to believe in the impossible, and she did it because she knew Rhendal would approve.

And so did the fire in her very essence.

She could see it all now, as though a veneer of cloud had been torn from her vision. They were her enemy, yet they were the same as her. Not a popular belief, where murder and war and genocide were concerned. Not a thing to think when ignorant generals deemed these necessary things as well. She wept with each painful stroke into the sandy, dusty ruin, and she did not deny herself this release. She cried for her life, for the waste. For this war, for the cruelty. She cried because there was nothing to be truly joyful about anymore in this world. It wasn't fair, but that was war, and she was sick of it. Oh, aye, she could still despise the Anguished One for the cruel deeds done in his name, for the fear of his demonic power, for the murder of her comrades in front of her. But these dead she searched for were simple folk who were crushed in soul and body by a war in whose making they had played no part. For which they had no need, either.

She dug for hours and could not stop herself. She dug until her body became drenched in sweat. Until her fingers ripped open and her body became a volatile furnace, ready to release. Even as the sun crossed overhead and the first fading of the day allowed a chill to creep up her back.

"Are you there?"

Silence.

"Do you still breathe?"

Silence.

"Would you forgive me if I left?" she whispered, and nothing but the wind replied.

And then she dug a little more and came upon a hand outstretched. She did not hesitate; she ignored the sting, the chill, the panic and the knowing of the darkening hour. She dug around that cold hand, talking to it, and as she did, she felt that dreadful burning come upon her even more, and she denied it.

What am I doing?

Why can I not stop?

Eventually, with the sun slipping away, she fell still and took that hand in hers and knew the futility of her actions. Still, with burning hands that might warm the blood back into the body, she gripped hard and pulled with all her might, and with a sudden violent give, she fell backwards holding tight that arm as it tumbled with her and then the true horror of her actions came upon her and the enchantment broke.

You wasted too much time.

They were better left forgotten.

You will be hunted down.

The limb was long drained, though no doubt it had been fuelled by a heart desperate to do its duty until the crushing end. She did not recognise the limb, but she wailed for her keepers' deaths. She wailed that she had not fled from this place and reached the gates, and her army, and her salvation, by this late hour.

And suddenly, she wanted to flee. To survive and live on. Instead, she placed the arm back in the rubble and covered it up with rocks, and slate, and wood and brick, and then, with a silent prayer to the Seven, she slipped away from the ruin of a house and, looking to the darkening sky, began to run towards the gate, knowing the foolishness of her actions.

What was I thinking?

You were thinking like a human, seeing more to this world than the cold lies of your leaders.

She held those thoughts as she sprinted and felt laden with the world, and every step was a harrowing march towards the end.

I am alone.

I am unimportant.

I will matter little.

All her life, she had desired importance. To be part of a greater thing than herself. For a time, it had been a gang in the streets. Before then, she couldn't remember much of her life save that it was rightly spitting shit. For a time, she had found a life among the rebels. Just as a runner at first, and then, as she grew older, she'd ranked up to become some bright-eyed fodder.

Though she still believed in their better cause, she no longer desired to be part of this rebellion. Not as little more than a grunt, running into a mountain of flame and a cyclone of demon smoke.

And black fire too.

She desired more than that. She desired orders that mattered, that would echo in the days beyond. But first, she wanted to be free of this dreadful city, and thereafter, she might find herself once more. She almost laughed as these thoughts spun in her mind, and she wondered if every soldier thought like this in the days before they went absent from duty.

Anything to justify cowardice.

Distantly, she heard the first howl of the monsters, and she did not fret. She saw the gate in the distance, and she knew the beasties would need to pick up her scent immediately to reach her before she reached that monstrosity and kept running.

Let the furry curs deal with a hundred thousand soldiers eager for a fight after that, she thought, and then, infused with hope and a desire to release herself from this pilgrimage, Erin sprinted faster and farther than ever before. She ran until her lungs burned and still, she chased the night, and although she should have kept running, a dim blue hue caught her eye as she passed the shell of a building, somehow still standing despite nearly all of its support beams having been blasted away.

Keep going, fool.

Near the end of the march.

Just a little more, is all.

She knew better. Her mind was not hers. And then, she spun and ran from the path towards the gate and into the darker ruins towards that dim blue light. Her body burned brighter in terrible fire, yet she could not stop herself as she ran.

Until she came to the old man, sitting upon a large boulder embedded deep in the ground. He was older than the most ancient fiend she'd ever seen, but there was an energy to him she found potent and alluring. She'd never come upon a man like this, and she was intrigued. He sat with hunched shoulders upon the rock, and as she came upon him, the hue disappeared as though it had been a trick of the darkened light.

You are not of this world, are you?

His long white hair was like wire sticking up, standing wildly on end as though frozen in a morning's frost. His skin was so deeply wrinkled she could barely tell if he smiled, or grimaced, or wept. His head was low as though he'd been beaten fully by life, and truly he looked a withered wretch, ready for death. He was but skin and bones wrapped in a ruined cloak that was torn and loose, charred as though it had set alight as he wore it. But it was the fresh scar upon his body that struck her most. Burned and pink and bubbling ever so, down his neck the wound travelled like a nasty cancer running wild in delight, and she wondered what horror had befallen him.

He nibbled at a crusty piece of bread and the effort looked like agony itself, and she felt a kinship to this wretch for he looked how she felt inside.

"Are you alright, old man?" she called out, stepping from the shadows into view.

He chewed for a breath and looked up, his entire body creaking as he did.

"Who is that?" he asked, and she wondered was he actually blind. He looked around, past her, hesitated, and after a breath, looked back to her. "Wait... Is that you?... It can't be... although it most likely could." He tried to rise and dropped back down where he sat. He looked at his bread and slowly placed it in a pocket inside his cloak.

"I am no one at all," she said, and her words felt heavy.

"You are a strange beauty... a beauty, alright... beautiful..."

"Um, thank you?" She stood before him and smelled the burned flesh on him. He looked ready to rest his head. To give up. To die.

Too old.

I never want to be that old.

I probably won't ever be.

"I had near given up sitting here... finding myself..." He

began to chuckle and it was a horrifying thing. "Fixing myself... so I might die..."

"I see," she said, and looked to the path, to the darkness around them. Her body began to burn inside again, and she held that pain and allowed it to fester. She did so because she was so very tired, and for a moment she wondered if she really was here, out in the dark, talking to a demented old man about nothing important at all.

"I find it so very strange that I can barely see you... friend," he whispered.

"I stand before you. Perhaps you are just a little tired."
From dying.

"Perhaps you think these demonic burns... took my sight?"

"I think nothing, old man. Only that it is late, and these ruins are no place to be."

"I have walked these ruins three nights... or two... somewhere among them. I fear no glorified hounds," he said, sniffing, and again, she could sense a terrible strength from him. "I think they are coming... for you alone... or me... Who knows?"

"Who are you?"

"I am a Crimson Hunter... or... at least I was... for a time... They are no more... burnt and gone... I did not see that coming... I'll tell you that."

"I see," she said, and wished she had water to offer, or a better morsel of food to give him. Instead, she listened to the wind and the piercing cries as they grew more insistent. The enchantment upon her began to fade as the need to survive took over. He was mad, but those words about the beasts hunting her alone resonated. Why? Because that's the type of thing that would scare anyone who was out here this late, when they could have been safe behind the wall, eating more than rotten bread, talking of this strange book that affected her. "Is there a place you hid these last few nights?"

"I sat right here... since I fell in ruin... after I was burned... after they all were..."

Despite herself, she reached for him. "Perhaps we might find a place to hide among these ruins, old man. Can you walk? Can you run?"

He laughed, and that sound too was a mucus-filled horror. He fought her grip, though weakly. "I will go for a little walk, but not where you rush to. Not with you at all... though you could come too... It is so strange I cannot see you... Everything else... the fading sun... the growing moon and the shimmering stars... but to you... in this light... I barely see you... and I wonder is the world spinning to right itself?"

"You are so fuken strange," she said, before she could help herself, and that terrible fire took her again, held her in its furnace grip and near burned her to a crisp, all from the inside. She wanted to scream, but the pain was tolerable; moreover, it felt welcomed. She did not know why, but at this, he opened his eyes fully and gazed at her. Into her soul.

"Oh, my girl... You are here... aren't you?"

"Yes... yes, I am... um... here," Erin said, looking to the path, edging a step away. If the beasts hunted her, perhaps if she started running, she could draw them away.

"Does it hide you... the book?"

How does he know?

She looked around, fearing this was a trick of her mind to delay her escape. "Will you hide from the beasts? Then I might lead them from here," she said, and he climbed to his feet and peered at her again. He was smiling, and fuk it if he didn't appear a few decades younger.

"You are here... and she is asleep... How very fortunate... Erin?... Is it Erin...? Are you she?"

"Am I asleep? What...? Wait, how do you know my name?"

He grabbed a long pole and leaned upon it and looked to the path. He appeared positively glowing. He held his fingers out, and there was a dim bluish glow to them. "If you come with me... things will be easier... but you might be better off on your path..." The old man looked to the path and nodded. "Perhaps he is indeed waiting for you... Wouldn't that be lovely?"

"I don't understand any of this," she whispered, and a tear formed in his eye and spilled down his cheek.

"Perhaps they fell from fire. Perhaps it's not all over... Though I'm probably wrong about these things... I usually am."

"Who are you, damn you?"

"I am a Crimson Hunter... perhaps still... though she does not desire me to be... but she's asleep now... Can't take the pain of my recovery... Easier to take from two souls... don't you know."

"Who the fuk are you?" she roared, and distantly, the Venandis's screams grew, as though they heard her, and he simply smiled.

"I will be seeing you soon... dear friend, at the end of it all, when those souls need to be freed." At this, he spun around and began walking towards the deep of the city, towards the echoes of the coming Venandi night hunters.

What is going on?
I must be mad.
That makes most sense.
That should make me feel better but it doesn't really.

Thoroughly confused, she began to run, and once she was back upon the path she felt better, her mind clearer. Soon enough her breath began to break against the effort, but she kept running, avoiding precarious snags, ducking shards of ruined wooden beams, all the while gazing to the darkened break in the wall where her army held, where she could rest, could eat, could weep for the misery she had endured, and after that, where she could flee this army altogether.

With every step, she heard the familiar call of the beasts, and soon enough the frenzy of the hunt grew in menace. She might have cowered or sought out a hiding place, but she refused to give in. Her foolish distractions had brought her to this precarious position; she refused to humour thoughts of failure. And besides, according to the strange old man, there was some man waiting for her. She wondered would he be good looking? She wondered would he be kind? She wondered if he existed at all. It was something to do while fighting fatigue and fear.

No less than a half mile from the gate and the first signs of an occupied territory, she came upon a massive barricade beneath the battered ruin of a tall tower. Its remains stood weakly against the night, no doubt battered by boulders before the rebels stormed the city. Slowing to a jog, she saw movement within, and her heart began to beat in excitement.

"Who goes there, cur?" a soldier called out, and gratefully, she raised her arms and marched through the barricade into the warmth of her former comrades.

"I am Erin, of the fifth, seeking shelter," she called, and dozens of soldiers with swords appeared along the barricade. It ran the length and breadth of the tower, surrounding it, all secure and fortified. It was a fortress within a war zone, and she recognised the outpost exactly for what it was: the line of hostile territory, and these wonderous fiends holding back the night were welcoming her in. "Under Captain Rhendal," she offered, and swords were eased, barrels were rolled out of the way and she was bade enter by an impressive... man.

She immediately felt camaraderie behind the barricade, among the few dozen soldiers. They sat in front of campfires, watching the night, watching for threats. They laughed, joked, they cooked and they cursed, and she felt so rightly at home that she near began to weep with relief.

The captain of the watch stood before her. He was twice her age, and that was no matter. He was clean shaven, but there was a hardiness she recognised immediately. "I am Captain Rusk. Where are your brethren?" he asked, and she collapsed to a knee, gasping, as the squeals of hunting Venandi filled the night. At the sound, the soldiers immediately drew their weapons once more, fanned out along the barricade and fell silent but for a few muted curses, a few uneasy jokes, a hushed number of orders.

"I am all that remains; lost the first night. Rhendal fell this very dawn to those cursed beasts," she said, mid-gasp.

"You aim to get back to the gate?"

"Yes sir, I do. Am I allowed to do so?" she asked, catching her breath, standing up straight, finally offering a salute, which he returned. Somehow, it felt better to be among those she had once called family. Easy to feel like that in the dark with monsters running around, she knew. She wondered how she would feel come the dawn.

"The war is not going exactly as we hoped… but we still hold the gate," he said. "Though there is a break in between the lines where those beasties sometimes hunt, so better you stay here until they pass through," he said.

Distantly, there came the sounds of shuffling as hundreds of nasties emerged from the shadows, and immediately, the soldiers lit torches and cast them back into the darkness where they caught fire in pools of blackwater and lit up the night, creating a small defensive barrier.

"There are more than usual, sir," a soldier called.

"We have enough to stand firm," Rusk called out, and he was imposing and reassuring.

The beasts began to howl mercilessly, and Erin's fear returned. She thought of the old man out in the dark, likely dead by now, no matter what he claimed. She looked around at the hardened soldiers, all assured in this watch, no doubt, and ready for an assault from these beasts from behind the walls of this bastion.

"More sir, coming around the rear," another soldier called. The young soldier lit a torch and tossed it out into the night, illuminating the beasts as they tested the boundary ever so, and Erin felt a dreadful sinking sensation.

"It's not the first time these bastards have come sniffing," Rusk declared. "Those with a bow, get ready, and we'll give them something to feed upon," he roared, and though she should have felt more secure here among the ramparts and fighters, she suddenly wished she was back in a room with Rhendal, reading a book in the belly of the beast. Or among the enemy's people, eating watered gruel, listening to true horror.

"Sir, these beasts are acting strange," another voice called.

"Don't worry, they are just bitter that they missed out on a little meal," Rusk assured them, and Erin stepped away from the line, deeper into the tower, towards the centre. She wanted to find a ladder to climb. Seek shelter in a level above, or the one after that. Perhaps, if she got high enough, they might lose her scent.

Perhaps.

"But be vigilant and prepare yourselves, lads, and we'll see whose teeth are sharper," Rusk roared, and the beasts charged as one down upon them all.

The Shadows

"Pull it out, fuken pull it out, by the gods of thurken spit, will you pull it out."

It sounded like an order and Derian considered it. He also knew the rules of warfare and welfare, and that pulling that barbed bitch from Lorgan's chest was going to kill the man if he wasn't already dead. Saying that, dying was never a particularly worrisome problem for the Crimson Hunters. A bigger problem was avoiding a strike from Lorgan for the pain inflicted on him. Lorgan could do a lot of damage with a careless blow should he decide to take it out on Derian. Still, though, it was an order.

The shadows loomed and Derian's heart sank. These barges were not painted black as the Dellerin air brigade were. Instead, they bore spatterings of green and gold against the darkness of the night, and Derian could see they were rebel units. All sneaking about in the clouds, all waiting to hunt down an unsuspecting airbarge eager to catch a breath.

Though only six accosted and surrounded the

Mongoose, there were at least a hundred similar shapes in the clouds around them. They loomed like demons of distant smoke and horror. Who knew how many were up here in the air, hidden in the clouds beyond.

Leaving their comrades to burn below.

No doubt, they were waiting for the proper moment to spring an attack while the Dellerin brigade were rightly distracted with their eyes on the cannons below, Derian mused. It was a plan conceived by a general with no concern for his own losses, and Derian ground his teeth irritably.

Another few longbolts shook the barge as they struck again. Only half a dozen came this time, as the soldiers aboard no doubt wondered why the barge did not immediately flee from the greater numbers. Derian was interested to know as well.

As was Lorgan.

"Let's get this fuken bird moving, Kesta," he bellowed from his pinned position upon the deck.

"Derian, get over there. Pull that fuken thing out before he dies all over the deck on us," Natteo cried, bringing his longshot to the rear as one of the barges hovered into his firing line. He looked ready to fire, but held off, even as the airbarges moved around the *Mongoose*, trying to pen her in, readying their barbs for another assault.

Seren knelt beside Lorgan, her hands flashing in a healing enchantment, but she did not pull the barb free. She was many things, but being strong enough to do such a thing was beyond her. And that was fine. Nobody gave a fuk about such a thing. Nobody thought less of her, either. "Come on, Derian," she demanded as her weaving engulfed her in a bright glow.

Suddenly three more longbolts struck the barge's hull. Another skidded past Derian's shoulder, losing itself in the night, while another bounced over the galley roof and landed upon the deck, where it lay spinning like a fallen coin in a wager's toss. It spun and fell still and it shook the mercenaries to life.

"Alright, alright, I'll help," Derian cried, finding his feet and sprinting to the edge where Arturo stood watching over Lorgan. The old acolyte looked positively intrigued as Seren caught the crimson, stemming the flow before it left through the front and rear of his body. She became an invisible dam against a relentless tide, and she groaned with the effort of her soul eating itself.

Derian could see it was a deep cut, and he swallowed his wariness as he considered how best to pull the heavy barbed metal pole from the battered mercenary without tearing him completely apart. He did not meet Lorgan's eyes lest the older man see the terror in Derian's face. Lorgan, though, looked fit to kill, looked to have a fit, and looked like he'd just been killed. It wasn't a good look to him at all.

"Why did you get in the way of a bolt, boss?" Derian asked, reaching around and feeling where the iron barb had gone through, tearing his back apart and embedding itself in the edge of the balcony as it did. A lesser man would be dead, and perhaps, had Seren not caught his bleeding as he was struck, they'd already be seeking a new leader for the group.

A new leader.

Derian had always considered himself a leader in the making. He also liked to think he was improving as a warrior. There was also that whole demon-monster type thing inside of him. That was rather polished for the average mercenary, and probably good for asserting his leadership among the more restless of the underling mercenaries.

A brave and honourable leader.

He thought on Lorgan's leadership and truly, in that moment, realised how strong a leader he really was, even if he had more failures to his name.

Failure and kindness.

These failures had led them to this very place. Any other mercenary leader would have left Derian far behind in the first few months of marching. And a hundred times since. Aye, although neither failure or kindness were traits welcomed in any good leader, in Lorgan they were in abundance.

I don't want to be leader.

I'm not at all ready.

Yet.

It was in this moment that Derian truly admired Lorgan for the man he was. It was also in this moment that he ran out of things to think about while performing field surgery on the deck of an airbarge. So he gripped that barb and pulled, and it was slimy and warm, and sharp and embedded, and he groaned as he failed in his efforts, but he kept at it, for the man was fading.

"I think these bastards aim to kill us," Natteo called. It wasn't helping matters.

"Well, kill them back," Lorgan roared, and cursed loudly for his efforts and Derian's too. Seren began to falter as she healed, and Derian could see the strain of keeping him alive. It appeared far more difficult to keep a person alive as death wrapped itself around their body, than simply healing the wounds of the fallen. Derian thought that interesting too.

Derian gripped Lorgan by the front of his shirt and looked into his eyes as he finally pulled the barb free of the deck, before turning to the true terror of removing it outright from his dying body. "Stop your shouting," Derian demanded.

Don't die.

"It isn't too bad at all."

Don't look down at your ruined chest.

"I've got you, Lorgan."

"I've got you, Dad."

Wait, what?

As though a beast took his will and did it for him, he pulled it free, taking all manner of sinew and blood and bone with it. It was the smoothest surgery under the circumstances, but devastating all the same.

"I'm so sorry, boss."

Lorgan swung and struck Derian across the chin. It was a devastating blow, and the younger mercenary collapsed as though the deck was taken from under him. The world spun and went black, and somehow, he stayed awake long enough to watch as Lorgan died in that breath.

For a breath.

For Seren caught him, raising both her hands and pulling him from the night just as swiftly as he himself had slipped overboard. She wailed as she did, and Derian saw the streaks of grey appear throughout her beautiful black hair as she weaved from her own soul for a breath. For his breath. And a breath after that was all it took to send the cur coughing, gasping, reaching to stand.

"Hey, idiots," Natteo cried to the nearest airbarge daring to hover into range for a clearer view and a better shot from the rebels upon the deck. "You fukers... over there," Natteo continued, gesturing to the barge and then to the banner they flew at the far end of their bird. It was a perfectly adequate mock-up of a mercenary banner. "Can you see it...? Look at it... idiots."

After incurring the wrath of the Dellerin air brigade, Lorgan had insisted they leave a banner to warn of what hissects' nest might be stirred up should they come under fire. It should have worked, and Derian had been rather proud of his needlework given the merely adequate materials he'd been provided with. The flag hung weakly at the rear without the rush of wind at their tail. Still, though, anyone could see the white and black outlines that suggested the mercenaries were protected by the Guild. "Hey, stop firing and listen to me," Natteo demanded, but they weren't listening at all, so he smiled his most deadly smile hoping it would hold their eager trigger fingers. He might have been right. He had a godly smile, or so he claimed. Peace was founded on lesser things.

"We are on your side... your side," Natteo screamed into the night. He might have needed an enchantment upon his words, for they were lost in the wind and the whirr of engines.

"I don't think it's working... Wave louder... comrade," Arturo suggested from across the deck, and Natteo spun around.

"Is Lorgan back up?... He's not dead?... Great stuff...

So, Lorgan…We are on their side, aren't we?… I mean, we don't like the king… but… we aren't at war with him… I mean, they have a point, don't they?… Hey, Lorgan… the rebels… you know… those fuks in the barges shooting at us." He seemed confused. "We probably shouldn't shoot at them… right?… Lorgan?… Hey… don't gesture at me like that."

Suddenly there was a slight explosion from the cockpit, followed by a little smoke, a little fire, too. "It's alright. It's completely alright. I have this," Kesta shouted, opening the hatch to let more smoke escape. She didn't need to. There was ample air flow around her. There were also loose wires upon her shoulders, and all manner of sparks where other wires met and separated throughout the little cabin, and she looked rightly flustered, yet also completely in control. "They hit my controls, is all," she added, and Derian could see where a barb had struck through a small section of glass and caused terrible problems within. It had stuck into her chair, too, and nearly lanced her like a pike. Lorgan was a larger target. She was lesser. It had missed her by a deep breath, and she didn't seem at all fazed about this. Merely annoyed her baby was a little fuked. Eveklyn had already begun hammering at the long, barbed bolt with her axe as though it owed her money. "In a moment, we'll be good," Kesta pledged, and Derian's rising panic took over as another tiny explosion engulfed her for a breath. "Ow, fuk it… ow… It's alright… I mostly have it… mostly," she said from within the cloud as it streamed out into the night.

Another barrage of bolts tore across the deck and one of them would have skewered Derian but for Arturo catching the barb mid-air and directing it wide, into the darkness, with a wave of his long, outstretched fingers. Emboldened, he attempted to stop another barrage, but the bolts merely wobbled in the air before landing throughout the *Mongoose*, ruining her finish in a dozen places. Distantly, Derian heard Kesta curse loudly again.

Arturo dropped to his knees, and if Derian were to wager, the old whisper of a man didn't look fit to last a week. At this rate, it wouldn't be the night.

Get us flying, Kesta.

From deep within, Derian suddenly felt a stirring of purest anger and he wondered did his beast stir. He sought that monster out. A beast like that would have no problem leaping from barge to barge, tearing apart everyone who tried to stop him. He'd not feel guilty about killing them, either. Derian, too, would feel no guilt.

"I'm feeling better already, girl. Save your strength," Lorgan said, grasping Seren's hand in his, and the healing eased and she shook her head.

"You are still rightly fuked," she said.

"I'm always in this state," he said, climbing to his shaky feet, and Derian could see the fresh membrane across the wound. It was raw and looked agonizing. "Tell you what, my dear. After this is over, you can tend to me."

"He's so fuken smooth, isn't he?" Natteo declared, as Seren allowed Lorgan to endure his agony without weakening her further. Perhaps he knew the value of having at least one healthy weaver aboard. A weaver was far more important than a ground-based warrior while they fought in the sky. "Hey, fearless leader, are we firing on these dickheads or playing dodge the death a little more?"

"Kill them," Lorgan roared, hobbling over to the

nearest longshot and strapping himself in. "You too, Derian," he ordered, just as all four propellors stopped with an alarming screech and the world fell silent for a breath.

"Fuk, fuk, fukety, fuk fuks," screamed Kesta as the barge began to drop like a flung stone.

It went from dropping, to falling, to deathly spinning in a breath.

The wind rushed in his ears, it rapped at his hair, and Derian felt his feet leave the deck once more as though he were floating, such was the drop.

This is bad.

Again.

Why always me?

The clouds disappeared above them, and Derian waved his hands in the air as though he were swimming. As he did, Keddy passed by, swimming his own way. He didn't appear concerned as he swung at Derian before pushing against the floating mercenary and using him as leverage. Then, miraculously, he managed to propel himself off the top of the deck and down one of the ladders into the great beneath.

"I fuken hate that cat," Derian cried as the *Fighting Mongoose* fell from safety back into a war zone.

TALK TO ME, GOOSE. TALK TO ME

"Alright, that's it... I definitely have it this time," Kesta shouted, but Natteo didn't believe her. He was swinging wildly with the pull of the wind, the force of the falling airbarge, or whatever it was that held him in its invisible grasp.

"We are so dead," he screamed to Derian, who had his own problems. He was floating just above the deck and drifting higher as the groans of the falling beast filled the air.

He's going to have a rough landing.

"Help me," Derian cried and reached for Natteo, who was at least a dozen swimming strokes away. He did as any drowning man would, and Natteo was helpless to do anything but watch and shrug.

I'll save you next time.

It was only Arturo and Seren who remained unmoved by the drop in the barge. They remained upright as the barge fell, their hands glowing with the juices of enchantments flowing through them.

I don't want to die like this.

"Dammit, Kesta, fix this bird," Lorgan roared as he too floated from the deck, though with one arm strapped into the spinning longshot, he looked somewhat in control.

The barge caught an unwanted gust and dipped forward upon itself, and this was a thousand times worse. As the clouds disappeared into a hazy darkness above, below them the ground, awash with fire and heartbreak, grew closer.

This is a shitty way to die.

"I don't understand. It should be working," cried Kesta, battering at the controls with the handle of Eveklyn's axe. The young girl was above her head, stuck to the ceiling, appearing both shaken and completely unsurprised in that same moment.

Maybe you should have stayed in Treystone.

He wanted to close his eyes as the ground became bright with fire and bombs. He wanted to look away as they missed the tail end of the bomber barges on another run. Instead, he could only face certain death as it crept up on them at an alarming rate.

Give me a sword in my hand and let me die on the ground.

By my own deeds and not through the actions of others.

I want off this spitting barge.

"I want off this spitting barge," he roared, and the gods must have listened. Or else Kesta's frantic solution to a desperate problem had worked.

It started as one solitary propellor spinning to life, and it was the most beautiful sight in the world to Natteo. He watched those spinning propellors disappear in a shiny arc, and he prayed that the rest followed. Immediately, the decline eased, but did not stop. Somewhere in the back of his mind, he recalled Kesta pointing that fact out. Regardless, though they continued to fall at an alarming pace, his feet touched down against the deck. Lorgan's too. Derian, far higher up, landed painfully, bouncing a few times as the beast slowed its deathly dive.

I don't want to die.

I don't ever want to die.

And definitely not on this spitting barge.

Wonderfully, a second and third propellor kicked to life, and suddenly they were merely dropping and Natteo felt the contents in his belly begin to settle ever so. He still wanted to throw up, but the urgency had passed.

"There we go… I knew I had this," Kesta declared, gaining control and levelling the bird off, just as the stench of burning reached his nose. Even without the fourth propellor kicking into life, the *Mongoose* began to fly again. She lacked the fluidity of Kesta's usual abilities, but Natteo was ready to kiss the woman, and the airbarge too.

Derian scrambled to the second longshot and immediately began to strap himself in. "I think I'll need this," he gasped, loading a longbolt as carelessly as Natteo did.

"So we are definitely going to use them?"

"Look up."

He did, and wished he hadn't. Dropping like a boulder could only get them so far away, and the hunting airbarges above were already in pursuit, dropping in single file, chasing them down.

"Dammit, get that last propellor going," Derian cried.

"Shut up, Derian, or I'll smash your head with a rock," Kesta roared. After a moment, she called out again. "That was a little harsh… I've just a lot of things on my mind."

"Are those 'things' getting the fourth propellor spinning?" Natteo asked helpfully. It was something to do while waiting for a half-dozen airbarges to catch up with them and shoot them to hell.

"Quiet, you," she hissed, and Natteo knew better than to tempt fate. Aiming the crosshair at the end of the weapon, he simply brought his longshot up to face the oncoming hunters.

Across from Lorgan, Arturo slowly strapped himself into the longshot. He did so with the carelessness of a sleepy man tying his shoes before a day's labour. Twisting the weapon around and testing the weight, he seemed more interested in the mechanics over actually firing anything, but after a few manoeuvres the effort got the best of him and he simply leaned upon the heavy steel as though it were the only thing that kept him afloat. He looked too ruined to fire a wave of weaver's fire, but dying at war was better than going to sleep and never waking up. That's how Natteo had always felt. Perhaps because he was certain he would die no peaceful death.

"It's us that this will fall upon, brother," Derian said quietly. It was no lie, and Natteo nodded sombrely. The pursuing barges spread out in lines three deep. So much for taking on each in a row and hoping for the best, he thought miserably. The two mercenaries stood at the rear where most of the fighting would occur. If any of the airbarges caught up with them and passed, well, that was Lorgan and Arturo's domain. Saying that, there would likely be more than enough for all to have a crack at killing, or to be killed by.

Spit on this shit.

"I suppose they're our enemy for now," Natteo said. The land began to rush wide of them as Kesta brought the *Mongoose* under her dogged will. She aimed for the city. A precarious thing, really, but Natteo wasn't going to argue. She neared the great wall and only just cleared it, dragging the airbarge wide of a high-reaching building and flying directly into a plume of smoke along the inside of the wall. There, the pull of the world was fierce as she suddenly changed direction, hoping to lose their hunters. On any other day, Kesta would have enjoyed the challenge, but with only three propellors, they hadn't a chance of outflying the hunting pack.

"Come on, you bastards," Natteo shouted, watching the airbarges chase down after them. For a breath he thought they were clear, but at the last moment their hunters caught the trail and followed after. "Ah, fuk it anyway."

"She's aiming for the Guild. I think we can make it," Derian said.

"It's too far. No cover. We really can't," argued Natteo.

"Well, even if we don't, at least we are getting to see the city in all its glory," Derian suggested, spinning his weapon to meet the incoming attackers. It was the silence before the storm at breakneck speed, and Natteo welcomed the company.

"Even on fire, she's as ugly as a fuk mule," Natteo offered.

"What's a fu... Ah, never mind."

As they raced along the city wall, Natteo caught sight of the remaining Dellerin brigade engaged in battle with a few hundred rebel airbarges that had also dropped from the clouds. Natteo couldn't help feeling the defending army should have engaged the Dellerin army long before they'd reached the city, or at least waited until they'd run the defensive gauntlet from the flak cannons a few more times. But what did peasants truly know about warfare?

Those with the best knowledge invariably ended up as mercenaries.

Better pay, fewer orders, less killing too.

"Aw, spit on me. There are plenty more targets in the sky. Could they not just leave us be?" Derian moaned as the rebel barges surged down towards them, staying clear of the cannons altogether.

"I shouldn't have smiled at them," Natteo suggested, grinning. He was getting used to tense moments with Derian at his side. There was something in his comrade's presence that stirred competence and confidence. It didn't seem quite as bad with the fool having his back and he his.

"You had to smile at them, brother. They were just asking for it," Derian mocked, and the screech of longbolts piercing the deck filled the night.

"Hey, no fair. We weren't ready yet," Natteo roared, and returned fire. It was a terrible shot that struck the barge's hull and had no effect whatsoever.

"I bet I get more kills than you," Derian called through gritted teeth.

"I bet I live longer than you."

"Oh, I'll take that bet," Derian cried, dropping low and pulling a second bolt from the ammunitions. "Hey, assholes… Aim at him, will you?"

"Come wipe away my smile, you spitting curs," Natteo challenged. It was terrifying being at someone else's mercy. But with a trigger at the finger and skills to be tested, there was a welcomed sense of control. It was harder to be afraid when you were trying to kill.

The world slowed, though their actions did not. With shaking hands and lurching bellies, they went to war against the swooping airbarges as Kesta alone tried and failed to manoeuvre away from their chase. That wasn't to say she wasn't skilled as she danced the *Mongoose* around the burning city, avoiding towers and grandiose houses, dropping low, darting high, all the while having faster, agile birds in pursuit.

She tried to make it to the Mercenary Guild. She really did. And in truth, she actually did make it.

Theirs was a precarious last effort over low-built buildings with little cover, and they were nearly blown out of the sky for their efforts, but they reached the Mercenary Guild. It was hard to see in the smoke, but at the last moment, as sanctuary called, there appeared a light-blue glowing shield blocking their way. Natteo knew it was a shield because it shimmered, but also because of the three wrecked mercenary airbarges below, which had failed to notice the barrier swift enough. Desperately, and with a force that near took Natteo from his feet again, the *Mongoose* reared like a mount and surged high, clipping the pinnacle of the massive blue weaver's shield as she did.

Knock, knock.

For a breath they circled above this massive thing, desperate to see if it would open for them, desperate to crack a code that might welcome them in, but they were the Crimson Hunters and luck was never far away from fuken them over royally. The shield remained and the pursuing airbarges cleared it as they flew. In fact, they rose higher above them and circled, seeking the perfect kill shot.

"Fuken go, go, go," Natteo demanded, and Kesta, cursing their luck, answered. The *Mongoose* surged off into the city once more as they sought to lose their assailants, but they knew their last card was played.

"Probably should have seen that coming," Derian said.

"Almost predictable, that," Natteo said in agreement as they watched the Guild disappear behind them.

"Well, at least we still have our health, and all our limbs," Derian declared, ever the positive voice.

"All this smoke is wreaking havoc with my throat. Either that or a nasty flu is coming upon me," Natteo said.

"Well, let's go kill them all, and then put you to bed."

"That's one of your smoother chat-up lines right there," Natteo suggested. "Hey, Seren, I think Derian has something to say to you," he called out, but Seren wasn't listening; she was lost in her world, watching the smoke and fire around her. And in her hands.

"I think I'm fine about that," Derian said, shrugging. "I think she's not for me."

"I told you, brother, she cast a fuken lure upon you," Natteo said in excitement, and he believed it too.

"Well, it's a good thing it's worn off, or broken, or

whatever," Derian said, lining up a shot as the barges screamed through the air, readying a fresh bombardment.

"Don't worry. We'll find you someone, dear Derian." He shrugged. "Perhaps she's somewhere below in all that fire and flame. Maybe you could save her."

"Now that mercenary tale is way too predictable," Derian said, taking the shot and missing widely.

"Nothing wrong with a little familiar tale if it works."

"I do enjoy these conversations at these times. By the way, there's a barge creeping up on your right."

"Aw, you bastard."

It became routine, despite the terror: both mercenaries calmly loaded and reloaded their weapons while longbolts landed all around them. It felt inevitable that they would fall to the barrage eventually, that something would have to give between the fighters, and eventually it did.

"Curses on you," Natteo cried in delight as Derian struck a fine blow to one of the barges.

It was his sixth or seventh strike, though he would have claimed it was his second. The shot had appeared to fly well wide, but as though guided by the gods, or perhaps Arturo's whispered hand, the chasing airbarge, which had been swooping to the left, pulled a harsh right, avoiding a sudden tower, and flew directly into the incoming barbed pole.

"I meant that," lied Derian, watching the pilot's cabin explode in a crimson smear, and the barge immediately shot off into the sky before dropping suddenly.

"That's going to be an awful wait," Natteo cried as the airbarge began to plummet to the ground.

"It needed to be done," Derian said coldly, but Natteo knew it hurt. Monsters and demons and even grand demons were one thing, but killing your own was a sobering, soulless thing.

"Hey, Lorgan! Derian just took one out," Natteo called.

"Get another," Lorgan called as he himself was attempting to strike out at an airbarge creeping through the gloom on their left flank.

"He deserves a pat on the back for that one," Natteo offered as the stricken barge gathered speed in its final dive.

"Aye, he probably does. Remind me after," Lorgan said as his own shot went wide. No doubt he'd been blinded by the sudden explosion of the airbarge on the roads below.

Natteo's words had distracted Derian enough that he hadn't seen the barge's end. A good thing too.

"Thank you, Natteo," Derian said, reloading just as three bolts flew between the comrades and embedded themselves in the deck behind.

Fuk, that was closer than close.

"As if I'll ever remind him," Natteo roared, swallowing the fright, and went to war once more.

It was Seren who took the next barge from the sky. She looked rightly spit n polished doing it, as well. With the wind rushing, drawing her hair and dress back in spectacular fashion, she moved across the deck firing fireball after fireball upon one barge that attacked from above.

Without the need to be strapped in, she was able to follow her prey more easily, and her steps brought her between both mercenaries. She looked at the bolts embedded in the deck.

"Hello there," she said, and cast a ball of fire upon her target right as it dipped down towards them. The two warriors upon the deck, who suffered from Derian and Natteo's lack of accuracy, were hit directly, and both exploded in flame and fell from the deck like fire hissects igniting in the light. "Ooh, that was pretty," she added, then fired again as the barge dropped too low and became penned in by two of its comrades for a pulse of time.

She delivered hellfire upon them, screaming as she did, and the fireball scorched through the deck and continued going.

"Nice shot," Derian cried, and the fireball exploded, taking the barge with it.

She stood proud for a breath, looking like the elite warrior goddess she could be, and Natteo could only be impressed. Especially when she giggled. "Did you see that? That was the most beautiful thing I've ever seen," she bellowed, taking great joy in the dozen or so flailing, burning bodies as they fell to the ground, surrounded by burning metal airbarge innards. "I hope there wasn't a cat aboard."

Natteo never got a kill, but he didn't die either, so it was a win-lose moment. And for a time, it looked like everything was going to be fine. Until everything got so much worse.

For suddenly the airbarges broke from their pursuit, but the *Mongoose* continued on its way, blind to what was happening below.

"What the fuk is that?" Derian cried as an eerie green emanated from the darkness of the palace.

"Where have our friends gone?" Natteo asked.

"I don't know, but I think they were the smarter ones," Lorgan cried, leaning out and looking over.

A great chorus of a thousand different voices echoed across the palace, across the deck, across the entire fuken city, and drove deep into Natteo's soul where something powerful stirred.

"I see you there," the voice roared, and the entire world shook.

The Destroyer of Worlds

The beast awoke and he was fierce. Vengeful and consumed with hate, he sensed the turning of things and he hated it. Stretching in the darkness, he felt his nimble limbs pop and flex and he felt good about himself. He always did, for he was the destroyer of worlds.

Xanthor, the Destroyer of Worlds.

They didn't call him by his true title, but that was fine. That was expected. These lesser mumbling beings were too distracted by their goings-on to understand the force he truly was. But some day, perhaps this day, he would rise above them and show them all.

And they will all suffer for it.

From his transient bedding he rose, and the darkness was his ally. He stretched out once more and his fangs pierced the air as he yawned most powerfully.

I am not pleased.

He was most wretchedly famished, and Xanthor, the Destroyer of Worlds, the title he had given himself, stepped forward from the night, seeking prey, seeking sustenance, seeking a little death too.

The tunnel through which he wandered hummed and rumbled, as the manbeasts and womenbeasts went to war throughout his domain. He thought these insignificant creatures so pissing tiring. Oh, aye, they could be manipulated easily, but it was such an effort. There was only so much a god like himself was willing to do. Sometimes he accepted their adoration up close and personal, but mostly, he desired to be left alone, to be worshipped from afar, to be left an offering or two as well, that he might choose to gorge himself upon. If it were worthy, that is.

Though the world spun and the screams of the dying filled his ears like music, he sought out his food. To his dismay and disgust, he came upon his altar and there waited for him no offering, as he would have expected, and Xanthor, the Destroyer of Worlds, felt a great anger come upon him. He desired to kill, to scream, to rage and to punish. Instead, he pissed upon the ground in defiance of their actions, or lack thereof. Let them understand his dissatisfaction. Let them pray to him and beg for mercy lest he bare his wretched, jagged claws and tear their flesh from their bones.

Above him, the land rocked as violence took it and he was not afraid. In fact, he very much desired to step upon the field of battle and deliver his wrath. And they would speak of his coming and they would worship him once more.

But first, libations.

These days, famine was more prevalent upon his darkened lands. It was his doing, and he felt a pride in his actions. They praised him for his brutality, but they didn't understand that he also killed out of desire. And oh, he liked to kill in front of his worshippers so that they might see his deeds, that they might take his gift afterwards, and gorge themselves upon the remains while he walked away.

I must kill afresh.

The world shook again as though in an earthquake of ancient times and he did not stir, or fear. He simply walked through this darkened domain, sniffing the air, seeking sport and blood.

For miles, it felt, he strolled, alone and unattended to, through his chosen tunnels where no humanbeasts dared to tread, and he sought game high and low, until, deep in the darkest region of his domain, he came upon the scent of beast.

Rabid, diseased beast at that, and so very succulent to the touch.

I am stalker.

I am divine.

I am death.

He did not walk as beasts did; he glided effortlessly and in silence, and Xanthor, the Destroyer of Worlds, came upon his hunting ground and it was intoxicating. Saliva dripped from his mouth as he sniffed the air and listened for the rumble of prey. Around him, the thunder of noise and death and fire and suffering should have kept his prey in hiding but good fortune was with Xanthor, the Destroyer of Worlds.

I am starvation.

Foolish beast of black and claw was no easy kill at the best of times, and Xanthor regretted that the kill would be swift and brutal. He much preferred delayed and torturous and brutal. Such a kill was a true slice of the divine. But he was no foolish little youngling. He knew well that a careless killer could suffer quite the injury when cornering an alert beast like this. Despite himself and his better desires, the act would be done in the twisting of a breath and a hiss or two after that.

He climbed high above the nasty, delicious, clawed feast and hid his scent beneath the reek of the machines of manbeast. The creature itself was out hunting for its own sustenance. A common thing upon this territory. All the more to draw the game in.

Silently, and from above, Xanthor flew across the darkness and landed with claws and fangs sharp and perfect. The beast screamed in horror for a breath, and it made the flesh tastier. He dug his claws in deep and, sinking his fangs deeper into the creature's throat, killed his prey before it could foul itself, before it could fight back, either. A good kill, but Xanthor moaned a little that he couldn't have enjoyed the slaughter a little longer.

Drooling and dropping in pleasure to be closer to the blood as it streamed free, the Destroyer of Worlds gorged as the manbeasts might in the morning beyond when they came to feast upon the carcass. What was left of it, of course.

His eyes rolled in their sockets as mouthfuls of delicious flesh and fur and bone were chewed upon. It was the snapping of cartilage he liked the most.

You would be alive if they had left me an offering.

Tearing and ripping and taking the innards in his mouth, the Destroyer of Worlds took his time as he sated himself. Eventually, he pawed at the carcass and then, satisfied he had left enough that the manbeasts would tend to their own banquet from his kill, Xanthor decided to answer the calls of death.

Through his domain he glided, unwavering, as the world shook around him, all the while seeking the freshness of the night air somewhere above. It was something to do, he supposed, climbing up to the man and womanbeasts. Instead, he sat for a moment, wondering if they deserved to be graced with his presence. He even considered lying fully down and sleeping away the goodness of his feast. Instead, the dreadful noise piqued his curiosity. As did the howls of panic and pain from above.

It sounds like death.

I want it.

Leaning on all fours, he spread his scent behind him and it was a welcomed thing. No beast would dare get his scent and come upon his domain.

Nobody else's.

Travelling through the last of the tunnels used only by his kind, Xanthor, the Destroyer of Worlds, emerged into the night of panic and it was a pleasurable thing.

There was so much to see, and his eyes danced from one vision to the next, for the world was alive with many burning things below and away. Further below, the land spread out for a thousand miles each way, and he knew it could be his, if he desired.

However, he did not desire this land.

He was content with his moving domain.

For now.

But let them be warned.

Stretching back and licking his shoulder a few times, he climbed up a wooden pole and sat upon his perch, taking in the wonderful humanbeast violence all around him. His mouth watered at the scent of blood and the knowledge that death was upon them all. He did not fear death; in fact, death cowered at his claws, eight times over. He knew this, for all his kind knew of this knowledge, and Xanthor had little interest in dying this night. No matter how wildly and fiercely the manbeasts and womenbeasts tore each other apart.

He purred at the violence and the dancing creatures in the night sky. He suddenly wanted to fling himself at them and make them his own, but instead, he sat and watched and considered having a quick sleep upon his wooden perch where nobody would disturb him.

And then, from nowhere, the world spun upon itself. It was a peculiar sensation and one he had become accustomed to these last few weeks since his older humanbeasts had died, or gotten lost, or perhaps been eaten. Those interesting brutes had not known his given name either.

They had called him Phillip, and Xanthor had disliked that name, but he had accepted it, for they were generous with their meat and they rarely dropped Xanthor's domain from the sky, or spun it around as frequently as these foolish new humanbeasts did.

Unsurprisingly, as the world blurred on either side of him as they fell from a great height, Xanthor was taken off guard. A foolish thing on his part, for he lost his grip on the perch and he was cast aloft into the night air.

This is fine.

Flying high was a godly thing, reserved only for his

kind. He knew this because he was not scared. He floated upon the deck, and those foolish humanbeasts did the same. They screamed, they panicked, and Xanthor floated past them, quite sure he would come upon an escape from this peculiar sensation.

He looked to the ground far below, and considered his chances if he needed to leave these idiots behind. He'd never come upon a fall harsh enough to kill him; he doubted he ever would. His eyes narrowed as he formulated his plan, but then he thought better of it. The land was on fire, but more than that, who on the land would leave him offerings so plentiful...most of the time? He was happy to stay a little longer. He was happy to float for a time and worry about it after. He was happy to see how pissing things went before he made a move.

He floated a little further and, arching his perfect back and flapping his tail, he realised he instinctively knew how to traverse this floating fall, to allow his natural momentum to send him right where he needed to go.

The houndbeast understood momentum less.

He was no fan of houndbeast, even though the houndbeast tried pathetically hard with him. At least at the beginning. As Xanthor floated beside him, he could smell the hound in him, could smell it coming upon him too. This didn't worry Xanthor at all. He didn't pissing fear anything.

"Keddy," screamed the little one, and Xanthor spun as he fell, and she was as high as he was, though secured to the roof of the little cabin bedroom, where the lovely motherbeast with the lovely hair usually sat. Xanthor liked motherbeast. Loved playing with her lovely hair. Xanthor also really liked little human. She was probably his favourite. He liked her style. And sometimes that was enough. He didn't despise the name Keddy either. It sounded noble and pissing terrifying. He'd been called far worse in his time.

"Meow," replied Xanthor in the tongue he reserved for humanbeasts alone, and he floated towards houndbeast. She should have recognised this tone as one of annoyance at there being no food left for Xanthor, but she never did, and that was alright. Once little humanbeast found a way to climb down from the ceiling, she'd put out a nice bowl of cream and everything would be alright in the world.

As it was, Xanthor was getting sleepy and a little irritated. Using houndbeast as a wall, Xanthor dug deep into his thigh and pushed himself off. But not before swiping at houndbeast first.

And why did he swipe at him?

Xanthor hadn't a reason.

A beast like Xanthor didn't need a reason, and the humanbeasts accepted it without question.

Leaping towards one of his tunnels, Xanthor used good fortune as his most trusted ally, and he flung himself perfectly through the little tunnel, down a ladder to the level below, where near tragedy struck by way of a slight stumble, before leaping upon a curtain in the main luxury bed place.

For a time, he swung happily on the curtains and ripped them gleefully as he did, until the slow decrease of weightlessness allowed him to land gracefully, at which point he immediately found the nearest cushion and curled up on it.

He fell asleep right away, rocked to sleep by the movement of his domain floating and flying against the night. It was a wonderful short nap, and his dreams were of rats and mice and blood and death and an ocean of horror, and he licked his lips as he purred.

Eventually, it was the sudden stillness that drew him from his slumber.

The beast awoke and he was fierce. Vengeful and consumed with hate, he sensed the turning of things and he hated that too. Stretching in the darkness, he felt his nimble limbs pop and flex, and he felt good about himself. He always did, for he was the Destroyer of Worlds.

He listened to the rumble of distant death and decided to see what the sudden silence was all about. Taking the tunnel that no humanbeast ever used, he climbed out into the night and there was further delicious ruin of blood and bodies all around him, and his back tensed, his tail went wide and he knew monstrous things were afoot.

No more so than the manbeast standing with his hooded back to him.

He was not welcome in Xanthor, the Destroyer of Worlds', domain at all.

And Xanthor, the Destroyer of Worlds, decided to do something about it.

ERIN'S END

hy did they hunt me alone?

Why do they seek out only me?

All around them became a surging ocean of fur and muscle and massive deadly paws built for tearing. They were thousands in number, and they came storming towards the light as though it were a welcoming beacon, and Erin could only take a step back while the soldiers, sure of themselves and their domain, prepared themselves.

To die.

I did this.

She still felt the effect of the sprint. Her body ached; her breath was shallow. It had been a desperate last effort to reach this sanctuary, but the race was truly lost right at the end, and truly, Erin knew she had brought doom upon these fine soldiers who had done little more but be at their post watching for stragglers.

"Stand firm and we'll hold these bastards," Rusk ordered, drawing his sword. If he was terrified, he showed little evidence of it on his grizzled features. If he knew they would be overcome, he showed none of that either. It was a good look to any man or woman in command. He did not hide, either; instead, he climbed upon the top of the barricade watching the monsters, leading by example.

"Sir, they keep coming," a soldier called. "From all sides, without any let-up." The soldier spoke casually, as though it were a simple problem to be overcome.

"They will let up and we will earn our stripes, my fine lads. For we have fire, we have steel, we have this fine blockade," Rusk roared above the growing rumble. "Remember this, lads: we are the true nasty bastards out in the night tonight. Give no ground. Kill them all." They were fine fighting words, but words were words and the chatter of snapping teeth grew, as did the demented, piercing cries of the Venandi night hunters discovering their prey at last.

I am death to all.

"Alright, line up, set yourselves and... release," Rusk roared, raising and dropping his hand suddenly, and a dozen arrows shot out into the growing darkness, piercing the night and the flesh of their murderers. Half of the shots fired were killing blows. A suitable number to start on any given night. Those beasts that fell tripped twice the number following after, who were crushed by their charging brothers behind. It was wonderful chaos, and Erin held her breath lest releasing it might distract their wall of defiance.

A second volley released, and they were closer this time, and nearly a dozen fell on all sides. Those behind were again tripped and crushed, and it was an excellent defence, and Rusk rewarded them. "That's it, lads, that's good. I'm proud of you. Now, keep on firing." His sword quivered ever so, in fear no doubt, but also in preparation for battle, and Erin thought him a rightly impressive man. At the end, with death so very close, she thought it perfectly acceptable to desire some wonderful, slithering, sweaty act with another. She knew it was only natural, and she wondered again, was Rusk the man who waited for her? And was it possible he waited in other ways too?

Control your head, idiot.

Those fierce archers continued to fire, and as the monsters closed the distance to a few dozen feet, they exhausted their ammunition, but they did not give up the fight.

"Watch them—they are clearing the fire," Rusk warned as the monsters overcame the small defensive line of fire.

It's already over.

For a savage moment, Erin considered running out from cover, drawing the beasts away, making a sacrifice worth dying for. She'd never once in her life felt like tempting doom this way, and she found herself eyeing her route, counting the steps she might make before they might savage her. But that next step never came, and she felt shame as the monsters closed the gap and all she could do was be saved by the soldiers.

I cannot even raise my blade.

Through the lines of fire the Venandi charged, snapping, howling, no doubt demented by the human flesh on offer. Her human flesh most sweet. Many suffered in the defensive flames, catching their paws in the sticky, burning fluid, roaring and hissing and dying long before they reached the barricade. All too swiftly, though, the flames were snuffed out as dozens upon dozens of the brutes charged through them, forgoing any self-preservation in favour of killing. The world's warmth and light diminished to faded shadows as they came a-hunting, and Erin's own inner flame ignited and began to burn something terrible. She wanted to release this agony but had no way to do so, and she stepped further into the centre of the barricade, shivering as she did.

If they rip me open, will they find fire in my veins?

"Come on, you curs," a voice roared from the furthest part of the barricade. "Come on," he demanded, as the first beasts climbed over and met steel for their effort.

"You are nothing," another soldier cried as the beasts gathered and surged up. "To the fires with you," he screamed as a dozen claws pawed at him, desperate to drag him over.

"Spit on you, fuks," another cried, and Erin thought these heroic warriors the finest of their kind. They did not yet know their doom. They would not accept it, either. They merely swung their blades as a neat line of devastation and held strongly in those first few terrible moments.

If there were a dozen of you, Rhendal, we would hold without effort.

These soldiers were no old captains though, gifted with experience, knowing to conserve energy, read the flow of battle, and spot the changing of the wind. Aye, they had greater stamina and youthful exuberance as they plunged and cut without losing a breath, but their efforts were for nothing with those numbers surging down upon them. Rhendal would have come upon a better plan to stem the tide. She was sure of it.

"That's it, lads," Rusk roared, swinging as he did, but there was a weariness in his tone. He was covered in their blood, he gasped for rest, but still, he swung and killed without giving ground, and Erin wondered if stubbornness and belief might just be enough to challenge the odds.

"Okay, time for the fire to the far line," Rusk suddenly roared, and those who were capable cast fresh torches back into the mass of monsters, setting alight another line of blackwater she'd not seen. It was a clever ploy, for immediately, a line of fire streamed out, surrounding the barricade in a golden glow, cutting the attackers' route off for a few breaths so that they could kill off those closest and earn a reprieve in the hope they could whittle down the numbers sufficiently to see the bastards off, or at least get a second wind for murder.

Please burn all night.

It worked, as the stragglers were cut down all for the cost of no lives, and there were a few cheers as those Venandi who charged headfirst through the fire met an end instantly.

But as the soldiers took a breath, the Venandi, as one, as though commanded by some invisible master, all charged again headfirst into the flames, snuffing out the fire with their dying bodies. The stench of burned flesh rose up, and Erin knew it was for nothing.

"Sir, can we still hold?" one of the soldiers furthest forward asked. Before him charged a dozen burning Venandi, followed by three dozen more behind them looking rightly tanned and little else.

"Sir, they just took Seth," another voice cried. "I can't reach him, I can't..." Erin stepped back further into the dark, towards a thin ladder that reached to the ruined roof above. Each rung looked weakened and unsuitable for any weight, but regardless, she took hold and that terrible flame erupted inside her, burning and taking her sanity, and she collapsed on the ground and no one noticed. Why would they? For around them, there came the terrible turning of the battle. And each soldier could see it. Though they had killed many, the enemy's numbers were barely affected.

The burning took Erin terribly, and she gasped in agony.

Let it all out.

Just let that fire burn the world around you and be done with it.

She wanted to, she really did. Instead, she rolled on the ground as Rusk leapt from the top of the barricade. Three Venandi monsters streamed over after him and met a swift end at the hands of those covering his retreat.

"Right, lads, we are lost in here," Rusk cried, spinning and meeting another monster on top of the barricade. With a deep plunge, he killed the beast where it lay and delayed the next few brutes by a precious few breaths. "You, you and you," he roared to three soldiers, holding the line in a fluid act of defence. "Stand firm, right where you are," he ordered. "The rest of you, back to the ladders," he roared, dooming those three to die in the delay of a desperate retreat. "Come on, right fuken swiftly as well," he roared, and Erin could take no more of this agony. She wailed as the soldiers streamed past her, desperate to climb to the next level where they might hold the monsters a little longer. A solid tactic and perhaps one they should have considered the moment the fires gave them breath.

Leave me here and I might delay them.

Boots hammered around her and Erin couldn't breathe.

She gasped for breath but with such terror, with so many bodies stealing her air, with such dreadful burning making her clench inside, she merely lay upon the ground, curled up, holding herself as she waited for the inevitable death upon four paws.

These brave soldiers took to the ladders, screaming orders as they did, and Erin could hear no more save her own whimpers. She was no hero, she was afraid of the world and she knew she was deserving of this fate.

Screams erupted as the defenders selected to hold the line were overcome. They did well and Rusk might not have seen their bravery as he climbed the ladder, but Erin did. It was all she could do. Through the boots she saw the first soldier fall, and a gathering of monsters streamed through the barricade, howling and panting and shrieking in delight as the scent of their kill suggested she was right before them.

"Piss on you," she gasped.

Within a breath, she could see only paws, scampering and racing, charging upon the masses who fled, and their noses were upon her, seeking her out, ready to gore her and feed upon her flesh, and Erin was terrified and she allowed herself to let go. To give up to the terror and the pain within. And from her fingers there came a bright white light that stunned and blinded her for a breath. A stolen breath that her lungs gorged upon.

What have I become?

Suddenly that light became purest fire that danced upon her fingers, and the pain began to ease as though the release had brought relief.

To the fires with me.

Suddenly, she could release, and she did, and it was no

trickle of warmth that she released, but a torrent of flame that became a pure sphere of fire, and it erupted from her every limb, from her soul, and it was fathomless.

I will not hold this in a moment longer.

She thought of the book upon her back, safely in her bag, and she weaved something incredible. The fire was eternal and it was beautiful and she wielded it with all her might, even as she lay crumpled upon the floor waiting to die.

She thought of the sins of her comrades invading this beautiful city. She thought of them levelling the ancient buildings and slaughtering so many. She thought of a building demolished in a breath and innocent broken people within. Mostly, though, she thought of Rhendal and his fate most cruel. She was no soldier anymore and she did not care. She was Erin and she was far from unimportant.

This is my vengeance.

The woven white fireball pulsed from her body, dazzling her and entrancing with its brightness, and it kept going. It burned brighter than anything she could have imagined and she allowed it, and did not know how she did this, but it felt so perfectly natural. Like picking a flower in a meadow and leaving it to float in the wind. It was effortless.

I am possessed by this book.

I am linked to that tale.

The fire erupted fiercely around her; it danced like a wave upon an ocean, covering every surface, reaching high into the stone around her, seeking further height through the levels above. It charred the ground she lay upon, it burned at her clothing, and she forced it further from her body until, with a desperate wail, the world remained bright for a breath and she looked out to the sky and the grand beacon she delivered to the clouds above and then she fell still and so did the world.

Silence.

Dreadful silence.

Gasping, and grateful for her breath, she panted and savoured the emptiness in her soul. The fire that had pulsed through her body was all but diminished, and she was empty and somehow alive.

But for the pack upon her back, which was still heavy and untouched, her clothes were a ruin, burned and charred to sticky nothing, but her skin was unblemished. Pink and proper in all the right places. She covered her shame where they had fallen away, wary that all the soldiers would see, and she thought it was humorous that she would care about such a thing.

Twisting her head, she looked to the barricade where the trio had stood and died and the monsters were burned away to nothing, but her relief was short lived.

For only in the sudden quiet did she realise the soldiers around her, desperate to climb the ladder and flee, were still where the fire had touched them, torched them, charred them to nothing. They were frozen like statues, their faces caught in the fear and agony they'd felt when she burned them. Killed them.

They did not even smell of cured meat; they were ashen ruins, and as she climbed to her feet, they broke into dust around her and she whined for her murderous act.

"Hello?" she called.

Silence.

"Is there anybody up there?" she yelled, but she knew the truth. Knew it as the bodies fell around her in dusty near-silence. They fell from the ladder too, and she climbed the first rung, and further after that, feeling dust upon her naked body and being disgusted as the ash stuck to her.

I'm sorry, I'm sorry.

I'm so fuken sorry.

I had to.

But I didn't know how.

Scrambling up in the dim light, she saw Rusk for a moment. He had made it up and was a statue looking out over the darkness. He'd not seen the fire coming from behind him. That was a mercy, but still, she wept for her murder of him. Of them all.

Everyone I meet dies.

Up this little bit higher, she could feel the chill in the breeze, and rooting through the ash and decay of the destroyed building, she found herself a thin blanket, worn and marred, but enough to cover her modesty and stave off the cool of the night.

She turned to look at the destroyed bodies of the Venandi. In the dim light she took a delicate pleasure in seeing them as charred as her comrades, spreading out in a perfect circle around the barricade.

"To the fires you went," she hissed.

In reply, there came a distant howl, and another after that, and her heart dropped. That fresh panic came upon her as the howls grew in volume and numbers.

Please, no.

They came upon this scorched sanctuary in no time at all, and as before, they surrounded the barricade and continued. She could only look on in terror as they filled the entire first level, howling and thrashing upon each other, sniffing the air, seeking her out.

"Where are you coming from?"

"Why are you so many?"

"Why are you coming after me?" she cried, but she knew it was the book they sought. Or else the power inside her.

Or else it is amazingly bad luck.

Like worms of fur and teeth wrapped in delirium, they thrashed, and as more and more surged over the barricade, they began to fill the room, climbing upon each other, snapping up at her, reaching the gap where the ladder entered the next level.

She was empty. Without fire. Without desire either. She wanted to stand where she was, to give up and be done. It had been too much these last few days, and this was the end, she knew.

Instead, she leapt upon the nearest ladder and climbed to the level above, as the first beast climbed through and sprinted after her, leaping at her, snapping and salivating as she climbed.

It was colder still up here. It was a small space to occupy as well. It wouldn't take too many of the scurrying bastards to reach this level, and there was only one more level up after this, and she fought that panic something awful as she listened to the monsters pursuing.

Burn them again.

Burn them all.

She sought that fire, and there was nothing within, and she panicked anew.

"Come on, girl," she roared, flexing her fingers, all the while keeping an eye on the level below as the monsters raced in, rabid and frantic, seeking her naked flesh. "Do it again—come on," she screamed, but she knew how long it took to muster such power. She was no weaver, blessed with the ability to weave her soul. She was something else entirely.

On all sides of the outer building, she could still see the monsters streaming into the fallen sanctuary and she knew they would keep coming until the end, so she climbed once more and reached the top of the ruined building. Some boulder had likely come right through the top level and left it open on all sides but for a long walkway petering out across a distant drop. She wondered if that walkway hadn't been some old corridor at some point, leading to another wing that was long since demolished. Looking below, she couldn't even see the bottom, and she wondered if that wasn't a blessing, such was her fate.

Strolling across the top, Erin let go of her blanket and let the breeze take it off the edge, where it dropped to nothing below. She came into this world naked, so she would leave it the same way, having never known family in between. She didn't want to think of them at the end. They didn't deserve it, and she didn't either, so she stepped quietly further into the night.

"This is it," she whispered to the wind and no one in particular. Stepping along the swaying walkway, she wondered if her weight might send it all plunging to the bottom. That would be a fine end as well.

Better that than being ravaged alive.

"It's almost beautiful from here," she whispered. She

could see the outline of the ruined city from up here. Beyond that, she could see the gate and she realised how close it was.

A girl could try and make a dash for it.

Below, she saw the beasts swarming ever nearer, and she was broken. Alone at the top of this walkway, she knew her fate was determined. She reached the edge of the walkway, no more than twenty feet from the ruined building awash with hunting monsters, and gathered her thoughts and her will.

With tears streaming down her cheeks, she cast her pack into the night beyond. She listened but never heard it land, and she felt somehow heavier without it.

She remembered seeing some cliff divers as a child. A blurry memory that had reared its head throughout her life in her quieter moments. She knew those who cared for her had been with her that day, watching the divers leap into the glistening unknown. Though she'd always wanted to, she'd never leapt from a cliff into warm, salty seawater. She had barely even stepped into a river, either, and it was no matter.

I remember the waves and laughter.

She remembered being warm and content in that moment, watching those gods of flight leap into nothing and do so with style and grace.

"Fuk it," she whispered and thought them suitable final words. Behind her, the hounds began to storm up, but she was far enough away that she wasn't worried.

Not anymore.

She looked to the darkness below and wondered how it

would be. She was terrified but strangely settled and at peace. No more running, no more being afraid.

She leapt as she remembered the divers did. Flipping backwards, she propelled herself out into the dark. For just a moment she wondered what mysterious power she had, that fire erupted from her form. She wondered if she had the power of flight that would ease her fall and deliver her to sanctuary, nude and all. As she flipped and faced the darkness and plummeted and nothing happened, she thought it a shame she would never know more of herself.

What a shame.

The Gathering of Fools

"I see you," the eerie, evil voice boomed across the land, and Natteo shook despite himself. There was a primal rage in that voice. It was no simple enchantment, either. This was something else entirely. It was unearthly, it was a warning, and Natteo wondered if the Anguished One wasn't going to appear and cause all manner of mayhem. Deep within, that festering anger reared its head. Anger was a gift in times of great terror.

He knew now was probably a time to be wary and watchful and wise, and use less of the lip he relied upon to carry him through the worse parts of his life. "Well, I fuken hear you…" he bellowed, but his voice did not carry across the land, and truly, he didn't mind if no one heard his wit. It was probably a bad idea to start a fight with a voice that sounded so powerful. Nevertheless. "… You prick."

"Don't start a fight with a phantom voice, Natteo," Lorgan called.

"Well, he started it, sounding all perverted and seedy."

The *Mongoose* hung in the air above the palace as the

smoke from the burning city grew around them on all sides. The palace itself was a thing of beauty. Tall thin towers stood out among a dozen grand domes of marble, and with such wealth on display, it was no surprise the rebels had issue with the world's king.

Through the thousand and one glass windows surrounding this magnificent palace, there shone a great deep light, and its glow spread out into the night, bathing the world in an eerie green glow. Taking the sudden silence for what it was, Kesta kept the barge still as she went to task repairing the mechanics. Natteo watched for any sudden airbarge appearing from behind the smoky veneer, but for just a moment it felt like they were the only people in the world—until he leaned across his longshot and gazed down at the countless squirming people below.

War most beautiful.

And wasteful.

As the airbarges battled with themselves in the sky, there was an entirely different battle on the ground, and the battle was swinging only one way. The rebels stormed through the battleground in great numbers. An impressive sight. "Looks like they won't need you to lead them, after all, Seren," Natteo called to the girl watching in dumb silence, and shrugged to himself. He wondered did she resent this sudden turn of events. He also wondered if her claims to be important were just a weaver's imaginings. Such a thing wouldn't surprise him at all. "Looks like we have a front-row view of the falling of a king," he added to anyone listening.

Not many were. They were watching the soldiers storm through the front gates of the palace. The large metal structure crumpled under the barrage of a ram within a few blows, crashing open wide for the rebels to surge on through the royal courtyard towards the palace's main entrance. Though they'd broken through the city, they were still made to work for the last few feet of the march.

"It looks so easy," Natteo murmured, and it did look easy. Even if the royal guard stood their defiant last as their domain was overrun. From behind barricades, they fired crossbow bolt after crossbow bolt and cut down the charging soldiers, who foolishly relied on swords as their only defence.

"This could have been over by now if the rebels had used their heads," Lorgan said.

"It's almost mesmerising," Derian said from beside him. Like Seren, he appeared terribly unhappy at what he gazed upon.

"All to a wonderful glow of green," Natteo muttered, watching the light pulse ever so. "Whatever that is, it can't be very good."

It wasn't skill that drove that battalion of rebels forward, but murder by numbers. They took the bolts, and watched their comrades fall in front of them, yet they did not stop, no doubt believing in their leaders' tactics, and their own importance.

Fuken peasant tactics.

"They should be attacking from the flanks," Derian pointed out irritably. A fair notion, for no mercenary enjoyed peasants throwing their lives away over foolish strategies. "Not just the fuken front."

"Why not go down and tell them?" Natteo suggested.

Derian might have replied, but suddenly his eyes

narrowed, and, unhooking the longshot, he smelled the air, all the while gazing out into the mass of soldiers storming forward.

"What is it, Derian?"

"I cannot help but feel I should be down there," he muttered.

"What do you mean?"

"Something in me is compelling me to be down there."

"Are you serious?" Natteo cried. "We already started a fight with the rebels. We don't need to start a fight with the king."

"Perhaps we do, brother."

Natteo didn't like that tone at all. Not one bit.

"It was only a matter of time before they appeared," Arturo hissed. From the palace doors there suddenly appeared a dozen figures clad in faceless armour. They stood out from the rest of the defenders by their weavers' cloaks, similar to Arturo's.

"Are they the acolytes?" Derian asked.

"Aye. Bastards, the lot of them."

"You could also go down and say hello," Natteo suggested.

"Those I knew are long since drained and dead."

Natteo didn't know how to respond to this, so he shrugged and watched these bastards get to killing.

As though controlled by one hive mind, as one they brought fire alive around them. "Look at those curs... desperate and cruel and fierce." Despite his withering form, Arturo hammered the edge of the barge's balcony fiercely.

Suddenly the palace courtyard was alight in screaming and fire. Rebel soldiers were blasted back in the first wave, and Natteo's heart dropped at seeing this dreadful slaughter just as they believed victory was theirs.

Only Derian reacted. He calmly loaded his longshot and fired down upon them. He did so without emotion, and Natteo watched the bolt catch in the wind and travel further than any longshot should have travelled accurately.

"That's a good shot," Arturo said aloud. As he did, the longbolt struck one of the weavers through the head, dragging him backward and pinning him messily to the palace gates.

So it's treason, then?

"Oh, Derian," Lorgan whispered. He might have raged, condemned, but it was a fine act by the young mercenary, thought Natteo, and truly something the Guild should have done a long time ago.

"Well, I suppose we are at war with them as well," Natteo said, and Seren hopped upon the barge's balcony, where, through more than balance alone, she leaned out, watching the smoke around them as it began to thicken. From her hand she drew a great ball of magenta flame and effortlessly she cast it down upon the line of acolytes. It flew straight, untouched by wind or distraction, and when it reached them, it blew three of the fiends to nothing. As impressive as Derian's strike was, this was a godly shot and perhaps gave hope to the attackers below that they weren't alone. Even if, technically, they might have been at war with them too.

"Perhaps they won't notice," Lorgan said, loading up Natteo's longshot, preparing a shot of his own.

"They noticed," Seren cried and dropped down,

forming a blue sphere around her. As she did, Arturo stood up beside her. He whispered in her ear and she nodded.

"What is it?" Derian asked, loading another longbolt. As he did, the palace's green glow suddenly dropped to nothing. It was the prelude to very bad things, for from the smoke there came massive moving shapes, and they fanned out and floated across the sky.

"Um... why is the smoke... um... doing that?" Natteo asked, feeling a terrible dread. Deep within him, there was curiosity; deeper below that, that terrible rage for this smoke-shaped beastie.

"They are coming," Arturo said coldly.

"Who? Who the fuk are coming?" Lorgan demanded.

The shapes continued to fan out across the sky. They moved as though blown by a gale and then accelerated to tenfold the speed after that as they became nasty creatures.

"They are the spirits of grand demons," Arturo whispered, and Natteo somehow knew this. He did not fear them, either. He merely wanted to take his blade to them and discover whether demon souls bled.

"Is that any worse than what we've already faced?" Lorgan demanded.

"They are the controlled, they are his vessels, they think for themselves, but they are his to wield, and he wields them upon those who walk upon his territory," Seren cried, and the demonic shapes became as black as the night, but with fire for breath.

A great creature like a serpent appeared above the palace, wrapping the largest tower in its embrace before slithering across the sky, forming up as though about to bite, and then blasting a terrible black fire upon the rebels below.

Derian fired upon the thing and the longbolt disappeared into the smoke without effect, and Natteo's anger rose once again. He hated this beast primally. It was almost familiar, and he wondered had he dreamed of such a thing? Had he witnessed it one of the times he died?

"All who march will die this night," that terrible voice cried once more as the flame erupted among the rebels, burning them alive where they stood, and Natteo found himself screaming in horror.

"This is not our fight, Kesta," Lorgan roared, and immediately, the *Mongoose* reared to life, and for a breath they began to turn until another of the smoke demons formed up in front of them. This fiend was far smaller, but oh, Natteo could sense its power.

It appeared as an Anculous demon. Twice the size of a large man, humanlike but with greater muscles and long additional bones like sharpened blades running down along the outer parts of each arm. The beast floated before the barge for a few moments. It did not attack; it merely stared upon them. Tendrils of smoke drifted out from each side of it and wrapped themselves around the propellers of the barge, and immediately the barge held. From those tendrils a greater line of smoke appeared, encircling the entire airbarge, filling out across the sky, entrapping them within like a terrible prison.

"To the fires with you, monster," Derian roared, and the beast grunted in reply. It paid Derian little attention. Instead, it looked to Seren and it hissed a terrible threat, floating closer to stare through her. She brought that shield up to protect herself, but the ball of flame that appeared upon her fingers remained where she held it. Perhaps she knew it would have little effect.

"Get us away from here, Kesta," roared Lorgan, hammering at the pilot's cabin as she fought the beast's hold.

"Silencio," the unnatural voice roared from deep across the world, and the smoke demon spun away in irritation. "What do you hunt, Silencio?" that voice roared again, and Natteo's hate burned real fuken bright, and he drew his daggers as it turned to look upon him. At this, it howled and there was black fire upon its breath, and Seren drew her shield wide across the front of the deck, protecting what she could.

"... Sillllllencioooooo... Answer me..."

Natteo knew that name from his survival guide, and that wrath fell away to be replaced by terror as the demon named Silencio floated towards the barge, shrinking ever so as it did. At last, it came upon the shield and cast it aside, like ripping a page from a book with a terrible twist.

"Stay away from this place," Seren ordered, to no avail. Natteo really hated that as well.

"You will know death if you step upon this barge, Silencio," warned Arturo, standing beside Natteo. He had become a shield of flesh and blood and bone and hardly anything at all.

Still, thank you, friend.

The demon didn't care. It glided upon Natteo, shoving Arturo aside, sending him across the deck, and with one of its clawed hands reached out and caressed Natteo's cheek and it near burned at the touch.

"The fuk away from me," Natteo hissed, but he was terrified, and angry, and confused, and strangely exhilarated. He wanted to fight this beast. He suddenly wanted to tear its smoky, demonic body from the sky and chew upon it, like Derian would in his beastly form.

The grand demon did not reply. It hissed a whisper and caressed Natteo's chest, stopping to place its finger upon his heart, and Natteo was too frozen in shock to stop it tending to him as though he were a pleasure boy in Castra, chosen as the meal for the night.

He didn't want to feel like that, and so he swiped fiercely with his dagger across the beast's throat, before driving the other dagger's tip through one of the bastard's beady eyes, and suddenly he realised what he was doing. He half expected to miss. Or to come upon little more than an illusion of smoke, like firing a longbolt into nothing. He didn't expect to feel the leathery resistance of flesh, or feel the implosion of gelatinous awfulness, and he most certainly didn't expect the beast to howl in horror and pain as he drew blood that spilled itself upon him. Its stench was of ancient decay and misery. He did not know how he recognised such a stench at all.

Within a breath, the demon retreated from Natteo's assault, disappearing back into the smoke, leaving the barge free from its grasp but not from the larger prison they hovered in.

"I'm not sure you should have done that," Derian suggested.

"Fuker had it coming. I regret nothing at all," Natteo countered, but he did regret it. And he did know he shouldn't have done it.

"Crimson... Company," that voice roared again, and it was less distant than before, and Natteo fell away from the longshot as the acolytes took flight, and with them their master.

———

He was dressed in his finest, most daunting armour. She saw the green glow of his chest and thought it wonderfully familiar. He stepped through the ruins of the courtyard, gazing up at the barge, barely noticing the bodies burning at his feet.

Seren recognised that voice. That vile voice had invaded her dreams, and now, she felt it dreadfully familiar. She listened and hated, and feared, and was intrigued. She thought less of herself for it, but she couldn't help being drawn to it, either.

Why do I welcome this?

Who am I?

Lorgan stood beside her and she felt stronger with his presence. She wanted to confide more to him than she already had, but she was wary of how much he could hear. She wanted to tell him more of the feelings that stirred within her, but also how that dreadful voice cut through her.

But she had said all she needed. For now.

She could barely see the scorched world below, where Anguis's grand demons had poured fire upon the masses, such was the thickness of the growing wall of smoke. She could see Anguis the Dark One floating above them all, his hands releasing that fire most black, and it was crude and cruel and devastating.

She wanted to weep, for this was so dreadfully familiar, and she felt the flames grow in her fingers, ready to release. She wanted to save those poor fools who were routed by ungodly things, but she couldn't. These pathetic, retreating soldiers looked like hissects, all alight, and she was mesmerised by the power of the man who commanded such violent things. She dearly desired to look upon his face. To know him.

So I might kill him more intimately.

She heard that voice in her mind once more and it spun her apart, tore her mind asunder, and she was terrified of what she saw. Visions of a darkened life in chains. Her soul wrapped in a spider's web, and a fierce warrior breaking her free, even though she was venomous and ready to snap. She saw a life in that world; she saw a life lived beyond that world as well. She saw herself as a beast and more; she desired to taste that world, and she was ashamed.

I am who I claim to be.

But she really wasn't.

I am a warrior of virtue and nobility.

But she never had been.

I am here to kill this beast.

But she was not capable of such a thing.

Not yet.

Not yet.

"I am here," she screamed, and her voice carried across the night, but not far enough. She demanded a fight. She demanded blood. She demanded him.

Because I must hate him for what he is.

For just a glimmer of a breath, she felt herself slip into the darkness. She took no steps; she merely called out into the darkness those words, so that he might hear, he might listen, he might come for her.

She did not know why she did this.

She only knew she needed to do it.

Is this Bereziel's command?

Is this his doing?

Am I his slave?

Was I always?

"I know you," the voice roared suddenly, and once more the palace was illuminated in that hazy green glow for the briefest moment, until it disappeared fully, giving way to the prison of smoke around the barge. Distantly, she heard Kesta scream in frustration and she wanted to tell the mothering hen that all was alright. She was finding herself. She was still virtuous. She merely had to see this man and be done with him.

Probably through battle.

Probably.

Bereziel's teachings played in her mind, even as she saw this striking, ungodly man, and Seren's heart began to hammer as she waited for him. And he came to her. For he had been waiting a lifetime or more. And he had been expecting her since she stirred him with her sleeping wanderings.

"Fuk me," cried Derian as the Anguished One rose up from the fire, carried upon a wave of smoke of his own. His cloak billowed out behind him as he flew, and she thought him less an anguished fiend and more a graceful warrior.

"Is that him?" screamed Natteo. "Did I do this…? Fuk… I'm sorry," he cried.

She shook her head and eased Natteo's guilt. It was her words that had summoned him. Her challenge too. "I am the one who brings the Anguished One, friends," Seren said dreamily, and truly, her knees felt weak. She'd already seen this in her dreams and woken unfulfilled. She looked to Lorgan longingly, and nearly dropped to her knees begging for his help, his mercy, his understanding, and his forgiveness too, for not confiding these stirring feelings and this connection to another man.

He might have been jealous.

Might.

"What have you done, woman?" Arturo cried, spinning upon her and she could see the betrayal in his eyes. In her eyes. She wondered was the other soul within stirring.

What is happening to me?

"It's alright. None of this is a worry," she insisted, for she was confident in this moment.

And suddenly, he was upon the side of the deck and no mercenary dared to move. Everything in the world froze, and somehow Seren knew it was the end of all things. She could feel his power, even though he spoke no words, even though he simply took her in without meeting her eyes.

The Anguished One of the Seven.

He hung his head as though the effort to look up was too much, and she stirred deep within, for she needed to look into his eyes and feel nothing. For if she felt something she would be doomed. They all would have been, these wonderful comrades. These wonderful friends who were her family now. They alone had earned the right to be the only family she knew.

Are they, though?

"I sense many things here," he whispered in the voice of a human alone, and his voice was smooth and silken and beautiful, and her mind raced to another time, another life.

She felt no serenity staring at this man, but she couldn't look away. Didn't want to look away. She wanted to greet him, and perhaps kill him. But mostly, she needed to understand him. And perhaps herself too.

I am not myself.

I never was.

And he looked up and drew his hood back ever so, and he was beautiful, and she wanted to moan for the awfulness of it all.

"You are not welcome in this place," hissed Lorgan, and she thought him impressive too, and somehow connected to her, and to the Anguished One as well. She desired to know all, but knew she would be left unfulfilled.

Unfulfilled.

She suddenly felt betrayed by Bereziel's absence. She felt alone in the world and, worse than all that, helpless, and she wondered if he had cast a cruel charm upon her to warm to him, be mesmerised by him. To desire him?

Unfulfilled.

Beside him, there suddenly appeared two of his acolytes. They landed upon the deck, their faces concealed behind heavy iron masks, and beside her, Arturo stepped forward and she sensed his fierce power growing. He was a mercenary now. But at one time he would have stood upon this deck, enjoying eternal life. No former partner ever wanted to meet the new lover. Not even to kill them.

Usually.

"I was invited by my heart," the Dark One replied, smiling, and he was charming. His chest glowed bright green as he spoke, as though it infused his words, and he looked down irritably at the light before wrapping his cloak tighter around himself.

I am not ready for this fight.

Bereziel did not prepare me enough.

It is all his fault.

It is not mine.

No matter what he said.

"Well, not by me, and I speak for the Guild," Lorgan warned, stepping forward as she should have. She thought Lorgan beautiful and brave. As her mind grew to itself again, she realised such things. Lorgan had an old soul, and she, well, her soul was older than anyone else's aboard. Even Anguis's.

"Look around you, Lorgan. You think you will leave this place to whisper your little evils to the Guild?"

"I aim to leave here," Lorgan countered, and she wanted to warn her dear friend to stand back, to avert his gaze from the Anguished One, for he was divine and cruel to those who stood in his way, to those to whom he owed a killing debt. The thick plumes of smoke had gathered around the *Fighting Mongoose*, enough that the world outside was a blur, and she could only imagine that if the Anguished One chose to burn this barge where it hovered, no one would know. No one would ever whisper a thurken word. "Wait... how do you know my name?"

"I know you well, killer," Anguis snarled, and as his voice rose in anger, so too did voices tinged in anguish and hatred rise with it.

At least seven of them.

"King or no, you have no right to call me that," Lorgan growled, and his face was red with rage.

"I will call you and your Crimson Company whatever name I desire," the Anguished One hissed, and it was a threat, and Lorgan fell silent, although he was fierce in the face of a being powerful enough to diminish him with a breath.

"Daria, I have searched the darkness for you," Anguis said, suddenly turning to her and staring into her soul as though there was no one else around, and truly, it felt as though there was no one else in the world. Just her and the monster. Connected. "I see you before me, and I fear this lie," he whispered, and his words spun her mind, and distantly, like in a dream she could not wake from, she knew that name. It was fierce and beautiful and desired... and unfulfilled.

I am not who you speak of.

I am so much more.

I am no longer wrath.

I am no longer hate.

I am serene.

I am Serenity.

"I am Seren," she whispered, and he stepped to her and she was ashamed of her actions. Of who she was. Her knees went weak and she was not herself at all.

Who is Daria?

"You are lost, my dear," he growled, and he stepped

before her and nobody reacted. "But I will take you home to me," Anguis said, and she was ashamed and she wanted to scream, to cast flame upon him, to hate him with all her heart, but there was a terrible drawing to him she couldn't resist. An appeal to return home. To find her mind completely. To love.

"What is all this?" Lorgan hissed. He reached for Seren, but the acolytes raised their hands and a grey tinge of frost came from their fingers. She knew how to counter that nasty weaving. She only had to allow herself. "Are you his ally? Seren? Have you betrayed us?" Lorgan roared, and she would not look into those weatherworn, beautiful eyes and lie to him. She was a whirlwind of emotion and lesser for it. She wanted to be away from here. Embraced in Lorgan's powerful arms. Comforted, cared for. Fulfilled. Loved.

"If you come with me now, my dearest companion, I will spare these, fools," Anguis warned, and she wanted to scream, to fight, to deny him. She also wanted to know him better, and herself too.

It was no offer, but she would take it.

To the fires with Bereziel for not being here to help her, as he pledged he would.

She stepped forward, and the monster, hidden in the night, suddenly attacked.

———

All of this was Eveklyn's fault. She had been so sure of herself and so certain she could fly this bird and keep them all safe, but instead she'd unwittingly flown into an army of airbarges above. A better pilot would have seen the signs.

Taken her time rising and caught sight of the numerous beasts above and avoided this grand meeting, which had led to the invasion, which had led to this trap in the smoky clouds.

I should have been more careful.

I should have been smarter.

I should have chosen my moment and done it right.

Eveklyn kept these thoughts in her mind as she crept along the edge of the barge to where this evil man stood before them. She had never been more scared in her life, but having spent much of her recent life in ultimate terror, it was a small matter. Her battle axe was in her hand. It was never far from her. It was as good a friend as any of the legends on this airbarge, and she would not be without any of them. For she loved this family that had taken her in. Every day, though, she was becoming fiercer, becoming better skilled to belong among them. She had only arrived, and she did not want to leave just yet.

Kill the evil man.

You'll feel better.

As she stepped closer and they spoke of things she did not understand, they ignored her. And why wouldn't they? They were engaged in hearing their own words, but she knew that words exchanged upon a deck invariably led to violence. It was simply a matter of who spoke last and who struck first. It was war, and it was acceptable, or something like that, according to Lorgan. Lorgan said a lot of things, frequently with bad language thrown in. She wasn't able to remember absolutely everything the big man said, but she was trying, and he was understanding, and she loved him for it.

No one will see it coming.

Eveklyn was a mere shadow and she was ready. She didn't understand why they bothered to argue as they did about things she didn't understand, and about people she didn't know. She would be ready, and she would do better than getting knocked out by a soldier thug, or battered by an oversized crab.

I will be swift and no one will see it coming.

It had been her father's battle axe. It had been his father's before that. He had christened it with a name, but she couldn't remember what it was now. It was a word that never played smoothly upon her tongue. Her father had religiously tended to it every year, though he'd never once carried it into war, for he had been a good man. A kind man. A poor man too, and she had been told never to be ashamed of such things.

And she wasn't at all.

Even when he'd placed her high in the rafters to sit and be silent while those monsters hammered at the door and walls and windows all around them that dreadful night. She had never been ashamed of him, for he had been kind, and caring, and reassuring. She had never been ashamed, even when he had been unable to protect them when the monsters broke through. He had swung and missed and been savaged for his ineptitude. As had her mother, and Eveklyn had watched from the safety of the rafters in silence, weeping silent tears as the beasts ate those she cared for as they screamed for mercy that never came.

At dawn, with the monsters long gone, she had come upon the axe, snagged in the side of the wooden wall, where her father had driven it in panic. It had taken a time to unsnag the flutterbye-shaped weapon, and she hadn't let it go since, nor would she, ever. Her new family might suggest she master an easier weapon better suited to her size, but Eveklyn was determined to make a name for herself using this fine heavy weapon. No better way to do that, she reasoned, than to strike down the evil man they all feared.

Perhaps, once she did that, she wouldn't find herself crying at night with the lights out and no one to hear but her cat.

She felt that heavy, reassuring grip and she was aiming to swing when, suddenly, the world exploded in motion as a monster attacked. A cat at that. Eveklyn screamed in horror as Keddy leapt upon the evil man in the middle. She knew Keddy was inclined to strike out, and she had been at the mercy of a few of his more vicious strikes for the sin of rubbing the beast too long at his tail, instead of at the back of his neck where he liked it most. So the fact that the cat attacked the evil man was not too surprising.

They called him the Anguished One, and she despised this thurken cur for his evil deeds. She really hated him for catching Keddy as the cat leapt upon his back, biting and snapping at his neck. The evil man looked ready to wring Keddy's neck as he pulled the beast free and held it in one hand, and Keddy snarled and hissed and she was proud of the beast for the sneak attack, even if it took the element of surprise from Eveklyn on her own adventure to attack the brute.

She would not let that cat die.

Much as her Crimson companions would not let her die.

Without thinking twice, she sprinted at the evil man

and swung her axe fiercely. As she did, the cat luckily broke free from the evil, anguished man. With a howl and a swipe and an aerobatic leap that near sent the beast over the side, Keddy landed, hissed, and darted for one of its tunnels and safety after.

The evil man's accomplices might have attacked Keddy before it fled, but Eveklyn was too swift. She ran at them, swinging, and incredibly, she reached the evil man and earned her legacy. Swinging fiercely, she struck the man as hard as she could. It was a sublime strike. But she was still only a child surrounded by adults.

It took him at the arm and he roared as she cleaved into him.

"Leave us alone," she roared, and the axe clinked off the metal armour he wore beneath the cloak. He spun to face her and his cloak opened and she saw a strange bandolier upon his chest. She counted seven vials of burning emerald light, and she thought them most beautiful, yet also tragic. She did not know why, only that they distracted her—and he struck her with an open palm across the face.

"This is no place for a child," the evil man roared, and she wanted to tell him she was a mercenary, that she was no Crimson Companion, but a Crimson Hunter. Alas, the force of the strike sent her to her knees, and one of his companions turned to her. He fired upon her with ice, and she lifted the large axe to protect her face as it landed.

"You had your chance," the companion roared as ice blasted around her. She held that axe and it was reassuring and blessed, for it saved her in that moment. The ice merely seared the skin along her arms and fingers, and she screamed for the stinging pain.

It's just a scratch.

A mercenary would get up.

Her family did not take this lying down, and she was proud. It was Derian who reacted first, and he was fierce. He leapt upon the evil man, gnawing at his face, tearing at what flesh he could, and she screamed in delight despite the pain.

It was Seren who accosted her attacker, and with a pulsing ball of magenta fire, she blasted the cur to a charred corpse where he stood before delivering a blow to the second man. Though this strike was less successful, it earned Eveklyn a moment to roll away from her burned attacker.

Without hesitation, she charged the evil man once more, swinging and striking him a second time, and then tragedy struck.

It was an axe built for war and violence, but not for taking a blast of unnatural ice and the melting of a fireball, for as she swung, it split in two in her hands and she froze as though that ice had taken her.

Memories flooded into her mind, and for a breath she realised her age, her skill, her horror and her tragedy. She felt little more than the lost girl reaching for a friendly hand as it swung past. She was suddenly alone and afraid, and she was inept like her father, and she was ashamed for letting them down, much as her father had let her and her mother down.

And Natteo suddenly grabbed her, and he was brave and heroic, and he pulled her from the savagery and down across the deck where Kesta was tending to the controls as they struggled in the gripping smoke.

"You are our second pilot, little one," Natteo cried, and she believed him, for why would he lie? "We can't have you getting killed out there," he added and charged back as the evil man began to fight back.

———

That fuken cat.

He just couldn't thurken mind his own business.

And now we are all doomed.

And betrayed brutally.

"On me, you wild fuks," Lorgan roared, seeing the child struck and hoping to inspire one last suicidal charge. A terrible rage came upon him, and he followed its fuel. He stormed the Dark One, not caring if he was flayed alive for his actions or if the Guild decided to flay him for starting on the king.

Lorgan should have been used to betrayals and heartbreak and terrible things occurring where his passion was concerned, but he could still smell her perfume where he'd held her, despite the smoke, despite the scent of death, despite the right awful stench of nearby grand demon and all. He'd always believed himself capable of undoing the great evils he had started, and up until this moment, had actually believed his actions were blessed and for the better good. As it was, he had brought nothing but ruin to himself, his companions and perhaps the rest of the world.

Failure, failure, thurken failure.

He wanted to collapse on the deck, bitter and distraught, suffering the cut of true betrayal, but that simply wasn't in him. He was incapable of giving up, even if all was lost, and truly, this moment felt like everything was truly lost. So he did what any foolish mercenary would do. He grabbed his sword and he went a-swinging in the hope he made it out alive.

He made it three steps before Derian reached the Anguished One first and kept going. He was more fang and ferocity than his usual docile self, and once more Lorgan was grateful he had the legendary fool in his group. It was probably the only correct decision he'd made in a half-dozen or so years. Aye, he was more trouble than he was worth, but such things didn't matter when one had a seeva beast to call upon at the darkest moments, when he was entrapped in a smoky prison with the most powerful warlord in Dellerin. While the rest of the world burned in grey around them, Derian was a rightly welcomed comrade to call upon altogether.

As Derian savaged the leader of the world, Lorgan attacked his acolyte companion. And a moment too late he reached him, for the brute emitted a fresh bolt of ice and, desperately, Lorgan tried to knock the blast from the sky as it struck. He missed completely, taking the blast directly to the chest.

Take it, cur.

Never give up.

Even when it's over.

Even though it really feels like it's over.

So just get on with it.

He willed himself to rise, even as the acolyte attempted to strike him down for good. It would have been a deathly icy blow, too, but for Seren and Arturo waging their own war upon the dark weaver. For a few frozen breaths, as

Lorgan struggled to breathe, they fired fireballs and electricity back at each other as all three weavers battered each other to ruin.

Struggling, Lorgan rose despite the frozen limbs and hobbling and charged the weaver who struggled under Seren's onslaught. He swung his blade and struck the brute down, only to see the face mask knocked free, revealing angelic features underneath.

She was half the age of Lorgan and destined to get no older. She hissed and spat and Lorgan could only swing again, delivering a blow to her ribs that caused her to gasp in bloody horror. It was never easy to kill a human, but Lorgan struggled with a woman even more. It was a lifetime ago that his mother had told him to respect women for the strength they carried, and he did respect them, and he respected them even more in warfare and death.

Unsurprisingly, she died well, still fighting, hating and hissing.

She weaved one more blast of ice for her troubles and fired it directly into Lorgan's heaving chest. She did so, knowing Arturo had her in his sights and that she was unprotected. The electricity shot through her, burning her deeply and sending her over the edge, where her screams echoed and then fell silent.

A good kill in death.

And Lorgan felt his death as her strike hit. Falling to his knees, Lorgan hated his luck, and his life. He looked to Seren, who was spinning from the acolyte to stare down the Anguished One, and he hated her with his faded, beating heart.

You lied.

You betrayed.

You cutting bitch.

I want to hate you.

She moaned, seeing the ruin Lorgan was, and spinning from Anguis, began to heal Lorgan once more.

"Get your weaving away from me," he roared, for stubbornness and pride were his only allies at the end. He could see the seeva and Anguis struggling and ripping at each other, and truly, from the blood spilled, Derian was doing rather well. He had drawn his sword and was plunging it into the Dark One. All the while Anguis's chest pulsed in a brilliant glow, and he savaged Derian back with a sword of his own and a hand of blackest fire.

"My dear Lorgan," Seren cried, and he struggled from her grip, even as he welcomed the immediate healing.

She's getting better at it.

Must be all the practice.

"Spit on you, Seren, or Daria, or whatever," he roared, but it came out as a tentative gasp.

"I'm sorry, my Lorgan, I was unprepared. I didn't know. I'm sorry. You must believe me," she whimpered, and he despised her. Despised himself for trusting her as well. All those comfortable conversations. Just the two of them for hours through the night and on into morning. Revealing everything to each other of what they knew. Slowly becoming friends and such. Greater than mere friends as well, he would have thought. In secret, so no one else would mock their delicate words of understanding. He was her strength; she was his belief.

All lost in a breath.

He wrenched himself from her grip, and her words still stung, and that was worst of all.

"I should have sold you to the mercenaries," he cried, and Derian flew past him, bleeding and broken. He crashed against the galley door and rose immediately despite a broken arm, and likely a dislocated knee. They appeared to pop back into place as he gripped his sword, and, steeling himself, charged the Anguished One as though on a hunt.

"Fuken get him, Derian," Natteo roared, wheeling around the Anguished One with wristbows loaded, waiting to take a shot. He wasn't alone, for having removed the acolyte from the battle, Arturo joined the fight as well. He fired all his finest weavings upon the Anguished One, who seemed to take each devastating blow with ease.

Why aren't you fighting, anointed one?

He looked to Seren and reviled her, and still he tried to stand. And then he tried to run. And he was fierce. Anguis finally faced him and he wouldn't be stopped.

Fuk you, cur.

"Spit on you, cur," he roared, and took that black fire across the chest, and it did little to him, and he wondered was he killed in that moment, and this was a dream in the dark beyond. He was strong as he charged, and he leapt upon the Anguished One, hating him with everything he had, all for the sin of twisting Seren to his will. He lost his sword along the way, but that didn't matter. Derian had been cutting into the cur throughout the battle and already, Lorgan could see the recovery brewing on his torn skin.

Heal from this.

He drew a fist and drove it down across the smaller anguished cur's jawline, and it was a sublime shot. He felt a tooth break loose, and then felt the pain of that tooth embedding itself in his knuckle. It was the last victorious moment he had, for Anguis, spitting blood, reared upon him, rising above Lorgan by way of unnerving black smoke, and driving his fists down upon Lorgan and battering him like no man had ever done before.

He has the strength of ten warriors.

Or at least seven.

Gripping him and dragging him aloft, Anguis continued to batter at him, and the strikes were like the blows of a hammer and just as rhythmic, like he was beating a post into the ground. As he near fell to unconsciousness, he heard Seren scream out aloud.

"Stop, Anguis. I agree to your offer."

Almost immediately, Lorgan was dropped to the deck where he could do little more than bleed. She was upon him, attempting to heal him, but Anguis roared across the lands. "Leave the Crimson to his injuries."

She leaned across Lorgan once more and kissed his forehead, and Lorgan struggled and recoiled, and she left him. She stood to Anguis, taking his hand and, without looking behind, allowed the cur to wrap himself around her. Together, they floated from the deck.

"I am spent," whispered Lorgan, knowing nothing could save the world from this tyrant. "I am a failure," he whispered, wanting unconsciousness to find him. He had delivered into his hands a potent ally and once again doomed the world.

"I am a killer."

———

"You failed them baby, terribly, and now they are lost."

Arturo wanted to retort. To reply with harshness, but she was not lying. She was positively dancing around his mind and soul, celebrating the victory, and there was nothing he could do. She had not tried to interfere in the battle, for she knew how precarious his reserves were. She still served Anguis after all these years, but she was still allegiant to Arturo, and to herself as well, if truth be told.

"Oh, my love, do not be like that," she whispered, and he was furious. Not with her, for she was as she always had been, and part of that fire was what made him love Edel so very much. *Until death parted us, that is,* he thought.

"We will not die, my old silver fox, at least not yet."

Sometimes, when he was careless, she could read his mind. The same could have been said for her, but somehow that mattered less. "I feel like dying," he whispered, and she fell silent for a moment. She never approved of his weakened self; she considered it a distasteful thing. It was one of the lesser traits of his that she endured, however. Sometimes endurance was love.

"Yes, it is, my love."

He dropped to the deck, spent and ruined. In defeat as well, and his constant little voice in his mind cackled at such a thought. He might have argued more, but what was the point? He had fuked up everything, and now Seren, or Daria, as he'd first known her, was back under Anguis's watchful gaze and all manner of terrible things were afoot.

"You think he will simply let you be, darling? Come, get to your feet and protect these fine fiends," she ordered, but he shook his head. He could feel the dark calling. Could feel the slipping of the sands a grain at a time, all in a breath.

With a broken heart that matched Lorgan's, he watched Seren give herself away for nothing. "Come, my dear," Anguis roared as he slipped from the *Fighting Mongoose* and disappeared through the smoke, but not before casting a deceiving enchantment upon them all.

"It was never in him to keep his agreement. He's a right bastard," Edel growled in his mind and it was no comfort hearing her speak ill of her greater master. Nor was it any comfort that she was right about Anguis's deceiving behaviour. *"You battered his pride ever so. He'll not let that go lightly,"* she added, and Arturo knew that to be true as well.

It wasn't the simple devotion of his soulmate, his love, his half everything; it was her practicality. She had seen a world beyond the fall of Anguis. Just a flicker and just the potential, like any future of a thousand others, but it had scared her enough to favour a lesser being, a lesser evil. In case the real darkness came.

"When the real darkness comes."

She believed that, when the real darkness did eventually come, only Anguis and his gathered demons and souls were vile and fierce enough, to prevent a far worse hell from coming upon the seven isles of Dellerin.

"And not even thurken Karkur will remain defiant, either," she added, and he shrugged.

"Well, we'll likely still be dead, my love," he offered, and she didn't like that at all. He was her carrier. Her vessel upon these lands. It was that or the nothing, and she appreciated their grouping. That he had been foolishly in love with her before her death was merely a fortuitous thing.

That she had grown to love the fool was probably a

necessary thing. No doubt grown from sorrow and loneliness and desperation.

"Do not think of yourself like that. You are a great man, my love. I would have fallen for you eventually, in body and in soul."

"Now is not the time, my darling," he insisted, and she envisioned herself standing before him naked and taking to him, and she giggled, and it was delightful. As it always was. Even after all these years. It was perfect and lovely, and he was so spitting tired of sharing this mind.

"Perhaps I shall sleep soon so you might have a little time to yourself," she offered, and he nearly took her up on the offer, but there came that dreadful green glow from behind the smoke, and it did not dissipate as he had hoped it would. *"Anguis will kill us all."*

The smoke turned ever so swiftly to black fire, and Arturo dropped his head in horror.

Around him the Crimson Hunters were screaming in horror and fear, in wrath and in jealousy, in anger and in betrayal, and they were a noise he couldn't take.

The fire pinned them in and began closing in fiercely, and Arturo climbed to his feet as Edel insisted.

"Let's you and me escape," she joked, and it was a half joke. But also, it was a plea for life. Also, it was an acquiescence to his actions.

He did not hesitate; he merely climbed to the edge of the deck.

"What are you doing?" Lorgan croaked, and he knew the cur needed healing, or a real spitting long rest away from warfare. Yet still, the battered man reached for him, and Arturo leapt into the fire as it surged towards them.

"My man," she cried as he leapt, for she was proud of his heroism. And she would offer what she could, for she gave part of herself to him. In soul, in essence. He spun in the air and hoped he was strong enough to break this nasty fire weaving. *"I'm proud of you, even if you choose the wrong side."*

With that, he felt the energy of both souls course through him, and he drew out all his power and blasted it outwards upon the flame of black as it pierced and burned him. It was a devastating weaving on his part, and he felt himself die but for her desperate soul giving him all he could take in as fragile a vessel as his.

"What a spitting rush," she squealed as the awful fire scorched him through, and he was empty and falling into the night below.

"It's all I have," he cried and hoped his wonderful, foolish companions would see his sacrifice. He'd always believed himself destined for important things, and saving a barge with a godly thing, a savage seeva, a burgeoning legend and a lucky cat seemed a worthy cause.

"It was incredible," she whispered, and he could tell by her voice that he had failed. He spun in the air and looked up as the cage of fire remained intact, repairing itself where he had broken through and supposedly shattered apart. *"I'm so proud of you, my love."*

"I suppose this is the end," he whispered, and fought the dreadful burns upon his body. She assisted where she could, and he delivered love as the ground drew nearer.

"There is always hope, my brave old fox," she whispered, and it was soothing. *"I will do what I can,"* she insisted as the ground was but a few smoke-filled feet away. *"Don't*

close your eyes, my hero. Face this terror and survive," she ordered, and he faced the ground and hit hard.

It's just fire.

It's just fire with a little shade of colour difference.

Hellfire that's coming in closer and closer.

Going to eat us up.

A rightly shit way to die.

Kesta looked to the fire around them and that terrible sinking feeling took her. Around her, the box of fire floated like a wave, ever moving, ever shrinking, ever growing in intensity. She could feel the warmth even from inside her cabin. They had but one option: to fly through it. And were it perfectly normal fire, she would have hated every moment, but she believed the *Mongoose* would survive the ordeal. This spitting fire, though, burned savagely hot.

She watched Arturo abandon them and she was unsurprised.

Betrayers and cowards.

She thought it telling that those who betrayed were those who weaved enchantments.

Must be due to losing all their souls that they commit such deeds.

The Crimson would recover from these betrayals, even if it hurt more for others. She looked to the ruin of Lorgan and her heart dropped further. He had fallen unconscious upon the deck where Anguis had battered him near senseless.

You are going to feel the sting of their actions, aren't you?

Lorgan was a dreadful companion when humanity let him down. It was a frequent occurrence.

He was insufferable when he was right about humanity letting him down. This too was a frequent occurrence.

Arturo had chosen openly to flee the fight and save his own skin, over standing firm, maybe weaving a shield or two to her hull to get them through the flames.

Just fire.

Hellfire.

She watched the flame recover itself where Arturo had leapt through, and she fought her anger something fierce. Anger would serve her badly if the moment arose. Better to have a mind as cold as ice.

When about to die.

She doubted she would live through this last flight, for there came the loud crackling rush of the flames piercing the night as they drew in closer.

Fuk, fuk, fuk.

"Are they stupid?" Eveklyn said from beside her. "There's a wall of flame attacking us, and still, they remain upon the deck."

"As usual, little one, you are correct," she whispered, smiling. She was growing into a right confident one, and fuk it, but it was endearing. "Get below, Eveklyn. Strap yourself in, but not before you douse your bedding with a tankard of water and wrap it around you," Kesta added. Her eyes were upon not just the ruined connections of the controls, but the large gaping hole that should have protected her, even if they crashed to the ocean below. Fire was going to get through that and burn her to a fuken husk, and she was damned if she would sacrifice the child.

"No, Kesta, I wish to stay with you," she insisted, and Kesta hissed her away.

"I will not survive this, but I will land her, and you might well take over for me," Kesta said, and it was an order, but the child shook her head and fell silent again. "I am the commanding general now," Kesta added, and the child's eyes whitened and she stood up, knowing her place. Heartbroken or no.

Suddenly, across the front of the deck, there appeared the demon once more. He floated against the fire as though it infused him, and Kesta could see his injuries were still fresh, and she thought it peculiar that a simple dagger could do such damage.

Unless it was enchanted, like Derian's blade.

She might have thought on this more, but the demon suddenly bellowed a great roar and Kesta grabbed the stubborn controls as they fought her touch, lest the demon return to simply flay Natteo where he stood.

To his credit, Natteo did not flee, and perhaps he should have. Down into the hold where the flames perhaps might not pierce him. He stood away from Lorgan and Derian and beckoned the demon attack him alone.

Instead, the demon roared to the wall of fire above them, and this time the world shuddered as he did, and with a crack, the flames began to lessen above them. With a third blow, the top of the fire cage dissipated completely and Kesta couldn't believe her luck.

Things never work out for us.
It's a nasty fuken trap.
Then again...
We have had a good run of luck these last few days.

Piss on this.

Piss on it all.

Fuk it, let's go.

"Hold on," she roared to the child as she kicked the *Mongoose* into life, and immediately it began to suffer from the sudden motion. Despite this, they rose swiftly, and below she heard the demon roar as the fire fought its weaving. The gap that had grown so wide immediately began to recover.

"We can make it," screamed Eveklyn, looking out at the deck, and she saw Derian and Natteo lying upon the deck as before, holding Lorgan, lest he suffer from the sudden movement.

That's my boys.

Upwards they soared, and the hiss of wind and hum of propellor overtook the crackling fire, and above, Kesta could see the burning amber of the morning come alive and she wanted to believe with all her heart.

Things work out for us.

They always work out for us.

They nearly did work out for them, for as the fire closed in, the fourth propellor began to churn. As it did, they surged that little bit further, and she willed them higher and faster.

Suddenly, they broke free of the gap, but not before striking the edge of the barge along its right side. With a shower of sparks and explosions, two propellors creaked and seared, struggled to spin. As they did, the barge twisted, but she kept rising, away from the fire prison, away from the palace, away from any watching airbarges ready to put them out of their misery.

"We are losing the front propellor," Eveklyn said calmly, strapping herself into her chair. Kesta looked to the churning propellor alive with smoke as it began to splutter and stall.

Immediately, Kesta dove the *Mongoose* back to the smoke, aiming for the Guild. It was one thing crashing the barge; it was another crashing the barge in a war zone without any backup.

"I think the second one is going," Eveklyn added helpfully as the propellor caught fire and outright died. "Shouldn't we do a sudden dive to put the fire out?" the child asked as though in a lesson. She watched the fire as it caught in the breeze and seemed to take note of its growing intensity. The child didn't need to know all it would take was a loose spark down one of the blackwater pipes and they'd be done for. Nor were they capable of pulling out of a dive while trying to extinguish the propellor fire, either.

Kesta should have been terrified, for she knew how precarious these next moments were. Instead, she chose to be grateful for this astonishing beast and all it had accomplished under their watch. "You will carry us, won't you, *Mongoose*?" she whispered, and the bird shuddered in reply.

"She sounds in trouble."

"She's just catching her breath."

Looking to the recovering far propellor and the one fully operational propellor behind it, Kesta fancied her chances. Shitty as they were.

"That fire is getting worse."

"It's alright. This bird will get us home," Kesta said, bringing the shuddering barge across the buildings towards the Guild and hoping to the gods they didn't explode in a fireball as they went.

"Isn't this home?" Eveklyn asked. It was a wonderful question.

"Yes, it is, little one."

———

"Get downstairs! Get some water," screamed Natteo, and Derian could barely move. He was frozen to the spot; his muscles ached and his head spun something terrible. Every breath was an aching ordeal, and the simple act of running downstairs to get some water was a task beyond him. "Are you listening...? He's not listening... Fuk's sake, Derian, will you listen to me?"

The barge shuddered as it neared the great blue sheen of the Guild, but Derian knew they were going to make it. Kesta was too assured, and this barge had taken too much as it was. They only needed to walk a few steps more. They would make it. He knew it in his aching bones. He still had the taste of Anguis's blood on his lips and he knew he would taste it again. He did not know how. Nor did he know why he needed to be off this airbarge. Out in the war zone. Hunting down something or someone very important.

"Derian, I think I'm going to piss on this engine fire. Will you join me?" Natteo cried, and Derian could only lean over the edge and gasp as his body tried to recover.

I remember everything.

It felt natural.

It was the first time the monster had come upon him

and he had been fully part of the fight. His limbs had been his own, though infused with fury and wrath and fierce power. It had been intoxicating, and the monster had surrendered to his will as much as he had given himself in reply. He still felt the monster deep within, but it was a presence now and less a commanding beast ready to take him over.

"We are the same."

We are each other.

I love it.

"I love it too."

At this, he began to gain his strength again and he wondered if he wasn't recovering at a rapid pace. A monstrous pace. He wanted to stand, to fight a little more, to seek out that scent he'd caught while flying over the battle.

"She's out there."

"It's out there, too."

In those precious few moments, he understood himself that little bit more. He was no mere mercenary for hire; he was a hound. He was a guardian. He was *her* guardian, and he would seek her out. Even if he lost everything doing so.

"I need to get off this barge," he said suddenly.

Natteo began closing up the front of his pants. "Well, that didn't work too well at all," he muttered.

Any reason to take out his manhood.

Or take a piss anywhere.

The fire continued to puff despite Natteo's best efforts. He raced back to the galley and returned a moment later with a heavy rug, dipped haphazardly in water. "Fine spitting help you are," he mocked, casting the rug across the flames and holding it there for a few breaths. Immediately, the fires began to lessen, replaced with heavy black smoke, and Derian was suddenly snapped out of his trance.

"Here, pull it back over there," Derian called, grabbing a corner and pulling the smoky rug along the turbine where flames still crackled. As he did, Natteo recovered the bucket from the galley and carefully climbed out and poured it over the smouldering rug to finish the job.

"Look at you, doing the littlest amount to get the most attention," Natteo said, pulling the rug away and watching through the smoke for a sudden eruption of fire.

"Look at us—heroes, saving the day," Derian countered, and Natteo grinned.

As they did, they came upon the Guild and the largest airbarge they'd ever seen floating above it. The shield was still mostly intact but for the top, where a clever airbarge might slip in and find cover underneath.

"Fuk me, is that the Dellerin brigade?" Natteo cried, leaping back over the side. "Now, I could be wrong, but aren't we now officially at war with them?"

"I don't think it's them. I think it's something far worse," Derian pointed out.

With a desperate struggle, the *Mongoose* tried to fly up to the barge and clear the gap in its shield, but the third damaged propellor gave up the fight completely and they began to drop at a slightly worrying speed.

"Oh, spit on me," Natteo cried. He didn't seem to notice they were dropping rather swiftly. As he spoke, he knelt down to the stricken, unconscious Lorgan and wrapped him in his arms. Unsure of what else to do, Derian did the same as the shield flittered alongside them.

From the rushing wind and the loud curses of Kesta, they understood they were about to have a rather impactful landing. Regardless, Natteo's mind was elsewhere. "How the fuk did they get that?"

"I don't know."

"I mean, that is insane," he continued.

"It is."

Along the hull of the dreadnaught barge, there were crudely painted letters in writing as large as the *Fighting Mongoose*, the name of this awe-inspiring bird.

"Death of the *Crimson Hunter*," Natteo said, reading them aloud as they fell away towards the war zone.

"It's a terrible name for an airbarge," Derian agreed.

"They really can't name things very well, can they?"

"How could they afford to buy something as big as that?"

"Not to mention keeping her afloat," Natteo said dreamily.

"I guess it pays well to be the most famous mercenary group in Dellerin."

"I wonder is Boab still mad," Natteo mumbled.

"You will find out soon, but yes, I reckon he wants you dead like the rest of them."

For a time, they sat holding Lorgan, listening to the wind rush past them and the increasingly lurid curses of Kesta as she struggled to "drop this rock."

Until, at the gates of the Mercenaries' Guild, they landed, and it was brutal.

The world spun, and for a breath Derian was near thrown upwards and over the edge. Again. But Kesta earned her keep and turned with the *Mongoose*'s momentum, and they settled in a roar and fell still.

Neither said a word for a time. Instead, they looked to the massive airbarge hovering over them, and the surrounding desolation. Behind the shield, the entrance to the Guild was pristine and untouched. It was an enticing thing too, but Derian smelled that aroma again and he knew it was his monster sending him a sign. That path was not his, at least not yet. Leaving Lorgan to moan, Derian stood up and gazed over the railing to the scorched ground below. As he did, Kesta and Eveklyn emerged from the cabin in both delight and disappointment with the landing.

"It was the best we could have expected," the older pilot said, and her protégé agreed with a few delicate nods. "Once the Guild grants us access, we can begin repairs." After a breath, she looked up to the daunting shadow of the new and improved airbarge of the Army of the Dead as it hovered above the city, summoning all mercenaries to come on home, offering a warning to any army considering a sneak attack and all. "That can't be good at all."

"I don't know how they beat us here as well," Derian mumbled. He needed to leave. Not because he was scared, but because that need was growing like a lure itself.

"That beast could be more than just a hulking bitch," Kesta muttered, eyeing the airbarge as though it was a cherry to be picked. A smart mercenary would have been wise to keep her far away from that barge, considering their history.

"I have to go," Derian said. "I have to be away from this place."

"What? You can't leave us? We can fight off the Army of the Dead together," she lied, and it was a fine lie.

"I do not fear them," Derian said, stepping over the edge. It was a long drop, but he fancied his chances.

"Nor do I," Natteo professed unhappily, looking up at the barge longingly.

"You both can't leave us. Not now," she cried, but Derian could not be swayed. He looked to Natteo, who grinned warily.

"There is something out there that I must tend to," Derian said, and it was the truth. She could see it in his eyes. "So I'm stuck with you, too?" he said to Natteo.

"Until the end, brother."

With that, they dropped from the barge and took a painful landing that matched the crash of the *Mongoose*.

Kesta leaned over and appeared crestfallen. "You'll return to me, my boys," she called.

"I give you my word: I'll be back," Natteo declared. "And I'll try to bring him, as well." He dropped his head. "Make sure Lorgan is tended to."

"He'll be on his feet by day's end."

"So will we," Natteo said, and carrying nothing but their weapons, the two trudged away from the airbarge without looking back.

They walked in silence for a time, playing at being mercenaries, listening to the world and its ruin around them. Eventually it was Natteo who spoke first.

"So, do you have any idea what we are doing?"

"None at all," Derian said without hesitation.

"Oh, that's just spit n polished, that is," Natteo cried. "You know we'll probably die out here."

"Course we will, and it'll be your fault."

"No, brother. It's your turn to get us both killed."

"I'll see what I can do."

Silently, the duo disappeared into the war zone, hunting something they were unaware of, and completely unprepared for. As they did, the world spun as things fell into place and the lures were tested to their harshest limits, and the beginning of the end finally began.

EPILOGUE

The girl spun elegantly in the air. She raised her hands to meet the ground as a diver might into an ocean, but she knew there would be no plunge deep into water most refreshing. She closed her eyes, and to her horror felt her momentum carry her spin a little further.

Suddenly she was falling as though from a short height, feet first, and it was here that she landed, and it was awful.

It was no rubble or pathway she landed upon, but indeed water. A dark pool in the middle of a war zone, almost deep enough for such a dive, and she plunged deep into freezing water and hit the bottom fast and the pain was immediate. It shook her body, took her senses, soared through her quivering body.

The instinct to splash and pull with her arms drove her to the surface, where she spluttered and gasped and moaned for the agony and the denial of her death. She had been ready, but now she raged against such an end. She wanted to live. For a few breaths more.

This life, though gifted, was one of pain, and she let out

a wail and immediately regretted it, for there came the terrible, familiar sound of a savage group of monsters in pursuit. They came from the dark, and the girl knew she would never see dawn again.

Bobbing in the water with legs unnaturally still and heavy, she made her way to the edge of the pool, pushing the floating debris out of her way as she did. She did so naturally, without thinking about it.

It took her a moment to realise the floating debris was not planks of wood and such, but rather the frozen corpses of the many dead. Raising her hand in the eerie dim light, she realised that the water she swam and struggled in was more crimson than clear, and, spluttering in horror, she sank beneath the surface once more.

Struggling to breathe, she coughed, swallowed and recoiled from the horror and the taste. Around her, the monsters began to appear. Like a dreadful pack of beasts, they gathered up and sniffed the air as she eased herself ashore to meet her end.

Strangely, she came upon her pack at the edge of the large pool. Sitting upright and saved from the water by a pair of dead floating women entangled with each other, the girl moaned and dragged herself along the bank where countless bodies lay strewn where they had been cast. The pack should have felt better in her arms, but it felt heavy, and she wanted to weep, to scream, but she was too tired. Too beaten. Too close to death. Too ready for the end.

With an effort, she pulled herself fully ashore and tended to her knees and was horrified with her injuries. She could see the bones, bulbous, shattered and out of place. Seeing such horror brought about fresh agony and fresh tears for none of it was fair. She had given her all and was lesser for it. She was alone and lost, and she simply wasn't ready for the next cruelty the world would place before her.

Around her the hound-like monsters began to howl and spit and moan as they too came upon this awful pit of the dead.

Pits of the dead.

They were not soldiers. They were citizens. Many hundreds of them, spread out across the surrounding area. Tears streamed from her eyes at seeing such atrocities up close and all personal like, for nearly every dead person lay with their eyes open, their faces locked in grimaces of terror and their throats slashed from ear to ear.

They killed everyone, regardless.

My people killed them.

I am a part of this.

She hated those who had committed such acts. She thought of brave soldiers burned to death, and the sins upon their souls as they had fallen, and she hated them, despite her guilt.

She lay among them, unable to move, unable to scream. As she did, the monsters came upon her. She knew they hunted her, but a great pit of the dead was apparently too enticing a thing to ignore, for they sniffed at the corpses before tearing into the bodies, frantic with the feast that it was. They took to the more rancid first, and she wondered would that be her saving grace, for they left those floating and, instead, ripped apart the corpses furthest away.

Slowly, slowly.

Real pissing slowly.

Ever so slowly, she edged back into the pool, sliding

silently over rocks and rubble that scraped and added to her maddening pain. Silently, and with a held breath, she slid halfway down into the water until she was up to her waist, and, wrapping frozen stiff limbs about her body, hoped desperately to outlast the night.

She could never say how long she lasted, lying there quivering and dying, holding her stomach from retching at the smell, all the while surrounded by hundreds of delicacies that were slowly decimated before her, but it was the sound of boots that drew her from her horror first.

They were heavy, assured and driven.

He walked through the monsters and she thought him most impressive, if not a little diminutive. The monsters separated where he walked. They did not hiss, they merely allowed him through, and she wondered was he their cruel master.

His cloak waved in the breeze as he hastily climbed down through the bodies to where she lay, seeking her out. She hoped.

She tried to call for him, but her voice was so very weak. He must have sensed her, for he rummaged through the corpses, seeking and hunting, and she tried to move, but she had nothing left. He came upon her, and she gasped a call out into the night that he couldn't have heard.

Regardless, he pulled the dead from her body and she could only shiver. Roughly, as though he was seeking something beneath her, he spun her over and she displayed everything she had to him, and he hesitated and drew his hand back.

"You are injured?" he asked softly, and she looked into his eyes and if there was feverish desire, he hid it behind a pretty jaw. There was only a softness and compassion in those eyes, and she feared he enchanted her in that moment.

"You are beautiful," she finally gasped without the weight of the dead upon her, and he grinned and she felt safer for a breath as he unclipped his cloak and carefully wrapped her in it. Weak and broken, she could only look at his face, stroke his chin and hope he smiled at her.

"And you are far heavier than I expected," he said softly, and lifted her from the water.

"Am I dead?"

He looked around as the monsters snarled and growled under their collective breaths but did not snap or squeal or attack.

"Not quite yet, but let's get you to a safe place," he said, carrying her from the pit towards the distant light.

The End

The Crimson Hunters are not yet done.
They will return in *A Breaking of Lures*.

To be the first to hear when it releases,
join the Robert J Powers Outcasts at
www.RobertJPower.com

THANK YOU FOR READING THE GATHERING OF FOOLS

Word-of-mouth is crucial for any author to succeed and honest reviews of my books help to bring them to the attention of other readers.

If you enjoyed the book, and have 2 minutes to spare, please leave an honest review on Amazon or Goodreads. Even if it's just a sentence or two it would make all the difference and would be very much appreciated.

Thank you.

Find Out How it all Started

They were sent to stop the Dark One. They Failed.

Set thirty years before the events of The Crimson Hunters, The Seven; The Lost Tale of Dellerin takes place in a grimdark fantasy world where evil reigns, demons roam, and enchantments cost your very soul.

"A truly dark work that is not for the faint of heart" - Readers Favourite

"Characters that feel alive with soul, the author captures true human emotion" - Amazon Reviewer

GET EXCLUSIVE MATERIAL FROM ROBERT J POWER

When you join the Robert J Power Outcasts you'll get the latest news on the Spark City and Dellerin series, free stuff, exclusive content and new release updates.

You'll also get a completely FREE BOOK for a limited time only.

Join at www.RobertJPower.com

ALSO BY ROBERT J POWER

The Spark City Cycle:

Spark City, Book 1

The March of Magnus, Book 2

The Outcasts, Book 3

The Actions of Gods, Book 4

Raven Rock

———

The Dellerin Tales:

The Crimson Collection:

The Crimson Hunters, Vol I

The Gathering of Fools, Vol II

The Lost Tales of Dellerin:

The Seven

About the Author

Robert J Power is the fantasy author of the Amazon bestselling series, The Spark City Cycle and The Dellerin Tales. When not locked in a dark room with only the daunting laptop screen as a source of light, he fronts an Irish rock band, despite their many attempts to fire him.

Robert lives in Wexford, Ireland with his wife, son, three rescue dogs, and a cat that detests his very existence. Before he found a career in writing, he enjoyed various occupations such as a terrible pizza chef, a video store manager (ask your grandparents), and an irresponsible camp counsellor. Thankfully, none of them stuck.

If you wish to learn of Robert's latest releases, his feelings on The Fallout series, or just how many coffees he consumes a day before the palpitations kick in, visit his website at www.RobertJPower.com where you can join his Outcasts You might even receive some free books, hopefully some writing updates, and probably a few nonsensical ramblings.

www.RobertJPower.com

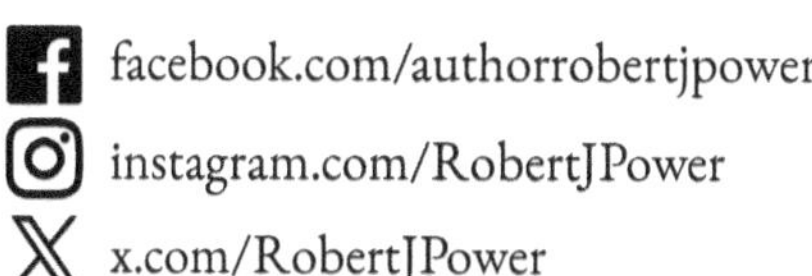
facebook.com/authorrobertjpower
instagram.com/RobertJPower
x.com/RobertJPower